The Wind of the Khazars

By the Author

The Book of Abraham

Marek Halter

THE WIND OF THE KHAZARS

TRANSLATED BY

Michael Bernard

The Toby Press

First English Language Edition 2003

The Toby Press LLC
POB 8531, New Milford, CT. 06676-8531, USA
& POB 2455, London WIA 5WY, England
www.tobypress.com

ISBN I 59264 028 I, *hardcover*

A CIP catalogue record for this title
is available from the British Library

Typeset in Garamond by Jerusalem Typesetting

Printed and bound in the United States by
Thomson-Shore Inc., Michigan

Ask those of generations past,
Pay attention to the experience of their fathers.
For we are of yesterday, and we know nothing,
Our days on earth are nothing but a shadow.

Job, VIII, 8–9

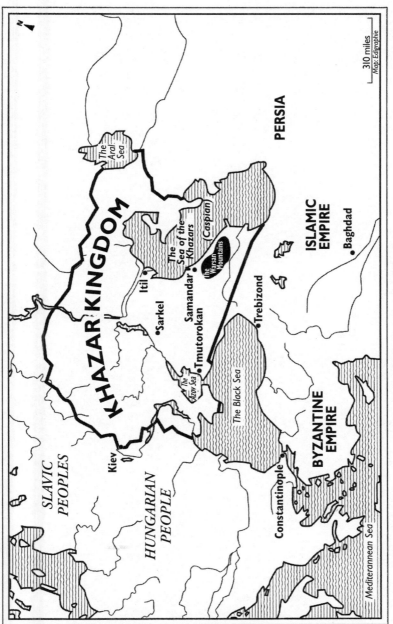

THE KHAZAR KINGDOM

Chapter one

Sarkel, 939

Attex pushed her foot deeper into the mud. She lifted it suddenly with a plop, leaving a perfect imprint. It only took a few seconds for the footprint to fill with water and disappear. Frowning, Attex lifted her foot as high as possible and crashed it down with even more force into the soft earth of the riverbank. The imprint was much clearer, much deeper. But the water filled it even more quickly and wiped it away without a trace. The little pockets of water began to ripple in the breeze. Attex raised her eyes from the river. Just beyond the bay where she was standing surrounded by thickets of wild roses, happy laughter broke out. On the bank, servants were washing wool in huge wooden tubs. The oldest of them had lifted up her skirts and tucked them into her belt, displaying her fleshy thighs. She entered the water and stretched out her hand to the young girl.

"Princess Attex! If you go too far into the river, it will carry you away!"

"If the river carries me away," replied Attex in a mocking tone, "my father will chop off your head!"

"Exactly!" the servant sputtered. "And I don't fancy that! My head does very well where it is, thank you!"

Attex heard a shout; in the cherry orchard bordering the river and stretching to the hill, her brother Joseph was training for combat with the greatest of the Khazar warriors, the worthy Borouh. As he was only thirteen, his horse was smaller than Borouh's and his sword shorter. Attex was full of pride to see how secure he was in the saddle, galloping between the trees with as much agility as the warrior.

"Attania," she asked, slipping her fingers into the servant's large hand, "why can't I go to the synagogue with Joseph tomorrow?"

Attania sighed, shaking her head. "I have already told you, Princess. Tomorrow is the day your brother becomes a *Bar Mitzvah*, the day Prince Joseph becomes a man. Only men have the right to enter the synagogue on that day, not little girls…"

"It's not fair!"

Attania smiled. "That's life! You are a princess and I am a servant. You are beautiful and I am already an old hag with no teeth. That's how things are, fair or not!"

Attex studied Attania's large and tender features. She wasn't as old as all that, and she was only missing two teeth. Huge gold earrings dangled from her ears, and her eyes sparkled with kindness. She had a mouth made for eating cakes and giving kisses.

"It is true you are not very beautiful," she teased, to anger Attania. "When I grow up, I will be very beautiful. The most beautiful woman in the world!"

But Attania was not angered. Full of sweetness, she slid her fingers through Attex's red curls.

"Yes, I am sure you will be."

Disappointed, Attex withdrew her hand and made the water splash out from under her feet as she ran up the edge of the riverbank, jumping like a goat.

"I am a princess, I am the most beautiful princess, and I am bored!" she cried. "I want to be thirteen like my brother and go to the synagogue!"

Attania and the other servants burst out laughing. Attex also burst out laughing. She wasn't really bored, she was never bored. But she really wanted to see what was going to happen to Joseph in the synagogue the next day! She sat down on the bank to dry herself in the sun. Behind the crest of the hill, she could see the tall towers of the fortress of Sarkel, and a little bit to one side, a long caravan of camels approaching the town.

As she brought her gaze back to the river, she noticed strange bundles of leafy branches coming from upriver. They were floating gently in the current. The branches did not appear dead; on the contrary, they still carried all their leaves, as if they had just been cut. These bundles of floating greenery were not in the center of the river, but appeared to be carefully following the meandering shape of the bank. Attex stood up to get a better view. There were about fifteen of them. In the middle of one of the branches she was sure she could see a horse's nostril and the yellow reflection of its teeth.

"Attania!" she shouted, pointing at the river, "Attania! Look!"

⁊⅃

Joseph heaved on the reins and forced his half-blood to pull up short. In his right hand he held his scramasaxe up to the heavens. It was a short sword with one cutting edge, but its blade, thick enough to ward off the most violent blows, weighed very heavy in the hands of a child. Borouh turned his mount in response to Joseph's move. He was far enough away for a fast gallop back between the cherry trees. With a measured gesture, he drew his long sword from the saddle scabbard and pointed it at Joseph. A ray of sunshine reflected off the gold wire encrusted on his silver helmet and flamed from the polished scales of Hun iron on his leather body armor.

"*Yyyaah!*"

When Borouh spurred his charger, Joseph distinctly saw the ground and tufts of grass shake under his hooves. With each bound, the thoroughbred spat out white spume from its foaming lips. Joseph could see Borouh's fierce black eyes. His fear transformed into a joyous rage. His heels, the points tipped with silver, jabbed into the belly of his little steed. He took off like an arrow. His spirit became that of a warrior.

They closed quickly. Borouh lifted his sword high in the air; Joseph pulled violently on his reins and threw his body to the left. The bit cut deep into the half-blood's mouth. Throwing its forelegs

3

forward, the horse moved out the way at the very instant that Borouh's blade sliced through the air, finding nothing but emptiness. Joseph then swung his sword with all his might. Borouh, pivoting in the saddle, had no time to parry the blow. The metal struck so hard that Joseph felt the shock right to his toes. Borouh followed his movement, swinging his blade with a circular motion. The heavy scramasaxe slid down, taking the child's arm with it. A stumble by his little horse made him lose his balance. His feet left the stirrups. He fell to the grass with a shout of anger.

Without even stopping his thoroughbred, Borouh jumped from the saddle. He took off his magnificent helmet, displaying high cheekbones and slightly almond-shaped eyes. His hair, utterly black, was pulled back severely in a thick bundle and held together by a silver clasp. A long mustache emphasized his full lips.

"Prince Joseph! Anything broken?"

Backside on the grass, the child raised his steel visor and flung his helmet away angrily.

"I did what you taught me, Borouh!" he grumbled. "As you say, 'Cunning is the strength of the weak!' If I were as big and fat as you, you would be dead and...." He stopped himself. Shouts from the riverbank. He recognized Attex's voice.

෨

Below, very close to the bank, rising out of the water like sea-monsters, a dozen horses appeared. A huge mass of branches hanging from their necks and saddles obscured dripping cavalrymen, soaked red turbans hiding their foreheads. Almost as one, they raised their arms. Above their heads, long leather ropes knotted to round stones began to whistle. The servants were shouting again, abandoning their barrels of washing in their attempts to escape. Attania screamed, "Attex!" and reached for the young girl. Alone on one side, immobile as a statue, the small princess watched as the assailants charged their horses through the shallow waters of the bay.

"The Petchenegues!" exclaimed Borouh, incredulous.

Joseph had already gathered up the reins of Borouh's thoroughbred and hauled himself awkwardly into the saddle. His legs were too

4

short to allow him to place even the tips of his boots in the stirrups, so he grasped the horse's mane and gripped with his knees while the powerful beast plunged down the slope. Down there, at the edge of the river, one of the servants had fallen in the water, her ankles caught by one of the leather thongs. Gasping out cries of horror, she was trying vainly to stop two Petchenegues from hoisting her onto a horse. The others were galloping after the remaining fleeing women. Attania had managed to reach Attex and was protecting her with her body. Still at a distance, Joseph spotted a barbarian swinging his lanyard at less than ten paces from them. Without thinking, he let out the war cry of the great Khazar warriors.

Almost completely covered by Attania, Attex heard Joseph shout. She looked out and saw him, his left hand glued to the horse's neck and his great sword held high. He was galloping toward her. Borouh was following more slowly on the smaller horse. She was no longer afraid. At that instant, Attania pulled her in closer, squeezing her tightly. The Petchenegue's lanyard whipped into Attania's skin. The stone crashed into her cheek. She screamed. Blood gushed from her lips. Joseph was still a few feet from the bank. Attania wanted to run. The lanyard tightened and they fell in the water. Attex slipped under the surface of the river, drifting with the silt. Panic-stricken, she closed her mouth and clenched her eyelids. Attania turned around just as the young princess came to the surface. Above her hovered the mocking face of the Petchenegue holding onto the lanyard securing Attania. Letting out furious groans, her mouth full of dark blood that overflowed and dripped into the river, the servant fought to disentangle Attex from the leather thong. At that moment Joseph arrived.

Attex had visions of a terrible bird moving through the sky above her. Then the pointed sword held at arm's length. And then Joseph's flaming eyes. The Petchenegue raised his eyes. With a tearing noise, the sword entered his stomach. Carried forward by his own momentum Joseph tumbled with him into the water, clinging on to him in the mud. Attania emitted a horrified scream. Joseph, hands red with blood, stood up and lunged over to save Attex.

"I'm here! Sister, I'm here! They won't take you!"

Attex held his face to her neck. Only tears could express her relief. For a few minutes more, there was nothing but noise and confusion while Borouh put the thieves to flight. Alerted by the guards at the fortress, other Khazar cavalrymen charged up to join him. Joseph recognized the white hair of his grandfather, Benjamin, and heard him giving orders. Attania staggered and collapsed unconscious on the grass, her jaw broken.

⁊ₑ

The Petchenegue speared by Joseph took so long to die that Borouh cut his throat to stop his agonized moaning. Withdrawing his sword from the body and brandishing it, he approached Joseph, his face beaming with joy. "Prince, this is a great day for you! Tomorrow, you will become a *Bar Mitzvah*. You will read from the Torah in front of Rabbi Hanania, our king Aaron—your father—and all the great people of the Kingdom of the Khazars. But today, the Almighty has shown us how highly He regards you!"

He stopped, his voice trembling with sudden emotion, more sincere and ardent than he himself expected. "You have punished the wicked and you have saved the life of an innocent! You will be a great warrior, Prince Joseph!"

"You will be even more than that!" boomed a loud voice.

Joseph jumped as Borouh stepped to one side of him.

"Grandfather Benjamin!" exclaimed Attex, holding Joseph's bloody hands in hers, "I wasn't afraid … Joseph has just saved me and I wasn't afraid!"

The old man nodded his head, laughing. He wore a long robe of skins embroidered with silver thread. On his large face, a long scar cut across his left eye, crossing from one side to the other and deforming his fleshy mouth. His one good eye was fixed proudly on Joseph. A simple black cloth skullcap was pinned to his hair. Borouh knelt on the ground and bent his head low. "May the Eternal grant you long life, Benjamin, father of our Khagan. This attack should not have been possible. It is my fault. I did not place any watchmen higher up the river this morning!"

Benjamin looked at him coldly. "Yes. It is good that you are aware of it."

6

He raised a hand missing half its fingers, lost during a battle against the King of the Alains, and pointed at Attex, still holding on to her brother. "Take the Princess back to the fortress. And have that poor soul Attania carried back to be cared for."

As Borouh bowed a second time, old Benjamin grimaced and smiled gently at Joseph. "You are right, Borouh. My grandson will be a great warrior. But he will be something else as well. It is time that he learned everything he needs to know to be ready for the day he will be Khagan of the Khazars."

Chapter two

Amigo Hotel, Brussels
April 2000

Mr. Sofer, you wrote in one of your novels that we are incapable of sharing our dreams like we share bread and love. Coming from a novelist, isn't it rather strange to believe that we cannot share our dreams?"

The woman who asked the question was seated in the third row from the stage. Marc Sofer knew that she had asked just the right question, at the right moment. She knew it as well. A smile hovered on her dark red lips. Her green, ever so slightly almond-shaped eyes and her prominent cheekbones spoke of an oriental origin. She looked barely thirty years old and her short deep red hair accentuated the delicate pallor of her skin. In truth, her beauty was so striking that from the moment she had entered the conference room, Sofer had been drawn to her above all the other women present.

There were about a hundred people in the audience, the majority of them women, as usual. Faithful readers who followed his plots from book to book, and who, once again, were giving him that strange and unique mark of respect that readers bestow on an author they love. There was something intimate and even familial about it and, as on all such occasions, some of these feminine faces displayed a most ambiguous tenderness. A good audience, then, as Sofer had experienced hundreds of times before. One of those meetings that comforted him, revivified him with a breath of the excitement of yesteryear. From the time when he believed, as cast in stone, that a writer could change the face of the world and, above all, bring peace.... Sofer started, realizing his answer was tardy. Like a bird fascinated by a snake, he had been lost in the green gaze of the beautiful questioner while the room awaited his reply. Escaping the all-encompassing gaze of the red-haired woman, he looked around the serious faces in front of him and said at last, "You are correct. I believe I did write that dreaming is the only activity we cannot share. We dream alone. We can only share the memory of a dream, or what remains of it."

"But, in your stories, are you not trying to share your dream?"

He was sure she had shouted. Her voice, like her skin, was so fine and yet slightly veiled. Serious and attractive. Disconcerted, Sofer glanced around the room to assure himself that it was only he who saw something personal in this exchange. He was. His listeners were as attentive and benevolent as before.

"When I write," he replied, this time confronting the beautiful stranger, "it is not to share a dream but to share a story, to transmit an idea, or knowledge. That may cause my readers to dream, but it will be their dream, not mine.... Yes, I have long believed that to write results in the magic of sharing. I have always hoped that my work provokes a sort of dance between author and reader, that it allows us to live the emotion of our dreams at the same tempo, with the same choreography. And that also we three, you the reader, the book, and me, can drag our dreams into reality, with the aim of altering it at the same time as we transform ourselves...."

Sofer sensed the uneasiness in the room. His words contained too many assertions and double meanings. He halted, smiled, and to include the other members of his audience, swept up his right hand in a theatrical gesture.

"But I know today that a novel is fiction. We only share the fiction, the echo of our dreams! Even a novelist must recognize, one day, that he is not God. He only fashions characters of dust to be dispersed by the first little breeze that manifests itself...."

There were several laughs, appreciative of the writer's change of tack, but the beautiful redhead was not even smiling. Her green eyes were elsewhere. The misdirection had been lost on her. Playing with his pen on the black baize covering the table in front of him, Sofer was concerned that he had upset her with his response. Looking at her face, he was fearful he had unwittingly misled her. He decided to continue without further precautions, as if he were talking only to her. But from his first word, his tone was much sharper and more urgent than he would have liked:

"It is true that I have not only written novels, but many essays and articles and numerous protest pamphlets. Doubtless I have shared not only the dreams but the hopes of thousands of my readers scattered throughout the world. However ... if that is the meaning behind your question, then yes, I am disappointed that I have not been able to effect the least impression on reality. I have written page after page about the lives and history of Jews. I dreamed that these pages would help them, would help us all, Jews and non-Jews, to live more peacefully together, with ourselves and others. Now, after so many words, pages and books, peace is no nearer. Neither in Israel, nor in our hearts...."

This time, the gorgeous redhead managed a smile. She briefly nodded her head before interjecting in a clear voice:

"Is that why you don't want to write any more?"

After a stupefied pause during which he held back an angry response, Sofer found the strength to display a placatory smile on his lips. "Let's just say that I haven't any inspiration at this particular point in time...."

The stranger reached out her hands toward him. The movement was so gracious that it seemed to Sofer as if she were really going to touch him. She looked at him as if they were the only two people in the room. Some of the women in the audience frowned, but the young woman was not intimidated in any way.

"If you were to find a dream or a hope big enough, mad enough, a cause just enough for you to sponsor, would you agree to write about it and defend it to the whole world?"

She put so much more vigor and fire into her question than he had put into his answer. It awakened the old well of cynicism in his soul. What did this beauty want? To sacrifice herself on his altar, to be his inspiration, his muse? What was this mad, grandiose dream she was proposing? Was she actually just hitting on him? What the hell? Perhaps she wanted to drag him off to one of the bedrooms in this fine hotel! Such games were not for him at his age and in any case, he'd already played too many. He took a deep breath, focused on the gentler expression in the eyes of an older couple and declared, as calmly as he could:

"One day, a man, whose name I forget, went to look for his destiny. He traveled the world and, many years later when he was very old, he returned home, grumbling his discontent. On the doorstep of his home, he was amazed to see destiny awaiting him, and he died. I am too old not to know that you don't chase your destiny. Destiny chases us—when it feels like it!"

The whole room laughed, as if relieved. A very bald man whom Sofer recognized as the editor of a distinctly partisan Jewish magazine stood up and posed a question on the partition of Jerusalem. He felt his muscles relax. The conference had returned to normal.

Chapter three

O
Sarkel, 939

n the eve of Prince Joseph's *Bar Mitzvah* ceremony, the soldiers were making their rounds on the high walls of Sarkel, the merchants were displaying their wares in the maze of leather tents, the boatmen were steering their heavy craft laden with fruit and cloth between the eddies of the River Varshan, the young women were washing clothes on the riverbanks; and all of them saw the old Khagan and the young prince walking, hand in hand, around the fortress. While the sun moved toward its zenith and the hot air became unbearable, Benjamin was replying to his grandson's questions and encouraging more. His one eye, slanted like that of a Chinaman and from which he derived the nickname *Mongol*, shone with a fervor that his injured fingers tried to transmit to the child.

"I am proud of you, Grandson!" he uttered in a shaky voice. "All the Khazars in Sarkel are proud of the courage of the young Prince Joseph!"

Below them, the town of tents spread out along the river. Smoke climbed straight up in the sky. Climbing with it were shouts and calls, the groaning of carts and the raucous bellowing of camels. A caravan had arrived three days earlier. The market extended into the distance along the gentle bend of the Varshan, in a southerly direction toward the Sea of Azov. Russians, Magyars and Muslims, subjects of the Vizier Ahmed Ibn Kuya, hawked their wares; their cloth, their weapons, their beasts or slaves. The air hummed with exuberance. Benjamin pointed to the hundreds of brown tents.

"And they will love you, because tonight there will be dancing in your honor."

"Can I go with them, Grandfather? Can I dance with them?"

The old Khagan appeared surprised by the question. A little laugh escaped his lips. "No, my child, you cannot! On the eve of becoming a *Bar Mitzvah* a prince must stay in the fortress and prepare his mind for the ceremony. Have you really understood what tomorrow is about?"

"Certainly, I know!" exclaimed Joseph, disappointed. "I am going to read from the Torah. I am going to sing for you and my father...."

"Is that all? What will happen after that?"

"I will have the right to march at the head of the Khazar warriors, the right to take a bride and to become Khagan when my father, Aaron, retires...."

They had climbed part of the path leading to the white brick walls of the fortress. Reflecting the sun, the strongest of the citadels of the Khazar kingdom burned their eyes. Sarkel seemed to be carved from alabaster, impregnable and eternal. On the paths around the top of the walls, only the leather helmets of the guards and the shiny metal of their fine lances were visible.

As Benjamin continued on in silence, Joseph asked, "Am I wrong, Grandfather?"

The slanted eye of the old man screwed up even more than usual. He did not reply immediately. Instead of continuing on toward the fortress, he guided Joseph down between an outcrop of rocks, leading him onto a steep path that linked parts of the north of the town like a dozen shoelaces. He slowed his pace, as if he needed to regain his breath. Holding the child's hand firmly, instead of replying directly, he asked:

"So according to you, you will soon have nothing but rights. Is that what it means to become a *Bar Mitzvah*?"

Joseph did not dare raise his eyes to meet his grandfather's. He had only one desire: to run toward the town that was full of sound and life and to join the crowd. But there was a snag; instead he had to listen to his grandfather's sermons. He loved and admired the old Khagan, his father's father, but he did not like these serious moments when he had to assume a serious air and think deep thoughts. If he had been allowed to return to the fortress with Borouh, they would have both been practicing with their bows.

"I know what you are thinking, Grandson," Benjamin went on, starting to walk again. "You are dreaming of life down there, with the merchants and the laundry-girls. You would like to be playing with the young girls who saw you fighting the Petchenegues a while back. You would like to see their eyes shining with admiration of Joseph, the courageous prince who has already killed a barbarian in combat on the eve of becoming a *Bar Mitzvah*...but you are Joseph, my grandson and son of Aaron the Second, the Khagan. You are he who, one day soon, will lead the Khazars in peace and war. From now on, you must learn to carry this load as a joy!"

Benjamin fell silent long enough to walk around a huge poplar tree. He left the path leading down toward the town and the river to take Joseph across the fields. Joseph knew that they were going to take a tour around the fortress along his grandfather's favorite route. While he searched for the answer to a problem, the old man was capable of walking around it ten times or more! Joseph smothered a sigh of exasperation. Tossing his long hair, he asked slyly:

"But you, Grandfather, you weren't Khagan for very long! You didn't like to bear the load, you shifted it onto my father...."

Benjamin agreed with a wry smile.

"Well said! And that gives me great pleasure, to see that you know how to use your brain as well as your scramasaxe!"

"Why did you not want to be Khagan any more?"

"Because I had achieved my aims and it was time to pursue another course. As Khagan, I had fought the Alains, who were hindering us from maintaining access to the Sea of Byzantium and who attacked our convoys, interrupting our commerce with Rome."

He stopped, let go of Joseph's hand and showed him his amputated fingers "I defeated them and made them our allies. As you can see, I paid a price for that peace. After that, there was no room in my plans for war. It was time to learn the teachings of the Torah."

Intrigued now, Joseph deliberately took hold of his grandfather's hand and questioned him, his voice full of doubt. "You think it is better to learn the Torah than to fight like a warrior?"

"A warrior fights with his body alone," Benjamin replied quietly. "He who studies the Torah fights with the minds and the hearts of a whole people behind him."

"The warrior who wins a battle gains the armor of the vanquished, and even his wife, his house, his land. What recompense does the one who studies gain?" asked Joseph.

"Recompense? Why, it is recompense without measure! He who studies can search all the shadows and enigmas of the world. And if he studies more and more, he begins to understand of what these shadows and enigmas are made. It is an inestimable happiness, Joseph, believe me."

Without having noticed, they had started to walk again and were soon under the shadow of Sarkel. There they could no longer hear the noises from the town or even the sound of the river. Joseph was listening more attentively to Benjamin's answers, and new questions were coming unbidden to his lips.

"But Grandfather, you never went to study in the synagogues in Jerusalem like Rabbi Hanania, did you?"

"Sadly, no! And I'm far from being a scholar like Hanania!"

"Do you think the Jews of Zion are different from us?"

"They are and they are not."

"I don't understand."

"The Children of Israel are the sons of Abraham and Moses. They are also the People of the Book and the Exile. Their history is different from ours. They gallop in words like we gallop over the steppe. They know how to listen to the knowledge of books as we do

16

the wind. They have been Jews for thousands of years, but they do not have a kingdom. We chose their religion less than three hundred years ago, but we are strong enough for the emperor of all Byzantium to wish to be our friend…. However, be you a Jew from Israel or a Jew from the Kingdom of the Khazars, we have faith in the same God, blessed be His name, and we respect the same Law."

They walked for a moment in silence until they came out of the shadow, and once again the noise of the town and the market became audible. Ten large flat-bottomed barges laden with fruit, jars of wine and sacks of rice were leaving the pontoons that served as a quay, pushing out into the swirling River Varshan. Joseph only gave them a passing glance. Ignoring the fortress gate guarded by a dozen soldiers, the old man and the child regained the path they had walked earlier. Frowning deeply, Joseph now wanted to know how the Books of the Torah had been written, by whom and for what purpose, and if the Jews from Israel would one day come to live on the steppes and in the rich valleys of the Kingdom of the Khazars. His grandfather answered with meticulous detail. Never before had the old Khagan Benjamin been as patient with the young prince.

When they passed the old poplar once more, Benjamin pointed to a flat rock. "Let's sit down for a while, Joseph. Walking and talking like this, I'm all out of breath." Joseph knelt down at his grandfather's feet. He remained silent for as long as it took a swallow to make a full turn around the fortress walls.

"Grandfather, why did King Bulan want us to become Jews?"

The old Khagan had led Joseph to the only question worth asking. With his undamaged hand he caressed the boy's cheek. Then, in a low voice, as if he was telling a secret, he said, "For the peace of his soul and his people. For our peace and our future, for all of us Khazars!"

He let his hand drop and placed it on the prince's shoulder, drawing him closer as the lad looked up into his face.

"Listen to me, Grandson. When our ancestor Bulan became king, the kingdom was not as vast or as powerful as it is today. To the southeast, the Grand Viziers of Persia and Baghdad were propagating their faith in Allah. Their religion was new and they wanted everyone to become part of it. On the other hand, the devotees of Christ left Byzantium to build churches right up to the banks of the Atel, where we had built our most valued town. The Russian and northern barbarians raided and pillaged wherever they wished. Some Jews, hunted by Muslim and Christian alike, came to beg for refuge with Bulan. Bulan himself did not believe in any god or believed in all gods, which comes to the same thing. Above all, like all great warriors, he bowed to the supremacy of the shamans, the medicine men and their amulets…."

Benjamin paused, his one eye sparkling with pleasure. Joseph rubbed his nose. The great Borouh was one of those soldiers who never went out to battle without several rabbits' feet and other magic tokens about his neck. He had given one to Joseph, an old silver piece from the dawn of time, originally from one of the deserts of China, which had been sewn into the lining of his tunic. The child restrained himself from touching it through the fabric, but he realized that his grandfather did not have to see it to guess it was there.

"Bulan was a thinking man. He said to himself, 'The people of the south are rich and powerful. They build palaces, cities and ports. Their sages are very knowledgeable, they invent machines and laws that disengage power from their kings when they decide whether to go to war or not. And they all believe in one God who helps and supports them…now, what do we Khazars do? We exhaust ourselves in vain wandering. We move our tents on the merest whim, sometimes to the east, sometimes to the west! True, we are courageous warriors and we win all our battles. But what good does it do us? When one of us dies, the shamans demand that we burn all his beasts, his belongings and his wives with his body. His wealth goes up in smoke. Nothing is left for his children! So, as rich as we may become, we remain poor forever, ignorant nomads…."

Benjamin paused to moisten his lips, dried up with so many words. Joseph immediately asked, "Bulan didn't believe in the Eternal, then?"

"No! Not yet. But he did something that was to change all that."

The old Khagan pointed his finger at the lining of Joseph's tunic, at the exact place where the good luck charm was hidden, and said, "He drove the idol worshippers from his lands. He forbade his family, his wives, his children and his servants from having the least contact with the charlatans and their amulets. He told his warriors that they would all perish in their next battle if they disobeyed him!"

"And the idolaters left?" murmured Joseph, very pale.

"All those that made a profession of it, yes. And those reluctant to leave were chased away with spears or drowned in the waves of the Atel!"

"Then what happened?"

"A few days after the last soothsayers and shamans had disappeared from his realm, Bulan received a visit from an angel in his sleep...."

In Joseph's curious look Benjamin could read the question he was formulating. His grandfather waited patiently while he composed it. "What is an angel?"

"Only someone who has been visited by an angel can tell you that, Joseph!" Benjamin responded. "Alas, the Almighty has never given me such a gift...."

The old man and the child both sat silently, deep in their own thoughts, contemplating the river waters, the rolling and bubbling spray, as if it was coursing again and again through all mankind's memory.

"An angel came to see Bulan," Benjamin started again quietly. "He said he was God's messenger: 'God has sent me to you because He has heard you rail against the idolaters and saw you send them away. He knows that you hope for a sign from Him and He wants to help you....' From the depths of his sleep, Bulan gathered up all his courage and answered: 'It would be an unmeasurable gift to receive a sign from the Almighty. There are all kinds of Khazars. If I was to go before them empty-handed, how would they believe He exists?' The angel replied, 'King Bulan, do what you have to do and you will have proofs in abundance. Your enemies will bend before you, you will have laws and precepts, your family will be blessed and your descendants will live long lives!' And that is what happened from the dawn of the next day."

"God made him win his battles?"

"Yes."

Benjamin leaned over, catching hold of the bottom of Joseph's tunic. A short-handled dagger flashed. With a quick and precise movement he slit the lining where the talisman lay hidden. The child cried out and jumped to his feet.

"No one ever goes into a synagogue with amulets hidden in his clothes," declared Benjamin, sliding his dagger back into its sheath.

Shamed and furious, Joseph opened his mouth but could not enunciate a single word. Benjamin's scarred face was magnificent in its severity. He held out his open palms to the child and spoke softly: "From tomorrow you will be a man, the covering on your head will be that of a man! Do you finally understand what that means? You are the descendant of Bulan, Prince Joseph. One day you will sit, as he did, on the golden throne of the Khagan of the Khazars. And like Bulan, you will have to avail yourself of all the wisdom possible when you make your decisions. You must sleep each night with a pure enough heart and pure enough hands that the angel of the Lord can come to visit and help you! You are not just a Khazar like all the others, son of my son Aaron!"

Tears shone in Joseph's eyes. It took all the strength at his command to withhold them. His heart was beating so fast he could hardly breathe. His grandfather's fierce look softened and he beckoned to his grandson.

"Come here, don't be afraid."

Joseph looked up. The dry old arms of the retired Khagan folded around him. Joseph relaxed into the embrace, biting his lips all the while.

"'Seated on the banks of the rivers of Babylon, we weep, thinking of Jerusalem,'" murmured his grandfather, gently rubbing his back.

There was a moment when there was nothing else but the embrace. Then Benjamin gently pushed the child away. "Listen to what I am going to say to you, Joseph. Yes, you will be given a sword and a magnificent horse. That is the law. And it is correct that this should be, because I know you will be a great warrior. But as I said to you just now, you will receive more than that. Much, much more! You are going to receive the power to be he who will bring peace to all the Jews in the world. Yes, perhaps you will even be the Khagan who welcomes the Messiah to your kingdom, he to whom God has designated the sacred land of the New Jerusalem. You must learn not only to be a good fighter, my grandson. You must learn to be the best of men, and the wisest. That's what it is to be a king. You must learn what the Torah and Rabbi Hanania teach you. It is your duty. Learn, learn and learn, until wisdom flows from your bones like blood!"

Joseph was shaking. He shut his eyes so tightly that they hurt. He wanted to close his ears similarly so that he could no longer hear the voice of his grandfather. Benjamin stood up. He murmured, with a smile of great tenderness, "Let's go down to the riverbank. You can throw your amulet in."

Chapter four

Hotel Amigo, Brussels
April 2000

The conference went on for another hour, in as normal a manner as it could. Sofer watched his beautiful questioner out of the corner of his eye but avoided looking directly at her. Surprisingly, she didn't seem to be more than vaguely interested in the rest of the exchanges and never again attempted to join in. The more time passed, the more Sofer's bad humor softened. From feeling just a while back that he was capable of noticeably shaking, he realized he was excited at the thought of being the hunted. After all, why refuse favors offered? Especially as this young woman had that *je ne sais quoi* that transported her beauty to the threshold of mystery. He began to fear that she might disappear by magic. While answering questions with all the amused distance he could muster under the circumstances, he decided to make the first move. He would find a way to say a couple of words to her as everyone left the hall, asking her if his answer had convinced her. Or even to which particular dream she had been alluding. Perhaps a more provocative remark.... Yes, why not? Trains left for Paris every hour, perhaps they could have dinner together. He would only have to postpone his reservation.... Sofer suddenly realized that he was smiling vacuously while the questions being posed merited a much more serious demeanor. He took control of himself and regained his composure, albeit more with a sense of irony than true seriousness. But nothing came to pass as he expected.

Ten minutes before the end of the seminar, the young redhead suddenly left her seat, excusing herself pleasantly to the adjacent listeners and heading, with feline grace, for the exit. Sofer scarcely had time to register that she was wearing a long, light-colored leather coat over a black mini-skirt, gently tailored at the waist in a way that emphasized the movement of her hips as she walked. As she reached the door, her hand on the doorknob, she turned around. Suddenly silenced in the middle of a sentence, Sofer thought he could see something resembling a smile of complicity in the flash of her emerald eyes, something that said *see you soon* rather than *goodbye*. That is, if he wasn't substituting his desires for reality. She was too far away for him to be certain. He hoped she would give him a sign, say one word, one pleasantry, but she offered nothing. And he couldn't in all decency run after her, even verbally, in front of this crowd! Without really believing it, he hoped she had not actually left. He knew about such things. Discreet women who disappeared from a room but miraculously reappeared as soon as he placed his foot on the pavement outside, pretending that some wonderful manifestation of chance had taken place.

※

That evening, however, it was a totally different manifestation of chance that occurred. After the room had finally cleared, an odd sort of man stood in front of Sofer, a smile on his lips. A smile that could not be ignored, composed as it was of pure gold! The man was large and looked about thirty-five or forty. From his appearance, he was obviously not used to wearing a suit. The one he was wearing was made from an old-fashioned cloth—probably twenty years out-of-date—into which his powerful chest had been squeezed. He wore a shirt of giant black and white polka dots and a wide gray tie with small pink and green flowers. His appearance was totally out of place in this fancy Brussels hotel of thick carpets and elegant decoration, reminiscent of the 1930s.

"Hullo, good day, I am very happy to meet you. They told me I'd find you here."

It took Sofer a few seconds to realize that he was being addressed in Russian. He took a step backward, as if to see the speaker more clearly. Narrow face, sunken eyes, an aggressive appearance. A look of the Mafia, as they say, but provincial Mafia.

"My name is Yakubov," he continued, extending his large hand. "I came to see you because I need you…do you understand me? You do understand Russian, don't you?"

"Yes, I do," acknowledged Sofer, intrigued.

"Ephraim Yakubov, that's my name," repeated the man, offering his golden smile. "If you would be so kind, I would like to have your address."

Just like that he asked for his address, and then immediately glanced suspiciously all around, frowning as he did so. A real caricature, thought Sofer, halfway between amusement and irritation. A Jewish name and a scoundrel's face; facts not always, alas, incompatible. And now this odd stranger had ruined his last hopes of running after the beautiful stranger. At least he would be spared from making a complete fool of himself.

The room was now practically empty, except for the two publicity girls patiently waiting near the door to be paid, and a handful of loitering readers still present who were devouring the Russian with their eyes. At least this meeting would enhance his reputation as a writer who had mysterious adventures, Sofer thought ironically.

"Why do you want my address, Mr. Yakubov?"

The man placed his hand on Sofer's arm. It was a hand that was used to being obeyed, to being a loyal and powerful tool. However, the gesture was neither a threat nor a familiarity, simply a way of demanding serious attention.

"I come from the Caucasus, Mr. Sofer. Georgia. You see?"

"I see only too well," replied Sofer, disengaging his arm.

He could see very clearly. For anyone who knew a little bit about the old Soviet Empire, Georgia and the Caucasus were synonymous with Stalin and mafiosi. Since the fall of Communism it had become rife with clan wars and mafias.

"And in what way can I be of assistance to you?" he replied circumspectly.

"They told me that you sometimes help gentlemen in my position…. I need papers. I entered Germany as a tourist. With my visa, they will expel me in two or three weeks. I don't want to go back to Georgia."

"And you want to remain in Germany?"

"Germany, Belgium, France—wherever! They told me that you…you could, for a Jew like me…."

Almost fascinated by the casual way the man was expecting his aid, Sofer asked, "Excuse me, but who are *they*?"

Yakubov leaned over and, in an almost inaudible whisper, murmured a name that Sofer knew extremely well. The Russian glanced at the remaining people in the room and breathed out, as if releasing a state secret, "I am a Mountain Jew!"

"A Mountain Jew?" exclaimed Sofer.

He would need to think about this. The Mountain Jews, who some called the Thirteenth Tribe, if not lost entirely, had lived in the Caucasus Mountains for centuries. Perhaps even for millennia, as it states in the Bible that at the time of the Assyrians, Jews were sent to the *Midii*, the borders of the Caspian Sea, into the region corresponding today with Azerbaijan. If Sofer's memory was not faulty, this people still used a language whose origin was unknown, called *Tath*….

"Do you know who the Mountain Jews are?"

"A little."

"Good, there we are then, I am a Mountain Jew and I have important things to tell you. That's another reason I want to see you. Not only for the papers."

"Would you like a drink?" offered Sofer, horrified to find himself already compliant, and feeling vaguely guilty.

"No, not here. In Paris, in your house. It is important."

"Can't you tell me any more?"

"You must believe me. It is important. You will find it important, Mr. Sofer. And for me, the papers are important."

"How did you get from Germany to here?"

"Oh, that was no problem. There are no frontiers in Europe, are there?" Yakubov smiled with all his gold teeth, happy as a child. "That's how I can travel to Paris to see you," he added.

Thinking hard, Sofer realized he had nothing to lose. The friend who had sent him this candidate for exile was no straw man. And this Caucasian was intriguing enough to merit a hearing, if not assistance. In any case, it was no more ridiculous than to be longing for an affair with a total stranger! He drew a calling card from his jacket pocket and handed it to Yakubov.

"There you are. Call me and we can have a chat. But I can't make any promises about your papers."

The Caucasian blinded him once more with a display of his golden incisors.

"In a couple of days! I will call on you within three days! And you will see, you will be pleased!"

As expected, when Sofer left the hotel, there was no sign of the redhead. It was a bit like a child's dream, Sofer thought. He began to feel as if he wasn't even sure he had really seen her, nor heard her solemnly seductive voice. Nevertheless, in spite of all the sarcastic remarks he could make to himself, he was disappointed. More than was reasonable. He caught the first available train for Paris, grumbling to himself.

Chapter five

I

t would soon be night. The sun was descending behind hills covered in dense forest. The walls of Sarkel seemed to be disappearing. With the last ray of sun, the long clouds glowed pink like lengths of vermillion-tinted silk and reflected off the surface of the river. Joseph felt the fresh air of evening on his neck. It was the east wind that came from the great Sea of Jordan and traversed the steppe from morning till night. The wind that the Muslims and Christians living in the kingdom called the Wind of the Khazars.

Attex shivered and hugged Joseph tightly. "They say Attania isn't going to die but that she will never speak again," she murmured. "And now she really won't have any teeth."

They were curled up in the recess of a tower on the path around the fortress. Joseph could hear Attex speaking but was paying no attention. At their feet the meandering river was turning red like the scaly body of a giant dragon. Joseph let his imagination carry him away. Far to the south, already covered in shadows, the dragon lifted up its immense and fearsome head. Its jaws opened to display huge teeth. Its eyes, flecked with gold, rolled in fury. A bifurcated tongue, like a thousand whips bound up in one, tore through the twilight air.

All the inhabitants of the town ran away howling. The camels stood up, bellowing their terror. The horses ran away, breaking down their enclosures as they fled. The mules, the dogs, even the geese and the ducks were fleeing. In their uncontrolled flight, they could see above them the dragon's head nodding gently, its muzzle lifted to the heavens, jetting out explosions of flame that were setting the leather tents on fire. The women, the girls, the aged and even the warriors on the towers of Sarkel were screaming with fear. Borouh came up to Joseph and said, "Prince, the time has come. You must help me. We must kill this dragon. Only you and I can kill him before he ravages the Kingdom of the Khazars!" Hastily, pale and shaking in every limb, they saddled their Arabian steeds. Heel to heel, they left Sarkel at a fearsome gallop, charging off into the horizon, lances at the ready, paying no heed to the demonic roaring of the monster.

"Hey," protested Attex, shaking her brother's shoulder, "why don't you answer me?"

Joseph sighed as his violent dream faded. There wasn't a dragon in sight. The darkness was already erasing the reflections from the river. Torches and peaceful fires showed between the tents, illuminating groups of crouching men.

"Answer what?" he asked.

"What do you think the Petchenegues do with the women they steal?"

"Slaves...servants...what would you expect them to do?"

"I would never accept that. I am a Princess, I can't be a slave! I would have drowned myself if they had taken me prisoner."

Attex spoke with grave pride. Joseph glanced at her affectionately. She was beautiful even at five years old, and she was almost as brave as he was. He liked to feel his sister's silken curls against his cheek. She shook his hand and added, "Now, I owe you my life. You will always be my guardian. And one day, I will save your life.... That's true, isn't it? Even when you will be Khagan, you will keep me safe, near you, won't you?"

"Yes," said Joseph sincerely.

He slid the ends of his fingers over the torn lining of his tunic.

Not being able to feel the weight of the charm made him feel ill at ease. He wished his grandfather had not made him fling it in the river. He would never be able to tell Borouh that he no longer had it. Although perhaps Borouh would guess. He was capable of it. He possessed that magic intuition that saves great warriors when arrows tear into their backs or enemies hide themselves. Borouh knew when to turn around in time to see through shadows. And in spite of that, Grandfather Benjamin did not want Joseph to be like Borouh!

"What are you thinking about?" asked Attex. "You look very sad."

"Nothing."

It was the worst response he could give his sister. Attex had an insatiable curiosity. She moved to the side and pouted. "That's not true! You are thinking about tomorrow when you will enter the synagogue, aren't you?"

"No."

"About the sword and the horse you will be given tomorrow?"

Joseph smiled. "Yes."

In the feeble light of the torches, Attex frowned with the air of an interrogator before asking for more. "What did Grandfather Benjamin tell you?"

"Things that they only tell to those who are going to be Khagan of the Khazars."

"Why?"

"Because, that's why!" groaned Joseph.

Attex screwed up her nose in disdain. From where they sat, they could just see families grouped around fires in the town. The echoes of women chanting and tambourines and lutes played by Arab merchants rebounded off the fortress walls. When it became really dark, they would eat their roast meat and drink their wine, children and adults, boatmen or longshoremen, they would all dance in honor of Joseph until the moon fell under the horizon as if it were going to fall into the Sea of Azov. The girls of Alain descent, with skin so clear that it shone phosphorescent in the moonlight, would turn in circles to make their skirts flair. But he, the Prince of the Khazars, the hero of the hour, would have to be content with listening to their laughter losing itself in the night.

"I know that Grandfather told you things you didn't like," replied Attex, kittenish. "I always know when you are unhappy. You can tell me."

He mumbled, "He doesn't want me to be a great warrior like Borouh."

"Why not?" Attex was sincerely interested.

"He says that the Khagan is first and foremost a wise man."

"Ah!"

"But he is wrong. A king is powerful and respected because he wins great battles, isn't he?"

Attex nodded her head in approval. "Yes, if you had not been a warrior, you could not have saved me today."

"Grandfather says that I should be wise, like the wisest of Jews," pursued Joseph, his voice trembling. "He said that perhaps I am the one who will save the Jews who will come here, driven out of all the other kingdoms...."

"Don't you want to?" Attex asked, impressed.

Joseph did not answer. They sat for an instant cuddling together, as if the wall of the fortress was only a frail bush out in the darkness. Joseph pointed to the fires at the edge of the river and grumbled angrily. "What's the use of being the Khagan if he must always be good! I don't want to spend my time reading and discussing. I just want to be a warrior, a great warrior like Borouh!"

Attex snuggled up to her brother and whispered at an almost inaudible level. "I know you are going to be the Khagan, like our father. And also a very powerful warrior. I know it. And when I am big, I will be like a wife to you."

Chapter six

Montmartre, Paris
April 2000

For three days following the seminar in Brussels, Marc Sofer occupied himself exclusively with the roses he cultivated with passionate attention on the huge balcony of his apartment high up in Montmartre, overlooking Paris, the city of his dreams. Despite the pessimistic warnings of professional horticulturists and thanks to meticulous care, he had succeeded in growing one gorgeous old variety of rose in an Italian pot: *Buff Beauty*. The petals of the young flowers were a delightful ochre color, which paled in color after the rose opened, and then became a soft shade of delicate pink, bringing to mind the shoulder of a young woman rarely exposed to the sun.

While gardening, Sofer gave nary a thought to Ephraim Yakubov, the Mountain Jew, but the memory of the beautiful face of his questioner in Brussels gave him no peace. He had pruned well, clearing up the cuttings as he went and surveying the buds of roses responding to the first warmth of spring. The green eyes, the red hair, the serious voice of the stranger came back to him, making him suspend the clicking of his secateurs. His obsession seemed shocking and unhealthy to him. He would soon be fifty, and had been with many women in his lifetime: beautiful women, always attentive, often intelligent, tender or passionate. Sometimes all those things at once, like a miracle or a gift from God. Sadly, all demanding more than one could give. At least more than he, Marc Sofer, could give. In short, beautiful and magnificent moments, pleasures to be remembered with delight. But adventures that ineluctably drew to their end before they properly began.

Sofer was one of those men to whom maturity offered supplementary charm. An age, people said to him regularly, that he did not show. He had slimmed down, and the wrinkles that creased his brow and the gray at his temples only added to his distinction. His libido was still present and sometimes rode out of control, although he was tiring of the roundabout of no tomorrows. He had even thought of growing a beard in an attempt to really look old, as nature seemed unwilling to accommodate him. In truth, what he considered his main disappointment in life was to know what a feeble influence he had had on real events. His decision to stop writing novels had also dried up his interest in games of seduction and their fleeting satisfactions, but he had savored his solitude as one would a wine, cellared for many years, that had finally achieved its perfect bouquet. And now, here was a woman who provoked such an extreme reaction in him, both as a writer and a man, and then disappeared so completely that he could not extirpate her from his mind!

"Old fool!" he muttered. The piercing bleat of the telephone interrupted his reverie. Sighing, he put down his watering can, took off his gloves and entered the room to lift the handset vibrating on his desk.

"Mr. Sofer?"

"Yes."

"Yakubov. You remember, Ephraim Yakubov, the Mountain Jew."

"I remember, Mr. Yakubov," replied Sofer in Russian.

"I am in the café below your apartment. I will be with you in a couple of minutes, just as I promised."

"Yes, but…"

The Caucasian had already hung up.

Grumbling to himself, Sofer went to wash his hands and had

34

hardly had time to slip on a jacket before the doorbell rang, heralding the arrival of the Mountain Jew.

"I did say three days!" exclaimed Yakubov when the door opened. "And it is now exactly three days."

He wore the same suit, the same shirt and tie. And he was still smiling his gold-laden smile. Sofer invited him in. Reaching the center of the room, Yakubov seemed intimidated for the first time. His dark eyes scrutinized every corner of the huge room, scanning the bookcases loaded with ornaments and photos, memories of a life of travel and meetings. Then, seeing the terrace, he stepped out. The presence of an arbor of roses on the tenth floor of an apartment block seemed more amazing to him than the fabulous view of Paris below.

"It's very beautiful here," he concluded.

"Vodka or coffee?" Sofer offered in acknowledgement.

"I'd prefer vodka."

The gold teeth shone once more.

"Sit down, please..." proposed Sofer, motioning to the armchairs on the terrace.

By the time he returned with the bottle of iced Zubrowska and two glasses, Ephraim Yakubov had taken off his jacket and undone his necktie. Sofer could not help but admire his visitor's facility to adapt. For Yakubov, who had spent his life in a village in the Caucasus, everything would be new, strange and complex. But he seemed capable of surviving all that was thrown at him. They drank the first glass in silence, then Sofer asked, "I don't think you told me where in Georgia you live."

"Kvareli. At least, a little village not far from Kvareli, in the mountains close to Daghestan and Chechnya."

"Did you leave because of the war?"

Yakubov looked at Sofer as if he had told a good joke. "The war? We Mountain Jews, we have lived with war for two thousand years. My father hid in the mountains when Stalin sent all the Jews from the Caucasus to freeze in Siberia!"

"What is it, then, that made you leave your home and your village, Mr. Yakubov? Why do you need my help and how can I help you?"

Sofer had spoken rather sharply and Yakubov was taken aback. He took some time to think, and finally asked, "Have you heard of the Khazars, Mr. Sofer?"

Taken aback in his turn, Sofer blinked. He knew vaguely about the Khazars. Koestler had dedicated one of his books to them.

"They had a kingdom near us," continued Yakubov, without waiting for a reply. "A large kingdom that stretched from the Caspian Sea over to the Black Sea and then to Kiev. Some size, eh? It was a long time ago, more than a thousand years."

"They converted themselves to Judaism...."

" Yes! A Jewish kingdom, right where we now live. Immense, very rich...a Jewish State, like Israel!"

Yakubov was obviously excited. His eyes sparkled as much as his teeth. How often had the Caucasian sat and listened to Mountain Jews telling this extraordinary story of a Jewish State in the middle of the Caucasus? How could one not be moved by stories of this people who, in the Middle Ages, had created a Jewish Empire?

Sofer refilled the glasses, touched by Yakubov's enthusiasm. "Yes," he admitted, "I have read two or three articles about the Khazars, but a long time ago. They were nomads, weren't they?"

"Originally, yes, nomads. Later they had a real kingdom, with towns, castles, markets. A state! And it was the only time in history that a whole people chose to convert to Judaism!"

Sofer laughed, as if the idea seemed ridiculous to him. Yakubov threw him a shocked glance and protested by shaking his great head. "They led the lives of true Jews, Mr. Sofer! They went to synagogue, learned the Torah and read the Talmud as we do. They were wise men!" He swallowed a mouthful of vodka and, leaning over the table, asked in his deep voice, "Do you know what they did to their kings?"

Surprised by the unexpected fervor of the Caucasian, Sofer shook his head and asked him to continue. With a knowing look, Yakubov explained. "Their kings followed inheritance rules, father to son. But only a Jew could be king. On coronation day, the Khazars led the future king in front of his people. Two men wound a silk rope around his neck, like this," he said, pushing the knot of his necktie upward. "They pulled hard. The guy could barely breathe. Then, you know what?"

"No."

"Well, squeezing his neck until his tongue hung out, they asked him how long he wanted to be king. He had to say a number. Five years, ten years, forty… And then, *oops*, they let go of the rope! But please understand, it was no joke! They really tried to strangle him and they didn't ask the question until he truly was on the edge of asphyxiation! Under such a regime a future king, aware of the terms, never dared say too high a number. And, if he said four years, after four years, it was over! If he insisted on keeping the throne they would cut his throat!" Yakubov burst out laughing approvingly. "Imagine if we could do that to our presidents, Mr. Sofer!"

Sofer smiled. "What is the link between your visit to Europe and the Khazars, Mr. Yakubov?"

"As I told you, my father never left the mountains all of his life. I know them like the back of my hand, but he could move around them in the dark, in the deepest winter snow, without ever becoming lost. Once he disappeared for two whole days. They thought he was dead…" Yakubov stopped, serious, as if he could see his father there before him. Sofer began to empathize with the fellow. He was beginning to think the Caucasian sincere, and he appreciated the sensitivity under the outer shell of hardness. Of course it could be that he was just a good actor, though if that were the case he was very good!

"My father discovered an immense cave," Yakubov began again in an even more solemn voice, looking at the roses. "And in the cave there were streets, houses, a synagogue…."

"A synagogue?"

"Yes. Built by the Khazars! I have seen it with my own eyes. It is huge, with a great library full of books."

"You have seen it yourself?" Sofer repeated, as an all too recognizable excitement overcame him.

"May God strike me down if I'm lying!"

"I believe you."

"A unique synagogue, like no other I've ever seen. Built in stone inside the cave, with pillars, chandeliers for lamps and candles, and the Star of David. And lots of wood covered in gold leaf."

"How did you discover it?"

"I already told you how the Russians, the Soviets, did everything they thought possible to make everyone forget about the Khazars. They wanted it to be like the kingdom had never existed. Therefore when my father discovered this cave, he said nothing to anyone. Nothing! Nobody! Only, from time to time, he went off into the mountains alone; he would disappear for a week or two. No one knew where or why. Well, one day I wanted to know. I followed him, walking, for two days. On the morning of the third day we reached a cliff-face full of holes. My father climbed up using a ladder. Once he disappeared into the cave, I followed. That's how I discovered the synagogue of the Khazars!"

Yakubov paused for a few moments, nodding his head gently to emphasize his story, then continued. "That's when I found out that my father went there to read the Talmud, the Torah! Can you understand? He went to that cave, alone, to that synagogue, lit the old oil lamps, sat down on a bench and poof! Hidden in the shadows, I watched him pray, rocking to and fro. I saw him, my father, his head covered with a *tallit* and *tefillin* on his arm. He prayed alone in that synagogue with the bats perched above his head! Can you picture it? He left us for that...."

"How can you be sure that the synagogue dates from the time of the Khazars?" Sofer asked.

Yakubov wiped his forehead with the back of one huge hand and his eyes held a look of guile. "My father never told us what he had found—that cave. Me, I've kept quiet too. But in the interior, apart from everyday objects, there were books; a Bible, some very old papers. And a trunk full of old coins. After two years of silence, I decided it would be idiotic to let all that rot away. I showed one of the coins to someone. That's how I know the place dates from the Khazars."

"Who?"

Yakubov hesitated. He appeared sincerely ill at ease. "I can't tell you that. I couldn't possibly...."

"Is that the link with your visit to Europe, Mr. Yakubov?"

"I've had nothing but bother since I revealed that old coin. There are some people who are demanding to know the exact location of the cave. But I don't trust them."

"Yet you trust me," Sofer smiled.

Yakubov looked him in the eye. "I know who you are. And this is what I propose: you arrange a visa for me—for two or three years it will cost you about fifty thousand dollars—and I will show you where the cave is. You will be the official discoverer. With all its contents. You can write a good story about that, can't you, not to mention newspaper articles! What do you think? It's a small price to pay…."

Astounded, Sofer let out a long whistle.

"Why don't you do it yourself?"

But Yakubov wasn't joking. His expression remained serious. "It would be better if you do it. You are a Jew. They wouldn't dare touch you."

"They?"

The Caucasian did not answer and Sofer watched him stand up without reacting.

"I will call you," Yakubov said, doing up the buttons on his tight jacket. "I'll give you some time to think." He plunged his hand into a pocket and pulled out a large coin with rough edges that rang noisily on the table. Silver, Sofer estimated at a glance, centuries old. On its face, well polished by years of handling, in relief, a very identifiable seven-branched candelabra—the *menorah*.

Chapter seven

En route on a very long and uncertain journey, the young
Isaac ben Eliezer arrived near Mâcon, in central France, one April
afternoon in the year 954. Having left Cordoba a month earlier, he
had departed Lyon the evening before and traveled along the banks
of the Saône on a capricious mule. The spring weather was stifling.
An hour before he caught his first sight of the city walls, the sky had
blackened like soot and the storm that had been building broke.
Lightning illuminated the shadows from above the immense forest
that covered the rolling hills. The noise of the thunder became so
violent that the earth seemed about to tear itself asunder. Isaac arrived
at the town soaked to the skin.

The great city of the Burgundy markets stretched up the
sides of a mountain. The crenellated walls, punctuated with circular
watchtowers, came down to the yellow waters of the river at several
points. On the central fortress hung a standard bearing the arms of
Othon, King of Burgundy and Italy. Hanging from a pole, immobile
and heavy with rain, it looked like an abandoned rag. Contrary to
Isaac's fears, the town guards let him enter after being offered one

silver coin, minted in Narbonne, and did not even ask him to open his saddlebags.

The storm had converted the streets into streams. Detritus accumulated on the uneven paving slabs and at the doorways of houses. Feathers glued to their bodies by the rain, chicken and geese were being chased by mud-covered pigs. Some of them were also snuffling through the heaps of refuse, grunting with delight. Apart from this activity in the streets there was not another living soul to be seen.

Isaac turned the mule into a wider street, which he thought must lead to the center of the town. He needed to find the house of the moneychanger, Nathan Judicael, a wise man of the Book to whom his friends in Lyon had commended him. Suddenly, a young man rushed out of an adjacent lane, staggering under a bundle of kindling wood as big as himself. Isaac had only just enough time to rein in his mule to prevent them from crashing into one another. Then, as he started to continue on his way, he discovered a toothless old man supping on a bran mash, sitting on a log in the shadow of a doorway.

Isaac smiled, saluted respectfully, and leaned out of his saddle to say, "Aged sir, a good day to you and yours, and may God be with you! I am looking for a shop owned by the wise man, Judicael, the moneychanger."

The old man gave him a rather vacant look. Without replying he plunged the wooden stick that served as his spoon back into the gruel. Isaac, a bit taken aback, wondered if the old man was mad, or if he did not understand Frankish. As he had less chance of being understood in Latin, he was just about to ask in German when the old man began to laugh, his mouth overflowing with mash.

"The moneychanger! Right now, he'll be with the Bishop!"

Isaac shivered. He hoped he had misunderstood. The old man's eyes narrowed and he pointed his poor excuse for a spoon at the travelers face.

"You, you too have the face of Judas! Today is Holy Friday, Judas! Get off with you! Go and serve the Bishop with the other Jews! They are all there!" Through the lane and the house walls, he designated a point in a northerly direction before once more plowing into his bowl, grinning.

With an icy heart, Isaac whacked the rump of his mule and moved off in the direction pointed out with a barely polite farewell. He could guess at the spectacle that awaited him. Nausea overtook him.

It was no longer raining when he entered the marketplace. The stalls were deserted. A few children played there, crouching under the planks, their backsides in the mud, stealing apples. Some of them came out from their shelters to examine him and hurl scarcely intelligible words at him. Held up high by strong ropes, the Christian Cross was affixed to the walls of the fortress of the Duke of Burgundy. From below Isaac could hear the chanting of a crowd. Taking no notice of the children following, his mule trotted on. Isaac crossed the vast marketplace.

On the right flank of the fortress, on a bare piece of muddy ground churned up like a swamp, it seemed that all the townsfolk were assembled, rich and poor alike, packed tightly together in prayer. The Palace of Christ was only a skeleton. The walls of the foundations, topped by wooden scaffolding, had only risen to the height of a man. At the eastern end, there was a rough pile of stones blackened by the rain, forming a scallop around a bowl cut in the limestone for the baptismal ceremony. A narrow platform overhung the crowd. On top stood a blue dais embroidered in silver. It supported a wooden statue of Jesus Christ, with staring eyes and a body painted in glaring white, gold and blood red. A dozen monks dressed in linen smocks and a bishop in a purple cape stood on one side. In barely comprehensible Latin the prelate prayed at length. Suddenly switching to Frankish that was heavily accented with Burgundy, he shouted out, "This is how it all happened: Pilate placed the crown of thorns on the head of Jesus and ordered him to be whipped! Then the Jews went to Pilate and said, 'We have a law. According to this law, the one you call Jesus must die because he claims to be the son of God. That is false! God has no sons!'"

The monks crossed themselves and a moan ran through the

crowd. Isaac reined in his mule and held still, hoping that no one would turn to look at him. The bishop, after having surveyed his audience, his manner that of a man used to causing a stir, continued in a raucous voice:

"Yes! That is what the Jews said! And, when Pilate the Roman really wanted to release Our Lord Jesus Christ, they said to him, 'No! No, you cannot let him go! That man wants to be the son of God and he wants to be King! You must crucify him. You must break his limbs and give him vinegar to drink!'"

A new cry of anger arose. Women began to wail. A squall of wind swept the square. The crowd surged forward, closer to the baptismal font. Shouting broke out everywhere. The bishop pointed his forefinger at the man they were pushing toward the dais. He was Isaac's age, scarcely more than twenty. His arms were tied to a beam that weighed his shoulders down. His head was bare and the hair had been shaved from his head. Seeing him, the monks fell to their knees, crossing themselves vigorously as if the putrefying smell of the devil filled their nostrils. The bishop shouted, "This is the Jew! This is the Jew!"

Far to his left, Isaac heard a muffled crying. A small group of men and women were squashed behind some beetroot stalls. Cold and wet, the family and friends of the wretched young man held on to one another while he played the role of the villain on the stage set by the Christian prelate. Cries issued from the throat of one young woman, her gown swollen by a belly containing tomorrow's child. Without thinking too hard, Isaac pushed his mount toward them while the prelate's voice swelled and echoed between the castle walls. Uneasy Jewish eyes turned toward him. He suddenly realized they saw only a stranger, and the fear of what he might do to them was in their eyes. He raised his right hand as a sign of peace and whispered loudly, so that only they could hear, "I am one of you! My name is Isaac ben Eliezer…"

He didn't have time to say anymore. The young pregnant woman screamed. "Simon! Simon!"

On the dais, the bishop was beating the young Jew with an

armful of brambles, tearing his face with every stroke. The crowd applauded, calling for more. The brambles broke in the bishop's hands, which made him beat Simon with even more passion, until the young man, arms and shoulders still bound to the beam, fell to the ground, unable to lift himself up. His wife strained to run forward, but her companions held her back, covering her mouth to muffle her cries. Isaac lifted up the skirts of his cape. Hammering the flanks of his mount with his heels, standing in his stirrups, he shouted and drew out his Toledo dagger.

The surprise was such that he was able to pass through the crowd like Moses parting the sea. The Christians were transfixed with amazement. For that moment they saw only a man of fine features—long honey-colored curls, a small and beautiful mouth, angry eyes more blue than the waters of a lake—standing on his horse. To their eyes he was as beautiful as the devil disguised as an angel.

Pointing the blade of his knife forward, Isaac rode up to the dais. Pressing his mule against the wooden structure, Isaac delivered the young Jew from his beam of penitence with a few deft cuts. "Come on!" he shouted, "Jump up behind me!"

The crowd had gotten over its shock and regained its sense of purpose. The women and a gang of youths turned on the group of Jews. Bending down in the mud, they began to throw lumps of earth at them, shouting, "Death to the Jews! Death to Judas!"

Slowed down by the weight of the bloodied young man and frightened by the noise, Isaac's mule hesitated and slowed to a trot. Brandishing his cross, the bishop shouted to the crowd to catch them. Some men waved clubs, others pitchforks or hoes. Isaac parried some blows with his sword, and kicked a few peasants in their snarling faces, but his mule was now hesitating, all ready to turn around. A ferocious cry drew Isaac's attention toward the group he was trying to reach. Some youngsters had got hold of the young woman's arms and were tearing her clothes off. Isaac felt rather than heard the terrified cry from his companion on the back of his neck.

"Don't harm her," the young man stammered as if everyone could hear him. "Please…no…!"

The young woman was practically naked. Children were trailing her skirts in the mud, laughing. Between the tears in her chemise the pale skin of her rounded, defenseless belly showed.

Simon jumped down from the mule and tried to run in the direction of his wife. Isaac tried to follow, but at that moment a huge man charged at him with a wooden fork. He beat off the first blow with his boot. The second he parried with his dagger, using it like a small axe. Two of the tines of the fork broke off, but goaded on by his furious fanaticism, the Christian managed to thrust the remaining tine into Isaac's thigh. Isaac groaned. The mule, terrified by the riot around it, then saved his life by carrying him away in a gallop through the crowd.

There was no more shouting, there were no more cat-calls. A heavy silence, like the shadow of death, hung in the air. Before Simon could carry her to safety, his wife had been assaulted with a large stone, pulled off the wall and smashed into her distended belly. She looked like a statue in the mud, nude and covered in dirt, unconscious. As if satisfied by the odor of suffering and death, the crowd muttered and turned away, ready to recommence its prayer that had been interrupted by the thirst for vengeance.

ॐ

Before nightfall, the low clouds began to clear. A ray of sunshine caressed the trees that covered the highest peaks. In an instant the ray became a beam, then a wave. The heat returned suddenly. The forest steamed, mixing its mists with the disappearing clouds. Light flared with a green luminescence. The world appeared immense, beautiful and peaceful. At any other time Isaac, leaning against the wall of a small country-house a league from the town, would have been moved to thank the Almighty for this sudden splendor. But now, in the depths of his soul, he could only feel anger and disgust. They had tended his wound, but in truth, his thigh hurt him less than his fury. The young woman was dead, killed together with the crushed child in her womb.

A small man of gentle yet sad appearance came and sat beside him. Emitting a sigh, he said, "When children lose their innocence,

46

the world loses its soul. I am Nathan Judicael, the moneychanger. We must thank you for your aid. Without you…"

"I didn't stop that woman from being killed," cut in Isaac curtly. "And maybe I even provoked it. Why are you thanking me?"

The moneychanger smiled bitterly. "For having refused that which we would have had to accept."

"It was no more than a reaction of the moment!"

Judicael swept away his objection with a gesture. "Each one does what he can…. They tell me you were looking for me?"

"Yes, I only have one purse of coins from Narbonne, and I am traveling far to the east…."

Nathan Judicael examined him attentively. "Far to the east? To Poland?"

"I was born in Poland," Isaac said reticently.

"You are very young to have traveled so far."

"My father was a scholar. He left to join the great Rabbi Hazdai Ibn Shaprut living with the Moors in Andalusia. He took me with him when I was ten."

"I feel certain you are already a wise man. I can see it in your face. You have the beauty of knowledge and intelligence. So, are you going back to Poland?"

"No, I am going farther than that. Beyond the Magyar country…."

The moneychanger started. "Beyond the country of the Magyars! But, my boy, there are only the Hungarians, thirsty for blood, beyond there! Mad barbarians like those that have invaded us incessantly ever since King Othon first failed to repel them…."

Isaac hesitated. On a day like today, he knew the weight of hope and dreams that his answer would invoke. But, perhaps, on a day like today, it was more necessary than ever that hope should stimulate dreams.

"I am going to a kingdom where the king is a Jew," he announced slowly. "They are called the Khazars and have chosen to observe the Laws of Moses."

At first the moneychanger registered no reaction at all, as if he had not heard. Then his lips began to tremble. He stood up, leaning on Isaac's shoulder. "A Jewish king! In the east…. A new Kingdom of Israel, are you saying? But, then—may the Almighty forgive me—does this mean that the time of the Messiah has arrived?"

Isaac avoided looking into the over-excited face staring at him and did not answer.

Chapter eight

D*uring* the two weeks following the visit from Yakubov,

Sofer's tranquility was disturbed by three things. According to the expert opinion of a numismatic specialist in Middle Ages coins, the silver piece really did appear to be of Khazar origin. Contrary to what he had promised, and against all logic, Yakubov had not called him. And for several nights the redheaded stranger had ruined Sofer's repose. He dreamed that she posed him the same question over and over again, and he had preferred to wake up rather than be driven mad. He began to hate the woman and to wish with all his soul he had the opportunity to tell her so.

જી

The expert had been Swiss and quite reputable, recommended by both Sotheby's and Christie's. He certified, in exchange for two thousand dollars, that his appraisal and opinion were valid for three months.

"This coin is pure silver, smelted using an ancient technique originating in the Euphrates basin. By ancient, I mean two or three centuries before the Christian era began. However, the coin itself is much younger, minted between the eigthth and the ninth centuries, I'm certain...."

He held a loupe under Sofer's nose and turned the coin over in his beautifully manicured fingers. "It's a Jewish coin, but you know that already, embossed as it is with the seven-branched candelabra. It carries two inscriptions in Hebrew denoting its weight, which at the time indicated its value.... This is what's so interesting, so surprising."

His varnished nail pointed to a group of three superimposed signs. He changed his tone and threw a conspiratorial glance at Sofer. "I had been thinking...a Jewish coin, an ancient mode of striking...that seems in order...perhaps a Syrian coin, or even a coin from the Jewish colony in Baghdad. Except that the inscription does not fit. It does not correspond with any of the languages used in that region or period. And then I remembered a coin identified some years ago...."

Without a word, one eye closed against the extremely strong beam of light emanating from the loupe, Sofer patiently waited to hear something of value. The expert left his desk and opened the armor-plated door of a burnished-steel cupboard. He fished out a tiny drawer from which he withdrew a coin similar to Yakubov's but slightly smaller.

"Look at this," he said, placing it under the loupe. "Do you see, there...?"

Sofer could see. The same group of signs, just as incomprehensible, were molded into the surface of the new coin.

"What do these signs mean?" he asked.

"Bulan, King of the Khazars!"

Sofer raised an eyebrow.

"They say that the only people apart from the Byzantines who knew how to mint money in the Caucasian region before the tenth century were the Khazars. They even minted them for their neighbors.... Bulan was King of the Khazars in the eighth century. According to legend, it was he who ordered the Khazars to adopt Judaism."

So, Yakubov had not lied. But still, to give the man fifty thousand dollars that Sofer did not have, at least not without complications, would require more details and, above all, a frank explanation.

Two weeks passed. Then half of another. Each morning, each evening, with growing annoyance, Sofer examined the coin on his desk. The expert had valued it at fifty thousand dollars. He could hardly believe that Yakubov was going to abandon it and disappear. It did not make sense. Especially since he had the air of someone hard pressed for cash and was the discoverer of the cave! Did Yakubov have other troubles? He had alluded to them. But what? And with whom? Did he, perhaps, have a box full of Khazar coins, just like the one he had left here? In that case, why did he want money? He would only have to sell a few, even at a low price, and his fortune would be assured.

Sofer sat out on his balcony and watched Paris offer itself once more to the spring sunshine. He detested unanswered questions. It was usually at such times that the desire to write overtook him. One morning, he made a decision. He abandoned his roses, which had no need of him, sat a pile of encyclopedias on his desk, and switched on his computer.

After wasting an absurd amount of time on the Internet, Sofer listed the meager information that he did have. It was as concise as it was poor. Information in the encyclopedias was sparse. Apparently, there were very few archaeological traces of the Khazars. Yakubov was right, again. All through their history, the Russians and Soviets had tried to make them disappear. The fortress at Sarkel, on the banks of the Don, had been 'inadvertently' submerged under a lake created as a reservoir in the 1950s. All the same, a few meager vestiges survived in the area of Itil, the great capital city of the Khazars, situated at the mouth of the Volga. But there was no record of caves or secret synagogues in the Caucasus mountains.

Of actual traces, three articles mentioned interesting details. There had been three letters written between 940 and 960. One of them had been dictated by a Khazar noble and addressed to the important Jewish community of Cordoba. Preserved in Cambridge, it apparently contained a great deal of information on life in the kingdom and on its subjects. The two others were even more important.

In the year 953, the great Rabbi Hazdai Ibn Shaprut, adviser to the Caliph Abd al-Rahman III and famed for his scienctific knowledge and his poetry, had sent a letter full of questions to Joseph, young King of the Khazars. An intrepid young Jew, Isaac ben Eliezer had been charged with the mission of delivering the letter and had crossed a Europe in total chaos, overcoming innumerable hardships. There was then a delay of seven years before the reply reached the hands of Rabbi Hazdai, again delivered by Isaac ben Eliezer. These two letters, also preserved in Cambridge, contained all the questions that anyone could ask about the kingdom of the Khazars, and even some of the answers.

⁂

Two nights later, the memory of the redheaded woman came back to haunt Sofer. He wondered where she lived. Was she Belgian? French? Sofer suddenly shivered. The meeting with Yakubov had so distracted him that he couldn't even remember whether she had spoken to him in French. No, that was absurd, he had replied in French. The whole room had understood and laughed.... Yes, true, but he did speak five languages and mixed them at will. If the beautiful redhead had spoken in Russian or Hebrew, or English even, he wouldn't have necessarily noticed. He could remember exactly what she was wearing: a light-colored leather coat and a black dress. No rings, no earrings. Only a silver necklace. A very reasonable type. Even as a child she must have been very sure of herself, always self-controlled. Seductive and capricious.... What was her profession? Was she single, married, involved with someone? Was she a mother? He could see her driving a car. A fast car. She would have money, lead a life of luxury. But how did she come by her money? By selling old Khazar coins?

Stretched out in the dark, Sofer smiled to himself at the turn his thoughts were taking, following a process set in motion in spite of himself, and one he knew only too well—that of shaping his memory to transform a stranger into a character. He turned onto his side and, to escape his obsession, let his mind wander to the Khazars. What could they have been like, these Jews from the ends of the earth, these men who decided to adopt the Law of Moses when it already signified exile and opprobrium in most countries? And why did they make such a decision? What did Judaism mean for them, there, lost in the Caspian steppes, their every move under surveillance by Byzantium? And how did they disappear? Why? How did they live, and love?

Sofer realized that his old demon was taking possession of him; whether he thought of the redheaded stranger or the Khazars, writing drew him like a lover. The demon whispered to him that plunging into the waves of written words in a novel was not so terrible. After all, one never broke anything real by writing it down. And anyway, surely it was better to be inconvenienced by accomplishing something than to dream useless dreams!

And then, the very next day, that is what happened.

He finally had the long-postponed lunch meeting with his editor. Prudently, Sofer presented himself in the charming surroundings of the patio in the Hotel Athena. His editor, as good looking as she was cultured, had the art of leading you to write books that you would never have dreamed of writing before speaking to her. Sofer feared the accusation that was not long in coming:

"Marc, how long is it since you finished a book?"

"Three years, six months and twelve days. You will have to excuse the odd hour or so I omitted."

"There you are, then! I think I have just heard a man deserted by the love of his life! Can you explain to me, now, the reason behind this silence? I know that you have not dried up, except perhaps financially. Would you like us to try and think of a subject together?"

"If I do need anything, it is most certainly not someone to take me by the hand like a senile old man," replied Sofer dryly.

He was picking nervously at his *coquilles Saint Jacques*, not wishing to spoil the pleasure of the excellent cuisine, when a voice made him jump. A laugh followed by an exclamation. A Russian exclamation! He glanced quickly around the restaurant. Behind a generous arrangement of potted banana trees and palms, he recognized a silhouette. The silhouette only, because the suit was unrecognizable; anthracite gray over a black shirt. No tie, but a canary yellow silk handkerchief in the top pocket. The outfit, this time beautifully tailored, disguised the breadth of the shoulders. When Yakubov turned around, Sofer wondered if he wasn't delirious.

"Good God!" he exclaimed.

"What is it?" his editor inquired, puzzled.

Sofer stood up, without replying. He walked around the patio zigzagging through the maze of chairs. At the same moment, Yakubov got up from his table as did the two men he was with, and they walked off in the direction of the reception hall. Sofer bumped into a young American, and without any apology, ran into the hall.

"Mr. Yakubov! Mr. Yakubov!"

The Caucasian paused while the men on either side of him turned around. Yakubov appeared annoyed. He looked quickly and imperiously at each of them in turn. They stepped aside, feigning indifference.

"Mr. Yakubov, you were to call me, no?"

With the face of a child that has been caught misbehaving, Yakubov squirmed and fidgeted.

"I know, but there was no more need for me to trouble you."

Sofer pointed at the suit mockingly. "It would seem your affairs have sorted themselves out! Nice suit, smart hotel…."

"Yes, fine."

"No more need of a visa? You found your fifty thousand dollars, then?"

Yakubov looked again at the two men patiently waiting beside the revolving door to the street.

"I am sorry, I ought to have called you."

"We can soon remedy that. Tell me where we can meet for a drink this evening and you can tell me all about it."

"That's not possible. I'm catching a plane shortly," Yakubov said, flashing his beaming golden smile.

"Oh well…. Are you returning to Georgia?"

"No, no. To Canada."

Sofer abandoned that line, stunned. "And the cave? The cave I was going to discover?"

"Sorry, Mr. Sofer."

"What do you mean, sorry?"

"I must go. You can keep the coin as a souvenir."

"The coin…. Good God, Yakubov!" Sofer exclaimed. "What the devil are you playing at?"

But the Caucasian had already turned his back. His two acolytes advanced to join him. Sofer understood: gorillas. Bodyguards, musclemen, hired by the day, the month…. Evidently, Yakubov had made good use of his moving family history and his Khazar coins.

Half the people in the hall were watching, silently. As the trio left the hotel, Sofer contented himself with muttering a few choice swearwords under his breath.

ॐ

That same evening, he looked up the name and telephone number, in Baku, of the president of the Association of Mountain Jews, Mikhail Yakovlevitch Agarounov. Agarounov answered on the fourth ring. He expressed surprise when Sofer introduced himself.

"It's a great pleasure to speak to you! Do you know, I've read three of your books in German!"

After some more civilities, Sofer told him of Yakubov's appearance and disappearance. Agarounov reflected for several seconds. "No, that name means nothing to me. I'd need to check our files to be sure, but if he comes from Georgia, it wouldn't be a surprise if I didn't recognize the name. Our association only applies to the Mountain Jews of Azerbaijan…"

"Pity…."

"What did he sell you?"

Sofer guessed the other was smiling from the tone of voice. He started to tell a shortened account of the story of the cave and the coin. Agarounov did not let him finish. "The Khazars!" he exclaimed. "That's extraordinary! Did you know that only yesterday there was an attack that damaged four oil-pumping stations in the Bay of Baku? Hardly an hour ago, the radio was talking of demands from a group nobody has heard of. You've got it in one, Mr. Sofer! This group calls itself 'The New Khazars!'"

Sofer closed his eyes while the charming Agarounov gave him as many details as he knew.

"And what did they want?" asked Sofer.

"It's not exactly clear. The demand letter was not read out on the radio. Money, for sure. But I can tell you, it's not good for our community...."

Sofer felt a shiver up his spine. He had to buy a train ticket for London and then on to Cambridge, so he could see the Khazar documents with his own eyes.

Chapter nine

T

he same evening of the terrible day that saw the death of
the pregnant young woman, the Jews of Mâcon attended a meeting
called by Nathan Judicael, the moneychanger. They met in a barn at
the edge of the forest, half a league from the town walls, a barn that
also served them as a synagogue.

"A secret synagogue," Nathan explained to Isaac. "It has to
remain so, for if not, a Gentile might think of setting it on fire. They
are convinced that we converse with the devil, that we eat children
and I don't know what other horrors!"

There were equal measures of bitterness and irony in the
moneychanger's voice.

A small bald man added, "But unfortunately, keeping our synagogues secret only feeds their suspicions. And the Christians would
just love to roast us! You see, brave Isaac, the Almighty uses many
means to put us to the test, most particularly, it seems, by squeezing
us between two stones, like the grain in my mill!"

"At least He teaches us modesty," sighed Nathan, pointing to
the bare planks all around them.

Some candlesticks had been fixed to the wooden walls. An oil lamp suspended from a rough beam cast a dull light onto a reading desk that supported a Torah scroll and some poor quality writing materials. There were no other tables or chairs, and no other sacred texts to study. Isaac felt his heart shrink before such poverty. How different from the beautiful libraries in Cordoba! Nathan Judicael pulled his prayer shawl over his shoulders and murmured, "The Lord is in this place, yet I am ignorant of His presence...."

Isaac, recognizing the verse from Genesis, added, "How special this place is! It is none other than the house of the Lord, and this is the gate to Heaven."

Nathan and his bald companion looked at him in admiration.

"It seems right that God, blessed be His name, has showered you with His gifts in abundance, traveler!" declared Nathan. "We shall say the evening prayer and then you can tell us the reason for your journey. Your news is so marvelous that everyone should profit by it and revitalize their souls on this day of sadness."

And that is what they did. Toward the end of prayers, about fifty men suddenly surged out of the night to appear within the weak and flickering light of the barn. They pressed around Isaac.

He told them first about the extraordinary lives that Jews led in Cordoba, in Andalusia. "The orange groves cover the hills with flowers whiter than snow. The perfume is so intense that in the heat of springtime evenings, when the sun plunges over the edge of the world, everyone has to breathe shallow breaths so as not to suffocate from the sweetness."

He also explained that Jews were treated properly and some were even respected for their great knowledge. "The Caliph, Abd al-Rahman III, son of Mohammed, son of Abd al-Rahman, son of Heschem, son of Abd al-Rahman, may God grant him long life, accords his confidence and mercy to the great Rabbi Hazdai Ibn Shaprut, who is his councilor and chief of all the Sephardi Jews."

"What is this Sephardi you talk about?" asked a young man with dark rings under his eyes and a face covered in scars.

Isaac recognized Simon, the same person the bishop had beaten with brambles, the very one who, in a flash, and in the most humiliating circumstances, had lost his beloved and the baby she carried. How had he the strength to come to the synagogue after such horrors?

"Sepharad is the name the Muslims give Andalusia," replied Isaac gently. Andalusia is the southern part of the continent of Spain. It is bordered on one side by the Great Ocean on which all the lands of the world float. On the other side, farther to the south, begins the other part of the world that goes all the way to Jerusalem...."

"Isaac, my boy!" Nathan interrupted impatiently, "don't make us wait. Tell us about this new Jewish Kingdom."

"It all started about ten years ago," Isaac began with excitement. "In the year 4710 since the creation of the world some merchants from Constantinople came to sell their cloth and other objects in Sepharad. One of them was hoping to sell a scroll containing the Greek rules of arithmetic to Rabbi Hazdai. You know what merchants are like; always gossiping, always telling tales. And so it was with this one, who claimed that there was a Jewish kingdom on the northern frontier of Byzantium!"

Isaac smiled, seeing the faces light up the darkness, with no need for candles or lamps.

"Continue, my son," whispered one old man with eyes so gray that he looked as if he could no longer see. "Go on, it's a good story."

"Rabbi Hazdai was astonished. He asked, 'How can that be? A Jewish kingdom? There was only ever one! There *can* only be one Israel, one Jerusalem! And they no longer exist, except in our memory and our hearts. They faded into shadow and tragedy because of our wrongdoings, even though God never took our special protection from us.' But the merchant protested vehemently. 'No, Rabbi,' he said. 'May the Almighty smite me if I am lying. There is a Jewish kingdom to the north of Byzantium. They assure me that it is populated with Jews who follow the Law of Moses, even though they are not sons of Abraham. Those Jews pay no tribute to any tribe of Gentiles and they are their own masters in their own land!'"

Isaac paused for breath before continuing. "Rabbi Hazdai Ibn

Shaprut is a true sage. He is not a man to believe the first wild tale he hears. He thought the story too good to be true, but remembered it, mentioning it to nobody so as not to raise any false hopes...."

Isaac paused again. "Eventually, he confided in my father, the astronomer Joshua ben Eliezer, because he trusted his judgment, but soon after that, in the month of Av 4712, my father died in the rabbi's arms. I was only a child, not yet thirteen years old, not yet a *Bar Mitzvah*. Calling on the Almighty to be his witness, his hand holding mine, my father passed the secret to me after making me promise not to divulge it. 'Hope, Isaac, my son,' he said, 'hope with all your heart that this kingdom exists and that it is waiting there for us. Hope, pray for it, but do not tell a soul.' That's the promise I made to the rabbi, and you must also keep it...."'

There were murmurs and nods. With a mechanical gesture, Isaac swept the long blond hair covering his forehead away from his eyes, and continued. "The market season passed and other details came to the ears of Rabbi Hazdai. Traders from Khorossan and Baghdad, from Poland and the Magyar country, confirmed the story first told by the man from Constantinople. They assured him they had met inhabitants of the Jewish kingdom, and it was called the Kingdom of the Khazars. Men with high cheekbones, like Asians, clothed in long leather tunics or linen depending on the time of year, speaking and writing in an unknown language. but also with enough Hebrew to be able to read the Torah...."

"Is this actually possible?" muttered the miller.

"More than possible," confirmed Isaac. "They said that they have kings whose names are drawn from the Bible, that the king reigning today is called Joseph, and that only his Jewish son can succeed him! They say these Khazars decided themselves to become Jews, that there are synagogues throughout their country, and that one can live there in peace according to the Law of Moses and—"

"You can't be sure!" a serious voice interrupted.

Isaac, like everyone else, jumped. The man who had spoken was tall and thin, but had a wiry strength. His eyes were sunk deep in his skull. A scar, which made his skin look as shiny as if it was covered in oil, marked the whole width of his right temple.

"What are you saying, Saul?" said Nathan, the moneychanger. "Do you know anything about this kingdom?"

Saul nodded his head and stared back at the stupefied glares all around him. "I, too, am a merchant. I too went, about seven years ago, to buy spears and knives forged by the Magyars. And there I heard this name, the Khazars."

"Then, why didn't you say anything?" asked Simon.

"Why should I have said anything?" Saul answered. "They only told me that there is a Kingdom of the Khazars east of the Sea of Azov, the one that reaches all the way to Constantinople. But nobody told me it was a Jewish kingdom."

The silence was so complete that they could hear an owl hooting outside. Saul turned to Isaac. "All I have heard is that these Khazars live in tents, ride horses and are continually at war with the barbarians to the north, the Russians. I swear that I never heard anyone say they were Jews! I have traveled far to the east, almost as far as Kiev. All I ever heard was that there are many Muslims in the Kingdom of the Khazars, and a few Christians and some idolaters. The kind that bring forth demons with their amulets.... No hint of a Jewish state in that!"

Silence returned, weighing down on the assembly. Nathan avoided Isaac's glance. Simon's young eyes flashed with fervor. Isaac opened the rucksack that he had been holding close. He drew out a leather tube.

"In this tube is a letter that Rabbi Hazdai Ibn Shaprut wrote to Joseph, King of the Khazars. The rabbi appointed me to go and place this missive personally in the hands of King Joseph. And I will do so."

"You are going there?" asked Simon.

"Yes. And even if someone were to steal the letter from me, I can recite it by heart to the King of the Khazars."

"And, if they are not Jews?" persisted Saul.

"They are." Isaac responded forcefully. "And there is one question that Rabbi Hazdai posed that must be answered."

"Which is?" demanded the moneychanger in a voice choked with emotion.

Isaac pressed the scroll case to his chest and began reciting: "'I ask one more thing of my master, Joseph, King of the Khazars; that he deigns to reveal to me what he knows of the miracle we have been awaiting these many years, as we passed from one captivity to the next. How can I be at peace when the destruction of our Temple throws us from one exile to the next? We are no more than a small number in the multitude. Deprived of our ancient glory, we have nothing to reply when they say to us that each nation has a country, and we, the Jews, have not even a piece of land that retains a trace of us! Also, my lord, in learning the news of the existence of your kingdom, the power of your empire and your army, our courage has come back to us, our strength revived. My lord, are you the king so much hoped for by us? Do you govern the country that this scattered people await, that signifies the ending of their servitude? Is the land of the Khazars that which the Almighty designated for the rebuilding of His Temple? May Heaven grant that this news be real. May the Lord God of Israel be blessed for not having refused the Tribes of Israel either a liberator or a country!'"

"Amen!"

The word echoed around the barn, uttered simultaneously by many mouths.

"It is a very long letter and contains many other things," added Isaac.

"None of us know with any exactitude what is beyond the country of the Magyars," acknowledged Nathan. "However, so great a rabbi would not have attempted to write to a king if he did not exist."

"I am sure that this Jewish kingdom exists!" exclaimed Simon, crying with emotion. "And I want to go with Isaac! I have nothing to keep me here and this cause means so much to all of us; even if I perish en route, that is better than to ever again submit to the bishop's hatred!"

"We must make a copy of this letter," intervened the old man with the gray eyes. "We will keep it here. Thus, in case of misfortune, someone else could take on your task and deliver it to King Joseph!"

The miller grasped the merchant's arm: "Saul, you are a traveler, you have been to the east several times. You know the roads and the directions. Go with Simon and Isaac."

"You ask that of me? A doubter who cannot be sure, like you, that this kingdom even exists!"

"Precisely! You will keep a cool head. Look at them! Isaac is courageous and knowledgeable, wise for his age. But his age is what it is. Passion will overcome him. He will always be liable to be foolhardy, like today. And look at our young Simon. He is nothing but wounds and pain. He has lost everything in one day, and with the first rays of sunshine, he will take his dreams for reality."

"While I, I can go and trade with the Khazars!" sneered Saul. "Is that what you mean to say?"

"Partly. It ought to give you the desire to go *and* return."

"The miller is right," Nathan interjected. "You could be of huge assistance to them, Saul. And think of the cause!"

"I would be happy to have your company," admitted Isaac. "And no doubt King Joseph will be pleased to learn how you carry out your profession."

With raised eyebrows, Saul looked at Isaac as if to assure himself that his words held no taint of mockery. He shrugged his shoulders.

"I will decide tomorrow."

Late into the night, they read and reread the long letter from the rabbi, committing it to memory. Then they copied it with care and attention. When they finally left the synagogue, in groups that huddled together in the darkness, the wolves were howling in the forest.

Chapter ten

N

Oxford, England
May 2000

obody dares approach the Khagan of the Khazars, unless it is for a matter of great importance. In that case, the visitor has to prostrate himself before the Khagan, touching his forehead to the ground, and stay in that position until the Khagan commands him to stand. All must remain silent until the Khagan indicates they may speak. Truly, the power of the Khagan of the Khazars is so absolute that his orders and smallest wishes are carried out with blind obedience. If he judges it correct to rid his court of someone, he summons him. The Khagan then says to this lord, no matter how powerful he is, 'Be gone from my sight. Your misdeed offends the rule of the Almighty. Go home and render up your life.' Upon hearing this, the lord returns to his house and kills himself."

Sofer sighed and closed his tired eyes. From within the silence of the luxurious paneled room, he could hear the comforting sound of the rain outside increasing in volume. Of course it would be raining; England without rain would be like New York without skyscrapers. Now a regular and light rainfall, it polished the leaves of the massive

65

clumps of rhododendrons and azaleas surrounding the courtyard of the Randolph, a typically vast Victorian hotel in the center of Oxford. Leaning his head back in the leather armchair, Sofer stroked the time-worn surface of the Khazar coin Yakubov had given him. Ever since Yakubov had given it to him, he'd carried it everywhere, like a talisman. Restless yet exhausted at the same time, he could not find repose. The preceding days had been trying.

⁊⁊

He had gone first to Cambridge, where the buses were disgorging tourists in noisy flocks. Swept up in the crowds, he had an interminable wait in a line before being allowed into Queen's College Library. Once finally in the holy of holies, he had been amazed when they had refused him access to the documents. In vain had he used all his capacity for persuasion; in the department of ancient manuscripts they made no exceptions. He thought to telephone the London publisher who looked after the translation of his own work, and the next day, like a miracle, the doors of Queen's College Library opened before him, with all the respect due to his calling.

"The originals, themselves?" Sofer had insisted.

"Certainly. Certainly!"

Of course, they would also be happy to furnish him with all the copies necessary. In addition, a specialist in these texts had been placed at his disposal for the whole day. The reference room had fewer than fifteen desks. Four high, narrow windows looked out onto the brick buildings of the college. An atmosphere of meditation reigned; so great was the tension that even the breathing of the occupants could be discerned. Here, reading was like praying. Sofer could not help but compare it with a *yeshiva*.

After a brief wait, a smiling young woman approached him pushing a silent trolley, like a dessert cart in a smart restaurant. It supported a glass cabinet that displayed four sheets of parchment.

"This is the document you asked for, sir," announced the young woman quietly. "The one we call the Schechter letter...."

The manuscripts were in good condition; only one of them was slightly cracked and showed some humidity damage. The ink, mostly brown and in some places almost purple, outlined square characters. The calligraphy was firm and thick. On each of the parchments the writing was divided into two columns. At first glance, Sofer deciphered signs of ancient Hebrew lettering, written in that manner so particular to the Middle Ages, of running the words together without any space between them to indicate punctuation or place for breath. To be here, before this physical manifestation of ancient times, brought a lump to his throat. These pages had been written more than a thousand years ago, yet they contained more of the essence of life in them than a glimmer of light at the bottom of a well. The young historian, close by, sensed his emotion. She smiled gently.

"These ancient manuscripts are always stirring. They make me think of an old family photograph album."

Surprised, Sofer raised his eyes to look at her. Up till then he had not paid her much attention, but now he discovered a sensual, intelligent face that immediately awakened another interest.

"Can't we open this damned box?" he asked.

"Unfortunately not, sir. We must avoid all contact with the parchments. They appear to be in good condition, but in open air they oxidize very quickly…"

She withdrew a folder from underneath the trolley. "These are photographs of the original, along with the translations Schechter made, as you requested. Would you like to know the history of these documents?"

Sofer riffled through the file and nodded. "Please, do go on."

"Like many of the ancient documents concerning the Jewish world, these came from the Cairo Geniza. In 1890, the researcher Solomon Schechter was working there. He found them and brought them back to Cambridge six months later. Today, we think that this letter was originally written right at the beginning of the tenth century, certainly before 955."

"By whom?"

"The identity of the author is in doubt, but the researchers are certain they have identified the mark of a very important person at the court of the Khazars in the document. A Jew, no doubt, and one who was residing in Constantinople when he wrote it…."

"How can you be certain of the date it was written?" Sofer interrupted her. "I can't see a date on it."

The young woman nodded her head briefly. "It is a simple enough piece of deduction," she replied, assuming an instructive tone. "It's not a normal letter, it's more of a report. The document summarizes the origin and history of the Khazars, and the situation as was then current in the Khazar Kingdom. It describes their conversion to Judaism, King Bulan's dream, his vision of the angel, the religious debate he organized between the priest, the rabbi and the imam to show which was the better religion ... certain facts contemporary to the author are also mentioned: the skirmishes with the Russians and the Petchenegues, and the difficult negotiations with Byzantium."

She leaned gently over to Sofer as if to tell him a secret. "It appears to be almost certain that this report passed through the hands of Rabbi Hazdai Ibn Shaprut in Cordoba even before he wrote his famous letter to King Joseph of the Khazars."

She concluded with finality, "thanks to this collection of data, we can specify that the date the text was written was before 955 CE...."

This last remark left Sofer dreaming. Involuntarily, his fingers caressed the glass cover protecting the manuscript as if he could feel the warm, smooth texture of the parchment, here and there scarred by the ravages of time.

"They wrote like this during the time of the pharaohs," he murmured. "With a twig of jonquil or rose sharpened to a nib and split down the middle. Something like the metal school pens we used when I first went to school. Except that these retain their legibility despite time, the same as pencil."

The young English woman observed him with a warm smile. Oblivious to her presence, Sofer continued his monologue. "That's how things were done in those days ... Jewish merchants journeyed between all the great cities surrounding the Mediterranean. They thought constantly about Jerusalem, its destroyed Temple, the exile, the dispersed tribes! And then, because of the hazards of travel in those days, several of them settled in Constantinople. For one reason or another, they had contact with the Khazar who wrote those words...."

Sofer tapped the glass and continued with scarcely concealed emotion. "Perhaps he was a merchant like them? Why not? And this man spoke to them about the Jewish Kingdom! Imagine their amazement. A kingdom for the Jews somewhere beyond the Caucasus Mountains. They surely would have thought of the Messiah. Instantly! They would have thought about Rabbi Hazdai, head of the most important and influential Jewish community of the time, and without doubt, the richest ... our merchants would have then made their way to Cordoba and told their story to the rabbi. Hazdai would not have been able to believe his ears: A Jewish king! He would need to know more...."

The young librarian tilted her head. This extraordinarily enthusiastic man, so anchored in his history, attracted her. She began to join in his game. "Rabbi Hazdai Ibn Shaprut sent a messenger to the Khazars," she interjected, "hoping that he would find the kingdom near the Black Sea. But, being affiliated to Rome, the Byzantine Emperor was leading a campaign against the Khazars; he wanted to conquer the kingdom. The Khazars were rich and tolerant; the elite were Jewish, but the Khazar people were probably Muslim as well as Christian or even pagan. A total anathema to the Byzantine Church ... the Byzantine authorities therefore forbade the passage of the messenger from Cordoba...."

Sofer took up the story. "After that setback, Rabbi Hazdai decided to send a letter written in his own hand to the King of the Khazars. To avoid the watchful eye of Byzantium, the new messenger would be required to risk the long journey across Europe...."

The young woman laughed, her face coloring. "Have you found the name of this messenger?"

"I knew it already!" exclaimed Sofer, proud of himself. "Isaac ben Eliezer!"

"Ah, you have seen these documents before."

"Only extracts. And I count on you to let me see them all!"

"On me?" The young woman stepped back, looking at him with

surprise written all over her face. "But, Mr. Sofer, you have made a mistake. The correspondence between Rabbi Hazdai and King Joseph is not here; it is at Christ Church College, Oxford!"

ϟ

Sofer left Cambridge a very disappointed man. Before he left, the young historian had contacted her colleagues at Oxford, to ensure that they would furnish copies of the 'Khazar correspondence.' It became obvious that this would not be simple.

"The original documents are not on display at this time," she told him apologetically, on her return to the reading room. "They didn't want to tell me why." Looking at Sofer's expression, she added, impetuously, "Wait a moment, all is not lost. I will speak to one of my friends. We do each other favors from time to time."

Once in her small paneled office, the young woman made a few more calls. Eventually, her face brightened. "It's okay, you will have everything." She chuckled. "But, it will cost you fifty pounds...."

Sofer raised his eyebrows. Gold-plated photocopies! How could he refuse her, after all her efforts?

He acquiesced. She handed him a slip of paper on which she had scribbled a name and a phone number. Then, timidly, she asked for an autographed copy of the book on the Khazars, as soon as it was published. "My name is Janet Woolis," she added shyly.

"Who said I was going to write any book?" he growled, surprised.

The young woman laughed, protesting that of course he was going to write it.

Sofer regretted his reaction. By way of apology, he would send her his latest book as soon as he returned to Paris. All the same his protest was not just caprice. Nothing was yet irreversible. He was only looking. He had not yet fixed on a target, not written one word let alone a sentence. He felt as if he were on the edge of an imaginary adventure, drawn and yet cautious, still sane enough to withdraw.

Seconds after arriving back in his room at the Randolph, he called the number written down by Janet Woolis. A cold young voice answered: "Yes, I know who you are. I can't talk to you now. Don't leave your hotel, I will call you shortly...."

The peremptory tone shook him. Why were such obstacles being put in his way to stop him seeing documents known for many years, and in which only a handful of people could possibly have any interest? He was almost at the point of going directly to Christ Church College, to make sure he was not being led up the garden path, but it was raining, and the journey from Cambridge via London had not exactly been restful. The comfort of the Randolph did not encourage excursions. And, after all, he had been asked not to leave the hotel.

He ordered a bloody Mary and several newspapers from room service. He had not even had time to unpack his bag before a waiter in a pristine white jacket knocked on his door. Sipping his cocktail, Sofer flicked through *The Times*, hesitating a few moments over the literary supplement. Then he opened *The Guardian*. In the inside pages he discovered a short article reporting the attack in Baku. Curiously, the paper made no allusion to the New Khazars, the terrorist group of which Agarounov, president of the Association of Mountain Jews, had spoken. The *Guardian* correspondent only reported:

> *The explosion caused very serious disruption. A collection pump drawing the oil from Baku to Tupsa on the Black Sea, and only recently installed by the Offshore Caspian Oil Operations, has been critically damaged. Technicians estimate that it will take them at least ten days to restore supplies to the Black Sea.*
>
> *At the moment, the police appear to have received the most fantastic of demands. None of them appear credible; the motives for this terrorist act seem undetermined. Some managers of the oil companies, meeting in their positions as exploitation partners in the* ocoo, *appear to believe that this is advance warning of a further outbreak of war between Chechnya and Daghestan....*

Pensive, Sofer remembered his conversation with Agarounov. He had certainly not invented that demand. The craziest of rumors were circulating in Baku and these New Khazars were no doubt one of the more fantastic demands *The Guardian* was referring to. The circumstances were troubling however. Yakubov and his story of the Khazar treasure, the secret cave, then his disappearance in a flood of inexplicable cash, that attack.... All this when those redoubtable Khazars have slept in tranquil obscurity for centuries. The circumstances were too consequential to be just chance, but he must restrain his imagination, so quick to draw threads between events that had no real links. Truthfully, he had reached no conclusions other than that luck was once again signaling to him...

"The luck of the Khazars!" He smiled, shaking his head. After another gulp of his bloody Mary, more vodka than tomato juice, his mind came back to the Cambridge documents. The fascination of ancient texts had always made him happy. For an hour, he attempted to decipher the original copy of the text given him by Janet, taking notes on an old pad.

> *"The King of the Khazars bears the title of Khagan. At his side, another prince directs the Khazar army; he bears the title of Beck. Even though his powers are considerable, the Beck is constrained to debate with the Khagan on matters of peace and war and, ultimately, he must submit. The princes who become Beck are chosen from among the best warriors, but they are not obliged to be Jews....*
>
> *The great Khazar towns were called Itil, Samandar, Tmutorokan, and Sarkel.... Itil, the royal capital, was built on several islands linked by floating bridges in the Volga Delta, at the time called the River Atel. Samandar, on the Caspian Sea, then called the Sea of the Khazars, possessed a huge market frequented by merchants from the Orient, Persia and Baghdad. The great fortress of Sarkel on the banks of the Varshan, today the Don, was built with the help of Byzantium. This was the least of the ambiguities in the relationship between the Khazars and Rome. Facing the Crimea, Tmutorokan controlled access to the Bosphorus, essential for passage between the Sea of Azov and the Black Sea, called respectively, at that time, the Russian Sea and the Sea of Constantinople."*

Constructed at the furthest end of the Caucasus, clinging to the first cliffs of the immense mountain chain, surrounded by gardens terraced right down to the sea, stood Tmutorokan. Sofer imagined it in all its splendor. It was a town that mattered to Joseph. Aged twenty, a very young Khagan, he won his first battle against the Russians there, supported and manipulated by Byzantium. He had won it, comporting himself so well in combat that his subjects considered him thereafter to be as great a warrior as his Beck, the renowned Borouh. This victory had marked the beginning of the legend. Assuredly, the Khazar Kingdom must have provoked great envy. Vast and rich, it was at the heart of the commercial routes running from east to west, north to south. This Jewish dynasty at the gates of rich and powerful Byzantium would only have profoundly displeased the devotees of Jesus Christ! The Jews must be made to submit, one way or the other....

The telephone rang. Sofer jumped. The brusque transfer from the imaginary to the present struck him violently. His hand was shaking as he lifted the receiver. He immediately recognized the voice.

"Mr. Sofer?"

"Yes?"

"I am Janet Woolis' friend. I have the things we arranged...."

"Good. Thank you for your assistance. Tell me where I may—"

"I am at your hotel, at the reception desk, sir."

"Here at the Randolph?"

"Yes. May I come up to your room? It would be more discreet."

The man who joined him a few minutes later seemed to have no neck, his face apparently forced down into the collar of his leather jacket. He held a large envelope in his hand. "We are not allowed to remove copies of the documents," he announced while Sofer closed the door behind him. "But I trust Janet...."

"Don't worry, I'll give you your fifty pounds!" said Sofer.

The Englishman did not seem to pick up on the irony. He opened the envelope and laid out twenty excellent photographs on the low table in the bedroom. Some were of parchment sheets and some looked like paper.

"This is Rabbi Hazdai's letter. That is King Joseph's answer...."

"It looks like paper." Sofer sounded skeptical.

The young man agreed, but with annoyance in his voice. "It is paper, Mr. Sofer. The Khazars made it. They learned the technique from the Chinese. They were writing on paper two or three centuries before the monks in Europe."

Sofer registered the information without comment, but asked, "Why is there so much mystery attached to these documents? There is nothing very extraordinary about them."

"Nothing unless one accepts that they are unique and the only documents attesting to the existence of the Khazar Kingdom."

"You are forgetting those at Cambridge...."

"Their author has not been identified with certainty. They are only second-hand evidence, so to speak. These documents here were written by one of the last Kings of the Khazars...."

"Very well," admitted Sofer, "but why can't I see the originals?"

"They were withdrawn from public display about four days ago."

"Four days ago? Why?"

The young man shrugged with disinterest. He was in a hurry and wanted to be paid. Sofer decided, however, that he wanted his pound of flesh, and waited for an answer. The Englishman shrugged again. "Someone demanded that they be allowed a re-examination. At least they didn't demand to take them for exhibition ... they didn't have the necessary techniques. They are very old documents, they have to be cared for."

"Who can demand that they withdraw such documents for a new specialist examination?"

"A respected expert of the period. You know, there are...." The young man suddenly interrupted himself, struck at last with the direction Sofer's questions were leading. "You are right ... it never struck me before, Mr. Sofer. But thinking about it now, it *is* strange. These documents have not been consulted for many years and now, suddenly, everyone is interested in them!"

"Everyone? What do you mean?"

"Yesterday, a young foreign woman asked the same questions of me. She also said she must have a copy and..."

"What did she look like?" Sofer cut in abruptly.

For the first time that afternoon, the young man's face opened. "Beautiful, Mr. Sofer. Very beautiful."

"A redhead, about thirty?"

"Redhead, yes. But less than thirty. I would say twenty-seven or twenty-eight. A foreign accent. Emerald green eyes. A small scar on her chin. There, like that, along her jaw ... what is it, Mr. Sofer? Do you know her?"

Chapter eleven

Tmutorokan, May 955

hey arrived during the night, like hyenas surging out of the shadows, and now their claws shine in the light of day." Borouh's voice was full of bitterness.

Attex shivered and wrapped her great embroidered cape closer around her. It was not the icy cool of the morning that gave her goose flesh, but the view before her. Immobile in the Bay of Tmutorokan, each one seeming as big as a mountain, half a dozen ships controlled the straits. Dromons! The formidable Byzantine war-machines, capable of spitting their terrifying Greek Fire more than five hundred cubits.

The waves hardly rocked them. In the mounting light of day, their long swans' necks with jaws of gold at their prows were sending out threatening flashes intermittently. The bronze blades immediately below glittered as the waves washed over them. Each the size of a man and solid enough to ram anything afloat, they cut through the surf. On the white-painted decks, men in armor were busying themselves around giant crossbows directed at the shore.

"They are not here just for an ambassadorial visit," declared Attex, disguising her fear. "It can only be for war...."

Borouh grunted and replied without even turning to look at her. "Kathum, ambassadors from Byzantium are never anything but another form of war. If the Greeks were so peaceful, they would have no need of these enormous ships to come and pay 'homage' to your brother the Khagan! It's now fifteen years that we've been at war and, today, suddenly they want peace?" Borouh slapped his fist against his leather armor and spat on the ground. "Believe me, I know, Kathum. If the Emperor of Byzantium holds out his hand, it's only to better deceive the recipient…."

Attex shrugged, annoyed by Borouh's tone of voice.

"Still, you always see things in black and white, Sir Beck."

This time Borouh turned to face her. His expression made Attex feel uncomfortable, but he bowed his head respectfully and answered.

"Perhaps you are right, Kathum."

Borouh was no longer the intrepid young warrior who used to fascinate her brother Joseph and herself in days gone by. His waistline had thickened with good living, and wrinkles had dug deep furrows around his eyes. His hair, still impeccably groomed, was now more gray than black. Only his mouth and his voice had not changed, both of them still hard and implacable. Even though he was the Beck, chief of all the Khazar armies, and the second most powerful man in the kingdom, his manners had always grated on her. The more time passed, the more stiff and ceremonious he had become. Recently, he had stopped using her name, using instead her title, Kathum, or 'Sister of the Khagan,' as if he wished to maintain a distance between them.

"Borouh, look!" Attex suddenly cried out.

A red sail had swollen in the wind. Between the dromons, a small boat with only one tier of oarsmen was approaching. Already they could see the regular movement of the oars.

"The ambassador's personal galley," muttered Borouh. "They aren't going to waste any time."

He turned around and barked a few curt orders. The twenty warriors behind them jumped up into their saddles. They were in full battle dress, lances in one hand, faces half hidden by pointed helmets.

Covering their coats of mail, a red tunic embroidered with the seven-branched candelabra signified their status as the royal guard. They came up to Attex and arranged themselves around her. The eunuch porters waited for a sign from their mistress and then lifted the poles of her chair. The cortege set off for the port.

In the morning light, the Sea of Constantinople appeared as white as milk. It was the time of day Attex loved best; the Bay of Tmutorokan seemed to her like a replica of the Garden of Eden. As the royal palace had been built to a traditional Greek plan, it was at the summit of a steep slope, with hundreds of terraces descending all the way down to the coast. From garden to garden, the velvety green of the fig trees succeeded the even more densely colored terraces of rye and barley. The gray shades of millet alternated with those of vines and olive trees. Clumps of rose bushes imported from China, hedges of laurels, multicolored flowers and lilies of various types bordered the roads. Every luxury that the earth produces could be found there, on slopes that had been softened by human labor.

On the very edge of the sea a spur of red rocks jutted out, protecting an extremely deep creek that formed a natural port. The town itself, mainly wooden houses, stretched away to the north, scattered on the lower slopes of the mountain, looking out over the immense plains and marshes running down to the Sea of Azov.

They arrived at the port just as the boat let go its anchor. A flat-bottomed barge went alongside. Half a dozen men stepped into it; remaining standing, they were taken ashore. When Borouh dismounted, Attex commanded her porters to keep her litter aloft on their shoulders.

Among the Greeks, the ambassador was easily recognizable. Displayed on his yellow toga was a large golden neck-chain that bore a medal with a picture of Emperor Constantine embossed on it. Tall and clean-shaven, he had an air of affluent authority. His thick nose and missing eyebrows gave him the appearance of a watchful wildcat. His eyelids seemed half-closed and his mouth, clearly outlined, protruded low on his face.

Behind him, standing apart from the handful of soldiers in armor, was a man dressed in black who had been crossing himself and mumbling away from the moment his feet had touched terra firma. A wooden cross hung from his neck. Attex recognized him as a Christian priest; the type who might appear modest and fragile but who were capable of spending years on the steppes, trying to convert anyone they met to their faith.

The ambassador raised his hands in the direction of Borouh. Two huge rings shone from his forefingers while he smiled with what seemed suspiciously like disdain.

"My Lord Beck, greetings...."

Attex was astonished to hear him pronounce these words in the language of the Khazars. He spoke with an unfortunate accent, but had a sweet and charming voice.

"It is always a pleasure to arrive at Tmutorokan. It is a veritable paradise!" His gaze traveled from the mountains over to Attex. He regarded her with surprise, as if the Kathum's hair of flame, simply caught back with a gold clasp, fascinated him. Close by, the priest continued his devout mutterings.

Borouh bowed slightly. "Welcome. The Khagan, Joseph, asked me to come and meet you with his sister, the Kathum Attex..."

The ambassador inclined his eyelids in Attex's direction. "It is a pleasure to meet you at last, Kathum. The Khazar merchants do not content themselves with only selling their fox pelts in Rome, they also sing your praises." He lifted his right hand to his heart, saluting in the Christian manner, but his gesture was as falsely polite as it was sarcastic. At the same time, his steely gaze hardened, and it was in Greek that he announced, "My name is Bardos Blymmedes. I bring to the King of the Khazars a message of friendship from Constantine, born in the purple, Lord of the whole world, Emperor autocrat and basileus of the Romans! I beg of you, please take me to your master immediately."

At his rear, the monk quickly traced the sign of the cross on his chest. In guttural Greek, Borouh said, "My Lord Ambassador, I will escort you to the Khagan's palace. But before that I need to assure myself that you know the rules of procedure for the royal salute. You may not see Khagan until after a day and a night of patience. When you do go before him, you must kneel and place your forehead on the ground. You must stay there silent as long as he does not question you...."

The ambassador squeezed out a smile of lordly condescension. "My Lord Beck, you may keep your day of patience, though the journey was tedious and I would love a rest. You are certainly well aware that the Ambassador of Byzantium cannot prostrate himself before anyone other than his master, the Emperor, however sincerely he would like to ... do not take this as an insult."

"There are no exceptions to the rule, my Lord Blymmedes."

"Oh, but there must be," the ambassador exclaimed. "I represent Constantine, born in the purple. The Emperor, personified by me, can only kneel before Christ!"

Borouh smiled, exposing his brilliant white teeth, and peaceably placed one hand on the hilt of his sword. "In that case, Ambassador, it would be better if you turned your boat around, because the Khagan will not receive you."

Fury as much as stupefaction caused Blymmedes' jaw to drop open.

A laugh from Attex did not give him time to find an answer. "My Lord Blymmedes," she exclaimed in limpid Greek, "come, do not annoy yourself over so little. I have heard that this thing you can only do for Christ, the men of Rome do willingly for their women. I will be behind my brother when you will come to pay your respects; you will only have to imagine that you are prostrating yourself before me...."

The silence was so absolute that everyone heard the groan of horror emitted by the monk. Borouh and Blymmedes contemplated Attex with the same confused horror. She signaled to her porters and announced in a calm tone, "Until tomorrow, Lord Ambassador. Excuse me, but it is time for my bath."

"Kathum!" groaned Borouh.

Attex raised her hand to bid him silent. "Nothing more. I must have my bath. Besides, tomorrow is my birthday. As a present, Khagan Joseph has said that I can do as I please tonight ... whatever I want...."

From the height of her litter, she beamed her most beatific

smile at Blymmedes. Borouh and the Greeks watched as she was taken off, carried by the robust eunuchs, as light and gracious as a dream.

"You Khazars," murmured Blymmedes, "you certainly have some strange manners. But that young Jewess, I must confess, is even more beautiful than they said."

❧

Attex's laughter rebounded off the tiled walls. The water in the great artificial pool in the rock was fed from a natural spring. It was so hot that pillars of turbulent steam whirled all the way up to the varnished brick roof.

"Borouh was very angry," she said laughing. "I thought he was going to murder me, right there, in front of the ambassador!"

"Your brother, the Khagan, will also be angry!" Attania scolded her.

"Why should he be? Tomorrow, Ambassador Blymmedes will lay his forehead on the carpet in the audience hall, with his fancy Greek airs transformed into a barbarian's supplication! When he stands up, he will look me right in the eyes, while I won't lift an eyelid." Attex laughed again, rolling herself voluptuously in the water. Her pale body disappeared for an instant in the hot liquid. When she surfaced again, Attania was running toward her flapping her old hands.

"Come out of there! You stay too long in that burning water! One day you will die in it!"

Eyes closed, Attex let herself float in the water, pretending not to hear the pessimistic warnings of her servant.

"It's true!" Attania obstinately continued in her guttural voice. "A bath that is too hot boils the blood, and you die suddenly. I have seen it myself! A young girl, just like you...."

Contrary to what the doctors had predicted all those years ago, Attania had regained her speech, despite her broken jaw. The Petchenegue attack which had almost killed her on the eve of Joseph's *Bar Mitzvah* was only a far-off memory. Enduring terrible pain, she gradually came to have sufficient mobility of her mouth to be able to form short sentences; sentences that she addressed only to Attex.

Unfortunately, with passing time, her face had continued to deform, because of badly set bones. Horrified by her own reflection, she lived in the Kathum's shadow, hiding herself under thick veils whenever she had to leave the palace. Her devotion to Attex had thus become her reason for living. With melancholy fascination, she had watched the young girl become a woman of perfection. In this blossoming feminine grace she saw the hand of the Almighty.

When whispers vaunting the incredible beauty of Attex came to her ears, Attania felt herself torn between pride and sadness. The hour was fast approaching when this admirable innocent, her pride and joy that had compensated her for all her bad luck, would be captive in the hands of a man, offered to the whims of his desires and his power. The splendor that was Attex would escape her forever. She would cease to enjoy her alone, the way one enjoys an undiscovered secret.

With a few supple movements, Attex approached the steps leading out of the bath. She shook herself, her long, flaming hair sparkling in the sunshine that engulfed the pool.

"Stop your grumbling, Attania! Go and look for your oils instead of repeating such stupidities!"

While Attania, grousing away, went into the adjacent small room, Attex called out.

"Hakon?"

An imposing eunuch, whose blue eyes and blond hair revealed his Nordic origins, appeared out of the shadows.

"Yes, Kathum."

"Bring me the towels, will you?"

She stepped out of the bath and waited, nude and dripping wet, while the eunuch returned with a large towel. Attania had not been far wrong; her fine skin, so supple, had become as red and swollen as a pomegranate." However, the smile she surprised on Hakon's face when he handed her the towel taught her that she was no less beautiful for the experience.

"The oils are ready," Attania announced brusquely, returning with a basket full of vials and pots.

Hakon arranged the other large towels on a brick bench, and Attex stretched herself out on it. With the corner of a towel, he wiped off the steam that covered the surface of a polished copper plaque that served as a mirror.

"That's enough, Hakon," scolded Attania. "We don't need you any more."

The eunuch looked for a sign from Attex in the hope she might contradict the order, but the Kathum contented herself with murmuring, "Thank you, Hakon. Would you prepare my tunic please?"

The blond eunuch twisted his mouth at Attania and left the bath without a word. Mumbling incomprehensible insults, Attania spread unguent on her palms and, baring Attex's back, began her massage.

"Stop picking on Hakon," Attex said suddenly, "I adore him."

"A Kathum cannot adore a slave, and even less a eunuch! She is merely to be served by him. That one has eyes that are far too curious!"

"He loves me! Can't you see how much he loves me?"

Attania rubbed hard.

"Hey! You're hurting me, old fool!" Attex protested, sitting up. Her eyes caught those of her servant in the polished copper. She added, "You are jealous. That's what you are, a jealous old … and you are right. Hakon is a good deal nicer to look at than you!"

Both of them fell silent, swallowing their anger. Attania's hands started moving again, helping the perfumed oils penetrate the skin. Attex, cooling down in both senses of the word, realized that the servant's hands were trembling. She searched for the woman's face in the copper mirror and discovered tears edging out from under her crushed eyelids.

"Attania!" Attex turned around, gripping the servant by the waist and squeezing her tightly, as she used to do as a child. "Attania, please, I beg of you! It's not true, you're not an old fool. You know very well it's not true!"

A sob escaped the jaws of the servant.

"I'm so sorry," repeated Attex. "I'm finished with Hakon! It's you I love…." With her fingertips, she smoothed Attania's deformed cheeks and tenderly dried her tears.

"Don't cry, Attania. I love you. You must never leave me…."

Attania pushed her back without a word and made her lie down again. She wiped her own eyes with a fierce swipe of her hand, then, lifting the red curls, she dripped a mixture of benzoin oil, asses' milk, macerated cloves and rose petals onto the princess's bare shoulders. Attex abandoned herself to the expert hands and repeated, "I swear it, nothing will ever separate us!"

But Attania was doubtful, and not easily appeased. "The man who takes you will not want me!"

"Then he won't have me!" Attex answered, laughing.

"Don't say such stupid things. He would be right. It is not good to have such an ugly servant."

"I will choose a man who wants you, I promise."

"Attex, my girl, don't be childish! You will choose nothing! Your brother will do it for you, you know that. It's the Khagan's law, the law of the Almighty. Even you must respect that."

Attex stood up suddenly, looking distraught, arms pressed across her chest. "I am frightened, Attania! I am frightened that I won't like him."

"All women are frightened before they know who their husband will be."

"I want to be able to love him."

Attania looked up into the vaulted ceiling and sighed. "Just hope that he loves you!"

"I really want him to be strong, handsome and respectful of the Almighty," Attex continued.

"Ah?"

"If he loves the Lord, he will have to love me a little, won't he?"

This time, a real smile drew sympathy from Attania's ample bosom. "I hope you don't say things like that to the rabbi."

"Attania! Do you think that I am going to have to wait long?"

"Before having a husband? Alas, I fear not, my darling little girl!"

⁂

In Tmutorokan the Khagan Joseph was holding an audience in a room with a floor covered in carpet and a ceiling supported by a veritable forest of sculpted and painted wooden pillars. His throne was a simple chair topped with a seven-branched candelabra. A canopy of leather embroidered with gold thread, very similar to a tent, covered the supporting platform. Holding himself erect, his beard trimmed short and hair swept back from his forehead like a halo, sat Joseph, proud and aloof. Thus, like all Khagans before him, had he learned to endure the audiences, for as long as was needed. He knew how to remain immobile, always master of his emotions. In the six years of his reign, his eyes had attained a gravity that was surprising in one so young.

Just as Attex had expected, Ambassador Blymmedes knelt and placed his forehead on the carpet. Alongside, two eminent Greeks from his entourage imitated him. Only the monk dressed in black remained outside on the patio, muttering his prayers in the fond hope that God would avenge such damning humiliation in this Jewish environment.

Immobilizing the Byzantine diplomats in their humble positions, Joseph maintained a stolid silence for some seconds. Attex could not help but smile. She searched out Borouh's eyes the better to savor her victory, but it was not the gaze of Borouh that she met, but that of Rabbi Hanania, his eyes sparkling with mischief.

Scarcely taller than an adolescent, and much thinner, the old man was almost invisible under his scarlet cloak, tied at the waist with a cord. His face appeared miniscule under a turban of white linen that covered his forehead. His mouth always seemed ready for irony or tenderness. Attex wondered how so much knowledge could be contained in such a fragile body.

"Stand, Ambassador," ordered Joseph finally, in a well modulated voice. "Welcome to the Kingdom of the Khazars."

Blymmedes, his face scarlet, stood up quickly, dusting his tunic with his hands as he did so.

"Khagan Joseph, this salute I have proffered is absolutely personal, and is a sign of my friendship for you. It is no concern of my master, whom I represent here, Constantine the Seventh, born in the purple, Lord of the whole world, autocratic Emperor and Basileus of the Romans."

Joseph's face remained expressionless, as did his voice when he declared, "You have crossed the seas with six of your dromons, Ambassador. I can only suppose that this was done with good reason."

For an instant the Greek hesitated, unsure whether he should follow protocol, but the watching eyes decided him and he proceeded straight to the facts.

"Peace, Khagan Joseph, that is the reason! The Emperor sent me to you that we might cast our ancient differences to the winds. He wishes you to know that it was against his will and against his advice that his Roman father pushed the Russians against you here in Tmutorokan…."

"And it was here he lost the battle!" Borouh intervened with barely suppressed fury. "Like all the Russians who tried to take Itil before him."

"We know that, Lord Beck. The Emperor Constantine knows it! That is why he offers you peace and the warmth of his friendship…." Blymmedes stole a glance at Attex. His smile was no more than a grimace. His eyes remained cold and calculating.

"I love peace, Lord Blymmedes, as long as it is not simply the silence preceding a battle. For, in that case, I prefer the battle."

Blymmedes waved his hands about as if he wanted to repel Joseph's words. "I know, Khagan Joseph, what a great warrior you are. We know of your courage. But we also know that, at this point in time, you are experiencing great difficulties in containing the Russians at your northern borders. Not a season passes without the army from Kiev attempting to capture your capital, Itil. To sleep in your palace seems to have become their dearest wish! Your kingdom is rich, Khagan. Your trade with the Orient flourishes. You are the master of the shores of the Sea of the Khazars, where great and rich merchant towns, which pay tribute to you, reside. The Russians are nothing but barbarians. Gold excites their appetites and their violence. Now, their excitation is at its peak, their appetite for the gold of the Khazars greater than ever. Emperor Constantine knows all this. He aspires to nothing more than a reign of peace and tranquility. Peace in the lands of Byzantium, but also among the neighboring peoples who are dear to us."

"Lord Blymmedes...."

The gentle, strongly accented voice surprised everyone. Rabbi Hanania moved out of Borouh's shadow to move closer to the ambassador, so close that the latter attempted a step in retreat. But the rabbi, with a smile that exposed his naked gums, placed his transparent-fingered hand on the Greek's arm.

"Lord Blymmedes, allow an old man a few foolish remarks ... the prince of Kiev is only a child of ten years ... is he not?"

Blymmedes nodded agreement, suspicious. "He is eleven. Sviatoslav ... it is his mother, Olga, who runs the kingdom. But—"

"They say here that Olga of Kiev has adopted the Christian faith of Rome. They say that, at this very moment, she is in Constantinople, where the Basileus Constantine himself is conducting her to the baptismal bath."

"Olga of Kiev became a Christian last winter, that is not a secret," responded Blymmedes.

The rabbi shook his head contritely, as if he had not understood. "Lord Blymmedes, be patient with the follies of an old man! For, you see, every day we receive here in this kingdom Jews fleeing from Rome. All of them deplore the brutality and the humiliation that the followers of the Laws of Moses are subjected to.... Why does Emperor Constantine want to live in peace with us, *us*, the Jewish people of the Khazar Kingdom, when he insults and degrades those of our people who live under his roof?"

"No! No! Emperor Constantine deplores the violence meted out to the Jews!" protested Blymmedes. He threw a glance behind him, assuring himself that the monk was out of range of hearing. He advanced a step and added in a quiet voice, "The Emperor is totally against it! But the monks are sometimes so fervent, Khagan Joseph, that we lose control of them. I am here to promise you that from now on Jews will be able to live in Constantinople in complete security. They will be able to engage in commerce as only they know how...."

The rabbi screwed up his toothless mouth in a malign smile and tapped the arm of the Greek. "That is very good news, Lord Ambassador. Excellent news, if it is true!"

"It is true! Absolutely! An alliance, that is what Emperor Constantine wishes to offer the Khagan of the Khazars! Close, fruitful, affectionate...."

"So close that you need to point the mouths of your flame-throwing dromons at our palace?" Borouh queried ironically.

"Don't you worry too much about appearances, Lord Beck! Make war with the Russians and sooner or later you will lose. Place your confidence in Emperor Constantine and he will ensure that Olga of Kiev restrains her warriors—"

"Ambassador," interjected Joseph, "why would he do that? Olga is his ally. Now she is of your religion and we know very well what importance that gives her. Why does he suddenly wish us to be friends?"

Blymmedes face was fixed in a most serious pose. His eyes were riveted on Joseph. He declared. "Byzantium has been at peace with the Khazar Kingdom for a long time. We have helped each other when necessary. Artisans from Rome constructed your fortress at Sarkel and your palace at Itil—"

"I know the history of our fathers, Ambassador," Joseph cut in, dryly. "I also remember that Byzantium supported us with soldiers when we repelled the Persian and Baghdadi armies."

Blymmedes tilted his head with a sly smile. "That is precisely what I am saying to you, Khagan Joseph! If Olga of Kiev and her son came by chance to conquer your kingdom, they would be masters of an immense nation. Immense, rich, powerful.... Only Byzantium can be immense, rich and powerful."

Joseph let the ensuing silence weigh on everyone, then he asked, "Why should I believe your words, Ambassador?"

Blymmedes raise his right hand. With a flash of his rings, he pointed at Attex, whom everyone else had forgotten. "An alliance, Khagan! A true alliance of flesh and love! This is what Constantine the Seventh proposes to the Khagan of the Khazars. To show his sincerity, he asks, with my presence and through my mouth, for the hand of your sister, the Kathum Attex, with the intention of placing it in the hand of one of his senior generals, Jean Tzimiskes."

A cry of surprise escaped the lips of Attex and Borouh simultaneously. Everyone, even Joseph, turned to look at Attex.

"Me, marry, me marry one of yours, Lord Ambassador?" she exclaimed. "That is your alliance?"

Silence answered her. Blymmedes was still smiling, while Rabbi Hanania, seized as though with a heart attack, could only gasp through toothless gums, lips opening and closing involuntarily. Attex searched out Joseph's face, but the Khagan was already standing, and declared in a calm voice. "Ambassador Blymmedes, I must leave tomorrow for Sarkel in order to visit my grandfather, Benjamin. You may follow us there."

Chapter twelve

Oxford, England
May 2000

A redhead, a beautiful woman, yes, what more do you want me to tell you?"

In spite of his persistence, Sofer had not been able to obtain any more information about the stranger from the young Englishman. She had come to see the copies of the ancient Khazar documents the afternoon before, that was all he knew. No, he had not taken her name. There was no need. She had simply telephoned, like Sofer.

"But how had she learned that you make copies?"

The other shrugged his shoulders. "How do you expect me to know that? She only had to ask."

Sofer smiled dubiously. His intuition could not be wrong. He was sure it was she, *she,* the stranger from Brussels. Why, how, he did not know. Perhaps simply because during the past few weeks he had not been able to erase her from his mind. She, the beautiful redhead who had asked him if he still believed in dreams!

As soon as the young Englishman had left, fifty pounds in his pocket, Sofer left the Randolph behind him. He was impatient to read the letter from Rabbi Hazdai to Khagan Joseph, but truly it was the thought that the stranger could still be in Oxford that literally impelled him outside, in spite of the intensifying rain. He walked straight ahead. He crossed the High Street, reaching the district where the colleges were located, then took a fork into Lodge Lane, then Merton Street. Carrying on to St. Aldates, he skirted the imposing walls of venerable buildings of science and knowledge, melting into the crowds of students and tourists, scrutinizing faces. In vain. He decided to go as far as the front of St. Giles, pushing through the crowds coming out of the museums and rejoining the commercial district at the bottom of Beaumont Street. There, he wandered around the bus station where the young people, hair long or completely shaven, metal rings encrusted in their lips, noses or eyebrows, calmly awaited buses to the suburbs. He suddenly had the feeling that he had changed worlds, jumped from one era to another.

It was late, darkness was overtaking daylight; the shops were closing, the customers leaving. Sofer noticed how even here in England, redheaded women were rare. And none of them, obviously, resembled the stranger. No, if truth be told, he did not think he had the slightest chance of finding her. Suddenly, he felt ridiculous. Running around like this, at his age, chasing shadows! She had certainly only come to Oxford with the intention of obtaining a copy of the Khazar correspondence. Just like him. But why?

So many questions, so many secrets, oddities! As if he was caught up in a spider's web that an unknown hand was weaving patiently in the shadows. He began to doubt his senses.

The rain had stopped, and the streets emptied as it grew dark. He asked for directions back to the hotel from an elderly man. It was quite a distance away. With heavy legs and a clouded brain, he pushed open the door into a coffee shop, sat down at a table and ordered tea. At least walking till he was exhausted had the advantage of having calmed him. Outside, through the coffee shop window, a few rare passersby crossed through the orange light of the street lamps. His gaze fell on a young girl jumping over the puddles left by the rain. Then, he saw her. She: Attex as a child, sister of Joseph the future Khagan. He saw her as she played at the river's edge under the walls of the fortress at Sarkel, more than a thousand years ago. He saw her plunging her foot into the mud, fascinated by the gray wave of the river that came to efface all her traces. And then, when she raised her face to the servant who warned her against the danger of the current, Sofer realized that the young girl Attex had the stranger's features. Oh, it wasn't more than a sketch, but already the beauty of the woman from Brussels was there: the emerald eyes, the shape of the mouth, the determined chin and, of course, the red hair.

"Damn! That's it! I have it! I can see them all," he exclaimed inwardly without noticing that people at neighboring tables were casting amused looks at this tourist talking to himself.

᠅

In a single bound, almost running, Sofer entered the Randolph. He ordered a bloody Mary, and once snug in his room he flicked through the sheets of correspondence between Rabbi Hazdai and Khagan Joseph. Then he turned on his laptop. He could hear the whisper of the story in his ear. Under his fingers the novel began to take shape. Soon he found them all on his screen.

Attex, first. Beautiful, complex, ironic, mocking. Uneasy at the desire for love that was rising within her without knowing whom God would send her. Joseph, more severe, more serious than his sister, with her grace, but with the added weight of responsibility. The burden of Khagan obliged him to make every word, every sentence, count. The prospect of being a spiritual leader did not enthuse him. Then the old Khagan, Benjamin, appeared, followed by Borouh, Rabbi Hanania, the servant Attania and Ambassador Blymmedes. They all came to life in the shadows of his hotel room. Finally, it was the turn of Isaac ben Eliezer, and his friends Simon and Saul. He saw them, traveling for months across Germany, Hungary, always pressing on toward the east. Autumn transformed the roads into potholes that pulled off their shoes. The cold was deadly. To reach a cottage with a fire where someone offered you a bowl of soup was a deliverance. Sometimes they slept out in the rain, covering themselves with dead leaves for protection. Sometimes they found an inn, a servant with soft skin, a bucket of warm water....

Once, they thought their end had come. They could hardly

sleep, lying under a large pine tree, the eyes of wolves shining at them in the black night. Simon was shivering with fear and Saul, for once in his life, was praying to the Almighty. The beasts came so close that Isaac, like Sofer, could hear their breath. One of them began howling, another responded. In just a few seconds their deathly howls were reaching the stars.

"We are done for," murmured Saul, furious. "I should never have listened to you, Isaac. To die en route to a non-existent kingdom! Very clever!"

Simon laughed nervously. "I just wish they'd kill me. Then I could rejoin my beloved."

Suddenly Isaac remembered his lute. Very cautiously, he withdrew the instrument from his bag. His frightened fingers plucked at the chords, searching for a rhythm. It only took a few moments before the wolves stopped howling. Responding to the sounds of the music and Isaac's plaintive singing, some of them started whining and slunk away. Others lay down in the frozen grass. That raised the siege until morning. Their journey continued to the sandy plains of Kiev. Saul did not want to idle there talking to the Jewish merchants after they confirmed that the Kingdom of the Khazars really existed and that the Khagan was indeed called Joseph.

Isaac was so happy that he danced around all alone as if he were drunk. Saul, for once in his life, was moved to pray in the synagogue. Simon, exhausted like a man delivered from a great torment, slept for four consecutive days. So well did he sleep that the small party did not leave Kiev till one day in May of the year 4715, according to the Jewish calendar. From Kiev, they would leave by the Gate of the Khazars; it would take two weeks, with good mules, to arrive at the Varshan River. There, if all went well, five weeks of good navigation would bring them to the fortress of Sarkel.

Sofer envisaged an impatient Isaac. Impatient to arrive. Sensing the end in the soles of his boots. Dreaming of his meeting with the king of the Jews. Already preparing his speech. Imagining the reply.... How could he, full of ardor and elation, gorged on hope and illusion, guess that destiny was going to fulfill and vanquish him, both at the same time?

Chapter thirteen

Sarkel, September 955

Benjamin smiled. His bloodless lips parted to display the four yellowed teeth remaining to him. In an almost inaudible voice, he whispered, "'There is a time to live and a time to die.' So says the Book of Ecclesiastes. That is what you taught me, Rabbi Hanania. This time it is my turn, I've arrived at the time to die."

The old Khagan halted, his one good eye closed, incapable of continuing. All his efforts concentrated on breathing. Eight naphtha lamps were kept alight permanently in the practically bare room, but they could not compete with the odor of death. It had been ten days now, on this eve of the New Year, that he had lain here on the wooden bench covered in fox furs that served for his bed. Benjamin's suffering only showed through the burning heat of his face and the occasional grimace twisting his lips. His white hair framed his face like silver smoke. His skin appeared extremely thin; stretched to the point of eliminating all his wrinkles, it seemed to want to melt into his bones, emphasizing his perfect features in a strange beauty.

Seated at his side, a Torah scroll resting on his knees, Rabbi Hanania appeared a great deal more fragile than the dying man. Under his large white turban his eyes were creased with sadness. Shaking,

Benjamin's three fingers stretched out to him. For a fleeting moment, Rabbi Hanania gazed at the horny nails, at the cracked skin. Finally he stretched out his own hand. The fingers of the two old men entwined. To the rabbi's surprise, Benjamin's was so burning hot that his own felt icy.

"Rabbi," the old Khagan gasped, "do you think I will receive the angel's kiss?"

The rabbi smiled. Without releasing Benjamin's hand, rocking gently like a woman rocks her baby, he began to recite the verses of *Berakhoth*:

"*When a man is about to leave this world, the Angel of Death will appear to carry away his soul. The latter resembles a vein that runs through the body. The angel seizes one extremity of the vein and pulls it from the body of the dying man. If the man is righteous, he is able to do so with no more difficulty than pulling a kid from a bowl of milk. If the man is wicked, his soul is caught as if in the cataract of a raging river or like a ball of wool caught in thorns: it is ripped apart.*"

Rabbi Hanania paused to release Benjamin's fingers. Then he spoke again in a clear voice. "Do not fear Khagan! The angel will come and you will be like a kid with milk...." After a moment, he added, "Khagan Benjamin, without wishing to contradict Ecclesiastes, and even if it is good to see a ship regain its home port, I must tell you that I am sad ... I am going to miss you."

"I will miss you too. But, above all, I regret never having reached the Land of Israel. These last months, I have often dreamed of Jerusalem." The old man was seized with excitement. A sort of laugh rattled in his chest. His hoarse whisper filled the confined malodorous air of the room. "Rabbi, I thought I had entered Jerusalem, and I even recognized the streets! I recognized the light on the roofs and between the tents! I recognized the smell of the mist and the perfume of the river at nightfall! Rabbi! I believed I was entering Jerusalem, but it is from Itil that I return."

There was a short silence before Benjamin whispered, "Itil, our Itil! The new Jerusalem. For Him! For His return, at last..."

"Amen," the rabbi said soberly, muttering a short prayer that such a hope should be fulfilled.

"Ah ... if only that could be! For he could come, the son of David, couldn't he Rabbi? He could reunite the Tribes of Israel, here, like King David did in the Land of Israel! We must repent, we must repent...."

Benjamin's exaltation sharpened his voice, and his back arched, but this time the rabbi did not answer, he simply rocked back and forth. After a few seconds, the Khagan's agitation subsided. His breathing eased and he looked clearly at his companion.

"I know what Byzantium is offering, Rabbi. Joseph must not accept. Emperor Constantine is playing with him. It is a trick. The Greeks are men without honor. Joseph must not deliver my granddaughter up to them...."

At that moment, Joseph's voice resounded in the room. "Grandfather, you should be resting or praying!"

Standing in the doorway, frowning at the smell, Joseph hesitated before approaching his grandfather's bed. Finally, jaw set firm, he walked over and bent down far enough for the old Khagan to place a hand on his forehead. Rabbi Hanania was struck by the resemblance of the two faces. Both had the same fine features, the same sensual, determined mouth, the high cheekbones of men from the steppe, and the almond eyes of their Oriental ancestors. But it was in Joseph's implacable irises that power was now concentrated.

"Joseph!" Benjamin continued, with renewed agitation. "Joseph, do you remember when you became a *Bar Mitzvah*?"

"I remember."

"The day before, Joseph, my boy, when you took your first steps as a man. It was for good against evil...." Benjamin paused, out of breath, a twisted smile of joy on his lips.

"I remember," repeated Joseph.

Hanania was surprised by the rude tone in the Khagan's voice. Benjamin gathered his remaining strength. His fingers gripped the fur edge of Joseph's silk coat as if he feared falling out of his bed.

"Joseph, you did not wish your sister to be carried off by the Petchenegues.... You cannot now agree to give her to the Greeks! You cannot!"

Joseph gripped the old Khagan's hand and, in a somewhat ambiguous gesture, authoritarian but affectionate, removed it from his coat. "Grandfather, you must not bother yourself with such things...."

"Your father, Aaron, may God in His mercy protect him, never ceded anything to Byzantium! He fought them! The Russians too! And before him, I too never gave in to the demands of Byzantium! They are treacherous. They promise peace to be the stronger in war. They say one thing and do another. They deceive for pleasure! Joseph! You cannot...." It was practically a cry of anger, but the old Khagan was now stiffened with pain. Rabbi Hanania stood up, eyes dilated, waiting for the moment of passage. Joseph's mouth quivered. He kneeled and pressed the dying man's three shriveled fingers between his own powerful hands.

"I hear your words, Grandfather," he whispered, "I know how wise you are. Be at peace. Nothing is decided."

The eyelids closed over eyes that seemed to want to sink into his skull. Benjamin shook his head painfully. Rooted to the spot, Rabbi Hanania saw tears roll down the old man's cheek.

"Joseph ... Joseph! If your sister becomes Christian, the Kingdom of the Khazars will no longer be Jewish. It will not be the Promised Land. The son of David will never enter Itil on his white mule!"

A long silence ensued, punctuated only by the raucous breathing of Benjamin. Neither the rabbi nor Joseph had the courage to break the silence this time. Outside they could hear voices, the comings and goings of the palace. Since the previous day, all the lords of the court had gathered in the fortress, ready to accompany the old Khagan to his grave. Around the fortress, three thousand archers of the royal guard formed an impenetrable belt, and all the foreign merchants had been sent away to the other bank of the river. In the town of tents, even those who were not Jewish restrained their children and talked in hushed tones.

Benjamin's voice was heard, so quiet that Rabbi Hanania guessed rather than understood the words being uttered. "May God grant you long life, Joseph. Remember that I love you as much as my son Aaron. Go and bring Attex to me."

⁊₷

Attex arrived at her grandfather's bedside in tears. Contrary to Joseph, she did not try to hide her sadness. Seeing her, the old Khagan forced a smile, but the discussion with Joseph had exhausted him to the point where he could hardly speak. Clumsily, he raised his hands to stroke his granddaughter's abundant hair. "You smell good, like an angel…"

As she could not find the words to answer, Attex stretched out alongside the old man, sliding her body as close as she could against his, holding him to her and placing her cheek next to his. The rabbi exclaimed in protest and extended his arm to catch Attex by the shoulder, to stop her assuming such a sacrilegious pose, but the old Khagan held her so tightly that the rabbi gave up with a sigh. "You must not be sad, Kathum. Remember Ecclesiastes: *Two boats were on the sea, one was leaving port and the other returning. The people rejoiced at the first ship leaving but not at the arrival of the second. A wise man who was there said, 'My opinion is the opposite of yours. You should not rejoice at the departure of that ship, for no one knows what wild seas, what tempests await it. But this ship which has just arrived, safe and sound, should fill you with joy.'*"

Attex sniffed and shook her head. "I can't be happy, Rabbi," she sobbed, looking at him reproachfully. "I can't."

Suddenly, the old Khagan coughed violently. Hanania seized his hand. He was frightened that Benjamin would die in crisis and pain, which would be a very bad omen. Attex hugged the trembling body to her. Benjamin opened his eye once more. A sigh of joy escaped his desiccated lips.

"You are the most beautiful on earth, Attex!" he murmured, "You are the messenger of the Lord, blessed be His name!"

His pupil dilated, and his body stretched out between Attex's arms like a piece of dry wood. "Ah," he groaned, "aah … the angel is coming, Rabbi! I hear the singing accompanying it! Oh, I can hear His voice…."

99

Attex could hardly hold him, as he thrashed about.

"Attex, don't go with the Greeks! Do not commit that folly! Attex, do not renounce the Laws of Moses!"

"No, Grandfather, you can be sure I will not!"

She never knew if he heard, for at that instant, his face wild with hallucinations, her grandfather closed his eye and passed away with one last sigh. Thus, on the morning of Yom Kippur, in the year 4715 of the Jewish calendar, the twelfth Jewish king of the Khazars died.

Chapter fourteen

Oxford, England
May 2000

It was just past four o'clock in the morning when Sofer allowed himself a break. Not a sound troubled the calm of the Randolph. The silence in his bedroom was so complete that he could hear the quiet rumbling of the mini-bar. Outside, behind the curtains, the night was orange-yellow. Oxford was bathed in sodium lamplight. It had stopped raining. Sofer opened the window and massaged his sleepy eyes. He was tired but happy, exuberant even. He felt very much alive, as if someone had poured something other than blood into his veins, or enlarged his heart. After all, he was still carrying the sound and the emotion of Attex, Isaac, Joseph and the others in his soul.

For an instant he let his eyes rest on the still image of the lawn, surrounded by the massive clumps of rhododendrons and azaleas colored ochre by the street lamps. He breathed deep gulps of the moist air. Then he realized. He wanted to breathe the wind of the Khazars. He would have to go there, see the sun on the Caspian Sea, the Sea of the Khazars. Yes, he must go!

He looked at his watch again. It would be nearly nine in the morning in Baku. A bit early, but acceptable, and perhaps a good time to catch Agarounov before he left home. He moved back to sit on his bed to dial the number of the president of the Association of Mountain Jews. While the different tones rang in his ears, he passed one hand over his rough cheeks. He had not shaved since yesterday. What he must look like!

"Da?" responded Agarounov in Russian.

Sofer announced who he was, said hello in Russian and explained that he was calling from England.

"I am sorry for calling so early. I wanted to be sure to talk to you...."

"No trouble, my friend!" replied Agarounov, always friendly. "You could never bother me. Funnily enough, I was just thinking about you yesterday evening."

"Yes?"

"The attack on the pipeline ... do you remember?"

"Absolutely, I—"

"The New Khazars, they blew it up. Astonishing, isn't it?"

"Are you sure, Mr. Agarounov? I have the English papers here, the ones that reported the attack ... and none of them mentions the New Khazars...."

"Bah!" Agarounov laughed heartily. "The English only report what their sources want them to believe. No, it is true. My sources are official."

"And your friends know members of these New Khazars?"

"That ... no. I don't think so."

"Rather odd, don't you think, to link it in with the Khazars?"

Agarounov laughed softly. "People around here have a need, from time to time, to revive the past. Above all nowadays...."

"Mr. Agarounov, the Khazars were Jews! Do you realize what this could mean?"

"Certainly, of course I do!"

Without knowing why, Sofer detected in Agarounov's tone a note of growing annoyance. Frowning, he again asked, "And what do they want? Do we know yet what they are demanding?"

There was silence. It lasted so long that Sofer was forced to speak again, a little brusquely. "Hello? Mr Agarounov? Are you there?"

"Yes, yes, I am here. But your questions are difficult for me to answer on the telephone."

This time it was Sofer's turn to fall silent, pensive, seeking to unravel the hidden meaning behind Agarounov's words. Finally, he exclaimed, with a light laugh, "Okay, my mistake! Besides, it doesn't matter much, you can tell me face to face! That is why I called you; I have decided to go and spend a few days in Baku. I want to see the Sea of the Khazars."

"Fantastic! Great news! That's really wonderful!" Agarounov's joy seemed absolutely sincere.

"It's just that I've started to write my little piece," Sofer responded, with a sudden need to tell someone.

"Your ... piece?"

"Yes. My book. A novel, on the Khazars, obviously...."

Suddenly Sofer could not resist the pleasure of briefly recounting why he was in Oxford. He described the documents he had acquired, the writings of Rabbi Hazdai and, above all, those of King Joseph.

"Maybe I'm presuming a little, because no one has said that the king actually wrote the answer in his own handwriting. I imagine he had some sort of secretary. Or a scribe. That's more likely. Besides, some researchers maintain that the rabbi's letter is also a copy. All the same, I can tell you, Mr Agarounov, it is very moving to have these ancient documents under my very eyes!"

On the other end of the line, far away in Azerbaijan, Agarounov was grunting in agreement and excitement.

"I will show them to you," Sofer promised. "I'll bring them with me."

"Marvelous," Agarounov enthused. "What a thrill it will give to our friends the Mountain Jews to see letters from someone who perhaps is a direct ancestor of theirs!"

"Speaking of which," asked Sofer, "any news of the mysterious Yakubov?"

Agarounov sighed. "None. We have searched the records of the Association. No Yakubov anywhere. I have questioned contacts on the subject of the cave. They know caves exist, and, if one of them did contain a synagogue, they would not be surprised, it would be nothing extraordinary. But they have no precise information. The Mountains are vast, obviously...."

"Obviously. Another question, Mr. Agarounov, if you will allow me. Do you know a young redheaded woman, very, very beautiful? I would say an extraordinary beauty? Do you?"

"Ah! A woman! A beautiful woman, you say?"

"Almost abnormally beautiful, if one can say such a thing."

"Oh!"

"Aged thirty, perhaps less. Emerald eyes, not very tall, dresses well. Red hair, like I said...."

"You are in love with her?"

"No, no! It is only..." Sofer felt ridiculous, as if he had told this fellow who was practically a stranger, in the first few minutes of conversation, that he was obsessed by a strange woman. He laughed, somewhat self-consciously, and said, "I am thinking of using her as a character in my book."

Agarounov was puzzled. "Nothing else? A name...?"

Sofer feigned indifference to curb the curiosity obviously stirring in Agarounov's mind. "No, nothing. Only an idea ... I'll explain when I see you..."

Hanging up, Sofer was embarrassed at how childishly he had acted. The fact that Agarounov had been so forthcoming and that he was the only tangible link to all the incomprehensible events surrounding him had made Sofer more garrulous than usual. Agarounov himself was an odd person. As warm as he was mysterious. What would he look like? And what would Baku be like? Fatigue suddenly seized hold of Sofer, and he hesitated at the thought of continuing working. He thought about taking a shower, but contented himself with stretching out, a pile of pillows under his head. The first sounds of the hotel stirring could be heard. Eyes closed, he tried to imagine what these New Khazars could signify. Who was hiding behind the name? Why destroy the oil installations?

Racking his brains about so many unsolved questions without being able to resolve any of them led him, once more, to evoke the unknown redhead—another mystery. A woman had posed several questions at a symposium. As she was beautiful and because, coincidentally, her questions had echoed thoughts that had been inwardly tormenting him for some time, he had created a whole story around their meeting. Nevertheless, at the end of his talk—perhaps even a little before the end, without even turning around to look at him—the unknown beauty had gone quietly home, perfectly happy that she had embarrassed that old bugger of a writer, Sofer. She would have had to call all her friends to recount the scene. At this time of day, she would be fast asleep in the arms of a lover or a husband. In two hours time, she would prepare breakfast for her children before going out to her own work, perhaps reading a John Irving novel, or some other equally romantic book dispensing dreams. Yes, that was certainly much more likely to be the real story! Feeling sleep engulf him, Sofer smiled at his wild theories. Before falling asleep, he just had time to realize that he had forgotten the stranger's face. From that moment, against the background of his closed eyelids, he could only see Attex, the Kathum Attex, bursting with youthfulness, impatience and that indecipherable something that could perhaps only be a fragment of the Divine incarnate.

❦

It was just past midday when Sofer awoke. The telephone was ringing, although it took him a few seconds to realize what had roused him. A friendly voice asked him if he wished to stay an extra night. He replied that he did not know, he had to arrange a ticket to Baku first. The friendly voice told him she could fix it for him, if he wished to call her in an hour, and offered him brunch while he waited.

Sofer accepted all her offers graciously and thanked her warmly. He did not totally awake until he showered. While shaving, he realized with pleasure that his features had changed; suddenly he looked younger, more alive. A keener look. Less baggy under the eyes. A firmer mouth. In total, a longer face, finely featured, all lassitude disposed of. A wide-awake face that he recognized: the face that appeared when he had something to write about! No comparison to the waxy features of the old, dying Khagan, and still less to those of the decrepit Rabbi Hanania. He had plenty of time to become as old as that! Now that he was freshly shaved, a woman could once again caress his cheeks with pleasure. Attex, for example. He had not yet imagined what Attex's hands were like. The hands of a princess, very white skin, not destroyed by making fires or washing clothes. Fingers longer than her palms. Alas, he was not Isaac. Isaac, the lucky one! Sofer, one hand full of lather and the other wielding the razor, stopped shaving and smiled at his own reflection in the mirror. Yes, absolutely yes: he *was* Isaac!

Chapter fifteen

Something is going on! Something bad!" Saul groaned. Standing on a seat in the boat, protecting his eyes from the sun with one hand, he anxiously scrutinized the water downstream, and the groups of poplars growing on the hilly banks. Hundreds of horsemen had begun to appear. Like a sash lining each bank of the river, they trotted forward in perfectly straight lines.

Sarkel, September 955

"It's not good! It's not good," Saul worried.

The horsemen kept on coming. Soon Isaac could see the bows strapped to their backs, the coats of mail shining in the sun over their embroidered tunics, their curved swords unsheathed, held in the salute position, their steel pointed leather helmets…. At the instant when he could distinguish their mustaches, someone in the convoy shouted in Russian, "Khazars! Khazars!"

Saul and Simon both turned to Isaac. Loud cries broke out among the merchants, all of them fearful.

"The Khazars! But why would they stop our convoy?" Saul asked no one in particular. Coming within arrow range, the Khazar warriors halted their horses. Some of them set their bows on the pommels of their saddles. The thirty heavy barges almost grounded onto the gravel of the riverbank of the Varshan enclosed in a pincer movement.

"Why do they treat us like Petchenegues?" Saul asked again. The large Nordic man who had welcomed them into his boat heard the question. With the expression of a man never surprised by anything, he murmured, "Who knows? That's how the Khazars are! They are the masters here. One day you are allowed to land at Sarkel, the next not. That's just how it is. And complaining will do no good...." He pointed to the line of soldiers. "I would advise you to stay away from them. Their arrows can kill a fly at a hundred paces as surely as you can snuff out a lamp flame with your fingers!" He mimed the gesture, eyes wide open.

"How long could they stop us from moving on?" Isaac asked.

"Who knows? A day, two, three ... ten, if that suits them!" Shrugging his shoulders, and taking no more notice of the Khazar warriors—now as immobile as statues—the boatman went to the back of the boat and flung himself down in the shade under a sort of tent that was erected there.

"Bah," Simon sighed. "What does it matter? We're in no hurry. As long as we stay in the boat we'll be safe."

"Apart from roasting in the sun! Bastards!" Saul exploded. "You seem to have forgotten your dreams! At least that's what it looks like to me. They were going to welcome us with fruit, wine, dancing and tears of joy! Look at them, your Khazars! Do you see Jews when you look at these brutes with their barbaric appearance? They look like Turks or I don't know what!"

Simon's smile froze. He looked at Isaac in search of support but Isaac turned away coldly. His companions were angry, the one as much as the other. The journey from Kiev had been much more onerous and uncertain than they had expected. Petchenegues infested the region, carrying warlike campaigns from one plain to the other, forcing the merchants to divert from the direct routes and travel in long convoys. These circumstances led Saul to expound on every difficulty he would have in taking back any items of valuable merchandise to Germany. His disposition, not the most loving or lovable at the best of times, had become even more anxious and sullen. He paced back and forth, holding himself as if at any moment someone was going to attack him, and not a day passed without him complaining.

Simon had a totally different attitude to life, and used his slight education and fragile spirit to the utmost. To him, their mission had become so sacred that it could not fail. He regularly assured them that the Lord, blessed be His name, would impose His will in that they would meet the Khagan, and that Joseph, without a shadow of doubt, would appear to them as the Son of David. Thus they would become the new prophets! Endlessly, he repeated the marvels that the merchants described as they spoke of the Jewish Kingdom of the Khazars: the riches, the splendor of the buildings, the king's golden throne, his white fortress, his science and wisdom, his courage in combat. Above all, Simon wanted to see proof that the Almighty protected the people and the lands of the Khazars in some extraordinary way. Even including the sister of Khagan Joseph, who was, by all accounts, the most beautiful woman any man had ever seen. As if that were not enough, he assured them that one night in the near future the stars would start to move, bringing a comet, the ultimate sign of the End of all Miracles—the Promised Time!

Inured to the bad temper of the one and the fantastic peasant faith of the other, Isaac was no longer impatient. Except that now, this morning, when they were no more than a half-day's sail from Sarkel, the first Khazars they had encountered were fearsome warriors who forbade them from approaching the fortress! For several minutes, the three of them remained disunited and unhappy, each giving free rein to his imagination, yet without daring to let it roam farther than the banks of the river, in which they plunged their hands from time to time to cool themselves. The first few hours of the morning passed in an endless wait. When the heat made the air shimmer and burn their skin, boatmen and merchants alike crouched down in the shade of the boats, buttocks in the water like chickens. The Khazar cavalry did not move a muscle, neither did their horses. Their coats of mail sparkled in the light, but they remained so stationary that one would have thought them made of stone. The barges of the convoy were side by side, the prows dug in to the shore. Some of them were stacked to the gunwales with fox furs, giving off such a stench that even the birds stayed well clear. Most of them carried slaves captured in the northern countries or sold by the Russians. Women, children, men, old, young, exhausted and treated like cattle, all were suffering in the sun; the leather straps that bound them to each other dug into their flesh, cutting like blades. Sometimes one would cry out and fall over, upon which a merchant would douse them with cold water from a large bucket, as one would wash baskets of cucumbers.

When the sun had reached its zenith, half a dozen men, apparently drunk on barley beer, slipped into the Varshan to cool themselves. They were laughing loudly, splashing each other and calling out. One of them, waving his arms, went a little too far from the bank, and in a split second, he was swept away by the current. His fat body bobbed like a straw in an eddy. He disappeared, then reappeared further downstream. They could see his head and an arm in the spray. Isaac imagined that he must be screaming with terror, but the noise of the rushing water was so violent that nobody could hear.

His companions leaped out of the water, shouting loudly and grabbing oars and ropes to try and save him. They ran toward him. It was then that Isaac saw four or five of the horsemen break their ranks. They approached the river at a trot. With one fluid movement they raised their bows. Silently, majestically, the arrows flew in a perfect arc toward the drowning man. They all landed on him at the same instant. He sank with the force of the blow, swallowed forever by the muddy waters.

"May the Almighty forgive me!" Simon whistled through his teeth, white as a sheet.

For once Saul was silent. He had no need for words. The boatmen and the merchants running along the bank stopped immediately. Not one of them dared move. The cavalrymen turned to look at them, bending their bows. The deadly points shone in the sunlight. The men from the north shouted, waved their arms, fell to their knees and showed every sign of submission, but the arrows were already in flight. They planted themselves in the ground right in front of them, forming a perfect grille. From one end of the convoy to the other, slaves, boatmen and merchants, no one dared open his mouth.

The noise of the river was all that could be heard. A cavalryman in a long red cloak, hair dressed in a long pigtail down to his waist, spurred his bay horse into a canter toward the kneeling group. Reaching them, his steed, wearing an embossed silver face-protector, gracefully reared up over them. Drawing his sword from its scabbard, he made the blade whistle through the air while he shouted at them. Isaac could not see and could only hear the angry shouts carried on the breeze. But the merchants and the boatmen stood up and ran back toward the boats while the Khazar horseman leisurely walked his horse back to rejoin the line of archers. Shortly afterward news traveled through the convoy like a puff of smoke on the wind. The Khagan of the Khazars was dead. No stranger could approach or enter Sarkel for the next five days under pain of death.

❧

It wasn't until several hours after dark that the mistake was rectified. After having plied anyone who could speak even a little Russian with questions, Isaac ran back to his friends laughing.

"Idiots that we are! It is not King Joseph who is dead! It's his grandfather, Khagan Benjamin!"

Simon cried with joy, though Saul was indifferent. Isaac drew them aside and explained his intentions to them. He was going to leave the convoy during the night. He would benefit from the darkness, and avoiding the Khazar horsemen's vigilance, would reach Sarkel by dawn.

"If you don't get lost in the woods, or if you're not eaten by the wild beasts that live there." Saul's pessimism prevailed. "At the very least you will probably travel in circles and find yourself walking into the arms of the cavalry!"

"I know how to travel by the stars," Isaac answered tranquilly. "My father taught me when I was a child."

"Why risk your life? Why not wait patiently for the convoy to arrive at Sarkel?" Saul asked.

"I promised Rabbi Hazdai I would give his letter to King Joseph, from my hand to his. I will do it."

"And then?"

Isaac swept his hand wide in annoyance. "Think, Saul! If the old Khagan died in Sarkel and we are forbidden to enter the city, that almost certainly means that King Joseph is in the fortress! It is incredible luck! That will save us traipsing round the whole country for months looking for him! Remember what the Jews in Kiev told us!"

"That the Khagan Joseph is so powerful that he travels from palace to palace, sleeping in tents, from one season to the next, all over the country!" intervened Simon.

"And, above all, that the Khazars themselves can live all of their lives without ever seeing his face!" added Isaac. "And he never appears except for important ceremonies and wars...."

"Ridiculous," Saul complained. "Nothing but the idle chatter of merchants."

Isaac sighed and pointed his forefinger at the Khazar cavalry-men still maintaining their perfect alignment. "Saul, look at them. Think of the man they killed only an hour or so ago! Look at what this Khagan is capable of doing to ensure that everything is quiet when the hour comes to bury his grandfather! That should give you some idea of his strength."

"All the same...."

"We will never be able to speak to him if we just present ourselves at the fortress door!" Isaac retorted, scarcely able to restrain his anger.

Saul's severe stare remained incredulous. He could see the merchants and boatmen installing themselves for the night, lighting fires, forming circles. Life had taught him the same rule it had taught them, that would let them live long: it is better to be in a group than alone.

"Let's wait until the boats can depart and we can present ourselves in a proper way, as the Jewish ambassadors we are! The Khagan will not refuse us an audience. Besides, if you do go there via the forest, what will you do? You don't know his language."

"I will speak in Hebrew! That will say everything that needs to be said!"

Simon's hand closed its grip on Saul's wrist. "Saul, my brother! Don't you understand that this doorway to the Khagan is an unexpected piece of luck? That the Lord is giving us a way to see King Joseph and to give him the letter?"

"Stop this nonsense, Simon," Saul growled. "Can you not understand, once and for all, that the Almighty, blessed be His name, is not just there to follow your actions and gestures? The only piece of unexpected luck that Isaac can look forward to, you bloody ass, is to have his belly pierced by an arrow!"

Simon shook his head firmly, indifferent to insults. "You are mistaken. The Almighty continues to help us. But you ... you have nothing but lead in your skull!"

Isaac broke up the argument. It was useless, he had made his decision and he needed to make ready. Ever since Kiev, he had worn the dress customary to these parts, baggy pants that reached just below the knee, with a cotton tunic embroidered in colored wool and a length of linen wound around his waist, rope sandals served as shoes. He hid the round leather case containing the letter under his tunic, stowed his Toledo steel dagger in his belt and filled a goatskin gourd with water from the river. When it was dark enough, he slipped under the stern of a boat that hid him from the Khazar cavalrymen. His companions joined him there.

"Let me come with you," implored Simon.

"It's better not ... you never know, Saul could be right. Stay with him, because I know that if anything untoward should happen to me, you will both be there to greet King Joseph in my place. You have a copy of Rabbi Hazdai's letter, you could give it to him...."

Simon's face was pitiful. Isaac hugged him tightly. "Take care of my lute, Simon. You will be fine."

Looking sad, Saul shook hands without a word.

Isaac cut short the farewells. The darkness made everything disappear as far as the stones on the opposite bank. He dropped down into the river as quietly as a water vole. Bent double, he ran along the riverbank in a northerly direction for as long as he could. Nothing happened. No whistling arrows. No shouts. No galloping horses. Nobody was pursuing him.

꒚

He had not lied to Saul. He had known for many years how to guide himself by the stars.

He climbed up the bank, easily following the meandering river. The night was very black because the moon, at this time of the year, did not rise before the early hours of morning. The longer he walked, the more accustomed his eyes became to the lack of light. He stopped stumbling into the hollows in the riverbank. When he at last made out a road that led to his left across the short grass of the steppe, he lay down on his back, his feet pointing downstream.

The ground was still warm and smelled dusty. However, the beauty of the sky sent a shiver down his spine. Above him, the immense path of the Milky Way ran to the horizon. The spray of light was so clear that he could almost count the stars. But that would no doubt have taken him more than one lifetime! Directly above him, in the part of the Milky Way that curled around like the bottom of a sack, he spotted Deneb and the constellation of the Swan. It was just as if he could hear his father speaking. "Isaac, remember these rules: When Deneb occupies the center of the heavens in the polar position, that is when one is in the last month of summer. Then the Milky Way indicates by its extremities the northeast and the southwest. The Polar Star is always in the north. Thus its axis with Deneb points out the south to you as clearly as goldenrod. Besides, you cannot possibly make a mistake, my son; in summer there are always fewer stars in the south than in the north." At that precise moment, Isaac could see clearly, below Deneb, the five bright points of the Dolphin and the conformations of Aquarius and Capricorn. He thought fondly of his father, blessed be his memory.

When he stood up, he discovered a brilliant star, right on the edge of the horizon, so low that it looked as if he should be able to reach out and touch it. He did not recognize it, but without understanding where his certainty came from, he knew instantly that it pointed to the way he should follow.

Thus, like a star-struck lover, he walked till dawn. The cool of the night gave him a new vitality. Step after step, eyes riveted to the bright star, he felt carried along a miraculous road, certain he would not become lost. Sometimes he had to walk around trees. Once he had to take a detour when the rope of his sandals became stuck in the mud of a marsh. Later, when he cut across a depression in the steppe, he nearly ran into a row of tents placed around dull, half-extinguished braziers. He hoped that none of the animals would sniff his scent in the air. Contrary to Saul's fearful prognostications, he did not encounter any wild animals. Sometimes he heard the slithering of a snake in the dry grass or the near-silent flight of an owl. Nothing that frightened him. He rehearsed what he would say to the Khagan a hundred times. The scroll case containing the precious letter rubbed through his tunic. He thought of Rabbi Hazdai and prayed that he was still alive. He regretted that he could not shout to him across the sky now that he was so close to achieving their mission.

Well before the first light of morning glowed, he reached the end of a plateau. Without realizing, he had been going down a long, shallow slope and suddenly found himself above a ravine. Once more he could hear the water of the Varshan. But four or five hundred cubits in front of him, above everything, apparently floating in the darkness, twenty or more torches burned. In their halos, he could see the outline of bricks. The fortress! Isaac stopped short. At that same moment, the very bright star disappeared as if swallowed by the earth, as if its task were completed.

Isaac wanted to laugh, to thank the Almighty with cries of joy, but he retained some semblance of sense, and contented himself with muttering a short prayer. He lay down. Only then did he realize how tired he was. He promised himself he would keep his eyes open, fixed on the torches, till dawn, but fell asleep without further ado.

❦

The sound of a trumpet woke him. The sun was high in the sky. He thought he was still dreaming. On a promontory partly encircled by the river stood the immaculate fortress, its crenelated walls at a height no ladder could scale. Four towers overlooked the roads in all directions, permitting surveillance for tens of leagues. Different from all the castles and fortresses he had seen in his travels, this one was built completely of white brick and stone. He could see no way in. The door of the fortress must be on the other side, toward the river and the tented town that stretched along the banks.

To see the fortress in front of him was a source of joy, but in spite of the assurance he had displayed to his companions, he knew just how difficult it would be to gain an audience with Khagan Joseph. How could he enter the fortress? How could he make them understand the importance of his mission? Who should he approach? A guard suspicious of foreigners, or worse? Saul was right; not being able to speak the language of the Khazars was going to make the task more difficult. He had flouted the injunction placed on strangers. Envoy of Rabbi Hazdai he might be, but he was more likely to end up buried at the bottom of a deep ditch than standing before the royal throne! Isaac noticed a group of soldiers walking around the topmost heights of the fortress. Supposing himself all too visible on the edge of the plateau, he rather unhelpfully hid himself behind a bush, but indifferent and sure of themselves, the Khazar warriors never even glanced at the surrounding countryside. They climbed a narrow staircase leading up to a tower and disappeared, their laughter reaching Isaac's ears. He felt ridiculous and angry at himself, but at that moment a whinny from a horse made him start. He bounded to his feet with a cry of alarm.

Ten feet behind him, a boy of about twelve was seated in the saddle of a half-blood, a bow grasped in his small fist. Long copper hair surrounded the high cheekbones of his face. Between slanted lids, gray eyes stared at Isaac. The boy's tunic appeared to be silk, gleaming with gold and richly embroidered around the neck. Also around his neck hung a silver chain bearing a large medal, like a coin. He was neither aggressive nor fearful. On the contrary, he had an air of calm grace that impressed Isaac. After a short hesitation, during which neither of them moved an inch, Isaac bowed as he would have done to any adult stranger.

The boy spurred his horse and had it advance a few paces. He said something unintelligible. Isaac recognized the sound of the Khazar language. He smiled at the child, making a gesture from ear to mouth to show that he had not understood. The child frowned and repeated what must have been a question.

"I don't understand you," Isaac said in Hebrew. "I am a traveler. I come from far away, from over there, where the sun sets."

Obvious surprise showed on the boy's graceful features. Isaac saw that he was thinking hard. At last, with a strange accent, rolling his r's, the child stuttered. "You speak the language of the rabbi and the Book of the Lord! Are you a rabbi?"

Full of happiness, choked with joy, Isaac's laugh resounded through the air. He walked toward the boy shaking his head. "No! No! I am no rabbi," he said, enunciating clearly. "I am a Sephardi Jew, from way out there to the west. And I too read the Torah, the book of the rabbis."

"You are a Jew of the Jews of the Book?" the child repeated, eyes shining with curiosity, as if he wasn't sure that what he was witnessing was real.

"Yes, if you like," admitted Isaac. "My name is Isaac ben Eliezer. What is your name?"

"Hezekiah." The child pronounced it in the Khazar manner and Isaac had to ask him to repeat it several times before he understood.

"What are you doing here?" the child responded, becoming suspicious. "Strangers are not allowed near the fortress today. My father is returning the body of his grandfather, Khagan Benjamin, to the Almighty...."

"Your father?" exclaimed Isaac. "Your father?"

"My father is the Khagan Joseph," Hezekiah announced proudly. "My father is the Khagan of the Khazars! And you, you should not be here...."

Isaac fell to his knees. Bowing from the waist, he thanked the Lord for His beneficence. All his aplomb recovered, Hezekiah advanced his horse. He drew an arrow from its leather quiver and, with the metal point, pricked Isaac's neck.

"If I want, I could cut your throat," he said with all the arrogance of a young warrior. "I have that right. Even my father and the rabbi would congratulate me...."

As Isaac looked up, he added, nodding toward the fortress, "I could also call the guards. As soon as they hear me they will come and get you...."

Isaac calmly nodded in agreement. He stood up and, pressing himself gently against the horse's flank, he gently grasped the young warrior's hand. "Hezekiah! I am a traveler who has come a long way. For nearly a year I have walked, crossing many countries, rivers and forests to meet your father, Khagan Joseph. You must not kill me before I have been able to bow to him."

"Why do you want to meet my father? Why is it so important for you to speak to him?"

Isaac pulled the scroll case from under his tunic. "In this there is a letter from a great Sephardi rabbi, Rabbi Hazdai! He is very respected in the west. He has written to your father because he respects and admires him...."

"A great rabbi?" interrupted the child, for whom these words seemed to have some magic virtue.

"Yes! The greatest and wisest rabbi of all the Jews!" Isaac exaggerated, silently asking the Almighty to forgive him.

"Greater than Hanania, our great rabbi?"

"Perhaps not," Isaac said diplomatically, "but just as wise as him. It is very important, Hezekiah. I promised to give this letter, in person, to your father the Khagan."

Hezekiah shook his head, twisting his mouth. "If you go to the fortress entrance they will not let you pass."

Just at that moment, Isaac noticed the design on the medallion worn on the child's chain: a seven-branched candelabra. "Hezekiah," he half whispered. "Help me."

The young boy frowned. He placed the arrow back in its quiver and pulled on the bridle. Before Isaac could stop him, he spurred his horse to a canter, jumping the ravine. Isaac did not dare call out to stop him, fearing he would alert the guards. In despair, he watched the boy make off into the distance. Suddenly the half-blood pulled up sharply. It pivoted and came back at a trot.

"Mount up behind me," the boy ordered. "If you are lying, the Beck Borouh, will have your throat cut."

His heart beating like a drum, Isaac jumped onto the horse. "How old are you, Hezekiah?"

"I will be thirteen next year. Then I will be given a real battle horse and a sword like my father's. And then I too can become Khagan!"

ঽ

The nearer they came to the fortress, the more formidable the walls appeared to Isaac. At the sight of the hedge of guards armed with pikes, bows and swords to prevent entry to Sarkel, he had to admit that he was scared. The gate was scarcely wide enough to let a chariot through and as high as three tall men. Its wooden door covered in iron was held up vertically by chains that disappeared through holes in the thick walls. It would take only a few seconds to let the door drop.

When they saw the horse approaching, the guards lowered their pikes. Hezekiah never slowed his steed. He shouted a few words. One young warrior with plaited hair pointed at Isaac. Hezekiah, without showing the least disquiet, shouted again and whipped the horse's neck with the end of the reins.

Isaac was aware of the guard's hesitation and surprise. However, there was so much authority in the young prince's comportment that he drew back, raising his lance in salute. A passage opened out in front of them, so narrow that Isaac felt his sandals rubbing against the guards' armor. Once through the hedge of guards, he did not dare turn around. Fearing the sound of an arrow seeking his back, he clung more closely to Hezekiah's waist, but worse than a heavy silence ensued.

They walked on in the shadow of the wall. The horses' hooves clattered on the paving stones. A sort of narrow lane wound its way between the vertiginous walls. Hezekiah rode his horse well. Isaac's heart was now beating fit to burst. It seemed to him as if he had just entered the most sacred place on earth.

The interior of the fortress was surprisingly cool. From high above, a trumpet sounded. Isaac could see the helmeted faces of ten warriors, bows at the ready. He understood that they were entering through a defensive labyrinth where it was easy to kill a would-be assailant. A stone portico in a perfect arch stood before them. Hezekiah slowed his mount to a walk as they passed through, entering a long narrow square.

Isaac saw small buildings, stores and armories, and a forge that sent flickering red shadows to the walls. Horses with men crouching on their haunches stood under cane awnings. Some of them rose when Hezekiah pushed his horse roughly through. Sowing stupefaction behind them, they reached the end of the square in a few steps. There, an imposing new door with arrow slots and sculpted pillars opened onto the northern part of the fortress. Shouts arose once more, as warriors placed themselves in front of the horse, waving their arms. The beast reared. Hezekiah stood up in his wooden stirrups, and Isaac felt himself sliding backward. Fearing he would take the boy with him if he fell, he let go of the lad's waist and slid over the tail to the ground. Frightened, Hezekiah's half-blood thrashed out with its hind hooves. Isaac rolled sideways to avoid being crushed but one hoof made contact, cracking his shoulder. He tried to move aside, one hand holding the broken limb. He received another blow, this time to his kidneys, and closed his eyes with pain as a further blow to his head stunned him. Immobile, he reopened his eyes. The point of a sword was being pressed into his forehead with such pressure that it had pierced the skin. He felt the warmth of his blood trickling through his hair.

The Khazar, without hesitation, placed the sole of his boot on Isaac's throat, suffocating him. Unable to see anything but the warrior's coat of mail and the blue sky, he heard the furious voice of Hezekiah, shouting again in the same incomprehensible language. Another voice replied angrily. The horse whinnied in objection at being kept on such a short rein, its shoes clattering on the paving slabs, sending vibrations through Isaac's back. Hezekiah's cries were sharp, he seemed to be calling a name, and for the first time, Isaac heard:

"Attex! Attex!"

A voice replied, commanding, but as feminine as a silk veil. Silence reigned through a moment of indecision. The pressure of the sword point on his forehead eased. Isaac took advantage of it; without considering the risk he was taking, he seized the soldier's boot that was still pressing on his throat, with both hands. With all his remaining strength, he lifted and twisted it, all in one movement. The Khazar, taken by surprise, jumped before losing his balance. Blood running down the side of his cheek, Isaac struggled to his knees. With quick reflexes he plunged one hand into his tunic and brought out the leather scroll case, while with the other he grabbed his Toledo dagger, pointing it straight in front of him to ward off the guards who were about to attack him. He shouted, "Shalom! Shalom!"

Only then did he have time to look around. The square was at least fifty cubits wide. Some extraordinary buildings were built against the walls; houses, trapezoid in shape, sculpted with seven-branched candelabra and supported by white marble columns with caps of gold. The Khazar warriors were now standing, directing their pikes and swords at him. Their faces were half-covered by round helmets ornamented with blue and white plumes. In their midst, hugging Hezekiah to her, was a woman.

A woman such as he had never seen before, not in the whole wide world created by Almighty God! Her green, slightly slanted eyes and her high cheek bones gave her an Oriental appearance. Her long copper hair hung down past her waist, framing a round pale face, skin so pale it seemed translucent. Her neatly drawn mouth was outlined in rouge. She was dressed in a long green tunic, a gold collar around her neck.

He was completely overcome by the look she gave him. Forgetful of the weapons pointed at him, and the stiletto he was brandishing, he stood up and held out the scroll to her, saying in Hebrew, "Help me, I beg of you! Khagan Joseph must read this letter."

Hezekiah looked up into the young woman's face. Isaac fell back to his knees. "I beg you! The Almighty Himself is watching over us!"

At that, a small warrior with shoulders like a bull and a mustache hanging well below his chin, barked a brief order. Isaac only had time to throw the leather scroll case at the feet of the woman before the flat of the soldier's blade crashed down on his arm. Isaac tumbled over backward, holding onto his own weapon. He jumped up again, exploding with anger at such stupidity, thinking of how far he had come only to be treated like this! He wanted to throw himself at the feet of the young woman whose mouth seemed to be smiling and whose eyes shone like the stars. He shouted, "You can't let them kill me! I have been sent by Rabbi Hazdai!" Amid the sound of these words he heard the whistle of weapons on the move. He wanted to prostrate himself, but darkness overcame him.

Chapter sixteen

BA Flight 786, London–Baku
May 2000

Sofer had, as usual, chosen a window seat. The man, without any hesitation and without consulting his boarding pass for his seat number, sat down beside him. Sofer had noticed him a little earlier, in the seating area at the boarding gate. He wasn't the type of man who would escape one's attention. Tall, clean-shaven, almost bald, he wore a raw silk and linen suit obviously tailored on Saville Row, a cream silk tie completing the ensemble. A gold signet ring glittered on the third finger of each hand. His thick nose and the strange absence of any eyebrows gave him the appearance of a wild beast, constantly alert. His eyes, coldly blue and unblinking, seemed to be scanning the pink pages of the *Financial Times* while in reality haughtily examining all the travelers around him.

For some obscure reason, Sofer was sure the man was going to begin a conversation with him as soon as he could. For his part, he had no intention of responding to the stranger and had no need for such distractions to while away the flight time. During take-off, he took advantage of his window seat by keeping his eyes on the runway. He particularly liked that part of a flight when the plane cleared the buildings, soaring like a bird, lifting him away from normal horizons.

It was a moment of exciting freedom, a time to be nothing, or at least, not yet part of something. With a little imagination he could believe himself in a time capsule suspended at an elevation where all paths seem possible, where a small computer error, a dip of the wings, or a moment's madness could dispatch one to Makhatchkala or Los Angeles, Samarkand or Paramaribo, or ... Baku.

However, on this occasion, he watched the unattractive Heathrow Airport buildings slip away with only one desire: to arrive at his intended destination. He had no wish for chance to divert them on even the slightest detour, and hoped that Agarounov would be there waiting for him that evening. One sign of his impatience, despite his fear of bringing bad luck, was that he advanced his watch to the time current at the Sea of the Khazars.

As soon as the aircraft achieved its cruising speed, he opened a book by D.M. Dunlop, *The History of the Jewish Khazars*. The study dated from the 1950s, but it had yet to be surpassed. Dunlop seemed to have been the only historian to have seriously researched and understood the eccentric conversion of the Khazars to Judaism. Sofer was already deeply immersed in his reading when a flight attendant offered him a meal. As soon as he looked up at her, the stranger beside him caught his eye and smiled at him knowingly. The flight attendant handed out the small white tray with chicken and rice dripping with sauce, chopped carrots, yogurt, and a synthetic looking Danish pastry. The glass and the cutlery were solid.

The man held the tray while Sofer put his book away. "Take your time," he said in educated English. Sofer thanked him, knowing he could not now escape the idle chatter of good neighbors. This began almost immediately when, having been served in his turn, the man ordered a real bottle of Bordeaux, a Côtes-de-Blaye that was only a little bit better than the quarter bottle of Australian plonk handed out 'free' by British Airways.

The man held the bottle at eye level, tipped the neck toward Sofer's glass and said, "Please, allow me ... it would be my pleasure...your very British chicken will not taste quite so bad...."

Sofer accepted. It was difficult to resist such an effort at conviviality.

"Are you going to Baku on business?"

The question was posed as if the stranger was only being polite. A gentle introduction, seemingly without the appearance of curiosity. Despite this, Sofer could not help resenting it as the first step of an inquisition. He smiled coolly, and said, "Yes, and no."

The Englishman gripped his glass, looking puzzled.

"Neither for business, nor as a tourist," explained Sofer.

The man laughed. A frank laugh, in spite of the distant look in his eyes. "Then," he said, slightly smiling, "I know only one other reason: a woman! Love!"

It was Sofer's turn to be disconcerted. For a few seconds, he scrutinized the stranger's face to see if he meant anything by those particular words. It even occurred to him that he might know something about the redheaded woman. Then the absurdity of his own thoughts reached him and he laughed too. "Who knows?" he exclaimed. "Who knows what one will find at the end of a journey?"

The man smiled politely. "Alas, nowadays such surprises are rare."

Sofer agreed and was about to use the platitude to put an end to the exchange, when the man asked, pointing at the book in Sofer's seat pocket, "Excuse my curiosity on one other thing, but isn't that a book about the Khazars you are reading?"

This time Sofer could not hide his surprise. "Yes.... Are you a historian? Do you know the story of the Khazars?"

The Englishman shook his head, vaguely amused. "Neither. I don't know anything about the Khazars, rather the opposite." He drew out a card from his jacket pocket and offered it. "It would be better if we introduced ourselves."

The card only had a name, Alastair Thomson, and *Lloyds International*. No address, not even a telephone number. Sofer hesitated a second before offering his hand. "Marc Sofer," he said simply.

Thomson's handshake was firm and courteous. He pointed at his *Financial Times* newspaper. "Read this," he said, pointing to a particular column. You will understand my interest."

The article described the attack on the oil installations owned by the OCOO in the Bay of Baku. It was almost identical to that in

The Guardian, with only two noticeable exceptions. First, it quantified the loss suffered by the consortium at several million dollars. Second, and above all, it mentioned the New Khazars "*…Among several fraudulent claims, the investigators seem to be considering that of the New Khazars with some seriousness, although, as of now, at least officially, it appears impossible to detect who is operating under this strange pseudonym…*"

"You don't look surprised," Thomson remarked, picking at his salad. "Did you already know about it?"

Without knowing why, perhaps only in self-defense against the Englishman's curiosity, Sofer lied first, then backtracked. "No! Well, yes … a friend in Baku told me about the attack. From reading *The Guardian*, I understood that no serious claims had been made."

Thomson looked him up and down, as if he were waiting for Sofer to continue. Eventually, he poured a little wine in each of their glasses. Sofer was now as curious about this Alastair Thomson as the Englishman was about him.

"Actually, nothing has been confirmed," Thomson admitted.

"Does the attack concern you professionally?" asked Sofer glancing at the business card sitting on his tray.

Alastair Thomson smiled proudly and said, "Lloyds insures 38% of Offshore Caspian Oil Operations. You have seen the estimated loss figures quoted. Between three and four million dollars. That may be a bit excessive. However, even a two million dollar loss is a hefty sum."

"And you, are you one of these investigators you read about in detective novels, an insurance agent tracking down crime-profiteers?"

"Something like that," Thomson agreed seriously.

They emptied their glasses in a silence that was broken by the flight attendant who asked if they were comfortable. Sofer accepted the perfumed tissue she offered to clean his fingers, and when she moved to the row behind, he asked, "What do you think, what do they hope to gain from the attack?"

"If you could tell me that, Mr. Sofer, I would give you a pot of gold!"

There was as much reproach as sarcasm in Thomson's tone. Sofer felt as if he had been accused of something. Evidently this Englishman liked to play with innuendo. Slightly aggressively, Sofer remarked, "Surely when people claim responsibility for an attack, they generally give their reasons."

Thomson agreed with a nod, but instead of answering he asked, "Would you tell me a bit about these Khazars? An ancient race? They really existed? Until yesterday morning I had never heard of them. Someone briefed me quickly. Then ... luck? You sit beside me reading about them!"

That's it, Sofer thought. In the check-in hall, the Englishman must have noticed the cover of his book, *The History of the Jewish Khazars*, after which he had made sure he was allocated the adjacent seat in order to pick Sofer's brains. He held back from remarking that luck was made, not found. In reality, the ambiguity of the situation amused him. "Originally the Khazar people were a nomadic tribe," he began, as if he were making the opening remarks at a seminar. "They have long been compared to the Turks. It is more likely, however, that they came from the eastern steppes...."

He outlined the picture using broad brush-strokes to describe what he knew: the development of the Khazars, the constant wars with their neighbors, the alliances—renounced and renegotiated a thousand times—their growing power, the originality of their culture and their extraordinary religious/political tolerance. The Englishman, very attentive, took notes. He only interrupted Sofer once.

"If I understand correctly, the exceptional nature of the Khazars was their conversion to Judaism. Am I right?"

"That is effectively their claim to fame in history," agreed Sofer. "To the best of my knowledge, there is no other example of such a choice having been made. Especially on the part of a state which, if it did have Jews within its population, was not principally composed of the descendants of Moses. Originally there was nothing Jewish about the Khazars: no memory, no culture, no language! It is even possible that, when King Bulan made the decision to convert, he knew nothing about Judaism! Under such circumstances, I find it extraordinary that the Khagans maintained their power and the integrity of the kingdom for over three centuries while still retaining absolute tolerance toward Muslims and Christians...."

"But why did they choose Judaism?" Thomson persisted.

Sofer smiled. He waited while the flight attendant cleared away the meal, which neither of them had touched, before answering. "I am going to answer as a writer, and cannot therefore give you a historian's reply. In my mind, one day King Bulan realized that rich nations are those that stop following the seasons. Under his reign the Khazars began to know wealth, and the strength that comes with it. Their kingdom was right on the great commercial crossroads, where East meets West.

"Rich nations construct towns: they build brick houses and put away their tents. They build a state with laws and institutions, because commerce prospers with stability and peace. Commerce also obliges intercourse with other rich and powerful people capable of buying and selling. Thus the Khazars needed to become sedentary, stable, powerful and capable of choosing alliances with care. If not, they would disappear. King Bulan must have known that. But he knew one other truth: alliances that had to be forged in order to live in peace could prove as deadly as wars. Three powers pressed heavily on the borders of his kingdom: the Barbarians, essentially to the north; the Muslim Arabs to the south-east, from whom the Khazars were partially protected by the Caucasus Mountains; and finally, the immense, all-powerful Christian Empire of Byzantium.

"Bulan knew that the time for nomadic life, shamans and amulets had run out. Barbarism had to be replaced, but with what? A priori, one of those monotheistic religions that protect the wealthiest nations. There were two that touched his frontiers. Firstly, that of the Christians in Byzantium: the masters of the world at that time. They ruled in commerce as in war. Bulan, however, had seen the Greeks at work. He knew that, if he embraced their religion, Byzantium would suffocate them! Perhaps then, he should lean toward the Muslim faith, which little by little was taking hold of the Arab world. But the result would have been identical. Even though the Khazars had often beaten the masters of Baghdad and Persia, on their own territory they had a good understanding with the Muslims, who were excellent businessmen...."

Thomson nodded his head, a thin smile on his lips. "I see! Your king decided to choose the sole religion that was not represented on his frontiers by any powerful state!"

"Yes, indeed!"

"Very shrewd. High voltage geopolitics, to coin a phrase!"

"But, unfortunately, untenable in the long term. Doubtless the Khazar Kingdom became too rich to avoid the inevitable clash with Byzantium. Nevertheless, in choosing the Jewish faith, Bulan obtained a respite of several hundred years. That's not bad...."

Sofer hesitated about continuing. By his own lights, such a choice, however politically motivated, lost none of its spiritual value by being influenced in this way. But he doubted if that would interest Thomson. Moved by an impulse, as if he wanted the Englishman to feel the reality and the power of the Khazars, he plunged his hand into a pocket. He brought out Yakubov's coin.

"Here," he said, "look at this."

Thomson took the coin.

"They minted their own coins," explained Sofer enthusiastically, after the Englishman carefully returned the silver disk. "A very rare skill at the time, so rare that they minted coins for other states, particularly for the barbarians to the north."

"Where did you get it?" asked Thomson.

Sofer noticed something sharper in his neighbor's manner. It was sudden, as if two pieces of a puzzle had come together. Sofer had not yet made a direct connection between that odd fellow Yakubov and the attack at Baku. For a fraction of a second he saw Yakubov's golden smile again, offering him the coin to convince him to help, swearing that he was being hunted, in danger ... then this same Yakubov in the Hotel Athena, having miraculously resolved all his problems, flies off to Canada in a Cerruti suit! Yes, the story of this Jew from the mountains would interest Thomson. However, whether from prudence, defiance or just to satisfy a curious feeling of solidarity toward these Jews of the Mountains of whom he knew little or nothing, he remained silent.

"A Jew who was interested in the Khazars and has done some research on the subject gave it to me as a present," he wriggled. Pocketing the coin with a smile he added in a self-deprecating manner, "This coin is my talisman till my current business is finished."

Thomson looked vague. Finally, he posed the question that Sofer had been expecting during the last few minutes. "Actually, you have not yet said; what is your business?"

"I write all sorts of things, serious and not so serious stories on the state of the world."

"Oh! A novelist?"

His reaction was one of condescension rather than surprise, and it annoyed Sofer. Thomson had probably never opened a book except at the end of a hospital bed when there was really no other option as to how he could kill time. Again, the Englishman demanded his attention.

"Do you know, Mr. Sofer, that the political situation in the Caucasus is not so very different from that in the time of the Khazars?"

"What do you mean?"

"Replace the trade in spices, silk and slaves with that of oil, and you have the same situation. Replace Byzantium with the Soviets for the main part, and us, the Westerners ... the Sea of the Khazars, Mr. Sofer, is the sea of black gold! Yes, you cannot imagine how close the parallel is."

Thomson stopped, a smile of satisfaction on his lips. The flight attendant offered them coffee that gave them cause for a break while they were served with the black foul-smelling liquid. Then Thomson asked sharply, "What do you know about oil?"

"Practically nothing. Not even how much they mean when they talk about a barrel."

"Zero point one four metric tons. To give you a comparison, let's say a daily output of one thousand barrels represents an annual production of fifty thousand metric tons."

He drank his coffee and continued. "Up until recently, they evaluated the oil reserves under the Caspian Sea at three and a half billion metric tons. An estimate, that's all. By comparison, the largest reserve identified in the world, Ghawar in Saudi Arabia, has an estimated ten billion metric tons. Mr. Sofer, the investigations that have been carried out around the Caspian Sea since the fall of Communism have revealed much, much more than anyone ever imagined possible."

He replaced his plastic cup as if he were handling real porcelain and fixed his emotionless gaze on Sofer. "One field alone, to the north of the Caspian, contains seven billion metric tons. That alone triples the known reserves in the area! Today, Baku exports a hundred thousand barrels of crude oil a day. In ten years, in 2010, it will be two million...."

"Per day?"

Absolutely! Two million barrels a day. If not, there won't be any gasoline for your car. But, you see, the difficulty in the oil business, contrary to popular opinion, is not the extraction of the crude, but its transport. Most of the time, it has to be taken miles from the well by road, in a continual daily cycle. It is heavy, it's a pollutant. Transport by tanker is no longer acceptable in our environmentally friendly era. The most economic solution, the cleanest and the most acceptable, is by pipeline. An enormous conduit capable of automatically propelling millions of barrels of oil, day and night, over thousands of miles, crossing many countries."

Sofer began to see where the Englishman was heading. With a wave of his hand, Thomson drew the Caucasus mountain range in the air. "Georgia, Chechnya, Daghestan, Azerbaijan ... from the Black Sea to the Caspian, these countries have become as vital to the West as the Middle East. Caspian oil concerns all the world powers: Europe, the United States, China, Russia ... all the main oil companies are represented in Baku. The Anglo-Americans with BP, Exxon, State Oil, British Gas, Mobil, Shell, Chevron, and anyone else you may care to name. The French are there with Total-Fina and Elf. And, of course, the Russians with Gazprom."

Sofer nodded. "Many people said that oil was the principal reason for the wars in Daghestan and Chechnya. A pipeline crosses both those countries, if I'm not mistaken, constructed during the Communist era."

"Exactly! At the start of the collapse of the Soviet Empire, all the countries along the Caucasus tried their luck for independence. Azerbaijan and Georgia only half achieved it; international pressure was strongly in favor of retaining Russian control. But there was no question of the Kremlin allowing Daghestan and Chechnya to profit in the same way from the oil passing through their territory. If so much as a drop of oil profit found its way to Grozny, Chechnya would feel the Russian boot.... And Europe, like the United States, distanced themselves from this conflict for the oil which did come to them from the Caspian, by avoiding that route. In 1999, a pipeline was laid directly from Baku to the Black Sea through Georgia. From there the oil could be carried unencumbered to Hamburg or Dunkirk...."

The Englishman was enjoying the attention his discourse was receiving.

"Charming..." murmured Sofer.

Thomson shrugged his shoulders. "The Russians lost out in the debacle, partly because of their own Mafia. They lost control of the Caspian oil. We are there now, us, the West, wealthier, better organized, and therefore stronger! We've been in place for several years now; they won't get us out. Ancient Byzantium has lost its golden goose to the New Byzantium. Of course, that makes these Russian fools furious. Chechnya paid the price for that anger, but who cares? Not even the United Nations, Mr. Sofer."

Thomson laughed quietly. His cynicism astonished Sofer. He was aware that Thomson was only expressing common political and economic imperatives out loud that ordinarily remained in the shadows. And, in some ways, he had said nothing new. Still, it sickened him. He didn't want to let the Englishman believe that he might be a willing or even an admiring accomplice. By exaggerating the movement of his hand toward his book, he hoped to signal clearly that he was not interested in further conversation, but Thomson leaned toward him. Sofer scented the luxury after-shave and the vague smell of wine. Thomson's eyes were shining, amused. A cat playing with a mouse, Sofer thought.

"I know what you are thinking, Mr. Sofer. And in some ways

you are correct. But listen to me, I am only doing my job, which is to understand a situation and to identify the threads before I can help them become different ... not only become different, but better. And, whether you believe me or not, better for the whole world."

"Are you trying to justify yourself, Mr. Thomson?" taunted Sofer. "What does my opinion matter to you? When one is a part of Byzantium, the opinion of clerks scarcely counts!"

The comment struck Thomson like a whiplash. It gave Sofer great satisfaction to see the Englishman's face flushing with anger. But the Lloyds inspector was a true Brit. He bit his lip, then quickly burst out laughing.

"Touché! Well said ... please excuse me if I have seemed arrogant in my explanations."

Sofer, always magnanimous, lifted his hand in a sign of peace.

"To return to the beginning of our conversation," the Englishman continued, "we had hoped that the attack on the oil installations in Baku was perpetrated by Chechnya. But now, it doesn't look like it."

"Are you sure?"

"With this type of thing, it is hard to be certain of anything."

"I don't see the connection with the Khazars, though. They disappeared almost a thousand years ago! I fear that the geopolitics of oil are just a little too recent for them."

Thomson had regained his composure. He pointed to the pink pages of his *Financial Times* and declared derisively, "How do you know? The people hiding behind the New Khazars certainly didn't just pull the name out of thin air!"

"So...?" asked Sofer, his heart beating heavily.

"Well ... nothing." sighed Thomson. "It is still too soon to be sure. But I must take every hypothesis into account." He had already plunged a hand deep into a pocket and was pulling out another business card onto which he wrote several numbers. "That's my mobile number where you can find me while you are in Baku. It will always be a pleasure to chat with you. One never knows, you may hear something, or have an idea...."

"I doubt it," murmured Sofer accepting the card nevertheless.

Thomson then said breathily, in a tone of warning rather than advice, "Mr. Sofer, nobody wants these attacks to get out of hand...."

"*These?* I thought there had only been one...."

"There will be others, believe me. Attacks never come singly. Those who commit them always have to repeat their action, even if only to show their determination. It's always the same. And that is really the reason I am on this plane. One thing you have taught me about the Khazars is that they were Jews. That is the outstanding feature of their history, isn't it? That is also the reason you chose to write about them. The Khazars were Jews. I can only conclude that the people hiding behind this pseudo-movement of the New Khazars are also Jews, Mr. Sofer. I say that without intending to shock you or hurt you in any way. Simply as something for you to think about...."

Sofer felt a surge of adrenalin; the sign of three old fears resurfacing. He nodded agreement and turned his face away, not wishing the Englishman to see his emotional state. Truthfully, he had been afraid of the possibility all along. It had occurred to him the moment Agarounov had first told him about the New Khazars. Up until now, Sofer had avoided thinking about it. But he knew Thomson was right. The New Khazars could be a Jewish movement. But which Jews, and why? And what should he do about it? He, Marc Sofer, who had come as far as the shores of the Caspian Sea to be able to better imagine his heroes whom he thought had disappeared centuries ago.

Through the window of the Boeing, the snowy peaks of the Caucasus appeared, beyond the metallic reflection of the Black Sea. The mountain chain was immense. Two massive ranges, the highest summits climbing into the sky like unassailable monsters, almost appearing to touch the plane. To the north, vaguely discernable through low clouds, extended the green and gray plains of the lands that had once been the Kingdom of the Khazars.

Had his worry been born out of the conversation with Thomson? He shivered. There, down below, Isaac ben Eliezer from Cordoba and Attex the Khazarian princess had been face to face, completely absorbed with one another. Incapable of finding words, of having the strength to name the sentiment that already engulfed them. That meeting had taken place one thousand and forty five years ago, but for Sofer, it was here and now.

Chapter seventeen

Sarkel, September 955

e is not going to die...." Hezekiah's voice hovered between question and affirmation.

"No," murmured Attex, "he is not going to die."

"They battered his head." Hezekiah sounded apprehensive. "He lost a lot of blood."

Attex watched the boy's fingers stroking the stranger's cheek, moving up to the edge of the bandage at his temple. The blond locks were blackened with dried blood. His tunic had been so covered in it that the servants had taken it away. A simple blanket covered his torso and its fine, pale skin.

"He is blond like the men from the north," chattered Hezekiah, "but he doesn't look like one of them. He is more handsome, don't you think so?"

He turned to look at her, to see if she agreed. Attex nodded approvingly. At that moment, Isaac's mouth opened slightly and let out a moan. They saw the stranger's eyes rolling under his closed lids. His lips trembled again, as did his fingers, but he did not wake. Worry showed on Hezekiah's face. Attex gripped him by the shoulders.

"Rabbi Hanania has read the letter he was carrying. He says

that it is a very important letter and that you did very well allowing this foreigner to come here. Your father won't punish you…."

"I know I did the right thing," Hezekiah replied proudly. "As soon as I saw him, I knew he was telling the truth. But Senek is too stupid to understand such things. He went for him as if he were a Petchenegue!"

"Senek only did his duty. Otherwise Borouh or your father would have punished him."

Hezekiah shrugged. Attania, who had been waiting at the entrance to the room, came up to their side and said in her raucous voice, "Ambassador Blymmedes is waiting for you to receive him. He is in the great hall. The courtyard is full of his servants waiting for your arrival in order to bring you hundreds of presents."

"Let him wait!" Attex replied. "I don't want his presents."

"The Khagan will be furious."

"I don't care what Joseph thinks! I am not just a piece of furniture in his throne room!" Attex met Attania's stare. In spite of her anger her cheeks reddened. She was wrong, and she knew it. She lowered her eyes to look at the stranger's face, as much to assure herself that he was still unconscious as to ensure she would not forget one iota of his beauty. "Take Hezekiah," she continued quietly. "He should not stay here. I will watch over the stranger. I think he will awaken soon."

"You shouldn't be the one to stay with him," preached Attania.

Attex pushed Hezekiah toward the old servant as if she had not heard. "Tell the Greek—and Joseph, if he asks—that the rabbi has asked me to carry out a most important task and that I can't possibly see him before tomorrow."

The grimace on Attania's deformed face rendered it uglier than ever. She shook her head, sighing deeply. Mumbling away to herself, she turned on her heels and led the boy away. Before leaving the room, Hezekiah took one more look at the unconscious foreigner. Attex returned the boy's smile as their eyes met.

Alone at last in the small room, she walked over to the window. Attania was correct; the patio of her small palace was totally occupied by servants. With the Greeks it was always like this, the excessive signs of wealth. They said that the Byzantine ambassador had arrived from Tmutorokan with a column of more than fifty camels to transport him, his attendants and the immense paraphernalia without which he would not have known how to survive a single day. The tent he had made them erect below Sarkel was, it appeared, as large as the Khagan's palace, and alongside it was an equally large wooden building of cedar, filled with furniture and even containing an ablution section as big as a swimming pool. All that pomp disgusted her. The presents, the presence of so many servants, the conversations Blymmedes had with her brother, the looks thrown in her direction by the ambassador, everything, everything about the Greeks disgusted her!

She knew only too well the significance of all this opulence. In the markets of Sarkel, Itil or Samandar other men showed off their wealth so they could buy the best flocks at the lowest prices. And that is what the Byzantine ambassador was doing, just what her brother, whom she loved so much, whom she had cherished and admired since he was a child as the greatest hero on earth, wanted to do; to sell her to the highest bidder. To force her into a Greek soldier's bed in exchange for peace in the Khazar Kingdom. At least he had not tried to lie to her, and she would not be sold and profaned at a total loss....

Did the Almighty truly want this? No, He could not. Rabbi Hanania had assured her of that many times. But Joseph no longer listened to the rabbi. No more than he had listened to the words of their grandfather Benjamin on his deathbed. She herself had sworn she would never submit to a Greek. She would not accede to that! She left the window to cross the room to the stranger's couch.

She had not dared show too much emotion in front of the child, but Hezekiah was right. How gorgeous he was! So handsome that she could not think of a comparison.

However, that had not been the first thing she had noticed about him when he tried to stand up amidst the guards, imploring yet defiant, ready to die to accomplish his duty. It was strange to consider, but true all the same, that when he stood before her, brandishing his leather tube as if it was a precious Torah, she became aware of his presence as if, for the first time in her life, apart from her brother Joseph, she were looking at a man. No, the truth was even worse; before she even knew who or what he was, where he came from or why, she knew that he had come for her.

May the Lord pardon her the thought, but in seeing him so ably defying the guard, fearlessly threatening all the others with his tiny blade, with blood running down his temple, and placing his life in her hands—unknown hands—it had seemed that this magnificent man was some sort of angel sent from the other side of the world to save her ... was this just pride? Was it a sin?

She had forced herself to gather all her strength so as not to tremble or cry. So much so that she had been incapable of expressing one word to restrain Senek. She had watched with horror as the chief of the guards approached the stranger from behind, raised his weapon and let it descend with all his might. She had not said a word, emitted a warning or complained. The stranger was struck down, right there before her eyes, because of her stupefaction. Not for a second was she afraid for him. Not for an instant did she think he would succumb to his injuries, so persuaded was she that the Almighty, blessed be His Name, would protect him ... and indeed, he was alive, unconscious but still breathing. She knew, at the bottom of her heart, with all the fervor in her soul, she knew that he would recover, that he would speak to her! Was she mad?

The tumult of her thoughts terrified her and filled her with joy at the same time. She held them in, not daring to tell them to another soul, not to the rabbi, not even to Attania.

Hezekiah had perhaps guessed; children sometimes possess the unusual gift of divining the invisible.

She sat down on the wooden couch where the young man was lying and pronounced the name that Hezekiah had told her: Isaac. That is what the foreigner was called: Isaac. She scrutinized every inch of the face that was slightly turned on its side, cheeks creased with the fatigue of a long journey and sullied with the blood and dirt that the servants had only lightly cleaned. Under the dust and the scars of his wounds, there was flesh and blood, life to rebuild his body.

She thought about calling for some water and washing him herself. If she did that, the whole fortress would know before sundown and buzz with rumor. Joseph would hear about it and his fury would be unleashed. But must she always subject herself and submit to the sermons of Joseph the Khagan?

The stranger's neck had something fragile and terribly attractive about it. His skin, stretched over the bones of his shoulders, was as fine as a girl's. Blood raced through it, pulsing quickly, reminding Attex that he was, after all, wounded and feverish.

She tried to wipe his wrist, but quickly withdrew her hand. A violent trembling seized Isaac at her soft touch. He shook. His jaw dropped, his mouth opened. His breathing was like a forge, pumping his chest. Attex was horrified, believing that despite what she had believed earlier, that he was going to die, then and there! She gripped Isaac's hand, squeezed it, murmuring soft Khazar words he could not understand. His breathing eased. She hoped that he would open his eyes, but he did not. After a quick glance at the canvas hung over the doorway, she finally made the gesture she had been restraining. Her fingers imitated those of Hezekiah a little earlier; they stroked Isaac's wounded cheek. They slid under his chin, ran over his chest in a slow sweet caress. It was she who shivered, heart beating so strongly that she could feel it hammering in her throat. Her fingers gently moved back up to Isaac's mouth, pressing his lips as if they carried her kiss.

He opened his eyes. Burning with fever, he looked at her as a man arriving in the Garden of Eden would delight in the immensity of the bounty surrounding him. Standing up, she whispered in Hebrew, "Blessed be the Lord, you are alive." She was not sure if he could hear her. He was breathing so fast that his breath was cracking the skin on his lips. His gaze was so intense that she thought she would catch the fever consuming him. He contorted his face, and she realized that he was trying to smile. In a deathly voice he said, in carefully articulated Hebrew, "I am Isaac ben Eliezer, I come from Cordoba. I was sent by Rabbi Hazdai to deliver a letter to the King of the Jews, Joseph son of Aaron, Khagan of the Kingdom of the Khazars."

All said in one breath, like a dying man close to expiring. A white saliva appeared like glue between his lips. He added, "You are as beautiful as the angel who visits the dead."

She laughed; a light laugh full of a thousand joys coming from the depth of her being. "You are not dead, and I am Attex, the Khagan's sister. We found your letter in its leather case."

An expression of extreme relief relaxed his features. For one short moment neither of them said anything, heard anything, did anything else but look at one another. Then Isaac fainted, a smile on his lips.

ᚵ

Attex called the servants. She looked after Isaac for the rest of the day. She had them wash him from head to toe, and ordered that they bring him new clothes and dress him. Attania herself placed the dressings and unguents on his wounds. In the middle of the afternoon, Isaac regained consciousness. He was suffering from a cruel headache that prevented him keeping his eyes open for long. With the aim of replacing some of the vast quantities of blood he had lost, they brought him barley bread, roast lamb, fruit, milk, and cucumbers in fresh yogurt. He was not hungry, but Attania's threats and terrible features convinced him to accept some of each. To his own surprise, he didn't find it bad and his headache even diminished. By twilight, all was noisy bustle around his bed. Throughout the whirlwind of activity, he searched for the eyes of Attex. In vain. She seemed to be avoiding his gaze, watching everything, occupying herself everywhere, but as if from afar, as mistress of the house, as a caring princess looking after a guest. She never once rested her emerald eyes on Isaac, never once bestowed upon him the fond gaze she had given him when he had first awakened. And as she never spoke to him, he believed he had dreamed it. A dream that became a nightmare to the wakened man. A dream of great sweetness that disappeared in reality. The violent pain that assailed his temples returned. A little before nightfall, he fell asleep, exhausted.

He wakened with a start. He felt he had only slept a short

142

while, but the two naphtha lamps that dimly lit the room contrasted heavily with the black night outside.

He searched for Attex in the shadows. The silhouette he discovered at the end of his bed made him jump. The man was very small, very old. The darkness emphasized his wrinkles and obscured his face. A turban enveloped his head in the Muslim fashion.

In spite of his nausea, Isaac sat up a little on his elbows and murmured, "Are you the Khagan Joseph?"

The old man chuckled. His gnarled fingers held the scroll of leather from Cordoba. He leaned nearer, showing his smiling pupils. "No. I am Rabbi Hanania."

His Hebrew was easy to understand, his voice old but alive, a bit dry, but used to being listened to. Isaac recognized his accent. He had heard it before, in Cordoba, from men who had come from the Orient. The strength of his emotion made his heart beat harder, and tears came to his eyes. He had crossed mountains and rivers, country after country, endured storms and frost, vanquished wolves, and at last, at the far end of the earth created by the Almighty, he was once more in the company of a rabbi! A rabbi who asked him, "Are you fit to talk, my boy?"

"Yes."

Hanania waved the leather scroll in front of his toothless smile. "This letter you brought is a good letter. But it poses many questions. You do understand that I will have to make sure of the messenger who delivered it...."

Isaac nodded, flickering his eyelids. "Rabbi Hazdai warned me that you would probably interrogate me for a long time...."

"Long, no. Did you know, before you entered the fortress, that we were in mourning for a Khagan?"

"Yes. Khagan Benjamin. The cavalrymen stopped our boats on the river...."

"You braved the ban on strangers approaching the fortress," the rabbi stated reproachfully. "You knew that you risked almost everything? Even death?"

Isaac sighed. "I have taken risks and avoided death every day for a year. If the Lord had not desired my arrival here, He had plenty of opportunity to prevent it."

The old rabbi raised his head. Encouraged, Isaac pointed at the leather scroll. "I promised Rabbi Hazdai Ibn Shaprut that I would personally place the letter in Khagan Joseph's hand. I must meet him…."

Hanania placed his hand on the cover. "One more question. Do you know this? When a man was at the point when he was about to quit this life, Adam, the first man, came to him and asked him why he was leaving the world in such a condition. The man replied, 'Unhappily, it is your fault. Because of you I must die!' To which Adam replied, 'My son, I only infringed one commandment, and I was punished for it; look at the number of our Master's commandments you have transgressed!'"

Isaac shivered. These were truly a rabbi's words. Words that he himself had heard from the lips of Rabbi Hazdai when his father died! If he had any further doubts, they vanished at this. He was now certainly in the New Kingdom of Israel! Head pounding, he took up where the rabbi left off. "'Rabbi Hiyya said, Even today Adam exists. He presents himself twice daily to the patriarchs and confesses his faults; he shows them the place were he lived in other times in celestial splendor. Rabbi Yessa said, 'Adam presents himself to every man at the moment he is going to leave this life in order to bear witness that the man does not die because of Adam's sin but because of his own sins, and this is why the Sages said, No one dies without sin.'"

Hanania remained silent. From his deeply lined face, his pupils shone so brightly that they reflected the flickering flame from the lamp. At last, an odd sound came from his throat. Isaac did not know whether it was a laugh or a sob. He saw the old mans' fingers trembling violently when the latter placed the scroll back on his chest. "Yes, you can give it yourself to the Khagan when your wounds have healed," he whispered, in a voice choked with emotion. "Sleep well, my boy." Without waiting longer, he walked away from Isaac's couch and made toward the doorway.

"Rabbi, Rabbi! Do you know where the redheaded princess who saved me has gone?"

Hanania turned and looked directly at him. A grimace—or was it a smile?—creased his features.

"She told me that she was the Khagan's sister!"

"Sleep, Isaac ben Eliezer. Rest yourself and don't dream about the Kathum Attex. Let the Almighty watch over your thoughts as He has done up till now."

The old rabbi left, a smile on his lips. He was not going to tell this foreigner that the fortress had been buzzing for hours with nothing but the scandal that had enraged the Khagan, so much so that the walls of the palace were still resounding with his cries. Since Isaac's spectacular arrival, not only had the Kathum Attex refused to receive the ambassador from Emperor Constantine, but she had announced, without deferring to her brother, that she refused to marry the Greek no matter what he promised politically. Blessed be the Lord!

Chapter eighteen

Baku, Azerbaijan
May 2000

The plane landed without incident at Baku. It was late in the afternoon, and the shadows were already long. A yellowish vapor hung over the suburbs surrounding the airport, along the seashore to the north of the town. The plane turned too soon to allow Sofer a first view of the Caspian Sea. The wing of the Boeing pointed at a dusty landscape, dotted here and there with hills and clumps of pine. The landing was very soft.

Thomson leaned over to Sofer. "Call me. Even if you have nothing very special to tell me. I might have some news that could be useful to you ... for your book!"

Sofer squeezed out a polite reply. They had hardly spoken to each other during the last hour of the flight. The Englishman was well-mannered enough not to persist when Sofer showed no more interest in pursuing their conversation. And anyway, he knew that his words had struck home, that they bothered the writer and that, one way or another, his insinuations were doing their work. He stood up as soon as the plane stopped. He pulled his leather bag out of the overhead bin and gave a final wave to Sofer. Sofer allowed him to take the lead. The passengers descended to the runway, where a bus was awaiting them. The warmth of the air surprised him. Even though it was only May, it must have been close to thirty degrees centigrade.

Sofer had visited countries in the Eastern Bloc and the Soviet Union before the collapse of Communism. He had become familiar with that rancid odor, a mix of heavy oil and fuel, that gripped travelers by the throat whenever they approached an airport. It had made him write in one of his books that Communism had a smell of its own. He had automatically expected something like it in Baku, but he could sense nothing except the humid dust and the stink of kerosene identical to every Western airport. And also, perhaps above all, a smell of new paint. The airport at Baku was completely new, not quite finished, but already displaying two huge advertisements; one for Coca-Cola, the other for Ford. Thomson had been right: ancient Byzantium had lost the war, the new one was taking over. At the entrance to the arrivals hall, even while he was absorbing all this, Sofer saw the Lloyds detective disappear into a Mercedes with opaque windows. It revved up quickly, driving off fast in the opposite direction to the main building of the airport. Alastair Thomson was evidently not subject to the formalities of normal passengers.

Sofer was. He rode with the other passengers in a yellow bus, and stood in line in the virtually empty Customs Hall, a striking building of brushed aluminum and steel. One thing, however, had not changed since the fall of Communism; ten dollar bills passing discretely from hand to hand to facilitate baggage handling and avoid fastidious and useless searches. Sofer traveled with only one piece of hand baggage. It deprived the customs official of his ritual baksheesh, and it saved waiting and argument. As expected, Mikhail Yakovlevitch Agarounov was waiting for him at the other side of the control barriers, in a light suit of Russian cut, white shirt and gray tie. Sofer recognized him immediately. He was just as he had imagined, rubbing his small plump hands together in a friendly gesture while a huge smile lit up his face. His small stature and hips as broad as his shoulders gave him a reassuring and familiar air, like a child's drawing. An apparently permanent smile hovered on his lips. His round face, cut in two by a powerful nose, matched his deep voice and refined Russian, so perfect that it was almost comical. Once the effusive greetings had been dealt with, Agarounov threw a deprecating glance at Sofer's little bag.

"That's all? No other bags?"

"It's enough! Don't worry, I've brought the documents."

"Maybe ... but such a small bag says that you are not going to stay with us very long!"

"No it doesn't." Sofer smiled, touched by the sincerity of the remark. "It simply means that I never carry too much because I never know how long I will stay."

Agarounov laughed, lifting the bag. "There's a car outside, Mr. Sofer. I am going to take you to your hotel...."

Sofer placed his hand, in a friendly manner, on Agarounov's arm. "It's Marc, and you are Mikhail, agreed? It's not worth bothering with ..." Sofer stopped suddenly. In spite of the moist heat, he felt his whole body break out in a cold sweat. Looking at him concernedly, Agarounov asked, "What is it? Are you unwell?"

She was there, at the other end of the immense curving hall, some fifty feet away. Like a dancing flame, in a purple dress as flamboyant as her hair, she was crossing the space to the glass doors. He would have recognized her walk in a thousand, just the same as when he had watched her retreat from him in the conference room a month earlier. Yes, it was definitely the same fluid walk, the same energetic and sensual grace, as if she were cleaving the invisible thickness of the air with her passage. He could only see her profile from afar, but he recognized her.

She joined a group of Asian businessmen dressed in dark suits, who were leaving the building. Before following them, she turned around, looking in his direction. It was her. It was her face, no doubt about it. The face he had borrowed to describe Attex. Goddamnit, he was raving! How could this be?! Without taking the time to think, he began to run, although the glass door had closed behind her.

"Where are you going?" Agarounov shouted.

Sofer hurled himself toward the nearest door, but it could only be opened from the outside. He ran along the transparent wall. Outside, his mystery woman was crossing the sidewalk full of people, passing between a row of taxis. Finally a door opened, but a family swamped him. Sofer was drowning in excited children and carts full of baggage. Agarounov had caught up with him and, panting, questioned him. "Marc, Mr. Sofer, what is it? Marc...."

As Sofer threw himself out onto the sidewalk, Agarounov shouted something about the car. Three policemen, in flat hats, kalachnikovs and bandoliers at the ready, were standing there. Agarounov made some sort of sign of appeasement to them. His smile traveled to a white Mercedes, and he nodded his head.

The woman had reached the other end of the forecourt. Sofer saw her disappear into the rear of a Japanese four by four that started up immediately. He raised his arm, on the verge of shouting out, but restrained himself. The car set off at high speed and quickly reached the exit ramp that led traffic from the airport onto the highway. Sofer wasn't certain of anything at that moment, but he could have sworn that at the last minute, from the rear window, the redheaded woman had smiled at him.

"I am not crazy!" he muttered angrily. "I am not. That was her!"

He suddenly noticed the worried looking Agarounov beside him. He turned to him. Behind him stood a tough-looking man, head as round as a billiard ball. He had a diamond in each ear, and dark curls escaping from a black and white shirt, the motifs of which could only have been designed under the influence of LSD.

"That was her," Sofer said to Agarounov quietly.

"Her?"

"The redhead I told you about when I phoned! The beautiful woman who ... who follows me everywhere," grumbled Sofer. "She was in England ahead of me." He shrugged his shoulders, conscious that it was impossible to explain what was happening to him. Agarounov frowned before gently nodding. Sofer added, as if to clarify, "Goddamn, I am sure that she was here for ... to see me arrive! She had no bags, the car was waiting for her...."

Agarounov's expression betrayed the incredulity and unease of a man who discovers a friend is ill. How could he understand? Sofer felt a wild anger rising inside. "Who is this man?" he asked sharply, pointing at the young stranger.

Agarounov jumped, then laughed a little too heartily. "Oh, may I introduce Lazir, a friend of my son. An excellent chauffeur! He knows Baku like the back of his hand. He is at your service as long as you need him."

Lazir offered a hand as big as a loaf of bread. He smiled, and Sofer could not help returning the smile; the chauffeur's eight incisors were of solid gold.

"I'm not a professional chauffeur," Lazir announced in a melodious voice, in perfect Russian. "I'm really an athlete. Greco-Roman wrestling…."

"Not just any athlete," Agarounov announced enthusiastically. "Lazir was the top boxing champion in Azerbaijan for six years. He was even invited to participate in the Olympic Games in Atlanta!"

"Sometimes it can be useful," Lazir commented modestly.

Sofer looked over to the motorway where the four by four carrying the redheaded woman had long since disappeared. Embarrassed, he said. "Okay, fine, let's go!"

❧

Lazir drove in the Azerbaijan manner: foot down hard as soon as he had a few hundred clear feet of sidewalk ahead of him, and the persuasive pugnacity of a prizefighter whenever he arrived at crossroads or changed lanes. It took them less than half an hour to arrive in the center of Baku.

They sped through a suburb of huge open spaces spattered here and there with modern buildings built like arrows, tall and straight. Those streets then gave way to avenues with lower and older apartment blocks. Carts and small trucks loaded with vegetables, fruit, plastic utensils or household furnishings could be seen from time to time. Baku resembled a Turkish town on which had been superimposed several layers of Soviet architecture; bourgeois and opulent where it dated from the 1930s, frenzied and imperialistic from the Stalinist era, and simply dilapidated where buildings had been constructed after the 1950s.

Sofer was not really interested in his surroundings. He could not stop avidly scrutinizing the route ahead of the Mercedes, hoping vaguely that Lazir's kamikaze driving might let them catch up with the four by four. In vain. Her driver was probably also some sports champion armed with golden dentures.... At the same time, he was listening with one ear to the program Agarounov had planned for the next few days.

"Tomorrow morning we will go to Krasnaia Sloboda, the Red Village. It is quite near Daghestan, on the river Kudial. It is an entirely Jewish settlement. Perhaps you will meet someone there who knows your Yakubov. There are only twenty-eight thousand Jews left in the whole Caucasus. They all know each other. If not the exact person, then his brother, his cousin, a friend...." Also they would visit some museums where they could find some small vestiges of the Khazars. And, of course, they must visit the oil fields!

"And the cave?" asked Sofer. "The cave containing the synagogue. Do you think someone could help me locate it?"

Agarounov pursed his lips, dubious. Sofer was surprised to see the curious look Lazir gave him in the rear mirror.

"We will need to make inquiries," Agarounov replied cautiously. "This cave Yakubov told you about seems to be in Georgia. It's a bit complicated. You will need a visa...."

They were entering the center of town. The traffic was dense and confusing. There was no more chance of seeing the four by four. Sofer felt resentful and, ridiculously, a sense of loss. Turning around in his seat, Agarounov related several anecdotes on the subject of the Mountain Jews, his constant passion. Sofer nodded repeatedly, a smile fixed to his lips, not paying him the slightest attention. The brief sighting of the unknown woman obsessed him. He could not work out why she had been at the airport, or how she came to be here at all. He could only remember the way she had appeared at the arrivals hall. It seemed to him that she had raised one hand and waved to him. If Agarounov would only stop talking, then he would be able to close his eyes and envisage her, a living flame, moving in front of him.

He wanted to memorize the smile that, perhaps, she had sent in his direction. An irrational, burning desire, was now being joined with a certainty that he was going to see her again, soon. Was he finally going to meet her? A small truck raced out from the left and cut in front of the starred muzzle of the Mercedes. Lazir swore as he slammed on the brakes. Agarounov and Sofer were projected forward, hanging on to the door handles as best they could. Agarounov laughed as if he was used to such events and settled back squarely in his seat. While Lazir steered the car back into the traffic like a player putting another coin in a slot machine, Agarounov pointed out a tall building, all steel and dark glass windows, further down the avenue.

"Your hotel!" he announced. "The Radisson Plaza."

"The best in town," added Lazir, winking. "Very luxurious! Just like in America."

His pride touched Sofer. The city center looked as prosperous as any European city. The pedestrians were numerous, young and old, and all well dressed. In the crowds, Western tourists, Americans and Europeans, were easily recognizable by the mediocrity of their clothes: jeans, polo shirts, tee-shirts, sometimes shorts on legs that were either too pale or too red. No elegant Thomsons.

"Anything new on the attacks, or the New Khazars?" Sofer asked suddenly. He got the feeling that Agarounov was taken aback, or unprepared for his question, and it was Lazir who answered with a light laugh. "It appears that all the oil companies have sent for their cops. If this goes on, there will be more of them in town than traveling salesmen! Or perhaps they will all disguise themselves as commercial travelers!"

Sofer smiled. He wondered if he should mention Thomson to them. But he kept quiet. No real reason, just that he didn't want to have to answer all the inevitable questions that bringing up the Englishman would engender. He had only one wish; to be alone. To allow his imagination full license to seize hold of the memory of the stranger he met in Belgium, scented in England, and now spotted in Baku, the one he called Attex.

As soon as they arrived at the hotel, he used his fatigue and his desire to make some notes as a pretext for refusing Agarounov's invitation to dine. They arranged to meet early the next day for their trip to the border of Daghestan.

❧

Once in his room, Sofer gave himself barely enough time to shower before leaving again. Within minutes, he found himself on the street, with a map of the city furnished by the hotel. The young woman at reception had indicated the route he should take to go down to the water's edge. It was quite simple, almost a straight line. If he got lost, he should ask for Nettchilyar Avenue.

Night was closing in and the heat had eased. He crossed a shadowy park, the air further cooled by half a dozen fountains. As in most Mediterranean towns, all the local youth seemed to have gathered there. Once again, Sofer was surprised by the slightly provincial, yet particularly elegant, look of the girls and young women. Even though he was in a Muslim country, skirts were short and dresses tight, hiding little. Lovers walked about embracing, leaving off their kisses and cuddles to look at stalls of trinkets, gadgets, confectionery and very Western clothes. He returned to Rasulzade, the long pedestrian walkway that lead to Nettchilyar, now busy with crowds of people. On the other side of the avenue, the sea front was lined with open air cafés, children's playgrounds with merry-go-rounds and a huge concrete kiosk that, during the Soviet era, must have been the site of many great celebrations. Now it served as just another restaurant.

The Sea of the Khazars was already plunged in darkness. To the southwest, Sofer noticed some lights on the offshore derricks. The Caspian was smooth, calm and peaceful, offering an evening's promenade to all, like an Italian lakeside. However, with his first breath he noticed the smell. Very particular, heavy like a piece of rotting fruit. The smell of oil. He sat down at one of the terraced cafés and ordered a glass of Georgian white wine, which was so light it seemed free of alcohol. Reflexively, he could not help looking at all the passersby, his examination jumping from face to face. He realized that it was mad to hope to find the stranger among this moving throng, but his desire was stronger than his sense.

Eventually, having consumed his first glass of wine, he relaxed. He contented himself with the thought that she was somewhere out there, in the environs of this large city. He surprised himself by concluding that he really had come all this way for just that. He would have to be patient. Was it not she who had said to him in Brussels, when she was heckling him, that man should not run after his destiny? He would just have to be patient. He would have to imitate Isaac ben Eliezer, and partake of a long journey before achieving its reward. To have confidence in the path and the time. To have confidence in the way life unfolds, in the Almighty, perhaps....

Night was obscuring his surroundings. Children were playing on wooden horses, pedaling with all their energy on plastic tractors, or proudly driving electric cars with winking lights. Sofer was thinking of the little girl in Oxford, playing in the puddles, of that instant when Attex the child came to him. But Attex, from now on, was obviously a woman. She refused to bend to her brother's injunctions. He could easily imagine the Khagan's pain and stupefaction. Stupefaction, then anger and sorrow. For the first time, Attex and Joseph were separate. For the first time, something had come between them, like the cold slice of a blade. In spite of his fury, Joseph knew that he was responsible for their estrangement. Still, how could he not accept the hand of friendship the Greeks were extending to him, even if he would have to conclude this alliance with the greatest circumspection and suspicion? Whatever Borouh claimed, whatever Hanania reminded him, he was a great enough warrior to recognize the truth: that his kingdom would not survive long if faced with the combined onslaught of the Russian and Byzantine hordes. If only Attex would try to understand him, it would render their enforced separation less painful. But no, she would not, and now, to add to his problems, she was infatuated with some foreigner under the pretext that he was a Jew who had come to her from the ends of the earth!

One morning, he decided to speak to her calmly, showing her all the love he had for her. The dawn had hardly started to lighten the sky. The fortress was still so silent that he could hear hens clucking outside the walls, in the town of tents. Ordering the servants to be quiet and still, Joseph went to the room Attex occupied. She was sleeping, her face and curls buried in some cushions. He sat close to her, staring at the opulent hair and, for an instant, was completely overwhelmed by his sister's beauty. Never had he seen such a beautiful woman. He had married the most beautiful of the Alain princesses, but when they stood side by side, his wife was a mere shadow in the splendor of the Kathum.

Attex opened her eyes, mumbling through a yawn. She smiled on discovering Joseph and, half asleep, cuddled up to him, kissing his hands. Joseph pushed her away tenderly and murmured, "Prepare yourself, Kathum! Ambassador Blymmedes is coming to have breakfast with me today. It is a meal of peace and farewell. You will be leaving with him tomorrow, for Tmutorokan…."

Joseph saw her eyes widen with fear, as if a serpent had just bitten her. She cried out, flung herself to the farthest edge of the couch. Standing up with one lithe movement, she spat, "Never! Do you hear me? Never!"

Joseph's heart filled his chest, fit to burst. Cold anger enveloped him. "You will do it, Kathum, because I want you to!"

A sort of laugh, more like a scream, vibrated in Attex's throat. "The great Khagan Joseph really wants his sister to open her thighs for a Greek he doesn't even know? Shame on you, Joseph! Shame on you!" She was laughing and crying at the same time, rattling out her phrases.

Then they looked at each other in silence, so apart they could not touch; so close that words would not have been worse than arrows.

"You are the Kathum and you must obey me!" Joseph persisted. "My decision is wise! How could you believe that I would give you to the Greeks if I did not think that it will mean life for all the Jewish Khazars in my kingdom?"

"Oh, a wise decision! A wise decision!" mocked Attex, her voice choked with emotion. "I remember the day you became a *Bar Mitzvah*. It was here in Sarkel. The evening before, the two of us were up there, high on the ramparts. You were upset with Grandfather Benjamin." She angrily opened a great wooden trunk containing ceremonial clothes. "I remember your words; I have never forgotten them: 'Grandfather said that I was to be wise like the wisest of the Jews. He said that, perhaps, it would be up to me to save all the Jews who would come to us, hunted from other kingdoms.'"

"Benjamin is dead, and I will not be the Khagan who saves all the Jews!" Joseph cut in cruelly.

Still pulling dozens of tunics and throwing them on the couch, Attex shouted derisively, "Damn sure you won't be! You aren't even capable of saving your sister from the Christians!"

"The Almighty, blessed be His name, did not create me for that!"

"How do you know, Khagan Joseph? Give the Jew from Cordoba an audience! The Almighty wanted him to arrive here, Rabbi Hanania himself said so...."

Attex fell silent, as a strange, evil smile grew on Joseph's lips. He asked, "Does the rabbi know what is pushing you into the arms of that stranger?"

Attex's cheeks flushed, suddenly as red as her hair.

"They told me how you looked after him. How you stayed with him, alone.... How even Attania had to pull you away from him, shaming your rank by showering caresses on him!"

"You are jealous!"

"A Greek waits for you to be his spouse, that's what motivated you!" Joseph replied, full of venom.

Attex remained silent, pressing a sumptuous tunic embroidered with gold thread close to her, and then said: "I will never go to Constantinople with Blymmedes."

"You will go. Or Borouh will incarcerate you in jail and deliver you to the Greeks in chains, as a slave!"

Chapter nineteen

U*nder a large vaulted ceiling ornamented with blue ceramics,*

Sarkel, September 955

Under a large vaulted ceiling ornamented with blue ceramics, ten men covered in prayer shawls were saying the morning prayers. In front of them, the curved silhouette of Rabbi Hanania accompanied the supplications with a gentle rocking movement.

"I call on You for Your reply, Oh God lend me Your ear, hear my words! I who know not how to contemplate Your face and from my awakening seek out Your vision! I who have confidence in You, Oh Lord..."

The words of the prayer were still resonating in the luminous air of the synagogue when the rabbi, arms stiff, turned the silver handles, reuniting the two halves of the scroll of the Torah.

The long roll of paper fixed to a fine silk backing rolled up with a soft rustle, as if the words were chatting to each other before concealing themselves. Hanania placed the scroll in a finely engraved steel coffer. When he closed the lid, the silence was absolute, so perfect that the rabbi, seized with doubt, turned around quickly. His companions in prayer had withdrawn, all except Joseph the Khagan. As was his wont, Joseph was taking his time removing the leather straps of the phylacteries from his left arm, then taking off the prayer shawl from his shoulders and folding it with care. When he removed the forehead piece, Hanania saw the fury imprinted on his features. His mouth was nothing more than a hard slit.

Without a word the rabbi hugged the box containing the scroll close to his chest and walked over to place it in a tall cupboard, the doors of which sparkled with gold. He stopped for a moment in front of a tapestry bearing an embroidered menorah. Along the height of the shaft of the candelabra, sewn so finely that they looked like paintings on parchment, were representations from the Sacrifice of Isaac to the Judgment of Solomon. With a mechanical gesture, the rabbi touched it with his translucent fingers. Only then did he go and sit down beside Joseph.

"I am listening, Khagan. Tell me your complaints."

Joseph was about to let his rage explode, but he decided to contain it. "Attex is not in the fortress, Rabbi! Borouh has searched everywhere, even among the apple stores…that monster Attania has also disappeared! They have disobeyed me, Rabbi! And the Greek will be here any minute now! He who will not even prostrate himself before me…."

The rabbi watched Joseph's hand open and close convulsively over the hilt of his sword. "And you think I know where to find them, is that it, Khagan? You even think I helped them escape?"

Their eyes met. The rabbi smiled, a smile that creased his face in a knot of wrinkles and bothered the Khagan. Joseph moved away. One might have said that he seemed scared to be too close to the old man. Was he afraid of his own urge to violence?

Hanania knew Joseph well, so it was in a peaceful tone that he addressed him. "You think I have conspired against you, don't you? That I have removed the Kathum from your authority. You think I have conspired to humiliate you in front of Constantine's ambassador. You think I wish your downfall. Yes, yes, I know what you are thinking. I understand what bothers your mind and has made your head boil!"

Joseph took the time to walk to the wall, fists clenched, before turning around.

"Actually, yes!" It was the snarl of a cornered animal.

The rabbi contented himself with a blink, then, eyes closed, he commenced rocking gently, back and forth. "The Bible says, '*He who is slow to anger is better than a hero.*'"

"I know that!" Joseph spat, his hands flashing nervously as if he were flinging the words from his fingertips. "But you, in your turn, must know that we need to ally ourselves with the Greeks. That nowadays, we are not capable of taking on Byzantium. No more than a toad can escape the hooves of a horse...."

"There is only one alliance on which you can depend, Khagan Joseph; that which your fathers and forefathers made with the Lord, blessed be His name. Do you remember the response of our Jewish brothers to Caesar in Rome? 'We resolved long ago not to be subjects of Rome or any other power, except for God, for He alone is the just and true master of man....'"

"Ah!" Joseph groaned, defeated.

"Your ancestors expect you to be faithful to their faith. It is not for you to push your sister into the arms of a stranger."

Joseph planted himself in front of the rabbi, his body as threatening as any sword. "It is not my faith in dispute here, but my authority! You did, then, help her leave the fortress?"

Rabbi Hanania acquiesced.

"Then you know where I can find her?"

Hanania shook his old head with the expression of a naughty child. "No, no I don't! Not a clue..."

"Why are you doing this?" Joseph demanded, seizing the shoulders of the frail rabbi. "I always thought you were my friend."

Hanania leaned forward. His hands gripped Joseph's wrists. He pulled on them to steady himself as he stood up. "I am your best friend. I love you, Khagan, and I admire you. I am just telling you that you are taking the wrong road with the Greeks. We know what they are. They lie without even taking a breath. And you, in wanting to be their vassal, you are running away. '*Lend me Your ear, hear my words! I who know not how to contemplate Your face and from my awakening seek out Your vision! I who have confidence in You, Oh Lord....*' Those are the words you have just enunciated in prayer a few moments ago, yet you flee from the power of the Almighty, you flee from the confidence and the power He has placed in your hands.

Forget this Blymmedes, Joseph. Read the letter the Sephardi Jew has brought you. Take account of the joy and hope that the Kingdom of the Khazars has brought to our brothers in creation! Build your strength on that...."

Joseph broke free sharply, but the rabbi did not give in and held him by the belt around his linen cloak. "Joseph, I beg you, give the envoy from the Sephardi Jews an audience. That boy has traveled for a whole year, has risked death a hundred times to place a thing of inestimable value in your hands. He is young, handsome, pure, naïve ... he would never have been able to succeed in such a journey unless our Lord wished it and gave him strength...."

A ray of sunlight penetrated one of the narrow windows that adorned the west wall of the synagogue and played for an instant on the king's black pupils. Joseph brushed at his eyes with the back of his hand.

"Is that what you told Attex? You made this lad out to be who-knows-what kind of messenger from Heaven? Rabbi, it is easier to fool a young virgin than a Khagan! Attex is a child who dreams of love. As long as he wasn't a Greek, you could make her think a donkey was an angel!"

The look on the face of the old man was mischievous. "Wouldn't it be lovely if those two were in love? Within the Law, of course ... They look so right together!"

"I will find her and lock her up!"

Rabbi Hanania chuckled happily. Then, suddenly his expression became serious once more. Between the tired wrinkles of his eyelids, his eyes sparkled like a lizard's.

"She has done nothing against the Law, Khagan Joseph. '*What is it that the Lord your God asks of you, if not to practice justice, to love true loyalty and to walk humbly beside Him,*' Micah said in chapter six, verse eight. No part of the Law prescribes asceticism, Joseph, but only moderation. It says that one must allow equal parts of soul to body, and nothing in excess. Khagan Joseph, nowadays you give far too much time to doubt, fear and jealousy. That corrupts your judgment. You no longer practice justice, for believing only in yourself, you do not place your doubts on the scales of the Lord. You do not love any more, because you are prepared to separate yourself from the one you love most in the world … after the Lord! And you no longer walk with humility, for you concentrate on your weakness and think of nothing but strength…." Joseph was scarlet with anger, but the rabbi refused to hear his protests. "I neither judge nor condemn you, Joseph! I know the load weighing on your shoulders and the fear you have for the future. I know your desire to be wise. However, the Kathum is right to refuse to sacrifice her faith and her body. In her innocent young heart she knows that love is the sign of the presence of the Almighty among us. What can you do if He manifests Himself as an envoy of the Tribes of Israel who lives at the other end of the world?"

Joseph did not have time to reply. The fortress trumpet sounded a long, loud and plaintive call. The door of the synagogue opened. A slave prostrated himself in the doorway and announced that Ambassador Blymmedes had entered the town. The slave retreated and hid as Borouh appeared. The Beck was in splendid ceremonial dress, a scarlet tunic under his leather breastplate, his long combat sword in his right hand. His eyes were red, as if his blood wanted to burst out. Joseph knew these signs of great anger. And he knew that extremely unpleasant news awaited him.

Chapter twenty

Baku, Azerbaijan
May 2000

I t was just past eight in the morning when the white Mercedes driven by Lazir left Baku.

Lazir was dressed completely in black. His gold teeth, bracelets, chains and other jewelry sparkled in the reflected light, and his Italian shoes were so highly polished he could have attended a ball in them. Mikhail Yakovlevitch Agarounov was wearing a light-colored suit, as smart and discreet as the previous evening. Sofer, who had no clothes other than those he brought from England, found them uncomfortable and badly suited to the Baku climate. For a brief moment he had considered asking his companions to give him time to buy a light shirt and pants, but scarcely had he stepped into the car than it sped away and he abandoned the idea.

No Angel of Prudence, divine messenger of the highway, had brushed Lazir with its wing. Although the traffic appeared to Sofer more chaotic and congested than London or Paris on Christmas Eve, it only took a few kicks on the gas pedal to take them to the suburbs north of town. As usual, Agarounov sat in the front seat. Turning around, he explained to Sofer the strange details of Krasnaia Sloboda, the Red Village, where they were going.

"Krasnaia Sloboda is the Russian name, of course. For Azeris, the name is Quba. And, like I told you yesterday evening, it's quite close to Daghestan. It will take us two or three hours, depending on the traffic. The town is divided in two by the Kudial River. One bank is Muslim, the other Jewish. Totally Jewish. The separation is so clear that one gets the impression that there are really two towns. You will see for yourself. I am positive you will return with some great memories!"

Sofer nodded in agreement, smiling happily. It was a pleasure to be on the receiving end of Agarounov's hospitality. With the deftness of familiarity he displayed his infinite knowledge on every aspect relating to 'his' Mountain Jews. Further, he seemed gifted with inexhaustible patience in making his visitor happy. Even so, Sofer was only listening with half an ear and wished Agarounov was not quite so overwhelming. He had not had a good night, troubled with dreams as upsetting as they were thought-provoking. He had woken up repeatedly for the most trivial reasons; he was too hot or too cold, a noisy air conditioning unit rattled his nerves. His mind seemed to grab at the smallest pretext to break his repose. Not once, however, did he have the courage to get up and do something useful, like work on his novel.

Numb from lack of sleep, eyes half closed, he watched the suburbs of Baku slip away at great speed. They traveled for about twelve miles on a main road planted with thickets of pines dense enough to hide the open air cafés lining the route. Where the trees were far apart or had been cleared, blue plastic tarpaulins or tenting revealed camp chairs, tables and barbecue fires between them. Some of the buildings had the look of prosperous and luxurious restaurants.

Lazir chuckled. He gestured toward a clump of pine trees with his chin. "Very nice in the afternoon. Or the evening, for that matter. Plenty of men come here with their wives. The ones you pay for ... or not...." He laughed as innocently as a joking child. Sofer and Agarounov were content to smile. Sofer's eyes met the boxing champion's in the rear mirror, and what he saw troubled him. Lazir's expression was not that of a man who had just cracked a macho joke.

Hard and vigilant, it revealed an astute man, always on the lookout. One word formed instinctively in Sofer's mind: Mafia!

Lazir not only had the appearance and tastes of a tough guy; his remarks, his sharp and sarcastic little statements were those of a *player* who wanted you to know that he was not what he seemed. But once more, Agarounov was demanding attention. "Do you know, on the new maps of Azerbaijan, the Caspian Sea is once again called the Sea of the Khazars? When the wind comes off the water it carries that strange odor of iodine and oil that is only found here, all over the continent. They call it the Wind of the Khazars. There is a lovely legend about it...." Agarounov raised his index finger like a storyteller trying to catch the attention of his audience. He turned around in his seat again. Sofer, for a split second, thought of telling him that it was not a clever thing to do at this speed; the road was chaotic, full of potholes, and cluttered with trucks swerving from side to side, but as soon as he formulated the thought he saw how ridiculous it would sound. By all accounts, in Azerbaijan, the expression 'to travel in an open coffin' ruled.

Agarounov pointed to the sea on their right, a thin blue strip beyond a dusty plain. "The legend goes, that when the Wind of the Khazars becomes a tempest, it will efface everything. Everything! All traces of animals and humans in the desert or from the mountains, man's handiwork, fields, culture, houses, it will reduce everything to dust ... in essence the Wind of the Khazars will erase all traces of what came before, like the Khazars themselves were erased. It will leave nothing behind but the odor of the sea and nostalgia for the past."

"It's a fine tale," murmured Sofer, sincerely appreciative. "Fine, but terrible!"

"Rest easy," Agarounov responded, laughing. "In all my lifetime, and I've been here fifty years, the Wind of the Khazars has not once blown a gale...."

Sofer was about to reply with a banal pleasantry when his eyes widened. "Damn! What a monstrosity!"

In front of them, as big as a town, a gigantic mass of rusty metal covered all the foreshore of the plain. Conveyors wider than the road intertwined with pipelines in a nightmarish tangle. Convoys of trains pulling ruptured tankers were surrounded by tanks as high as castles. Some of them were split open, their aluminum stays shining, brandishing metal tongues like huge venomous daisies. A labyrinth of hangars as high as apartment tower blocks sprawled down to the sea and, here and there, fixed among the chaos like giant nails, were gas burn-off chimneys just waiting to rot away.

"That," announced Lazir solemnly, "is the petrochemical complex of Sumgayi ... or at least, it was!" Of his own accord, he slowed down. They passed under a pipeline made transparent by rust that was three times thicker than the Mercedes. "The Russians store oil here that they pump to us. They partially refine and send it to the old Soviet Union, across Daghestan and Chechnya."

Lazir pointed vaguely in front of them, to the north. Sofer sensed evident antipathy in his voice whenever he spoke of the Russians, and real pleasure in showing this spectacular debacle, as if, by itself, it bore witness to the fragility of the Soviet power in Azerbaijan and the joy in its collapse.

"The complex was abandoned in 1992," continued the prize-fighter. "Can you imagine it? They pillaged the country for twenty-four years and in another few years this monster will have disappeared entirely! Without the Wind of the Khazars having appeared once!" He laughed sardonically, and winked at the embarrassed Agarounov. The vehicle managed to traverse the remainder of the rotting disaster of steel and concrete that was Sumgayi. It continued along the seaside plain, yellow and rocky, very like a desert.

"You will see, it is much more beautiful at Quba," Lazir predicted proudly. "It is very green, there are fields, vines and orchards! Nothing like here! When the people of Baku want a real holiday they go there, to visit us! It's the most beautiful part of the region, maybe even of the whole Caspian...."

Agarounov laughed, slightly mocking. "We, the Jews of Quba, consider ourselves to be descended from the most ancient Jews in the Caucasus. Our ancestors arrived directly from Jerusalem well before the migrations of the Jews from Turkey and Byzantium."

Sofer nodded. "Is that the reason the Mountain Jews claim to belong to one of the exiled Twelve Tribes of Israel?"

Agarounov nodded. "Yes ... the studies I have carried out on our language, Tath, seem to confirm that. It could be that the Mountain Jews were the original Jewish Khazars and then they became their last descendants. After the destruction of the Temple, they came here and installed themselves in the mountains. Several centuries went by. When the nomadic Khazars conquered the Volga plain, they naturally traded with the Jews. Over three centuries, the Khazar Kingdom would have represented a safe haven for them. Besides, when persecutions elsewhere became too severe or too frequent, they knew where to go. And more came from the Muslim countries and Constantinople ... but with the fall of the kingdom, it could be that the Jewish communities of the mountains once again settled in the Caucasus valleys."

"But we know that most of the Jewish Khazars were dispersed around Central Europe, where they mixed with the Ashkenazi community," objected Sofer.

"Yes, but it is also almost certain that a handful of the Khazar elite remained for some time in the Caucasus. Once there, nobody could dislodge them. It must have been very easy for them to hold out for centuries.... The Caucasus would have been an impregnable refuge at that time. It was their country of origin, so they would be returning to their roots. Nothing more natural.... And if that were the case, we, the Jews of Quba, would be the direct descendants of the Khazars!"

"Which takes us back to the untraceable synagogue of our friend Yakubov!" exclaimed Sofer.

"By my faith!" Agarounov uttered vehemently, glancing at Lazir, "Why not?"

Lazir laughed sharply. "It's only guys like you and Mr. Sofer, Mikhail, who would be interested in knowing who the descendants of the Khazars are anyway. In some ways, all the Jews in the region are, more or less. That's what matters."

Without being able to stop himself, Sofer asked the question that had been burning on his lips for quite some time. "Do you think the people who carried out the attack on the OCOO the other day, the ones that call themselves the New Khazars, are Jews from hereabouts?"

There was a short silence. Perhaps of embarrassment. Lazir concentrated on his driving and pretended not to have heard. He overtook an old Tatra and two Ladas that couldn't have been less than twelve years old. Finally the boxing champ's laugh exploded. His teeth shone. "Surely that's the question all the oil company cops are asking! Eh?"

"Probably," responded Sofer, thinking of Thomson. "Provided, of course, that these cops, as you call them, have the slightest idea what a Khazar is!"

Lazir shook his head. "The oil guys are not stupid, Mr. Sofer. With so much money about, the ones that fill their pockets are always intelligent."

The justice of the remark pleased Sofer. "Do you thing that the perpetrators of this attack, these New Khazars, could be Jews?" he insisted.

"I don't think anything of the kind! I don't know any more than I hear on the radio."

"They still haven't told us what they want," Agarounov added, without much conviction in his voice.

"And, of course, you know," continued Lazir, "anyone could call themselves the New Khazars! Even some pop group! Or the Chechyns."

"Or the Mafia!" Sofer added mischievously.

Lazir laughed heartily, slapping his steering wheel in delight, which gained Agarounov's attention. "Yes! A band of Moscow Mafia come to teach the Caucasus Mafia a lesson ... a good idea, eh! We know that anything's possible in these parts. Abroad, that's what they say: Caucasus equals Mafia! Stalin said it too, and he should know! Yeltsin and Putin say it: all Caucasians are bandits! And, remember, they have an end in view, don't they?"

They laughed and joked. Sofer laughed too, one of the boys. But, at the same time, he thought that Lazir knew who the New

Khazars were, but that he wouldn't reveal anything. At least not now. Not in Agarounov's presence, and perhaps never. Hoping to stir things a little, Sofer said, "Sooner or later we'll know. The oil companies will find out."

"Perhaps. The oil men are powerful. But if they find out they will keep it to themselves. They know when silence is worth more than truth, when it suits them...."

Another point for Lazir, Sofer thought.

"If they were Jews it could prejudice everyone against the community here," he continued, showing some annoyance. "Especially those who live in Quba...."

Lazir looked fiercely in his rear mirror. Agarounov half turned away, as if this turn in the conversation was becoming too personal.

"You know, Mr. Sofer," Lazir started coldly, "the Jews here have seen so much real trouble in their time that this kind of suspicion would give them no cause for alarm. Ask Mikhail...."

"That's true," agreed Agarounov, relieved at being able to return to the safer ground of the past. "Before the arrival of the Soviets in the region, around 1920, there were many Jews. From the Caspian to Georgia, there was a synagogue in practically every Caucasian valley, but during the war, when the Nazis threatened to reach the oil fields of Baku, Shaoimian, the strong man of the Caucasus, displaced thousands of Jews to collective farms in Crimea. A means, like any other, of disposing of us. What was to happen, happened; the Germans occupied Crimea and the Jews were exterminated. After the war, Stalin 'displaced' whole towns of Georgians, Chechyns, Daghestanis and Azerbaijanis. The Jews who had survived among them were sent to Siberia, like all the Caucasians. That's why there are only a handful of us left."

That, Sofer knew only too well. He accepted the information with a brief shrug, in silence. The sun, now high in the sky, reflected the copper in the cliffs rising up to the west. The light became dazzling. In a simultaneous movement, which made them smile and eased the tension created by Sofer's questions, they all put on dark glasses. The road surface was improving as they approached the Sea of the

Khazars. The sea was as smooth as a mirror, and of such a pale blue that it was almost white. Nothing was to be seen, not even a sail or a fishing boat. It was strange, like a sea in waiting, thought Sofer. As if uninhabited. Or too well inhabited by its underwater life.

Lazir had not lied. After a few miles the dust gave way to green, cultivated land. They passed fields of watermelons, apple orchards and immense walnut trees. Young children appeared on the lower side, waving and laughing.

"They sell baskets of nuts," explained Agarounov.

Soon afterward, as if he were relaxing, Lazir slowed the car, and then stopped in front of a few children in rags selling enormous baskets heaped with fruit, ranging from dark red to cream. It was not until the children pressed up against the car window that Sofer could see the luscious cherries. Agarounov bought a large helping. They drove on, sharing the cool fruit in silence. For the first time since he had arrived in Azerbaijan, Sofer realized he was in the Orient. The dark irises of the children's eyes, their high cheekbones, dark skin, bare feet and laughing mouths were the same as those of children from Samandar, Ispahan or Baghdad.

Behind the orchards, he could see the sea. That very ancient sea, almost empty, as in times long ago when only convoys of boats crossed it, loaded with all the wealth of Asia.

Chapter twenty-one

In Sarkel, the royal audience hall was small. It occupied a space

Sarkel, September 955

within a Greek-style building adjacent to the northern wall of the
fortress. The splendor of the marble and the columns made up for its
lack of size and overwhelmed most visitors. A cedar throne encrusted
with ivory, pearls and green semiprecious stones was situated on a
raised platform overlooking the hall. A thick carpet covered the seven
steps. Only the Beck and three royal guards had the right to be there
on the platform when the Khagan was on the throne.

Above, as at Tmutorokan, a leather canopy embroidered with
gold thread, was suspended, like a tent. Alongside the dais stood an
immense gold seven-branched candelabra, a replica of the one in the
Temple in Jerusalem that had been removed by Titus and taken to
Rome, reminding everyone of the affiliation of the Khagan of the
Khazars. Whenever the Khagan was in residence in the fortress the
servants, slaves and eunuchs maintained permanently lighted candles
in the candelabra. Due to the small size of the audience hall, the huge
doors leading to a courtyard of black, pink and white marble were
kept open. It was there that crowds of important visitors waited.

At dawn on this particular day, the Beck had set fifty guards to form an impenetrable hedge bordering the path to the Khagan's throne. They all wore round pointed silver helmets, and tunics embroidered with the menorah, the uniform of the royal guards. All had a steel breastplates, and held their bared swords point downward, between their feet.

Ambassador Blymmedes arrived, preceded by servants whose sole task was to clean the floor with the hems of their robes, kept extremely long expressly for that purpose. Four Abyssinian slaves held a palanquin above him to allow him to hide from the burning sun. He was wearing a short Greek toga, leaving his round knees and pink thighs exposed. His face and bald pate were covered in a mixture of chalk and almond cream. The strange pallor of this makeup smoothed out the crudeness of his features without softening the hardness of his blue eyes.

He appeared surprised at the positioning of the guards. Borouh, who was watching him attentively, saw him slow down. As his eunuchs continued to walk on, still carrying the palanquin, Blymmedes forced a smile and stepped out to catch up, chin raised. Behind him followed the monk in black robes and a handful of junior officers. Arriving at the doorway of the audience hall, the servants spread out in front of the guards, without any of the usual smiles or pleasantries. The silence struck Blymmedes. Above the scuffling of feet on marble, he could hear the peaceful gurgling of the fountains. The black slaves stopped at the threshold. Only Ambassador Blymmedes entered the hall, while the monk knelt down under the palanquin, muttering a prayer.

Blinded by the light, the ambassador did not at first see that the Khagan's throne was empty. When he did, his eyes opened wide and he half-swallowed a curse. He turned to his left, then his right, searching for a servant, but he could see nobody, only the impenetrable faces of the hedge of warriors. His right hand twitched nervously and his rings sparkled in a ray of sunlight. He pivoted, the bottom of his toga rising as he spun around. He was about to quit the royal audience hall, but he hesitated when a tall and powerful silhouette rounded the warriors and emerged from the shadows. Borouh stopped in front of the guards. Blymmedes started to retreat, shouting for help, the makeup exaggerating his expression to such an extent that he appeared grotesque. With his breastplate half covered by a long leather and metal-plated coat, his combat sword unsheathed, his headdress with steel wings projecting from the nape of his neck, his long mustache, and his angry determination, the Beck gave the appearance of a bellicose demon.

"My Lord Ambassador," he announced in his raucous Greek, "Khagan Joseph bids you welcome. He will not keep you much longer."

Blymmedes managed a smile of relief, so as to at least appear to accept the strange welcome that had been offered. "So be it," he said mockingly. "Has the Khagan of the Khazars forgotten that we were to dine together? I can see nothing but his empty throne, no tables, no plates ... and even less, the Kathum! My Lord Beck, can you explain these new protocols to me?"

"The Khagan will be pleased to explain the reason for the delay himself."

The delay lasted long enough for the shine to fade from the ambassador's makeup. He returned to the shade of his palanquin to rejoin the monk, swearing under his breath. A servant unfolded a portable chair into which he collapsed with an expletive. The two Greeks darted bright glances all around them, displaying as much fear as hatred.

The sun's shadows lengthened. On a discreet signal from Borouh, the two hedges of guards fell back at the entrance to the patio. In the heart of the fortress of Sarkel, the Greeks looked like fish caught in the folds of a net.

Suddenly, Joseph was there, standing in the shade of the canopy, at the foot of his throne. He held his son, Hezekiah, by the hand. The servants' murmurings brought the ambassador out of his torpor. Blymmedes, his face running with sweat, his cheeks underneath their makeup looking like the ravines of the steppe, jumped up from his folding chair. Holding the edge of his toga in one hand, he ran into the audience hall, shouting in a peasant Greek that no Khazar could understand. Without even a salute, he stopped short before Joseph, who was still standing there, holding out his hand in a peaceful gesture of friendship.

"Ambassador Blymmedes, I am happy to see you."

"I must protest, Khagan, against this humiliating delay to which you have subjected the Ambassador of the Basileus, Lord of the whole world and Emperor of Byzantium, Constantine the Seventh!"

Joseph took his time, an icy smile on his lips. "My Lord, through you I salute Constantine and wish him long life."

"This delay is—"

"Is equal to the time you take and the fervor of the salute you no longer render me, Lord Blymmedes! I have noticed that during our latest meetings you did not bow, as is required of all visitors to the Khagan of the Khazars. I have compensated for this, considering that the little time you waited on my patio was, from the bottom of your heart, a sign of respect that you would wish to offer." Joseph gestured toward Hezekiah and said, "I wanted this to be a lesson for my son. One day he will be Khagan. He must understand what his rank means and how to make people respect it."

Blymmedes did not need makeup to make his face livid white. "Khagan Joseph," he murmured, "this was to have been a meal of friendship before my departure, to seal our alliance, and in the presence of the Kathum, who is to accompany me!"

"Yes," agreed Joseph. He released Hezekiah's hand and mounted the steps to his throne. As he sat down, the child walked proudly over to join Borouh. Seeing the easy bearing of his son, a burst of tenderness softened Joseph's features, that still showed traces of his dispute with Rabbi Hanania. However, his voice was cutting when he declared, "The Kathum Attex, as you know, my Lord Blymmedes, wishes to wait a while before joining you at Tmutorokan."

"They say she has disappeared," hissed Blymmedes.

"The sister of a Khagan never disappears, my Lord Ambassador!"

"All right, Khagan, let's talk frankly. Since I have come here, I have had to accept nothing but humiliation from your sister. She has disdained my presents, sent by her future husband. She has refused to see me or my servants! Today they tell me she has disappeared from the fortress."

"It was I who asked her to leave Sarkel."

"You!"

Joseph pointed to Borouh. "My Lord Beck also knows what to do when he hears rumors on the wind."

"What is this new mystery?" exclaimed Blymmedes, as if he were dealing with naughty children.

Borouh approached him. Hezekiah observed everything intensely. When the Beck crossed the ray of sunlight coming through the doorway, the metal plates on his cloak and his headgear sparkled with fire. The child thought he saw a man of steel and stone, not flesh, advance on the Greek. Borouh's voice resounded from the ceiling vaults.

"The Russians, under Olga, have assembled two hundred flat-bottomed boats higher up the river Atel. Four thousand of their cavalry are protecting them as they gather."

"I don't understand!"

"That is what they need to do to launch an attack on our capital. They assemble many boats, a nucleus of cavalry, and wait for the rising river to carry them down to the sea, and then to Itil."

"Oh, I see! But, my Lord, surely you are not frightened by the buzzing of a fly? You must agree that that sounds like nothing more than a caprice of Queen Olga's. However, as our alliance is not yet consummated, I must say...."

"This time, Ambassador, there is something more. The Russians are installing arbaletes like we saw on your dromons. Arbaletes capable of firing Greek Fire!"

The Ambassador's eyes widened suddenly. "Greek Fire? But—"

"But only Byzantium knows how to make Greek Fire, the fire of war. You are correct, Lord Blymmedes," Joseph said softly, "the Russians are nothing but barbarians. They don't even use naphtha for their torches. How could they know the way to make or use Greek Fire if the Greeks had not shown them how?"

In the furnace-like heat of the midday sun, silence fell on the royal audience hall like frost in January. Even the monk's muttered prayers ceased. Hezekiah looked at his father in fearful admiration. When Khagan Joseph started speaking again, each word seemed to the boy like the blow of an axe.

"Olga is in Constantinople. You are here. The Russians are less than five hundred leagues from Itil. We talk about weddings like servants beside a well. My Lord Blymmedes, your master Constantine takes us for a hare to be eaten by his hounds!"

"Khagan!" Blymmedes cried out. "Khagan Joseph! That cannot be! Those are fairy stories, minstrels' tales … you know very well that none of the peoples that we … that we…."

"…that you dominate…."

"Ah … none of these peoples—neither the Russians, nor the Bulgarians, or the Magyars—Byzantium has never conveyed the knowledge of the Fire to any of them! No, I beg you, think about it, Khagan! These must be false reports!"

"We will soon know for certain," snarled Borouh. "In four hours we leave for the Atel River and our capital."

"And if we are mistaken, my Lord Blymmedes," added Joseph smiling, "then the Kathum Attex will join you as arranged at Tmutorokan. You know that we, the faithful of the Book of Moses, never swear. But you have my promise."

Blymmedes was indecisive for a moment, then suddenly bent his knee in an awkward salute, bowing his bald head to the Khagan.

Joseph's smile broadened, rejuvenating him for one sweet instant. He pointed at the monk, whose mutterings at the doorway to the room were reaching him. "I had almost forgotten; as a token of goodwill and to show you how well-intentioned we are, the monk who usually accompanies you will come with us as far as Itil. Maybe he would like to build one of your churches there. If we defeat the Russians…."

Chapter twenty-two

Quba, Azerbaijan
May 2000

The first view of Quba, the Jewish town, was a shock for Sofer. The Mercedes stopped on a shady street. Agarounov immediately left the vehicle and disappeared into a huge and unexpectedly luxurious building. Sofer opened his door and stood on the pavement. It took him a few seconds to realize that the awful sadness that engulfed him was nothing but nostalgia. Everything here seemed foreign yet familiar, all at the same time. Bordering the street, the houses had terraces covered with wooden or finely worked zinc canopies. The ground floors were built of stone while the upstairs was wood. The open staircases climbed up to the balconies. Zinc latticework decorated the roofs, all different, evidence of a long lost skill. Some bore motifs of a seven-branched candelabra, others the Star of David. Most houses were surrounded by wooden enclosures, behind which, among clucking hens, small boys played ball, their heads covered with skullcaps.

Seeing Sofer, they stopped to look at him. He waved to them. They responded with smiles that brought a lump to his throat, as if he had suddenly been plunged back into his own past. As if, all of a sudden, he had passed through the mirror of time. He saw these children in front of him and, somehow, he was one of them again! He took in once more everything he had thought gone forever; the smells, the shapes, the faces of his own childhood, here, in the Caucasus, among the descendants of the Khazars! How could time play such tricks? Quba reminded him of the *shtetls*, the Jewish villages of pre-war Poland. These streets and houses seemed as unreal as if they were images from a long lost world. However, they were real Jewish houses, real Jewish children, real balconies belonging to Jews of today, and in them he could see preserved a way of life into which he had been born and raised; had learned to be a Jew. And what that had cost!

Agarounov was suddenly at his side. "I knew you would be surprised."

"It's more than surprise," murmured Sofer, who was uncomfortable that his emotions had been so transparent. "I feel like I've come home!"

"We are often asked how this tradition of the building and organization of villages came to be here."

Agarounov was always ready to pass from emotion to reflection. "For instance, could this zincwork have been some late influence brought here by European Jews? However, when you think about it, you soon realize that it is one of the oldest traditions in the Caucasus, even among Muslims and Christians in Georgia. On the other hand," Agarounov pointed out a balcony with carefully carved balustrades, "the Orient has long been a source for that type of decoration. You can find it everywhere in the region, from the ancient Persian towns right to the Black Sea, from Turkey to the Crimea. Why not believe that in this instance it was the Khazars who brought the tradition to Central Europe?"

A short toot on the horn interrupted them sharply. Lazir's golden smile appeared in the window of the Mercedes. "Why do you always have to keep asking questions that don't mean anything," he laughed, "and, anyway, you never have any answers! I'm no professor, so I only have real questions. First, now that we are here, what are we going to do? Secondly, where are we going to eat? It's lunchtime and I'm hungry!"

Sofer and Agarounov laughed heartily. "I would like Marc to meet my friend Zovolun, the Mayor of Quba," said Agarounov. "They have just told me that he has gone to the cemetery. He is participating in the special ceremony marking thirty days since the burial of one of his old friends. It might be interesting for you to take part. That way, you could meet him and some of the Jews from the Mountains."

"Mmm, I see," sighed Lazir, without enthusiasm. "A traditional funereal meal! I tell you, Mr. Sofer, no *shashlik*, no *khajapuri*, no stuffed pancakes!"

❧

Quba possessed not one, but three cemeteries. Agarounov explained that all the Mountain Jews originating from Quba, even those who had emigrated to Israel or America, wanted to be buried at 'home.' The huge cemeteries were situated at the edge of a plateau overlooking the valley and the town. Each was opulent and meticulously maintained, with an overgrown field studded with simple traditional stone tombstones, souvenirs of times past.

The cemetery Lazir drove them to was the farthest from the town. At the entrance they had to pass through a compact group of women, their heads covered in black shawls. Discretely, Agarounov pointed out thirty or so men assembled around a new grave, their heads covered with skullcaps, or occasionally a folded white handkerchief. The faces, for the most part, were those of peasants, rough and marked by the sun and the frost, mountain men like mountain men everywhere.

As they approached, Sofer recognized the plaintive sound of psalms being recited in Hebrew. They waited at the back, joining in for the recitation of the *Kaddish*, the prayer for the dead, with the mourners. Then the group broke up and suddenly, in front of him, Sofer saw a small man, round and nervous, short hair plastered to his head with sweat.

"Zovolun Buruth Danilev," he introduced himself. "I am honored by your visit, Mr. Sofer. Mikhail said he would bring you to meet me. You know, the Khazars, we don't know too much about them here...."

The Mayor extended a slightly moist hand. His speech was rapid fire, his gaze steady and direct. Without knowing why, Sofer responded to him by smiling as one does at a salesman who assures you that the article you have requested is of such rarity that it makes it almost too precious to sell. The formalities of introduction concluded, they walked toward a plain breeze-block building, inside which the communal meal was being served. While the women waited outside in the sunshine, disturbed from time to time by the piercing wails of the oldest mourner, the men placed themselves around the tables. Following tradition, the cold food had to be eaten in sequence according to natural origins, just as light comes from the sky and sinks into the shadows of the earth. To begin with, Sofer received an apple, food of the air; then slices of cucumber, produce of the earth; then cheese, fish, and lastly a potato. Vodka was virtually mandatory with each course, this providing at least some solace for Lazir.

During the meal, conversation flowed. Astonishingly, considering the place and the event, subjects passed randomly from the cost of living to the quality of mobile phones, from economic hopes for the region to prices at harvest time. However, every so often the gathering fell silent, as one or other of the participants recited a psalm or one of the eighteen blessings: *"Lord be praised, our God and God of our fathers. God of Abraham, God of Isaac, God of Jacob...."*

Sofer hesitated several times before taking out the photocopies of the documents he had researched in Cambridge and Oxford from his inside pocket. The sheets of paper circulated from hand to hand; few of those present were able to decipher the ancient Hebrew calligraphy of Rabbi Hazdai and Khagan Joseph, but the emotion that lit up all the faces made up for their inadequacy. Agarounov came into his own, recovering from the seriousness of the ceremony that had subdued him. Typically, he interjected one of his thought-provoking statements a little too early in the proceedings.

"Isn't it extraordinary that we don't even know the origins of our own language, Tath?" he exclaimed. "Persian? Turkish? Khazar? A mixture of all three? Take the word *Kiev*. In Tath it means 'at the edge of the water.'"

"Also in Khazar," Sofer said with a smile. "Kiev meant 'at the edge of the water,' but in two words *Ki-Ev*."

"Exactly!" Agarounov was jubilant. "So does that mean that the name Kiev is Khazar or Russian in origin?"

"Both, perhaps, a belated effect of the influence of the Khazars in the region. Don't forget that Kiev was founded by the Khazars and not by the Russians, who only conquered it a century later."

The conversation became more general. Sofer, in a flush of excitement, brought out the coin Yakubov had given him. Like the photocopies of the ancient texts a few minutes earlier, the coin was passed from hand to hand, drawing gasps of admiration. The mayor's face became serious. After a few intrigued glances at Sofer, he finally asked, "How did you come by this coin?"

"A man—a rather strange man—gave it to me. Perhaps one of you knows him. He is called Ephraim Yakubov. He says he found it in a cave in Georgia. A cave large enough to contain a whole synagogue."

Sofer was going to relate in detail how Yakubov had contacted him and then disappeared, but he had hardly pronounced the name when a heavy silence enveloped the previously noisy room. There was a moment of unease, then Sofer heard the mayor's abrasive voice launch itself into the recitation of a psalm. He thought for an instant that his imagination was inventing a mystery where none existed. After all, was it not strange enough to have this type of discussion during a ceremonial meal in memory of a deceased person? He looked for Agarounov's reassuring approbation. But Mikhail Yakovlevitch continued to chew on a potato, eyes cast down.

The psalm ended. A thin man with black sunken eyes and heavy cheekbones seemingly held together by an enormous mustache, stretched his arm out over the empty vodka bottles and handed the coin back to Sofer.

"I think I know who he is, your Yakubov." His Russian was scarcely comprehensible, sodden with alcohol. "My brother knew him. They were butchers together in Georgia. They fell out. Your Yakubov, he was trafficking with the Chechyns."

"What kind of trafficking?" Sofer asked.

The man smiled, wiping his mustache with the back of his hand. "You name it, they trafficked in it. The Chechyns? Arms! The mountains are full of stories, if you believe them all. Yakubov? There are plenty of his type in the Caucasus…."

Sofer jumped at the unexpected sound of Lazir clearing his throat behind him. The boxing champ smiled. The gold in his teeth shone less brightly than in the sunlight, but his gaze hung heavily on the man with the mustache. The thin man lowered his eyes. Once more, Sofer felt a sense of unease permeate those near him at the same time as Lazir placed a friendly hand on his shoulder.

"The Mayor would like to show you the cemetery," he said gently.

"Now?"

"Why not? We have to leave the room anyway, so that the women can have their turn."

The heat of the sun surprised Sofer. Zovolun Buruth Danilev was bathed in sweat by the time they had crossed a large part of the cemetery. Sofer was quite disturbed by what he saw. Even though graven images were normally proscribed from Jewish cemeteries, a large number of the tombstones bore portraits of the deceased. Here was the face of a young, very lovely, woman, sweetly sad; a little further away stood a mother and a young son in uniform.

"In Quba, we really like to see the faces of our dead," explained Zovolun, sponging the nape of his neck. "But it is even more astonishing if you look at these."

The mayor took Sofer's elbow to turn him around. Absolutely stupefied, Sofer stood stock still, staring; on the reverse of some of the stones, seven to ten feet high, there were no photographs facing him, but rather men and women, mostly young, in their normal daily attire of simple dresses or jeans and T-shirts, smoking cigarettes or smiling, hailing a friend or reading. The realism was so complete that they all appeared to literally spring out from the ground, raising themselves from the darkness of their marble homes like a plantation of the dead on the point of resurrection.

Zovolun took Sofer's astonishment for admiration.

"It's beautiful, isn't it?"

"More odd than beautiful," corrected Sofer.

"We like it."

"It must cost a fortune!" Sofer commented, in order to change the subject. "These graves, the houses in Quba; you run a wealthy town, Mr. Mayor. May I ask how it's done?"

"America. Our children go there to do business. The United States, Canada. It seems that the Jews from the Mountains are particularly well-suited to business. But they stay away from their families for a long time, from their aging parents, sometimes even their wives. They are filled with nostalgia. They hope to come home one day, but to a large beautiful town. So they send money, much money, so their families can live as well as possible and so that when they return they will be able to live the American way. You see, it's all very simple."

Yes, all very simple, Sofer thought, holding himself back from asking the mayor what sort of hugely lucrative enterprises the Jews from the Mountains undertook in the United States. In any case, there would not have been enough time, for the mayor added, in a deep voice, "Since we are talking about money, it would be better if you didn't let anyone else see that Khazar coin you have."

"Eh? Why?"

"That Yakubov you told us about, I don't know much about him, but all the same, you don't have to be psychic to realize that he must have robbed a sacred place."

"The cave ... the synagogue! Yes...."

"If you show it to everybody, they will all want to go and rob it."

"But no one knows where it is!" exclaimed Sofer. "Somewhere in Georgia ... you think that's enough information?"

"You, you're a stranger. You don't know. Neither do I. But others may know. You can imagine how news travels in a small community. And we, the Jews from the Mountains, it's as if we live in a tiny country on its own in the middle of Azerbaijan!"

He made a gesture indicating a tiny space between his finger and thumb. "It wouldn't take much to make us disappear altogether. For some, it's not for lack of trying!"

"Who? Why? Mayor Zovolun, why won't you tell me openly what you know about this man, Yakubov? He wouldn't have anything to do with the attack at Baku, by any chance? The claim to be the New Khazars?"

The small man carefully wiped his face. Sofer thought, just for an instant, that he was going to open up to him. But he only screwed up his face and shook his head. "I don't understand what you are trying to say. What connection could there possibly be between him and the attack? As Lazir said, the mountains are full of rumors. If you believe them, you'll believe anything! Come on, I want to show you the old cemetery. It is all that remains of our community from the Stalin era."

⋇

Lazir and Agarounov returned Sofer to his hotel long after dark. He entered the grand marble lobby dreaming of a shower and ten hours of sleep. At the reception desk he was informed with a gracious smile that someone was waiting for him at the bar. His fatigue disappeared as if by magic. He was certain it was her. Why? By what miracle? Without being aware of it, he slowed his pace. He wanted to savor the moment. He tried to formulate his first sentence, his first question. He felt as if he were already under her emerald gaze. This time he was going to understand at last. Hear her voice. Breathe her perfume.

Damn! He was like a youth on his first date!

A double glass door slid open before him. He felt the marble give way to carpet through his soles. Looking around he searched for her red hair. But he did not see it. She was not in one of the deep armchairs that surrounded the low coffee tables nor on one of the stools at the bar. On the other hand, Alastair Thomson was there. Standing, his bald cranium reflecting the subdued lighting, he hailed Sofer with a silent gesture.

Sofer felt such anger and disappointment that all he wanted to do was turn his back and go to his room without acknowledging Thomson, but the stupidity of such a move, and some twinges of curiosity, restrained him. He advanced stiffly, feeling all his fatigue

186

flood back. The morose look on his face drew an ironic exclamation from the Englishman.

"I'm happy to see how much pleasure my visit brings you!"

He seemed in good form. He had traded in his Saville Row suit for a freshly ironed Sahara suit in khaki. A bow tie, dark blue with red spots, closed the collar of a light colored shirt, and his signet rings shone under the bar's spotlights, reminding Sofer of Lazir's jewelry. The writer fell back into an armchair, grumbling that he had had a long day and that the roads in Azerbaijan were not conducive to rest. As Thomson came over and sat down, his jacket flapped open to reveal the smooth handle of a pistol sticking out of a cloth holster. Thomson leaned over and pushed a large red box decorated with a sturgeon and the word CAVIAR across the table toward him. The gun was even more visible.

"It's the best, even for the excellent Beluga! I told myself that you probably wouldn't think of it. Baku is not only an oil town, it's a caviar town as well."

Sofer's surprise, as much at the gun as at the present, passed for polite protest. Thomson insisted with a sweep of his arm, making the ring on his right hand flash above the caviar box.

"Please accept it! I know I bored you with so many questions on the plane, and I would like to make amends. Anyway, in the market here, it only costs seven dollars for a hundred grams!" The Englishman's face cleared. "There, you see, if it had been my intention to bribe you, I'd hardly have told you the price!"

Sofer relaxed. Like the evening before, he was intrigued by this mysterious Englishman and horrified at how he never seemed to have a response ready for his verbal parries. He did not imagine for one second, however, that Thomson was wasting his time visiting the bar out of courtesy. He called the young waitress, ordered a Polish vodka and asked, "How did you know that I was staying in this hotel?"

"If it were only as easy to find out who is hiding behind the New Khazars," Thomson joked.

Sofer smiled politely. "Thank you for the caviar, I appreciate the gesture. But I doubt that you came here just to give me a charming gift. I guess you must have more questions to ask me. Still on the subject of the Khazars?"

Thomson took his time before replying. The waitress placed the glass of vodka in front of Sofer. When he raised his eyes he had the distinct impression that the look on his visitor's face was as icy as the glass of alcohol.

"It isn't really a question. I would like to share a theory with you, and discuss its consequences."

Sofer swallowed a refreshing gulp of Zubrowska.

"I'm listening."

"I explained to you yesterday how the Caspian region plays a role in the larger game…"

"Because of the importance of its recently discovered oil reserves. Yes, I remember."

Thomson nodded. "The fundamental condition necessary for successfully extracting and exporting oil is security in the region. The Americans, I dare say, invented the Gulf War for that very purpose; to sanitize the Gulf region and render it secure, neutralize the power of Iraq which at any moment could and would have helped itself to the oil as a means of blackmail. It's enough to understand the economic downturn, and therefore the political fallout, that is produced in Europe by a rise in the price of a barrel of oil from ten to fifteen dollars, for you to be convinced."

"Oh!" Sofer smiled broadly. "I'm convinced."

"Europe and all the West and anyone else involved in making economic rules need an abundant, and not too expensive, supply of oil," hammered Thomson. "Our standard of living as well as the durability of our values and our civilization depend on it! We must have security to exploit the oil here. Security now, and in the future—"

"It's the West's Achilles' heel, then," Sofer intervened. "Oil is a sort of weapon. In general, what you are saying is that whoever has an oil resource at hand—whichever dictator or group of determined men—they could embarrass the West … a West, it must be said in passing, that it seems to me, you are a bit too quick to confuse with the handful of oil giants that employ you! To define our civilization as that of Black Gold warrants some debate.…"

Thomson appeared surprised at the dig, but accepted it with a wry smile. "Oil is only a weapon for fools ready to submit to such pressures as the Iraqis already do. Saddam Hussein is mad, and he imposes his madness on all his people!"

"At least that is if you don't accept the other view, that the West would have imposed the same madness on the Iraqi people…."

"Please don't pretend to be naïve. We are wasting time. When a giant has sore feet, Mr. Sofer, he cares for himself with giant remedies. The microbes do not survive!"

"A good metaphor!" applauded Sofer, who was really beginning to enjoy the game.

But Thomson was barely amused. He replied dryly, "When I question myself about the identity of those who hide behind this ephemeral appellation, the New Khazars, I ask who really has a vested interest in introducing chaos into the Caspian oil exploitation arena."

Sofer, smiling, nodded. Thomson leaned over, his jeweled hand resting on the caviar box, and declared in a quiet voice, at the same time dramatic and threatening, "You don't see, you don't understand. You can't even guess at the number of bodies, Mr. Sofer. However, all around you, here in Baku, in this hotel, a war is raging! A commercial war! The most vicious, the most violent possible! In commercial wars the more deceitful the blows, the more they are worth their weight in gold. Just today I gathered some information that made me think that the beneficiaries of a well-orchestrated mild panic could be the Americans!"

Sofer opened his eyes wide, amazed. Thomson straightened up, proud of himself.

"I have already explained to you that the potential profits from the Caspian exploitation are colossal. The Russians are out of the game, and will be for some time to come. But the Europeans, that's another matter. Now, the attack claimed by the New Khazars destroyed only those installations owned by the OCOO, a consortium funded eighty percent by the Europeans."

"Are you saying that the American oil companies could have organized this attack?" exclaimed Sofer, incredulous.

"With the aim of artificially spreading insecurity through the region, yes. With the intention of scaring the European oil companies."

"But...."

"If the European companies give way to panic, they will reduce their ambitions and withdraw their funding of the Caspian exploitation. The gap would be immediately filled by American companies. Like a miracle, the insecurity would suddenly cease! No more attacks! No more threats. Calm would return and the game could continue; the Americans would have complete control of all the reserves in the region. If one adds to that those of the Middle East, it would be just as if they had their hands on the fresh air tap for the whole world."

"Do you think that's possible?"

"It is one hypothesis. We will soon know."

"How?"

"I told you the other day. I am pretty certain there will be another attack. It always happens like that. If my theory is correct, they will attack the ocoo installations again. Not the American ones."

Sofer looked around the room at the faces there. He began to understand where the Englishman was coming from. He finished his drink. With a shiver amplified by the alcohol and fatigue, he articulated the conclusion he had reached. "In that case, what you want me to understand is that the New Khazars are nothing but...."

"... a cover, a diversion. A manipulation!" Thomson was excited. "A Jewish group, Mr. Sofer, with a long and ancient history in the Caucasus, but that most of the world has forgotten; a group of Jews whom God-knows-who has promised God-knows-what and has been led into an adventure that will lose them...."

Sofer thought of Lazir's strange behavior in Quba, of his conversation with Zovolun in the cemetery, of the fruitful 'deals,' as the mayor had called them, that allowed sufficient money to come from the United States to maintain the town at a standard well above its normal means.

He asked, "Do you have any proof?"

Thomson shook his head but he was triumphant. "None. I

repeat, it's only a theory. But the best we have. If not, why else resurrect this name from the past, the New Khazars?"

Sofer was close to agreeing with him; nevertheless he shrugged his shoulders and said, "There could be another reason."

"There could."

Sofer picked up his glass before remembering that it was empty. He grimaced. "So what do want from me?"

"That you pass a message to your friends…"

"My friends?"

"I know where you were today. Oh, it's not magic; you are a Jewish writer researching the Khazars. It's natural for you to make contact with their descendants, the ones they call the Mountain Jews. They live an odd life, don't they?"

Sofer did not answer. He felt frozen from head to toe.

"Tell them to let it drop," Thomson continued. "Tell them they should not allow themselves to be led into making a second attack. For us it would be a sort of signal, and we would remember where it came from. And if some kind of explanation, absolutely anonymous, of course, came to our ears, that would be even better—with details implicating the Americans, if possible…."

"Why are you asking me to do this? I have nothing to do with this affair!"

Thomson stood up, laughing.

"Precisely! I am asking you because you're no more than a tourist on the periphery of this business. If I were a novelist like you, I would say that you are not even a character in the story. It's perfect!"

Sofer stood up. Thomson put a hand on his arm. "Have you found out where the cave is? The one where the coin you showed me came from?"

"No … I…. How do you know it came from a cave? I never told you that!"

"Oh yes, you did! A cave with a synagogue inside!"

Thomson tapped his forehead with two fingers. "I have a very good memory…."

For a fraction of a second Sofer felt like he was a mouse caught in the paws of a cat. Then the Englishman bid him farewell. "Have a good night's rest. And tomorrow, please telephone your friends. That will be enough. Remember to tell them it's the best favor you can do for them. And that we have nothing against them!"

He was already in the hall when Sofer remembered that the box of caviar was still on the table. For Pete's sake, why had he agreed?

Chapter twenty-three

T here will be great celebrations this evening," said Hezekiah. "There will be singing and dancing all night … it's always the same when a convoy of boats arrives from the north."

The Khagan's son was seated beside Isaac in one of the indentations in the wall at the top of the south side of the fortress. The town of tents was spread out below them. Khagan Benjamin's funeral was over. The boats that Isaac had left four days earlier were just landing in a little creek on a bend in the river, a sort of beach where the big flat-bottomed boats could come aground without damage. From their position high on the walls, they could clearly see the slaves leaving the boats, closely watched by the townsfolk. In spite of his efforts however, Isaac found himself too far away to recognize Saul and Simon among the crowd of onlookers, boatmen and merchants.

"You are sad," remarked Hezekiah. "Would you like to go and dance with them?"

Isaac shook his head without even a smile. "My two traveling companions must have arrived with the boats. I am sad because I cannot go to meet them. They must be wondering whether I'm dead or alive."

Hezekiah nodded seriously; he understood. With the old rabbi's assistance he had managed to convince his father to allow the messenger from the Sephardi Jews to go for a walk on the walls. Isaac ben Eliezer was now able to walk again without suffering from vertigo, and he needed some fresh air to help him heal after all the blood he had lost.

Nevertheless, the Khagan had only permitted this favor reluctantly. A handful of guards followed closely, bows in hand, keeping a sharp lookout. As unbelievable as it seemed, Isaac was a virtual prisoner, without really knowing why. The evening before, Senek, the chief of the guards who had clobbered him on his arrival, had announced that he could not leave his room, never mind the fortress, until he was granted an audience with the Khagan.

At that moment, Isaac had practically jumped for joy, for surely that could only mean that he was going to meet the Khagan soon. However, when the rabbi came to see him later, he advised him that, on the contrary, the meeting might be delayed for a long time. Why? The old man had dodged the question. The Khagan sometimes acted oddly, he had said. Isaac must be patient.

Hezekiah didn't seem to know much more. "It is true that my father is very angry with you. Nearly as much as he is with the Greeks. He hasn't told me why. Perhaps it is only because he is angry with everybody because of Attex's disappearance."

For that was the other bad news. More than bad; terrible, painful! Isaac could not bring himself to tell Hezekiah, but the Kathum's flight, and the cause of her flight, had nearly overwhelmed him with sadness. After having asked him to be patient, Rabbi Hanania had confided to him that the Kathum had disappeared and that he would be lucky to ever see her again.

"Why did she run away?" Isaac asked, amazed.

"Alas! Alas!" The rabbi told Isaac of the Greek's hatred toward the religion of Moses. He described the threat that Byzantium had posed to the Kingdom of the Khazars for centuries. Finally, in a quiet voice, he told him about Emperor Constantine's latest maneuvers: "Ambassador Blymmedes, with his sweet manners, soft words and many presents, was sent to take the Khagan's sister for marriage to a Christian, to make her deny the Book."

"And? Did she refuse?"

The old man's eyes were ablaze. "She did better than refuse! She disappeared, fled! Gone, out of sight. The Ambassador is furious. The Khagan, also!"

The rabbi's chuckle did nothing to ease Isaac's sad stupefaction.

Long after the rabbi had left he remained prostrate on the edge of his bed, not knowing what distressed him the most. How could it be possible? How could Khagan Joseph accept this humiliation of his sister, even collude in it? Could he not anticipate the reaction it would bring from the Almighty? How could he collaborate in a denial of the Law, the faith of his fathers, the testament of his grandfather? How could he sweep away, with some putrid accord, the hopes that all the Jews in the world placed in him? What deception!

Just when he had finally arrived at the Jewish Kingdom of the Khazars, everything was falling apart. His hopes, so strong, were no more than sand scattered by the wind, the dust of shame! For how could he still believe now that this inaccessible Khagan could become the David of all the Jews? Their King, their Messiah, so long awaited … surely it could not be. It could only be a blind aberration from one at the head of the flock. That's what it was, what it must be. Surely Rabbi Hazdai would die if he heard such news!

He too, Isaac ben Eliezer, felt he would die, here and now. He wanted someone to hit him on the head again. Properly this time, to finish him off! And this time, there would be nobody to care for him. No angelic beauty to watch over his bedside, to glide her fingertips along his lips, to encourage his breathing in and out. Death was sweeter than to lose Kathum Attex, may the Lord forgive him!

Oh, yes, he was relieved, greatly relieved, that she had fled, refusing to contaminate herself with this Greek alliance. He could only admire her courage. He was full of admiration for what she had done. And desperate. For some days now, he had lived only to be able to breathe the same air as her. To see her joyous eyes again, to sense her perfume, feel the rare contact of her fingers, hear the murmur of her voice, the rustling of her tunic. In truth, and blessed be the Almighty who had made it so, he had only regained his strength and fought back death to be alive next to her! She had resuscitated him solely with her presence, and the halo that the morning light had set around her head, and defined her lips. To know that the Kathum had fled for a just cause and even for the most sublime of causes changed nothing. He missed her, needed her, like fire needs air and deserts need rain. Her absence drew the strength from his limbs. It broke his heart, leaving nothing but a dead lump in his chest.

Where was she? What dangers was she facing? What would become of her? May the Lord protect her if He could; from now on she would be facing the unknown. Isaac would have given anything to be beside her, he would have changed into a dog or a wolf to protect her in her travails, to defend her from evil. So many dangers and threats would range around her like wild dogs around a wounded fawn.

Hezekiah was right, more than he knew; Isaac was sad, inconsolable. He suffered now more than he had ever suffered from the blow that nearly killed him, and to his suffering was added one more injustice—silence. He could not confide in either Rabbi Hanania or Hezekiah. Almost, he could not admit to himself the astonishing term by which his torment was named, his desire and his despair—love.

The boy uttered a cry and placed his hand on Isaac's wrist. "Look, down there!"

Far to the south of Sarkel, a whirlwind of dust was stirring in the breeze. They could just see a long caravan forming. The brown tufted manes of the camels, the colored canvases of umbrellas and shades, reflections from weapons or armor, traced the shape of an undulating serpent starting to climb the first of the hills bordering the river.

"The Greeks! The Greeks are leaving!" Hezekiah was jubilant. "What a pity Attex isn't here to see it! It would make her so happy!"

Isaac didn't have a chance to react to this exuberant declaration that turned the knife in his wounds; a warrior had crept noiselessly up and accosted them. Hezekiah left the niche where they had been sitting and translated.

"The rabbi wants to see you."

Isaac glanced over the fortress wall, and clenched his fist against the vertigo his movement induced. Rabbi Hanania was standing in front of the synagogue, a minute turbaned silhouette, waving his arms in an imperious gesture.

"You'd think he was in a hurry," remarked Hezekiah, smiling broadly. "He too will be happy that the Greeks have left!"

However, when they reached the front of the synagogue, the rabbi did not seem very happy. Gravely, he asked Hezekiah to leave him alone with Isaac.

"What we have to discuss is not for young ears, Hezekiah," he affirmed, throwing an angry look at Isaac. "The Khagan wants me to make doubly sure of what we know about the messenger from Cordoba. More than ever, he fears traps set by the Emperor of Byzantium. He wants to be sure that your arrival, Isaac ben Eliezer, which coincided with that of the Greeks, is not just one more subterfuge among the many that he knows the Greeks are capable of committing."

"But they have gone!" protested Hezekiah.

"All the more reason. The criminal flees leaving the poison behind him!"

"Poison?" protested Isaac in his turn, confused. "How could you accuse me…?"

The rabbi raised an imperious hand. "It will be explained to you in a minute. But you, son of the Khagan, leave with the servants."

Hezekiah sighed. He waved a sad goodbye as the rabbi pushed Isaac inside the synagogue.

"Rabbi!" Isaac exclaimed, bursting with anger and shame. "I am hurt by your suspicion. Do you really believe…"

Rabbi Hanania caught him by the sleeve to stop him. "I only believe in the alliance with the Lord, blessed be His name. Now stop your protests and listen to what I have to say—without interrupting!"

He led Isaac to the base of the holy ark, and took out a canvas bag from which he withdrew an exquisite woman's gown.

"Put that on," he commanded.

"That?"

"No arguments. You don't have much time and I don't want to discuss it!"

Puzzled, Isaac rapidly divested himself of his own tunic and put on the delicate garment. The rabbi passed him a piece of cloth embroidered with gold leaf. "Cover yourself with this veil. It will hide your wound, and hopefully your beard when you go outside."

"Outside? Do you mean outside the fortress?"

"Outside means outside! Do you think I'm dressing you like this to stay here and read the Torah with me? Come on, come on, hurry up!"

In spite of the harshness of his words, the old man's expression was becoming warmer by the second, eyes sparkling with humor. Isaac covered himself in the veil, showing only his eyes. Rabbi Hanania, opening his great toothless mouth, let out sharp cries of joy. "Very pretty! A very pretty young woman! You look like a woman from the Alain tribe. Watch out for the soldiers, Isaac, they could take a liking to you...."

He pushed Isaac toward the ark, pulling on a plank of wood that came away freely. An opening scarcely as wide as a man's waist appeared.

"I have no candles to give you," whispered Hanania. "A pity, but you'll just have to go in the dark. Anyway, the tunnel is straight, there's no risk of getting lost...."

"The tunnel...?"

"By my faith, what else do you think it is?! Get a move on! Someone will meet you at the other end. Be careful when you first appear...."

Isaac found enough presence of mind to protest. "Rabbi, I don't understand! Don't you want me to meet the Khagan?"

"May the Lord preserve us from thinkers!" the old man hissed. "Get out of here, Isaac ben Eliezer. Go to the end of the tunnel and then do what you are told. At least as long as your heart tells you that it's right! Hurry now, I must shut this entrance!"

❧

Whether it was all the questions whirling through his head, or simply the absolute dark of his surroundings, the tunnel seemed very long. Isaac's fingers, extended to detect whatever was in front of him, finally came up against a wooden door. It seemed so thick to the touch that he feared he would not be strong enough to move it, but a single push with his shoulder was sufficient to allow in the blinding daylight.

He cautiously widened the opening. He appeared to be surrounded by a pile of large rocks that were interspersed with very thick outcrops of a thorny laurel bush. He had to be careful not to tear his fragile garment as he struggled through them. Between gaps in the foliage, he could see the river at some distance below him. He was well upstream of the tent town, far below the fortress. He was just skirting the last thickets with great care, when a groan made him catch his breath.

He gasped, nearly falling as he squatted down behind a rock. The face that he could barely distinguish was clothed in female garb but had the appearance of a monster. Only the eyes and the forehead bore any resemblance to a human being, the rest was nothing but lumps and bumps; deformed jaws, twisted lips and a nose so misshapen that it had only one nostril.

"Come along," erupted a raucous voice in almost incomprehensible Hebrew.

Isaac recoiled instinctively. "Who are you?"

"I'm the one who looked after you..." replied the monster, pointing an unusually delicate finger at Isaac's temple.

He remembered incessant orders given by the Kathum Attex to her servant. Engrossed in Attex's beauty, he had paid little attention to the servant, who had in any case hidden her face under thick veils.

"Attex," he whispered. "You are her servant!"

"The Kathum is waiting," Attania concurred. "Hurry!"

"She is waiting for me?" repeated Isaac incredulously.

"Yes," confirmed Attania.

"Then ... the Kathum, Attex, has not run away? And that means, Rabbi Hanania...."

She was waiting for him! Blessed be the Almighty!

Isaac tottered and would have fallen to his knees again if Attania had not caught and held him.

❧

A boat was at the river's edge, a long thin canoe carved from a single tree trunk. The boatman steered it easily along the busy river, hugging the shores of the Varshan. Then, as they passed a sort of cabin surmounted by a wrought iron menorah, Isaac thought for one brief moment that he saw Simon in a beam of sunlight. Instinctively he raised himself from the crossbar on which he was seated, but Attania was watching. She made him sit down with a hand as strong as any farmer.

The village fell away behind them. A small fleet of merchant boats appeared as they rounded a bend in the river, which was now widening and deepening. Ropes wound around poplar tree trunks held the boats to the bank. The boatman managed his steering oar so that their boat slipped under the bows of the larger ones. Isaac saw a rope ladder suspended from the deck of one of them. Attania was already standing. The boatman only just had time to stop the boat with his anchor before she grasped one of the rungs. She didn't have to tell him to follow.

Isaac discovered a small wooden house, like a small castle, on the deck. It had no windows, but a door painted a pretty shade of blue. The servant pushed him unceremoniously in front of her. It was he who turned the door handle. Inside, he saw carpets, cushions, little low tables with bowls of fruit, a solid lamp and two beautiful swords with curved blades. And her. She was standing, face unveiled, smiling. The Kathum, Attex.

Attex, with her hair of fire and her gaze that went through you in the blink of an eye. The silk of her green gown was so fine that it seemed to be a second skin. She made a small gesture with her hand, and the door closed behind Isaac. He turned around; the servant had disappeared.

"Attania has her own quarters in the stern of the boat," Attex explained in a voice vibrant with emotion. "I am so happy you were able to escape!"

※

Afterward, Isaac could never remember precisely all that happened that night. He felt ridiculous in the garments he was wearing. Attex declared with a smile of complicity that she had chosen the gown herself. She bade him sit down on the cushions, so close to her that he inhaled her perfume with every breath. Isaac was concerned for her, but she assured him that she had nothing to fear, that neither her brother nor Borouh would find them. She asked Isaac if he knew why she had fled. He answered in the affirmative and told her how the rabbi had explained everything.

Eyelids lowered as if she doubted her own judgment, she nodded her head, then after a moment's silence, declared, "I knew at once that I would never marry that Greek. And when I saw you in the courtyard, with the letter from the Sephardi Jews, it was as if an angel had been sent with a message for me from the Lord! Sent by the Almighty to make sure Joseph did not give me to the Greeks. I couldn't believe that you were a man of flesh and blood—to the extent that I didn't even think to stop them from beating you!"

At these words Isaac felt his head whirling, and all his anguish and fatigue disappeared instantly. He replied stupidly, "It doesn't matter. I don't feel it any more."

"That's good," murmured Attex, smiling gently.

"No! I mean to say ... it is the same for me! When I regained consciousness, I saw you and could not believe my eyes!"

Attex stretched out her arm and placed one hand on his. "I am here, and I am not an angel. My brother and the Beck think I am a plague."

She told him of her dispute with the Khagan, her flight— thanks to Rabbi Hanania—and her hopes of going to the great mountains to the south.

"My uncle lives there in a cave so big that it holds a synagogue as well as houses. Nothing can happen to me there."

She hesitated for a second, then, letting go of his hand, added, "You could come with me."

Isaac was on the point of agreeing gladly, when he suddenly imagined the shouts of anger that would be directed at him by Rabbi Hazdai. He shook his head. "I cannot. I promised to give the letter from Rabbi Hazdai of Cordoba to the Khagan. And I will do it. I promised that I would wait for his response. Even if I have to wait ten years, I will."

Attex's reaction to this was strange. She leaned over, shaking her red hair so that it covered her face, and seizing both his hands, this time kissed them gently. For an instant, Isaac ceased breathing. His heart was pounding so loudly that he could no longer hear the rushing of the river water against the boat's hull.

"I knew it! I knew that you were one who would never lack courage to do the right thing. I knew it! Yes, you must convince my brother to read the letter from your rabbi, and to answer it! Then the Almighty, blessed be His name, will save us all!"

"Amen! Yes, I think that is what will happen!"

The idea was so beautiful that neither of them could help laughing, eyes shining with joy and desire, and dread.

Isaac became serious first and murmured, "It could happen like that, or perhaps not...."

Attex gazed at him with infinite tenderness, and she agreed with a slight nod. "Whether he reads it or not, you will eventually join me in the cave of the Great Mountains. I will wait for you there. Ten years if necessary!"

The words contained so many promises that Isaac trembled without being able to respond. After a short silence, Attex stood up and went to get a painted wooden box, exclaiming, "You must be dying of hunger!" She deposited the box in front of him and opened it. Isaac suddenly felt as if he were breathing in the odor of seaweed, or the very sea itself. The aroma came from a glass bowl within the box, filled with a mass of small black grains. "It may taste odd to you at first as you will never have eaten it before. But I am certain you will love it."

She laughed, seeing him restrain a grimace. "It is the best in the world. These are the eggs of a fish that lives in the Sea of the Khazars. It is called *khaviar*." She plunged a large wooden spoon into the bowl. Laughing, she offered it to him as one offers food to a baby. "Taste it! You will love it, I guarantee it!"

And he did. The grains seemed to evaporate on his tongue. The flavor was strange, full of memories of the sea, salty like tears, yet also sweet, soft as a memory when it disappears. Attex laughed to see him eating it by the spoonful. Her happiness increased Isaac's appetite, as if this curious food contained some of the same mystery as she. When he had practically emptied the bowl, she said seriously, "What you have just eaten is the love offering that women in the Khazar Kingdom give to the one they have chosen for a husband. I choose you."

Isaac was dumbfounded, spoon suspended in mid-air.

"And you," asked Attex very softly, "will you have me?"

"Yes."

He was not sure his mouth had pronounced the word, but then Attex leaned toward him, and caressed his wounded temple. Under her fingers, he closed his eyes. Then, with the tip of her tongue, she gathered the errant fish eggs around Isaac's mouth. Their lips came together for the first time. Attex placed her hand on the nape of his neck and prolonged the kiss so sweetly, so tenderly, that he felt enveloped by her whole body.

At last, Isaac's hands relaxed. He abandoned the spoon to the carpet and ran his hand up Attex's thigh, then pressed the small of her back, shivering with excitement. The green silk of the dress was finer than he thought possible. Through it the firm suppleness of the princess' body warmed his hands. Purring like a small animal, Attex kissed his eyelids and placed her forehead against his cheek. Isaac felt her pressing all her weight against him. She cuddled up to him as tightly as she could, as though worried he might disappear. She was as voracious and clumsy as a child; Isaac fell over backward onto the cushions, knocking over a small table in the process. Attex chuckled happily. Their two bodies pressed one another, thigh to thigh. Her breasts squeezed softly against Isaac's chest, tips hard.

He felt as though he would be torn apart by the intensity of his desire to fully realize everything he was feeling inside. Although he was lying down he became dizzy. He almost burst under the strength of the desire that was hardening him. His hands continued to caress her arms, her shoulders, then again her waist, her back, without really daring to approach her breasts, as if afraid of too large a flame.

With one bite, Attex tore the ridiculous garment still covering Isaac. She placed her cool lips on the base of his neck. He shuddered and felt his member become so hard that it was painful. Attex also felt it, suddenly hesitating. He pushed her back gently. She straightened up, kneeling. Only their hands remained touching. Her cheeks on fire, she observed him fearfully.

Like someone advancing in the dark, Isaac stammered, "I have never really looked at you before. You are so beautiful."

Attex frowned. "All men say that to me. Even the Greeks. It's not important whether I am beautiful or not."

Isaac blinked. His spirit returned. He knew what she had meant to say; he remembered it from the teachings of Ecclesiastes: 'Do not hire a man for his beauty, do not malign him for his ugliness.' That must be true for a woman, too.

"No!" he murmured, shaking his head slowly. "You are not merely beautiful in that way. When I look at you I think the Almighty has offered me honey from Eden. You are like His hand and His gaze, you are His voice and His sweetness. In you I see the lights of the stars and the rivers. With you, I know why I am happy to be a man!"

She smiled like a spoiled child, let go of his hands and swung gently back. With a few swift movements she was naked. In her eyes was neither doubt nor shame. "I am pure and you are pure," she said. "It is a real marriage. I know the rabbi will pardon us. The Almighty, too. Only Joseph will never forgive us. Too bad...."

Isaac knew that the sentiment he had expressed a moment earlier was becoming a reality; Attex's beauty was effacing all memories of other women from his mind, just as a cloth wipes steam from the shiny copper of a mirror. Naked, she sat on his thighs, her curls intertwining with his. Quickly, she divested him of his gown. The embarrassment he felt for his erection disappeared. She took his right hand and placed it under her breast, then she pulled down on his neck until he could kiss the dark exposed point.

Together, kiss after kiss, rocked by the rolling of the river, they invented their common body, the ineffable sweetness of the voyage of love, where time and the sure knowledge of death dissolved.

~

Later, wrapped around each other on the rug, eating fruit, cakes, and roast chicken, they talked at length. Attex wanted to know everything about his journey and the countries he had seen. He recounted how orange trees cover the hillsides of Cordoba with blossoms whiter than snow, so perfumed that in the evening, when the sun plunges off the end of the earth, everyone has to breath in small gulps to avoid being suffocated by the sweetness. He told of roads edged with cypress trees. He described white houses and patios with blue doors. Relishing her laughter, he imitated the cool murmur of majolica fountains, frogs croaking in the twilight, crickets clicking in the hillsides outside the Cordoba gates. He evoked the books and the immense libraries where one could spend hours learning and understanding.

He told about the learned men whom he admired; his father the astronomer, and Rabbi Hazdai Ibn Shaprut, adviser to Caliph Abd al-Rahman II, who had sent him to her.

Finally he described his journey and the sad events leading to his meeting with Simon and Saul, how they had crossed the snow-covered countries of the Magyar at risk of being devoured by wolves until he thought of playing his lute to them.

"I'm sorry that I haven't got my lute with me tonight," he whispered, kissing her breasts. "I would have loved to play for you. Unfortunately, I left it with Saul and Simon. I will retrieve it before we meet again in the Great Mountains."

His head resting on her bosom, Attex was quietly storing the words he had spoken in her heart, her dreams. Her light hand slid over her lover's body, his thighs, his hip bones, played with the undulations of his waist, the flat of his stomach, and the softness that was once more becoming rigid. She hoped that with every move of her fingers each caress would be inscribed in the palms of her hand and her memory. Isaac did not realize that she was crying.

"My brother the Khagan will be so angry with you that he will dream of nothing but your death."

Isaac hesitated before replying. "No. Rabbi Hanania will not allow him to lay hands on me. And I will convince him that he must reply to the Grand Rabbi of Cordoba. The Lord, blessed be His name, will see that it does not happen otherwise. The Khagan will give me an audience! Tomorrow, I will prostrate myself before him when he emerges from his prayers and he will have to listen to me."

Attex sat up, leaning on one elbow, and shook out her hair of fire, eyes full of sadness. "You won't be able to. He is leaving, they are all leaving: the rabbi, the Beck, the Royal Guard...."

"Leaving? Leaving the fortress?"

Attex nodded, stroking his scar. "Yes. For Itil, our capital beside the sea. Messengers arrived yesterday, warning us that the Russians were once more trying to conquer us. Tomorrow at the latest, perhaps even tonight, they will set off. Joseph will not give you an audience for a long time...."

Isaac closed his eyes to help him think more clearly. "First, I must find my friends Saul and Simon again. Then I will follow the Khagan—to all his palaces, if that proves necessary!"

Attex knew that he was not talking this way boastfully. Her heart was breaking because she could only admire and fear his determination. She smiled through her tears. "Perhaps you will succeed. When you have your precious letter, if you like, I could come with you to the Sephardi country. I could be the ambassador from my brother, and your real wife...."

She laughed as if that were a foolish hope.

Emotion burned in Isaac's eyes. He raised his hands to caress his lover's breasts once more. From that moment the night had neither beginning nor end. The taste of their flesh was the pure delight of love and they forgot all the pressures of tomorrow.

⁂

At dawn they were still asleep when Attania knocked on the door to tell them that the boats were preparing to move. Their farewell was sharp and quick. Attex had carefully prepared Isaac clothes in the Khazar fashion; a long blue and yellow tunic, a leather belt covered in cloth, and beautiful cavalry boots, so supple and light that they enclosed his feet and calves like a second skin. They did their best to hold back their tears and preserve smiles of promise.

Isaac left the boat, reaching the bank by a plank from the deck. In his hand, he gripped a large silver medallion just like the one that hung around Hezekiah's neck. A seven-branched candelabra was molded on one side and on the reverse, inscriptions that he did not know or understand.

"Only members of the Khagan's family possess these medals," Attex explained. "If you wish to return to the fortress, you will only need to show it to the guards. It would be more sensible of you to come with me or to leave the kingdom altogether. But I know you will not do either. May the Almighty protect you, my love!"

Isaac untied the ropes holding the boat to a poplar tree. The first flush of dawn was appearing, and the light was as beautiful as that of the first day of the world. The small boat left the bank, dancing on the water. It moved away slowly, slapped by the yellow turbulence of the river.

Isaac saw Attex's raised arms and her windblown hair. Her green dress and red hair became a flower that faded into space and distance, as if nothing that night had been real. But he could still smell the fragrance of her perfume on his skin. In the silence that penetrated the depths of his soul, he heard her whisper his name.

Chapter twenty-four

Baku, Azerbaijan
May 2000

S ofer wakened with a start at the strident ringing of the telephone. A quick glance at the phosphorescent hands of his watch confirmed that it was still the middle of the night. Ten after four! For an instant he thought of throwing the offending apparatus onto the thick carpet, to lose it in the pile and return to sleep. What imbecile would call him at this ungodly hour? He lifted the receiver and grunted, so as to leave his caller in no doubt of his bad temper.

"It's Lazir." The voice of the boxing champion resounded in his ear.

"The devil it is! Do you know what time it is?"

"Nearly four fifteen, Mr. Sofer," Lazir replied placidly. "I'm downstairs."

"Downstairs? Here, in the hotel?"

"Yes, just in front, in the car. The white Mercedes."

"What the devil are you doing here?"

"Mr. Sofer, you'll need to come downstairs and go with me."

"Go? Go where?"

"You will see. I'm sure you will be interested."

Sofer passed a hand over his face, felt his nascent beard under his palm. He woke properly. In the gloom of the room he could just see his clothes on an armchair and Thomson's box of caviar on a table. He had eaten some of it before going to sleep, partly out of anger at the Englishman's presumption. The memory also brought to mind the large amount of vodka he had consumed with the caviar and succeeded in breaking the last threads of sleep that were trying to restrain him.

"Is it important?" he asked.

"It's important!" Lazir's tone of voice left no doubt.

"OK. I'm coming," said Sofer with a sigh. "I'll have a shave, then be with you."

"Keep your beard, Mr. Sofer, there's no time for that! Just wear warm clothes; nights in the Caucasus are always colder than you would think."

⁂

It wasn't true. When Sofer crossed the street to the Mercedes, where he could distinguish the glow of the Lazir's cigarette, the warm, humid air almost stuck to his face.

"I hope this is really important," he started bitterly, taking the seat next to Lazir. Because you don't even seem to know the difference between hot weather and cold!"

Lazir smiled as pleasantly as his golden incisors would permit. "Don't worry," he said, starting the engine. "You won't be disappointed. You'll be happy when you see her. And … you *will* need your sweater!"

The vehicle was doing seventy miles an hour within seconds, literally hurling them through the empty streets of Baku, floodlit with yellow street lamps.

"Where are you taking me?" Sofer asked, although he thought he knew.

"Right now, to the port."

"And then?"

"I can't tell you!"

Sofer grumbled, trying to put on a mocking face. "What's all the mystery, my friend? And why are you taking me to the port?"

Lazir shook his head, running a red light with as many twists and turns as a swallow. "I can't tell you anything. Understand?"

"Oh, I beg of you, please spare me the children's games. It's the wrong time of day, apart from anything else, and I never did like James Bond, either!"

"James Bond?"

"Idiocies!" sighed Sofer. "OK, what are you Lazir? One of the New Khazars? Or just Baku Mafia?"

Lazir gave out a hearty laugh. He slowed down to turn right into Nettchilyar Avenue. They were doing ninety, the nose of the Mercedes, a little heavy, plunged to the right while the tail skidded around to join them. Tires squealing on the rough pavement, he braked to regain control then accelerated, foot down, in the direction of the walls of the fairground. The wooden balconies and town walls flew by as Sofer hung on and Lazir answered deliberately.

"Since you arrived, Mr. Sofer, you have been absolutely certain that I belong to the Mafia! Why? Do you need a Mafia character for that book you're writing?"

"What the hell are we doing at the port at four in the morning?" persisted Sofer, annoyed.

Lazir threw a quick glance at the dashboard clock and corrected him. "Four thirty ... we need to be on time! I can't tell you anything, sorry. Don't worry, relax. You will soon have the answers to all your questions. Please, believe me ... I don't want to upset you, I assure you...."

The avenue suddenly seemed to widen out before them. Sofer realized that they were driving along the shore that was still hidden by the night. On his left, the darkness was pricked with hundreds of points of light. The derricks, the famous oil wells! At the same moment, scarcely slowing, Lazir turned right again. The vehicle whistled like a tornado through a maze of narrow streets. They began to climb. The district was poorer, less well lit, but also more alive. Men appeared, on foot or on bicycles, pushing handcarts, or loading trucks. For them, the day had already begun. The Mercedes passed by unidentifiable open spaces filled with old abandoned cars, refrigerators and unused pipes. Lazir took a badly surfaced road, destroyed by too many trucks, that led to a large complex of buildings under construction.

The car was still climbing. Sofer could see the lights of Baku on his right. Soon they were traveling on what could only be described as a trail. Raising a cloud of dust in the pale dawn light, the Mercedes took a huge bend as it appeared to turn back toward the sea. Which is what they did.

"Here we are!" Lazir declared in a self-satisfied tone, as he cut the engine.

Sofer stepped out of the car, overcome by the spectacle. They had stopped right on the edge of a plateau overlooking the oil-bearing Bay of Baku. Below them there was nothing but steel pylons, derricks, and intertwining pipelines; an incredible metal forest surging in every direction. Here and there they could see huge valves where pumps joined, and giant cranes moved slowly but unflaggingly. At the foot of the plateau, on the bank several hundred feet away, huge cranes and barges—a sort of floating workshop—were illuminated by batteries of halogen lights. All around, the ground looked marshy. Black puddles reflected both the night and the artificial lights simultaneously.

"Two minutes to wait." announced Lazir.

Sofer began to wonder what was happening to him, but still he avoided trying to reason it out. He only asked, "Where?"

Far to the east, day broke. A luminous strip grew on the horizon, like bright spilled cream. And then, at his feet, an explosion engulfed the bank. Before even hearing the noise or sensing the percussion against his chest, Sofer saw the flames light up the sky. A ball of fire bloomed at the foot of a crane as high as a ten-story building. Then the noise of the explosion shook the air. The bright yellow flame dilated, lifted the crane, dislodged it, reducing its twenty ton beams to twisted blades of straw, tossing their burning embers out of the fire, throwing incandescent balls of fire into the air and outshining the dawn.

Sofer recoiled instinctively. Lazir whistled in admiration. For a few seconds the fire seemed to fill the sky. They heard the beams fall back one on top of the other, making sounds like a discordant xylophone, but already the flames were retreating into a loud hissing heap. They fell in on themselves, flaring up like a dozen braziers. There was a dreadful creaking. A barge that had been thrown in the air fell back on the bank like a giant tortoise.

"Well! This time they really have done it!" exclaimed Lazir.

Sofer breathed out heavily. He realized that he had been holding his breath since the explosion. Lazir's hand touched his arm. "Come on! We'd better not stay here too long!"

As Lazir launched the Mercedes back into the dust, Sofer saw the sky above the oil complex redden like the roof of a furnace. His conversation with Thomson the previous evening came back to him. As much despondent as exasperated, he had to admit that the Englishman had been right on every point. He was too late to stop the second attack perpetrated by the New Khazars. It had just taken place. At the thought that the Lloyds investigator could be right about everything, Sofer's anger and disgust mounted.

"Are these OCOO installations that just blew up?" he asked frostily.

Lazir looked at him, surprised. A sly smile exposed the gleam of his gold teeth. "Not at all! This time it was the American consortium of Exxon and Chevron that went bang! Each one in turn...." Lazir began to laugh.

Sofer's relief was so great that he could only join in.

"And don't worry," added Lazir. "There is no risk of pollution and there were no casualties. It was only a derrick construction and installation facility. They don't work at night."

Sofer smiled. Thomson was not completely right. Definitely good news! "I suppose someone is going to tell me eventually who these mysterious New Khazars are?" he ventured, full of curiosity. Lazir did not answer. He took a left-hand fork at the beginning of the building site, turning away from the street they had come by. A little farther on, the Mercedes entered a compound cluttered with diggers and other earth-moving equipment and came to a halt behind a black Nissan four by four that Sofer thought he recognized. Lazir pumped his horn lightly. A young man got out and smiled at them.

"Come on," said Lazir, opening his door without switching off his engine. "We're changing vehicles."

"To go where?" Sofer questioned without moving.

Lazir was silent. He got out of the driver's seat and the younger man took his place. Sofer did not leave his seat, and the young man stopped smiling. He looked anxiously at the boxing champ. With the look of a father trying to keep calm when faced with his son's waywardness, Lazir walked around the Mercedes and opened Sofer's door. "Please get out. We can't hang around here."

"I asked you where we are going. What gives you the right to dictate my movements as you feel inclined? What makes you think that I am happy to act as your accomplice?" The look on Sofer's face was as amicable as a knife blade.

Lazir shrugged his shoulders fatalistically. "Take your sweater with you, and your bad temper, too. We're going to Georgia. Fifteen hours drive, if we're lucky. But at least it's comfortable to drive through the mountains. There are people who want to see you there. One person in particular. But, it's up to you, you are free to refuse. We are not going to kidnap you. Just give this lad the name of your hotel and he'll take you there…."

He stopped, raised one finger in the air and winked. The howl of sirens could be heard waking the town.

"Here they come," he said, turning on his heels to settle behind the steering wheel of the four by four. "It's up to you."

For a few moments, as the noise of the sirens grew louder, Sofer looked at the youth, undecided. Finally, he gave him a gentle tap on the forearm, wished him a good day and went to join Lazir.

It was true. The four by four was slower and more comfortable. Sofer appreciated the change. Even though he had not given the impression of being enthused at this new turn of events, he was actually quite taken with the sense of mystery and adventure in the air. Not knowing where he was being driven gave him a feeling of being lighter than air, as if he should worry less about reality. As they left Baku behind them, he remembered that he didn't even have a notebook with him. His computer was back at the hotel. Tough luck! The book would have to wait. What he was now living was more exciting than any book.

Then he thought about Agarounov. They were supposed to meet in a couple of hours, and he wouldn't be there. Tough luck again! He would explain what had happened later.

He fell asleep before day broke fully, succumbing to the exhaustion of his disrupted night. He had a bizarre dream, no doubt reflecting the attack, full of fire and the chaos of war. When he woke, they were already halfway up a huge mountain. The road was barely wide enough for the four by four, and zigzagged under immense ash trees that had rays of sun dancing through them.

"Sleep well?" asked the indefatigable Lazir. "The radio has just reported the attack. Everything's fine...."

"Everything's fine!" grumbled Sofer. "If you say so...."

They crested a summit. The forest gave way to short thick grass. For hours, they twisted in and out of valleys, sometimes passing through small, isolated villages. When they drove through, the inhabitants stopped to observe them with as much surprise as if they had been traveling in a flying saucer. Cows and sheep grazed on the hillsides. From time to time they would pass a man on horseback, a hoe over one shoulder, a leather gourd on a strap over the other. They saw hay wagons and women in heavy cloth dresses with scarves on their heads wielding long handled wooden pitchforks. Not only was Sofer ignorant of his own whereabouts, he felt as if he didn't even know which century he was in.

In the early afternoon, just after they crested another summit, Lazir stopped the vehicle. The valley they were about to enter opened in front of them, providing a fantastic view to the west. The boxing champ lifted a sports bag out of the rear door of the four by four and offered it to Sofer.

"There's something to eat inside. Sausage, cheese and fruit. Some wine, too. You are French, they thought that would please you!"

Sofer failed to ask who *they* were, and Lazir pulled a small pair of binoculars out of the bag. "We are only a short distance from the border," he explained. "I am going to see what's going on there."

He disappeared down the road as Sofer discovered how hungry he was. The wine was sweet and syrupy, as he had expected. An old woman's wine, he thought. He did, however, drink a fair quantity.

He was definitely making sure that nothing disturbed his newfound good humor. He felt like a child being taken for a surprise holiday. Half an hour later, Lazir reappeared. He nodded sagely in place of giving any direct report.

"Are you not going to eat?" Sofer asked him.

"I'll eat tonight, on the way. That's the best time."

A bit farther on, he left the road and steered onto a trail that descended to a wild looking river. They crossed a ford with some difficulty, the four by four slipping and sliding on the wet stones. Lazir didn't look worried at any stage. They climbed up the other bank, a slowly rising grassy slope, and continued over rolling fields for a mile or so. Finally, another road appeared, full of potholes and very dusty.

"Welcome to Georgia!" joked Lazir.

"We are here?"

"Ever since we crossed the river."

"Is this how the Chechen and Daghestani fighters slip from one country to the other?" asked Sofer.

Lazir shook his head. "No. They keep to the roads. They pay for their crossing, in dollars, to the customs men. It's simpler."

An hour later they reached a plain that was as dry as a desert. Fallow fields lay at the foot of the mountains. Sofer saw several churches in the distance, and a few dilapidated buildings, perhaps old factories or unused warehouses. The road became more and more prone to potholes. Even though it was straight, Lazir regularly had to slow the vehicle and sometimes drove along the edge of the road, which was more comfortable. Direction signs in Georgian appeared occasionally, half in Latin letters, half in Cyrillic, hung on rusty poles. Going round a bend, they saw about fifty people, men and women, spread out in a straight row, hoeing a field.

"There are no tractors left in Georgia," explained Lazir to a bemused Sofer. "No tractors, no trains, no factories ... nothing since the Civil War in 1993. In less than ten years it's as if they have returned to the last century."

The feeling of desolation lasted until they left the plains running along the feet of the Caucasus. Twice they passed through villages that seemed abandoned, not even seeing a cat or a chicken. At the entrance to a third, from under a rusty canopy of corrugated iron, some women followed their progress with their eyes, disconcerted at the sight of strangers. Lazir drove along the outside wall of a small chapel, in a street shaded by eucalyptus and bordered on the other side by low houses with beautiful zinc or carved wooden balconies. Then they left the village behind to bury themselves in the mountains.

Scarcely had the village disappeared in the driver's mirror than Lazir stopped the four by four. He fiddled in his pocket and pulled out a tube containing two tablets. "Sorry Mr. Sofer, you'll need to swallow these."

"What?"

"Sleeping pills, nothing bad."

"Lazir, this is ridiculous! I don't know where we are, I don't read Georgian! Whatever is written on these signs could be in Chinese for all I know…."

"Where we are going they will be in Russian," Lazir commented.

"Listen … I…."

"Those are my orders. Take the tablets and stretch out on the back seat. You will wake up fresh and full of life. I am sure you will be happy to see…."

"To see what? Who? Damnit, where are you taking me?"

"Do what I ask," Lazir appealed. "It is late, I'm fed up with your complaints and I want to get there before dark."

Sofer took the pills, swallowed them and opened the car door. There was nothing near them but bushes. He wondered what Lazir had meant: 'You will be happy to see…'

Not worth the trouble asking who … obviously, *her*!

As he started to nod sleepily, it came to him, dreamily: this four by four in which they had been traveling for hours was the same one that he had seen *her* climb into the night before last, in Baku airport.

"Well then, are you coming or am I going to have to force you to get in?" demanded Lazir, starting the engine.

Chapter twenty-five

Itil, October 955

We will be in Itil in two days. What are you going to do then? Nothing! You will wait, just like you did in Sarkel. You will gossip with that good-for-nothing rabbi, but the Khagan, he'll never see you! Waiting, that's all you know, Isaac! All this for a letter that contains only dreams and errors…. I should never have come with you. I should never have listened to Nathan the moneychanger when he suggested that I go with you! May the Almighty blessed be His name strike me down if I am blaspheming, but your Khagan of the Khazars is not the Messiah, and never will be! He is not even a true king of the Jews. Would a real king of the Jews have treated you like he did, half-killing you, locking you up, refusing to see you? And, while we are at it, would a king of the Jews offer his only sister as a present to the Christians? Just think about it, if you are capable of thinking anymore…."

"Saul…. Please!"

"No, it doesn't please me. Nothing pleases me. Above all, you don't please me, Isaac! You must have been mad to undertake this mission, and the blow to your head has done nothing to improve matters! The truth is that your Khagan Joseph is no more than a warlord who scatters nothing more important than goat droppings about the country. They're all the same, always ready to cut each other up! And always, first, us Jews! That's the truth! I ask you, what use is this letter that you hug to your chest as if you want to replace your heart with it? Why do you persist in wanting this false Jew to read it, this man who doesn't want to read it, whose rabbi has ordered him to read it, yet he hasn't listened? I ask myself what I, a merchant, am doing here, other than wasting my time and my savings? I buy nothing, I sell nothing, and each day I remain here I become poorer than Job! That's what's happening! And all the while I'm mocked by Lord Isaac! He just replies by shrugging his shoulders. It doesn't matter to him if we are trespassing as long as we accomplish his precious mission...."

"Shut up, Saul!"

"No, I won't! I've got as much to say about you, Simon. It's not just that you've got the gumption of a donkey turning the wheel at a well, it's that I have had more than a bellyful of you venerating these damn savages around us. Have a good look! Look at these Khazars! Do you think they are Jews, with their Asiatic eyes, Hun mustaches, Chinese weapons and boots from way up north? Have you seen how they eat, without even draining the blood from their meat?"

"Shut up, Saul!"

Simon's words echoed so loudly over the noise of hooves that all around them the Khazar warriors turned en masse in their saddles, hands ready on their swords. Scarlet with anger, Simon paid no attention to the soldiers and repeated, hardly any quieter, "Shut up, or I'll rip your belly open, here and now!"

"There's no use arguing," Isaac intervened, trying to make peace, "especially since there is a lot of sense in what Saul said."

All three fell silent, eyes riveted on a wooded hillside overlooking the river. The twilight was illuminating its edges with a shade of molten copper. Most of the Khagan's forces were more than half a league ahead, no doubt already dismounted and preparing their tents for the night. The three travelers would have to content themselves, as they had each evening, with lying down near the rear-guard fires, with only the moon in the sky for cover. For the thousandth time, Isaac glanced at the chain that joined the bridles of their mounts. At least they weren't chained themselves, though their horses were, although that was certainly no less humiliating and equally as effective.

Everything had happened with great rapidity. After having seen the boat carrying Attex disappear, Isaac was taken to Sarkel where he had hoped to rejoin his companions.

He had hardly reached the first tents when a group of cavalry, lances at the ready, encircled him. He had no difficulty recognizing the chief of the Khagan's guard leading them, the one who had wounded him on his arrival. This time the Khazar contented himself by giving him a slap on the back with the flat of his sword.

Isaac pulled the medallion given to him by Attex out of his belt, the one that was supposed to give him unimpeded access to the fortress. He brandished it in the officer's face. The result was completely the opposite of what he had expected. The chief of the guards grabbed it, shouting. By the furious look on his face, Isaac realized the guard took him for a thief. Unfortunately, Jew or not, the Khazar officer did not understand one word of Hebrew. In spite of all his efforts, Isaac could not make himself understood. Without further ado he was escorted, steel lance points at his back, into the great courtyard of Sarkel. His surprise was complete when he discovered Saul and Simon sweating under the sun, chains around their ankles. His two companions were so petrified with terror that they didn't even look relieved to see him again.

In a few whispered words, they explained to him that at dawn a troupe of archers, as fearsome as those who had immobilized the convoy on their arrival near the town, had invaded the place where the foreigners were enclosed, where the boatmen and merchants were sleeping spread out on the ground. The archers had questioned the men of commerce and the sailors blanched with fear. It did not take long before fingers were pointed at Saul and Simon. After which, within moments, they found themselves chained up like murderers.

Isaac did not have time to answer their frantic questions. A giant of a man appeared in the courtyard. He wore a magnificent helmet, encrusted with engraved silver, lined with purple silk, with a velvet flap hanging at the nape of his neck. His mustache was nearly as long as the pigtail that hung down his back. His face seemed to be made of the same metal as the plates sewn onto his leather coat. Upon his appearance, the archers stopped their chatter, and stood respectfully at attention. Their officer ran toward this lordly personage, bowed, then fell to one knee. Isaac had no problem identifying he whom Hezekiah had spoken of with such admiration; the Beck Borouh, great chief of the Khazar warriors, was favoring them with a visit!

Borouh was at least a head taller than Isaac. He approached very close, looking him up and down as if wishing to reduce him to dust. Isaac noticed that he had a six-pointed star that some Oriental Jews called the Star of David hung around his neck. As the silence continued, and as he had not yet turned to dust, Isaac spoke first.

"I am Isaac ben Eliezer," he announced with as much strength as he could muster. "I am the envoy of the Grand Rabbi of Cordoba and in accordance with that, the ambassador of the Sephardi Jews. These two whom you have so shamefully chained are named Saul and Simon. Together we have traveled for a whole year across half the world in order to meet Khagan Joseph, to whom I must deliver a letter."

The Beck smiled frostily. His lips revealed perfect teeth, something very rare for a man of his age. Like a magician, he made the medallion Attex had given to Isaac appear between two of his fingers. "It appears that you have met the Kathum Attex, Isaac ben Eliezer," he remarked in a grave voice, using labored Hebrew. "This medallion belongs to her. Would you prefer me to think that she gave it to you, or that you stole it?"

"I know the Kathum. She cared for me with great attention when I was wounded by him," replied Isaac, pointing at the chief of the guards.

"I know that," snapped the Beck. "Don't take me for an imbecile, traveler. The Kathum fled from the fortress. She disobeyed our Khagan and risks death. But you, did you see her last night? I only need to look at you to know. Those clothes you are wearing come from factories in our capital. The Kathum gave them to you, didn't she?"

Isaac did not answer and did his best not to blush. The Beck took a step closer. Isaac could smell his sweat and the odor of warm metal and leather from his breastplate and cloak. Borouh raised the piece of silver.

"You must tell me where the Kathum is. If not, I will have you roasted like a chicken!"

Saul and Simon could only look on in amazement. Isaac, however, thought he could see a slight glimmer of amusement in the eyes of the Beck, a sign that perhaps the words were harder than the intent. Therefore, he replied in a cool, calm voice, "It is useless to search for the Kathum, my Lord Beck. She will not marry the Greek from Byzantium. She will not deny the Law of Moses and God's commandments to lie in a Gentile's bed. The Khagan should receive and listen to me instead of threatening me. His duty to the Almighty demands that he hear what I have to say!"

The Beck let out a curious sound, somewhere between a whistle and a groan, a laugh and a sigh. His icy smile reappeared. He threw a glance at the surrounding warriors as if to reassure himself that they would obey if needed. "This is a traveler who does not lack courage! But first the Khagan and I are going to slay the Russians, then I will deal with you."

"I won't tell you where the Kathum is, even if you do roast me!" declared Isaac. "The Lord will welcome me into His bosom!"

This time the Beck burst out laughing. "It's good to listen to you. I hope you're not just bragging."

"I want to see Rabbi Hanania!" Isaac demanded, vexed.

"I wouldn't in your place, Isaac ben Eliezer. I would want nothing to do with him! The rabbi left the fortress last night in a cart. He is on his way to Itil. Do you know that he too disobeyed the Khagan by letting you escape yesterday?"

"A rabbi can only disobey the Almighty!" Isaac spat, to have the last word.

And that is how they, in their turn, left Sarkel, all three on poor, chained horses, surrounded by a group of the rear guard of the royal army, not one of whom understood Hebrew, or even Saul's Russian.

⛭

For three days of hard riding, from the first light of dawn until nightfall, they trekked across the immense, flat steppe, continually battered by a dust-laden wind. At each encampment they had to accept the rough manners of the warriors without comment. They slept under the stars. In the desert, it quickly became cold, despite the incandescent heat of the day, and they found it difficult to sleep. To pass the long hours of darkness, Isaac told his companions of his entry into the fortress and all that had happened thereafter, or almost all, veiling the truth of his night with Attex under a white lie.

Simon had asked him several times to repeat his description of the princess's beauty. The descriptions Isaac gave enraptured him. But Saul just sank into a worse and worse mood.

"Beautiful or not, what good will it do us? You helped her to escape, sticking your nose into something that was none of your business! If this King of the Khazars is short of a reason to do away with us whenever he fancies, that would be a thousand times enough! You only think of yourself, Isaac, as always! It's a good enough reason for you to let the Khazars roast you for saving that girl. But me?!"

"Saul," protested Simon, tears in his eyes, "the princess did what the rabbi told her. She is as full of courage as she is beautiful, doing what every right-thinking Jewish woman would have done in her place. Would you want to see her in some Greek's bed in Constantinople? Don't you remember how my wife died at the hands of the Christians?"

"I am truly very sorry for you, my friend," Saul replied dryly, "but she wasn't the first and she won't be the last. Is there any reason why all the Jews in the world should burn at the stake in memory of her?"

Isaac could not think of a quick reply, or perhaps, he thought of too many, and he could not find the strength or the desire to express them. Truly, although he had already committed himself previously, he again put himself entirely in the hands of the Almighty.

More than ever, what he had said to Attex when she was in his arms seemed true. Perhaps it was out of folly, or delirious love, but he still bore with him, indelible, deep inside, the supernatural beauty of the princess. And that grace could be nothing else than the living memory of the Almighty in human beings, His honey from Eden, His hand and His gaze, His voice and His sweetness. How could he explain to Saul that he was sure that this faith, this complete love, could protect them better than all the archers and armor of the Khazars? What would happen that terrible night would certainly prove it.

⁂

That evening, as usual, the Khazar cavalry dismounted from their horses as soon as darkness obscured their view of the steppe. A little earlier they had come round a wooded hill and met the banks of the Atel. It was a river like no other Isaac had seen, so wide and smooth at this point that one could hardly see the other side. It could easily be mistaken for a lake, shimmering under the perpetual wind off the steppe—the Wind of the Khazars that raised whirlwinds of dust in the air. Oddly, they could see no boats, no sails, nothing afloat.

Was it the proximity of the river, the capital men said was near, or the rumors about the Russians? The Khazar cavalrymen, normally so sure of themselves, almost seemed nervous. When they set foot to ground, they did so in silence, unlike the previous nights. Half a league ahead, the campfires of the Khagan were already reddening in the mounting darkness. There, the warriors had the right to raise tents and light as many braziers as they wished. The rear guard had to content itself with decoy fires composed of a half dozen logs lit at intervals around the encampment. The cavalrymen used them to cook a little food and boil water for their tea, but nobody slept near them. Sentries fueled them through the night. Their lights were designed to attract would-be attackers, to lure them to the wrong place where they could be more easily attacked themselves.

Isaac and his companions had scarcely sat down, awaiting their meager allowance of food, when they heard shouts and movement at the head of their position. They saw the silhouette of a cavalryman trying to make his way through. The Khazar soldiers ran forward to stop him but immediately fell back, saluting him respectfully. Isaac suddenly recognized him. He stood up, amazed.

"Hezekiah!"

"Isaac!"

Quite as stunned as the warriors around them, Saul and Simon saw the son of the Khagan push his mount forward toward them and jump down from his saddle like a dancer, to envelop Isaac in a fraternal embrace.

"Is it true that you have seen Attex?" he questioned. "Did you see her?"

"Yes, she's fine!" replied Isaac prudently, not thinking too much about the truth.

"She's not going to marry the Greek?" Hezekiah persisted.

"No chance!"

"Ah, that's good!"

Isaac introduced his friends to the prince. Hezekiah pointed at the river and without taking a breath, said, "The Russians will attack soon!"

"Soon! How soon? Tomorrow?"

"No! Not tomorrow, this evening. They like to start war at night in order to use the element of surprise, and now, with their *Greek Fire...*!"

Isaac and his companions scanned the sky to the west. Darkness had already swallowed everything and the fires were glowing brightly. There was no way of telling what lay over a hundred cubits away. The Khazar warriors did not seem to be preparing for an attack, but all the same, quite a few had not removed the saddles from their tired mounts.

"Are you sure?" Isaac asked, sitting back down on a blanket and inviting Hezekiah to join him.

"I heard Borouh telling my father," replied Hezekiah, whispering. "He told him there are thousands of Russians, on horseback and in boats, just to the north."

"But that's not possible!" protested Saul. "Before night fell we could see for leagues over the steppe and it was empty. Just like the river!"

Hezekiah shook his head and replied, very seriously. "You must believe it. We can't see them because they are so good at concealing themselves, but the Beck has spies among them. He always works that way with the Russians, that's why everyone is afraid of him. My father and the Beck decided long ago to do it that way." Hezekiah looked at Isaac as if he was ashamed of this strategy. "Over there, they are ready. The archers are already mounted. That's how cunning the Beck is. He often acts this way, sacrificing his rear guard as bait before catching the Russians in his trap.

Saul and Simon threw fearful glances into the darkness around them.

"At this very minute, the Russians are watching us," added Hezekiah. "They are saying to each other that the whole royal guard is like this, making soup for supper...."

The noise of cooking utensils being stirred rose above laughter and the chatter of gossip. Goats were turning on spits, roasting on flames fanned by the guards. Fifty warriors were stationed close to the river's edge. Their plaintive chanting could just be heard. Isaac, surprised, realized, despite what he had previously thought, that they were chanting in Hebrew.

"Does your father know that we risk being massacred with his rear guard?" Saul asked bitterly.

Hezekiah acknowledged his question with a nod. "He is very angry with Isaac. He says that the Almighty Himself can decide your fate."

"Not much use wasting any more time then," Isaac said. "Move! Go! Move down to the river bank and follow it to the Khagan's camp."

"Why? How?" objected Saul. "Our horses are chained to the soldiers mounts…"

"On foot! Nobody will think you are trying to escape. Besides, nobody is watching us…"

"What about you?" asked Simon.

"I will go with Hezekiah to be near his father."

"I could try to get another horse," interjected Hezekiah. "That way you…." The Khagan's son didn't have time to finish his sentence. An unbelievable clamor, so terrifying it was as if the dark sky had split asunder, petrified them. There followed a brief silence, then the uproar erupted again. The Khazar warriors in their turn started to shout, brandishing their weapons, calling to one another to organize a front.

Once again the tremendous noise stupefied them, as if a thousand wolves were howling at once. They came out of the darkness, coming from nowhere and everywhere all at once, then they diminished. Isaac could hear the clash of pikes against breastplates.

The Khazars had extinguished almost half of the fires. The rest darkened down as the fanning stopped.

"Over there!" cried Hezekiah. "Look over there!" He pointed a finger at the hill and the shadows of the forest.

Like demons springing from nowhere, the Russian hordes rushed at them. Silhouettes in the night, they galloped forward, swords bared. The dim light of the rising moon reflected off their blades and helmets.

"The Russians!" muttered Simon, incredulous. "The Russians...."

Through the soles of his fine boots, Isaac could feel the vibration of the earth hammered by hundreds of hooves.

Hezekiah rushed to seize his horse's bridle, in case the chaos scared him and he would run off.

"Run," Isaac shouted to Saul and Simon. "Run to the river! Quick! Hurry!" he shouted, but a group of Khazar warriors, in their hurry to form a front, bumped roughly into them, and Saul received a savage blow that floored him.

At the very instant he stood up again, a terrible buzzing filled the air.

"Arrows!" shouted Hezekiah. "Try to avoid the arrows!"

The buzzing transformed itself into a hail of iron and death. Cries rang out all around them. One arrow with white feathers hit the ground only a couple of paces from Simon, who yelled. Hezekiah gripped Isaac's hand. The Khazar soldiers were crouched down behind their shields. When they were hit, some shields broke, while others deflected the arrows to do their damage elsewhere.

"My horse!" cried Hezekiah.

The beast was rearing and bucking in terror, lashing out with its hooves to such good effect that it had smashed one Khazar warrior's ribs.

"Hezekiah, take his shield!" Isaac called, flinging himself at the horse to catch its reins. Eyes staring, the beast tried to bite Isaac, but somehow he managed to grasp the long leather strap that was whipping through the air and pulled on it with all his might. At his back, he could still hear the noise of the Russians, this time much closer. While Hezekiah handed him the dead warrior's steel-covered shield, Isaac saw Simon watching him, eyes staring, incapable of moving.

"Don't stay there, Simon!" he begged. "Find a shield and run!"

The whistling of a new rain of arrows vibrated above their heads. Isaac squeezed Hezekiah next to him, kneeling in the shelter of the shield. He shut his eyes, putting himself in the hands of the Almighty. These were moments of hell; two, three, five times he felt the shock of iron points breaking on the metal of the shield. Others dug into the soil, or ricocheted, searching for more delicate flesh targets. Howls and cries of pain resounded all around.

Eventually the rain of death ceased. When he peered around the shield, Isaac saw two arrows less than a hand's breadth from his boot. Hezekiah, eyes wide with terror, trembled as if he had a fever.

"Saul, Saul...." Simon's shout rose above the new clamor of the Russians engaging the first lines of the Khazars in hand-to-hand battle.

"Saul!"

The merchant had completed the long journey to the Jewish Kingdom of the Khazars without having made one decent deal. An arrow was protruding from his left eye, having passed through his skull, knocking him over and pinning him to the ground. At least he had avoided suffering in agony. From that moment on, everything seemed to happen like a sort of nightmare, slow and inexorable, one that you want to wake up from, but you know you must endure until the end, for to wake is to die.

Isaac pulled Simon off Saul's body. He pushed him toward the river, shouting to him to find a horse. Hezekiah was already in his saddle, and Isaac jumped up behind him, holding the boy close.

Hardly had they reached the bank when they saw the charge of the royal guard cavalry. Some carrying torches, they galloped without holding their reins, advancing in a powerful line. Terrified, Isaac suddenly realized that they could not go north, where the Russians were ensconced, nor south from where reinforcements were coming. Holding tight to his shield and holding the reins of his nervous mount securely, he tried to sidle along the river's edge. Then the sky lit up.

A yellow flame flew from the river, forming a graceful curve and leaving a trail of stars behind. All the faces raised to the sky were illuminated, mouths open, cries strangled in their throats. The dragon's breath weighed heavily upon them. Then the ball of flame crashed on the plain, covering the combatants in sparks, transforming them instantly into golden silhouettes. Inhuman screams of pain emanated from the living torches.

"Greek Fire!" hissed Hezekiah, jumping down to find shelter behind his mount.

Still in the saddle and struggling to restrain the horse, Isaac saw two new balls of fire climbing to assault the sky. This time, with the night bathed in light, he saw the boats. Five Nordic longboats, rapid and maneuverable, each with two rows of oarsmen. In their prows the Russians had installed the deathly crossbows that could transform the sky and earth into fire.

The fire suddenly spread itself over the whole of the rear guard camp, even burning some Russian cavalrymen who had already arrived there. Expanding nearly to the banks of the Atel, the blazing flames left no way for Isaac and Hezekiah to pass.

The youngster dug his nails into Isaac's arm. "Look! Look!"

Swords flashing, the Khagan's cavalry, the Beck at their head, were coming around the fire. At full gallop, they did not stop to fight but charged on toward the boats. Isaac had to look away. An oily ball of fire burst less than one hundred and fifty feet away, sending a shower of sparks that quickly turned to blue flames on the water.

Isaac swung Hezekiah up behind him. "Hold on!" he shouted.

Whipping the horse's neck, he drove it into the river. To his surprise, the bank fell away steeply. The horse couldn't get his footing and started to float without trying to swim. Isaac slipped off the saddle into the icy water.

"I don't know how to swim," complained Hezekiah, half choked with fear.

"Hold on to my shoulders and keep your chin up!" shouted Isaac.

The cold gripped his chest, making him short of breath, then Greek Fire burst once more into the sky, warming his face. For a moment he tried to swim against the current, but he realized that it was better to allow himself to be carried along with it, so long as he kept near the bank. The explosions of fire all around them gradually decreased, but they were floating down the river more quickly than he had hoped. Isaac started swimming toward the bank, fighting to ensure that Hezekiah's weight did not sink them both. Heart laboring, Isaac felt the river bottom beneath his boots. They had just collapsed on the riverbank, out of breath, when Hezekiah shook him so that he turned around.

The Khazar archers had launched two salvoes of fire arrows at the Russian boats, tracing a line of light arcing from the river's edge to the center of the waterway. One boat burst into flames almost immediately. The fire on the deck spread to the barrels of naphtha. Everything exploded. An enormous ball of fire dilated violently, carrying away masts, seats and rows of oarsmen, throwing them like wisps of straw into the night. The hull split open like a walnut; a tongue of flame so pale that it appeared white, covered the surface of the water. A second boat exploded in its turn, and night became day. Isaac murmured a prayer. The Almighty had just saved the Jewish Kingdom of the Khazars.

Completely exhausted, shivering and dripping, Hezekiah turned to Isaac, smiling, and said, "Now that you have saved my life my father will have to see you and listen to you!"

Chapter twenty-six

W hen Sofer regained his senses, it was nearly nightfall. At least the thick darkness that enveloped him seemed to be that of night. Thirst tormented him as if he had just crossed a desert. His throat was almost sore. It was certainly that which had wakened him. He blinked, trying to pierce the darkness, listening for any noise that would tell him where he was. The silence, however, remained as impenetrable as the darkness. A sort of general exhaustion slowed his thinking processes as much as his tactile senses.

Under his touch, he felt the roughness of a thick blanket, perhaps linen. He spread his arms out, running his fingers over the length of the couch. His fingers encountered curious wooden sculptures. He tapped gently on the round bumps until he realized that they were the mountings on a four-poster bed. An old bed! The mattress was as hard as a plank of wood, but there was a blanket over his legs. Someone had taken care to remove his shoes. What was he doing here? How had he come here?

His furred mouth and a vague bitter taste reminded him of the sleeping tablets he had swallowed. Suddenly everything came back to him; the attack at Baku, the interminable journey through Georgia with Lazir, in the same four by four! *Hers!*

Her! Her, for sure! What had Lazir said? Eyes closed, Sofer searched his brain as if riffling through an untidy drawer. A smile hovered on his lips. 'You will be happy when you see her....' Yes, he remembered the words of the golden-toothed boxing champ perfectly. Anyway, where the devil was he? Sofer's mind started to function coherently, and slightly aggressively. He was angry at himself; he had accepted swallowing Lazir's drugs too easily. He thought about calling out, shouting, letting someone know he was awake, but the ridiculous nature of the situation held him back. He wasn't just going to call out in the dark like a child! Besides, call whom? After all, if the redheaded stranger had brought him here, waking him in the middle of the night, kidnapping him—well, almost—knocking him out with sleeping pills, it wasn't to get rid of him! He almost began to have doubts about whether this weird night had really happened, sitting alone in silence as if wrapped in cotton wool.

He sat up, his back straight. For a few moments he still had to fight against the tightness in his chest that was restricting his breathing. Thirst amplified his discomfort and oppressed him. "Damn!" he thought angrily. "That idiot gave me horse pills!" He pivoted to sit on the edge of the bed and put his feet on the floor. A light flickered in the darkness. At first he thought it a mirage, the result of his head swimming. He rubbed his temples, then his eyes, with clumsy fingers.

When he reopened them, he discovered that he had not been mistaken; in front of him, a few feet away, a yellow light was giving out irregular beams that were being swallowed up quickly by the darkness. Without thinking any more, he stood up, on still uncertain legs. He could feel the cool dusty surface of the stone under his feet. Cautiously, arms extended in front, he walked toward the light. What he discovered made him smile.

In a sort of vaulted alcove, a flaming torch as long as his arm was fixed in an iron ring. The flame was very low. It gave off a slightly rancid odor and light just sufficient to illuminate a copper bowl, a thick cloth, and an earthenware jug, atop a heavy wooden table. Behind it he could discern a curved white wall with small masonry supports holding a basin. Sofer walked up close. He saw his own reflection in the water, and broke the surface with one hand as if to break the mirage. He splashed his face and drew up water with cupped hands, drinking deeply without stopping to think if it were safe. Straightening up, he found he was completely out of breath. He picked up the towel from the table. The soft touch of a hotel bath towel would have been preferable; the cloth he held in his hands was rough and scraped his face like wire wool. Using it as gently as he could, Sofer noticed a design woven into the material, a seven branched candelabra with some signs and letters beneath it. The same design and letters as on the coin Yakubov had given him!

He laughed and thought, marvelous stagecraft! Suddenly he grasped what had been circling through his mind since he awoke. The cave! He was in the cave of the Khazars! That was where Lazir had brought him, that's why he had been drugged. The famous cave! But what a way to set the scene! He laughed again. He felt better. He was no longer thirsty, the oppressive tightness in his chest had disappeared. So she had a sense of humor as well as mystery. Preening slightly, he reflected that he did not know any other woman who had gone to such lengths to seduce him. The memory of the explosion in the port at Baku flashed through his mind and brought him back to reality. No, it was not for games of love that he had been transported here.

However, since he had apparently been invited to undertake his ablutions in this simple, ancient manner, he felt duty bound to continue, removing his shirt and energetically splashing his chest and neck over the basin. He wondered what his beard must look like. It was prickly, rough and uncomfortable. He looked at the shelf underneath the table. There was a piece of soap near the copper bowl, but no razor, or shaving soap. She hadn't thought of everything. The old towel was not very absorbent. He gave up and clothed his still damp body. Then he lifted the torch from its ring and crossed the room to the bed. In the meager light, he discovered that the room was round, although not perfectly so. It was empty apart from the bed, with its enormous canopy, and the table. The room narrowed into a sort of corridor leading to a dark wooden door.

It took him longer than usual to put his shoes on. He struggled with his laces with one hand while holding the burning torch high with the other, to avoid burning his face. When he finally approached the door, he could feel his heart rate increase. He was frightened the door might be locked—but it was not. The heavy paneled wood swung open with a single push. Sofer found himself in a corridor as shadowy as the room he had just left. To his right, a flight of worn stairs rose up from the white rock and disappeared into the darkness. Sofer decided to take the opposite direction and continued following the corridor. After a few more steps, the corridor turned at a right angle and light flooded in. A few more steps and he was outside in the fresh air. This time, his surprise was absolute. The beauty of what he saw astounded him.

He was standing on a platform only seven or eight feet wide, cut out of the side of a huge cliff. Spread out at his feet were folds of wooded hills covered in variegated green. Beyond, to the south, a long valley displayed chalky, desert-like fields. Ignoring a touch of vertigo, Sofer moved to the edge of the platform. Feeling like a bird in flight, he looked over a one hundred and fifty foot drop to the carpet of green-leafed branches at the foot of the cliff. Around him the rock appeared as smooth as skin, some bits white, others ochre, all striated with moist trickles. When he finally deciphered the strange chaos of shapes surrounding him, it took his breath away.

He realized that a huge area of the cliff face, perhaps fifty by three hundred feet, was sculpted like an immense mural. Dozens of caves opened into the side of the mountain. Some possessed wooden doors, and gray barriers that had been burnt by the sun and washed by the rain. Some had balconies with balustrades, some displayed verandas roofed with tiles. They were all connected by an intricate network of vertiginous stairways and passages. Where Sofer stood, a double staircase led to upper and lower platforms. It wasn't just a cave but a whole town that had been dug out of the chalk. Here and there, hanging onto the very edge of the sheer rock and dazzling in their grace, appeared actual house façades, similar to those Sofer had seen in Quba. Enormous vaults surrounded them, flaring deep into the rock behind. There was no regularity, rather an impression of disorder, a little mad, something like the labyrinthine vision presented by a termite mound unexpectedly cut in two. Above that, a thousand feet of rock took the cliff to its crest, so high that it seemed to disappear in the already darkening blue of the heavens. Short of breath, Sofer retreated a few steps.

He did not know exactly where he was, but he was sure he was somewhere in the Caucasus, about half way up to the highest peaks. His gaze shifted to the strangely dry valley beyond the forest. From down there it would be impossible to see the open caves in the cliff. They would disappear in the natural shadows of the rocks. Doubtless too, in the age of the Khazars, the forest would have been even greater than now, covering a goodly part of the valley, hiding this strange troglodyte city perfectly.

The whistling of swallows made him jump. The birds flew in tight groups, cutting violent arabesques close to the tree tops, snapping up a few insects brought out by the evening warmth. Sofer watched the sun descending toward the mountainous horizon, lengthening shadows and setting peaks aflame. How long had he slept? If his memory was correct, it had been getting dark when Lazir had given him his sleeping pills. Had he really slept for twenty-four hours? It did seem so—no wonder he had felt so awful upon awakening!

Sofer checked to see if he could identify the path that had led them here to the heart of this town. He hadn't noticed it when he first took in the view, swamped as it was by the vast horizon and hidden by the jumble of chaotic rock. Now the slanting twilight rays of the sun revealed it through a trick of the light. A whole curtain of rock, like a knife pointing to the sky, hung over the side of the cliff, opening up an empty space of forty to fifty feet below. On the point stood a well-designed building, open on all sides, very old and reminiscent of a Greek temple. Its double sloped roof, covered in slabs of chalk dotted with lichen, rested on a colonnade of twenty columns topped by little Doric caps. On the pediment, traces of bas-relief and round lumps were visible even though very worn and polished by centuries of intemperate weather. A wooden bridge with carved handrails joined the rear of this imitation temple to the first of the stairways that led, through perilous elevations, to the very platform where Sofer stood.

Sofer recognized that what he was seeing was both the gateway and the key to the troglodyte city. He guessed that winding behind the colonnades of the temple there must be a sort of drawbridge like one used to bring passengers off small boats at a wharf. Thus the occupants of the town could cut all links with the outside world at will. When the bridge was withdrawn, people who arrived uninvited at the end of the road would have no option other than to cool their heels thinking about the way they had been deceived. Better still, the narrow width and slope of the road made attack in large numbers impossible, and the use of arrows impracticable. Yet archers situated in the temple or postern gate would have all the time in the world to wipe out any imprudent invaders trapped in the path with no exit.

A town as secret as it was impregnable! That's why it had survived the centuries and still remained a mystery. And that's how he, Marc Sofer, suddenly found himself a model prisoner here!

The strong twilight lit up the crests opposite, making them glow purple and pushing the shadows into the valley like a dark sea. The beauty of the place acquired a disturbing depth. Emotion flooded Sofer's mind. What he was looking at was what the Khazars would have seen! If he were guessing correctly, the Kathum Attex herself had climbed this path one day long ago. Was imagination not always just the borrowing of a long-hidden truth? A throbbing sound brought him back down to earth. Far away in the reddening sunset, he could make out a helicopter, the noise growing as he watched it. For a moment Sofer thought it was heading straight for the cliff and wondered whether someone was searching for him, if the pilot could see him, if he ought to show himself or, the opposite, hide in the interior of the cave.

He was not given time to choose. The machine slowed, and hung above the forest, strangely immobile like some great clumsy insect. Sofer tried in vain to make out whether it was a military machine. He was certain they could not be very far from the frontier between Georgia and Chechnya…. Suddenly the helicopter swung round and, in the blink of an eye, disappeared to the north. The deafening noise of its departure was followed by the flight of swallows and clouds of bats. For the first time, Sofer became aware of his absolute solitude, and felt a little anxious. Nobody appeared to be worrying about him. *She* was not worried about him. Where was Lazir? Were they trying to frighten him by leaving him like this? Was it a game, as he still preferred to believe, or was he actually a prisoner? In a flash he recalled all the articles he had read on the numerous kidnappings in which the Caucasus had played center stage. Still, he couldn't really bring himself to be worried. When Lazir had picked him up in Baku, not for an instant had he seriously thought he was being kidnapped. No more than he felt any fear now, at any rate.

Something happened to him at that moment, something both extraordinary and marvelous. Something he had dreamed of ever since becoming a writer. He suddenly felt he had arrived at the heart of the story he had started to write some weeks previously, here in this nameless place petrified in memory and time. Unwittingly, by sheer chance, or destiny, he had somehow been deposited in the cave he had imagined and strived to describe since first putting pen to paper in Oxford. Now here he was, and he could stretch out and touch the rock. He looked around him at the daylight now mixing with night; and what he saw did not belong to the present day, but to the far away millennium of the Khazars.

He didn't need to think about it; there was no need to write the words on paper or on his computer screen. Princess Attex, Isaac ben Eliezer and Joseph the Khagan were real, and here. He was breathing the same air they had. He was listening to the same silence, the same swallows' cries, the same breeze rustling. It was enough for him to lower his gaze to the temple gate, to see the Khazar warriors hailing the little troupe that was hurrying to reach the end of the road beside the cliff before nightfall rendered it dangerous. Bows were already raised and arrow points directed at the new arrivals. The drawbridge, tied to a ring on the wall by a thick hemp rope, was raised.

The chief of the guards came up behind an archer and shouted, "Who goes there?"

It was Attex herself who answered. "I am Attex, daughter of

Aaron, sister to the Khagan Joseph and Khatum of the Kingdom of the Khazars!"

The echo of her voice rebounded off the cliff and seemed for an instant suspended in the cool night air. The chief of the guards was briefly silent; Sofer could sense his embarrassment. The man glanced quickly up toward the top of the cliff, as if he hoped for assistance, just as Sofer heard a scuffing of feet, a rustling of cloth behind him.

"Who is with you?" the chief guard eventually asked.

"Can't you see?" Attex replied, annoyed.

"I must ask, those are my orders!"

"Lower the drawbridge immediately!" Attex insisted. "Are you waiting till we break our necks on this road?"

"It's past the time for the evening prayer, I am under orders not to let anyone into the town!" the guard replied.

Sofer heard the roar of anger from Attania, who was waving her arms in the direction of the temple. "Lower that bridge, fool! You can see who we are!"

"That's Attania, my servant, who just spoke!" shouted Attex. "And you can see there are only five soldiers with me! Officer, we have been on the road for three weeks since we left Sarkel, and we are exhausted! If you are in any doubt, call my uncle Hanuko, since it is he who gives you your orders. But hurry up! It's getting dark!"

Sofer heard a laugh close behind him. Hanuko appeared beside him, draped in the long cloak of the Khazars, a gold chain around his neck, long white hair brushed out impeccably. In a clear voice, loud for one of his age, he said, "What's this niece, why are you making so much noise?"

"Oh, uncle!"

"Greetings Kathum! May the Lord be blessed for this wonderful surprise!"

"The surprise will not be wonderful, Uncle, if they don't let us over the bridge! We can't see an inch in front of us down here! I can't see where I'm putting my feet!"

Hanuko laughed again. At the same moment, another laugh made Sofer jump.

"Good evening, Mr. Sofer," said a soft, feminine voice.

He pivoted on his heels. And he saw her. It was *her*, Attex! Ten years older, perhaps, red hair held back with a small scarf, dressed in jeans and a large sweater. In her hand she held the torch that Sofer had left at the cave entrance.

"Good God! It *is* you!" he exclaimed. "I wondered if you were ever going to turn up!"

She laughed. "I've been standing behind you for some time now, Mr. Sofer, but you seemed so absorbed in your daydream! If I hadn't been afraid that you might fall off the edge of the platform, I would have left you to it."

Sofer felt a little dizzy, a dizziness that had no connection with the abyss plunging through the darkness at his side. His mouth was dry, his heart beating fast. He had woken in a mysterious forest and like a fairy tale, the princess had appeared. No humor, no self-control could moderate how he felt. It was *her*, the woman who had occupied his thoughts since the conference in Brussels some weeks before.

She was just as he remembered her, with the same slightly slanted green eyes and high cheekbones, moist lips, and hair a shade of red that accentuated the milky-white paleness of her skin. Hair that had not ceased to occupy his mind, representing this young woman whose image he had carried with him ever since, in everything he did, thought, and felt. The only difference between that woman, and the one who was even now walking toward him—an amused smile on her lips, hand outstretched—was that she was real!

Sofer remained paralyzed for an instant. Reacting like an automaton, he felt the cool touch of her hand and fingers against his own. He felt as if by that simple touch, she had completely absorbed him.

"I can see that you like this place," she said.

"Attex! You are Attex and you are *real!*"

She laughed and withdrew her hand to push back a lock of her hair. "No," she protested, smiling. "My name is Sonja Tchoban-zade."

Sofer smiled in accord. "Yes, of course, but to me you are Attex! I now know that you have been since the beginning."

"You must be hungry!" she remarked. As Sofer did not answer, she added with a light throaty laugh, "I am sorry. Lazir made a mistake with the dose. You slept for a whole day and night."

That he had slept a hell of a long time, Sofer did not doubt. What was less certain was whether he was now awake. The woman he had instinctively called Attex walked in front of him, holding the torch high. Currents of air wafted past, sometimes from their right, sometimes from above, as if they were at the bottom of a well. His hostess led him through a labyrinth of narrow corridors with the easy assurance of the mistress of a house showing it off to a visitor.

"I have prepared a little meal for you," she offered in the same melodious tone. "But before that, I want to show you something."

Her voice echoed from the high-vaulted ceiling. She walked with animal grace. The light of the torch, glancing off her shoulder and the nape of her neck, projected her moving shadow on the rock wall. From time to time she shifted her body, accentuating her figure, lifting her bust, emphasizing the tender curves of her breasts under her sweater. The enveloping silence of the rock was broken by the rustling of her clothes and her soft footfalls. It seemed to Sofer that he could even hear the flesh of her body. He was seized with an emotion he had nearly forgotten; the pull of desire. She was taking him out of his world. He continued to walk behind her, but on another plane he was completely inside his own imagination, transported by the sensuality of the moment. Each step she took before him, each time his arm brushed her side, invaded his consciousness. Her manner in avoiding an unexpectedly low rock ceiling, tipping her head to one side, the swaying of her hips, the gentle rasp of her breath … he tried to stop himself, finding his excitement ridiculous, but found himself increasingly subject to his desires.

"Careful," she warned him, "the steps here are a bit uneven."

A large staircase stretched out before them. They went up it side by side. As they climbed the stairs, Sofer saw they were approaching a much bigger space, poorly lit by a dozen torches. The smell of naphtha became stronger and stronger. Just before reaching the last step, he stopped.

He was standing at the entrance to an immense grotto, so huge that the vault of the ceiling disappeared in darkness, as if dissolving into the sky. In the open space before him, three buildings stood around a central courtyard. Real buildings of carefully sculpted and plastered stone walls, with roofs tiled as if built to stand in the open under the skies, and not in the heart of a mountain. Torches illuminated the whole without really dissipating the weight of the shadows. The front of the nearest building was composed of pillars supporting a triangular façade with huge doors beneath. Sofer could just see that the latter were covered in magnificently worked carvings representing the Tablets of the Law. It was the entrance to the synagogue! So the secret synagogue really did exist!

In his wonder at what he beheld he must have exclaimed out loud, because he heard his own voice echo from the roof of the grotto. The young woman turned to him, watching him kindly. "Come on," she said, "it's not a dream!"

In the light of the torch, the green of her eyes became clearer and her mouth rounder. Sofer searched for words, for an amusing anecdote to break the foolish muteness that had sealed his mouth. Nothing came to mind. He nodded and followed her. Even though the synagogue door was as thick as a man's arm, it opened easily. Its hinges hardly made a sound.

It took Sofer several moments before he realized what he was looking at. He felt paralyzed by amazement. The interior of the building was octagonal. Vast tapestries of green or faded blue covered the walls. Some were torn or had been slightly singed by the candelabras placed every few feet along the walls. At the center of the room was a piece of furniture that he recognized but which he had never seen before, even as a reproduction. It resembled a tall, large, gray wooden chest or cabinet, with handles coming out at both sides, standing on small feet. His heart pounding, he advanced toward it. It was, really and truly, an ark from Biblical times! Then he heard from behind him, "*They will make, then, an ark from the wood of an acacia tree.... You will cover it with pure gold.... You will make four rings on one of its sides.... You will make bars of acacia wood and you will cover them in gold. You will introduce the bars into the rings at its side to carry the ark with them....*"

"Exodus!" murmured Sofer. "The ark described in Exodus!"

He stretched out his arm, sliding his fingers timidly over the old wood, hard and smooth as metal. On top of each side of the ark were sculptures, damaged, cut or broken, representing small human figures. He smiled and said in his turn, *"Make a Cherubim for one end and a Cherubim for the other end..."*

"Yes!" she agreed, with a slight nod of her head. "An ark constructed strictly in accordance with the description given in Exodus. In acacia wood, and with the exact dimensions: two and a half cubits long, one and a half cubits width and height."

"I suppose it's true," Sofer thought aloud, "that the Khazars would have had the same needs as the original twelve tribes of Israel. Like them, they were always on the move. The whole steppe was their synagogue. They couldn't place the Torah in a fixed piece of furniture but in an ark they could carry with them."

"And when they became more sedentary, they would have preserved a custom that had become sacred for them," she concluded. "But look over here. Along the wooden transport poles as well as on all sides of the ark there is a series of small holes aligned, two by two, like sewing holes in cloth. That was where clips held the gold leaf," she explained. "The ark must have been totally covered in gold like it says in the Bible. That would explain why the Cherubim are in such bad condition—someone ruined them when they took the gold plating...."

While she spoke, Sofer was looking around, open mouthed, unable to stop himself repeating like a child, "I am in a Biblical synagogue, I am in a Biblical synagogue!"

Delicately, he pulled on the small wooden pin holding the foot-high door of the ark closed. To his great disappointment there was nothing but dust inside. But of course, it would be stupid to believe that a Torah scroll could have survived there for a thousand years.

She smiled, sparkling with fun. "The ark is empty, but this is not the end of your tour! Come on, follow me...."

He noted the pride in her voice, along with a self-confidence that surprised him, as if she had repeated this performance many times and had foreseen most of his reactions. He had to admit to himself that in other circumstances he would have already objected out of principle, demanding to explore such an extraordinary place at his own pace. He contented himself with smiling and admiring the grace of her neck gilded by her gorgeous red hair.

They crossed the courtyard to enter into the building closest to the synagogue. Inside was one long, low room. The walls were about seven feet high with several alcoves in them. With the ease of habit, the young woman lit some oil lamps that were laid out on a plank that was gray with dust, and gnawed away by rodents here and there. Suddenly illuminated out of the darkness, Sofer saw ten great chests banded with metal, silver or polished steel, high-backed chairs in sculpted wood, and some plain benches. Carpets rolled up, stacked in piles, boxes heaped near one wall, a jumble of casks, old blankets, wooden and copper buckets....

Walking forward to the center of the room, Sofer suddenly recoiled in surprise; inside one alcove was a collection of lances, bows and quivers of arrows. Many of them seemed in good condition, even the color of the feathers were clearly discernible. Sofer went nearer, but the contents of the next alcove caught his attention; two saddles, hundreds of spears glittering in the lamplight, and swords and scabbards leaning against the wall.

With a gasp of excitement he moved forward to touch the rough dry surface of the saddles. They had small silver plaques embossed and covered in thick blue cloth, and no pommels. The undersides were in brown linen lined with leather, and sounded like dry wood when tapped. Sofer jumped, hearing a squeak behind him. Attex had opened one of the chests. She reached in to pull out a silvery disk, which she handed to Sofer.

"I suppose you recognize this?" she asked.

It was a coin, as large as the hollow of his palm, heavier and thicker than the one he had. Sofer grasped it with emotion, guessing what he was going to see: the seven-branched candelabra, strange characters, and on the obverse, the Star of David. He searched in his jacket pocket to bring out the coin Yakubov had given him. Apart from the differences in size and weight, they were identical. Attex lowered her torch and he could see that the bottom of the chest was covered with hundreds of identical coins.

"Yakubov didn't get them all," she remarked, mockingly. "He was content with the small ones!"

Sofer laughed nervously. "I take it you know Yakubov, then?"

She nodded, amused. "Be patient for just a little longer, I will explain everything…." With a circular motion of the torch, she indicated the space surrounding them. "This was a guard room, probably for Khazar officers, but we think the rabbis may have used it as well. It seems that through the ages it has become some sort of hiding place, or secret warehouse. The weapons don't all date from the Khazar period, some are much more recent."

Sofer was on the verge of asking who 'we' were, but the young woman turned around and added, "That's not the end of your surprises … as they say, I've kept the best for last!"

They retraced their steps through the central courtyard in the huge grotto until they reached the giant doors of the third building. The panels, not as heavily carved as the synagogue doors, were covered with large sheets of steel speckled with rust. At the center were some large rings superimposed at irregular intervals. One only needed to move some chains to close it as securely as a safe.

For the moment, there appeared to be no other hindrance. But this time, Sofer had to help his hostess swing open one of the panels as the bottom scraped along the slab floor. Doing this they found themselves shoulder to shoulder for a couple of seconds. Attex's hair brushed his face. He breathed in her perfume, a mixture of amber, pepper and sandalwood. But there was no time for him to be transported by the sensual swell rising in him. As soon as the door opened, Attex moved forward into the darkness. Before Sofer could distinguish what the torch glow revealed, she leaned toward a plastic switch and pressed it. Half a dozen spotlights on tripods lit up. Sofer stood stock still, mouth open, dumbfounded.

Books covered every wall, to a height of twenty or thirty feet. A library such as Sofer had never seen illustrated or described in ancient books. Huge volumes in carved boxes, embossed copper or silver, inscribed and punched, quarto volumes in leather, piles of papyrus sheets, rolls of parchment, masses of painted-lettered tiles …

hundreds, thousands of works of all sizes, overloading the shelves in dark piles.

Sofer suddenly felt a stranger to himself. Even the smell that hovered in the hall was unrecognizable, a strange mixture of humidity, rancid oil, and the cool air of the grotto. Again he felt as if he were moving through time, as if the powerful visions of his memory had finally materialized before his eyes. He rubbed his aching temples. His gaze jumped from corner to corner, incapable of fixing on anything, wanting to absorb it all at once in case it disappeared, as it might in a real dream.

In a solemn voice, Attex announced, "The Khazar Library. It's all here. Everything the rabbis of the Khagans of Itil were able to read and know, is here. Each of these books, each of these manuscripts passed at least once through their hands...."

"It is marvelous," he murmured after a stunned silence. "Marvelous! There is no other word.... I can hardly believe it! How can it be possible?"

His eyes slid from the cluttered walls to the long table occupying the center of the room. It was also laden with scrolls, antique manuscripts, and leather tubes similar to the fine tubes florists sell to hold rose stalks. Stretching out, he touched several of them very gently. The browning papyrus was so polished by use that it possessed the smoothness of ivory. Sofer's fingers ventured over the bindings. To his astonishment, the first work he opened, made of thick paper and very well preserved, revealed double column printing. The left hand columns of each page bore drawings richly illuminated in ochre, gold and indigo, and writing in Hebrew, while the other column appeared to consist of Arabic letters drawn in beautiful calligraphy.

"That's the Pentateuch," explained the young woman at his back. "The Five Books of Moses in Hebrew and Arabic." She pointed to one of the distant shelves. "You can find other versions over there, in Hebrew and Coptic, or Arabic and Greek. They were gathered together and brought here by rabbis and scribes when the Khazars knew that the destruction of their empire was inevitable. Even before the occupation of Itil and Sarkel by the Russians, the rabbis took measures to empty the synagogues, especially the ones they considered most valuable."

"But how do you know all this?" exclaimed Sofer in a slightly skeptical tone. She pointed, and Sofer let his gaze follow her out-stretched arm. Totally anachronistic, he saw half-buried under the manuscripts and parchments on the table, two laptop computers, magnifying glasses, cotton gloves and a strange machine of polished steel that was almost certainly a small microscope.

"We've been here for months studying this library," she answered him in a slightly amused tone. "We want to make an inventory but we are less than half done. But I can tell you that in among all this there is a copy of the correspondence between King Joseph and Rabbi Hazdai Ibn Shaprut of Cordoba, the original of which is kept at Oxford. It is probably the copy made by the Cordoban messenger Isaac ben Eliezer himself! It was a common precaution at the time; they created multiple copies of important documents, having good reason to fear their destruction...."

She had come close to the table while speaking, gently touching the scrolls, sliding fingers down the spines of ancient bindings. Her red hair seemed to flare up in flames in the bright beam of one of the spotlights. Fascinated, Sofer could not prevent himself imagin-ing Attex, the young Kathum, having run away to this very place.... He made a huge effort to control the confused thoughts spiralling through his mind and asked, "Who are you?"

She stood up straight, head held stiffly as if she were insulted. Sofer looked her in the eye. She replaced the leather scroll cover she was holding among the untidy pile on the table and smiled a smile that puzzled Sofer. It was not a seductive smile, or even an amused smile. On the contrary, it seemed to tend toward sadness mixed with a little pride. Looking at her, Sofer suddenly recalled a long-forgot-ten passage from Euripides: 'It is not woman's beauty that bewitches, but her nobility.'

Without anwering, she walked over to the batteries to switch off the spotlights and proposed, in her coaxing voice, that they eat.

"When I was a teenager, fifteen years ago, Georgia bore no resemblance to what you saw coming here. Everywhere there were factories, cultivation, fields covered in vines, wheat, flowers ... there were tractors and agricultural machinery in motion all over the place. We seemed to be rich. Rich and secure. Every day we ate good food and we were sure it was going to last forever. My parents felt safe—but they were Jews, and during the war their own parents had been deported by Stalin—they ought to have known, and acted cautiously, but no! That was, without any doubt, the strength of communism; its ability to make people forget, even Jews! Under such conditions, anything is possible. We lived in a bubble, and it seemed on the inside that no one could possibly burst it. That's why my parents sent me to study in Moscow. They were very proud of me...."

She spoke softly. Her voice seemed to be absorbed by the night outside. She turned toward the rectangular opening, where a crescent moon was hanging, as if painted on the wall. Sofer was sure he could see the force of her emotions moisten her lips. She passed her fingertips mechanically along those lips. The rapid gesture fascinated him. Again he experienced the full force of his own desire, and as if ashamed of his immodesty, lowered his eyes to study the outline of the meal in front of him.

They were seated on either side of a narrow table, on benches carved directly from the rock. The long troglodyte room resembled the kitchen of an old farmhouse. A fire was burning in a half-covered hearth that held pots for cooking. Various niches were carved into the rock wall, the work as fine as a cabinet maker's, shelved and shaped to hold dishes and utensils. The woman he called Attex was again looking into his face and he was certain that she could guess his exact thoughts, but she waved her hand brusquely, and said, "Eat up! I can see that you are famished!"

Indeed, he was so ravenous that instead of becoming satisfied as he ate, he seemed to become hungrier with each mouthful. He devoured skewers of lamb, stuffed eggplants and cheese-filled crepes. He drank white wine eagerly, wine as sweet as that which Lazir had given him, scarcely more alcoholic than cider.

"To tell the truth," he admitted, smiling, "I don't ever remember being so hungry in all my life!"

She laughed warmly and allowed the silence to take over. Sofer was sure that, at that instant, he might have been able to reach out and stroke her cheek, her lips, perhaps even steal a kiss. But he instinctively knew that he ought not do it. Not yet ... he thought of the poor appearance he must be presenting; unshaven, eyes swollen from the long sleep he had been plunged into unwittingly, wearing the vacant look of a man who doesn't know whether he is delirious or not. He pushed aside his self-doubt and refilled their glasses.

"When you were at university, did you already know about these caves and the synagogue?"

"No, not a thing. That's not how I came to hear of it. Our village, Sadoue, is about twelve miles from here. In those days very few people would have ventured so far, perhaps only if hunting or looking for mushrooms. And the forest down there, at the foot of the cliff, had a bad reputation. For hundreds of years, they said it was infested with snakes, wolves and bears." She smiled, thoughtful for a moment before continuing. "It was probably quite true in the main. Especially in centuries gone by. But, now I wonder if it wasn't just a rumor passed down through the ages, spread about by the Jewish Khazars themselves to protect the secret of their synagogue ... whatever the truth, no one in Sadoue knew of its existence until very recent times. The Jews as little as anyone else. Until Yakubov and his crew..."

"Ah, Yakubov!" interjected Sofer, "the fellow who is here, there and nowhere! What do you know about him? Who is he?"

She shook her head with a slightly nervous gesture. "It will be better if I tell you everything in the correct order. At seventeen, giving great pleasure to my parents, I won a scholarship to the University of Lomonossov in Moscow...."

"On Mount Lenin!" Sofer chimed in, amused. "I took part in several debates there, just after Yeltsin overthrew Gorbachev. Plenty of nonsense was proffered then, same as every time people think they're at the heart of history in the making!"

He chuckled, but she answered him eagerly, saying "I know,

I was there! That's where I first came across you! I didn't think you were talking nonsense. On the contrary, you were full of life and optimism, we were encouraged by what you said!"

Sofer felt himself blush. He almost had the impression that the young woman felt that he had since committed some form of treason, but her eyes and her open face showed no aggression, very much the opposite. "And then ... what happened?" he murmured.

"I studied history and languages—English and French—for six years. Every holiday I came back to Sadoue. Part of our family lived then in Ducheti, a village north of Tbilissi, mainly Jewish. That's where I first heard about the Khazars and their conversion to Judaism—but I didn't believe it!" A grimace twisted her pretty face. "I simply didn't want to believe this story of conversion to Judaism and a great empire that had disappeared! At that time I was sure that I knew the truth. I believed that I knew the history of Russia off by heart. To me, the edifying story of the Khazars, that great and tolerant empire, the first to make paper in the region, to mint coins ... all that was just a fable. A nostalgic and reactionary legend that the Jews had passed down, not having anything better, to create a bit of legitimate history for themselves in this great country. I didn't realize that I was totally brainwashed by the official version of history according to the USSR!"

She paused, smiling, almost laughing at herself. "However, since my Jewish friends insisted, I decided to investigate. I first searched in the libraries. Profiting from the onset of perestroika, I wrote to several English historians. I will never forget the day I received and read the documents they sent me. It was as if I had discovered that someone had lied to me about my birth! When they say that the floor opens up beneath your feet, that's how I felt. Up till then I had been walking on a carpet of lies, which suddenly had been whipped out from under me. Yes, the Khazars had been a great people, converting themselves to Judaism even though they were not Semites. Yes, the influence of the Khazar heritage in Russia's formation was important. And yes, all serious studies on the subject had been forbidden, censured and condemned by the Soviet regime!"

"But why?" Sofer asked.

"Oh, for the simplest of reasons: Russian nationalism. It was inconceivable that this great nation could owe some of its heritage to Judaism! One Russian historian, Artamanov, attempted to write the truth in an essay he penned in the 1930s, 'The Story of the Khazars.' He showed the influence of the Khazars on the formation of the first Russian state. Artamanov noted this indisputable fact: that the Russian hordes who invaded and conquered the Khazar Kingdom were nothing but barbarians manipulated by Byzantium. It was through settling in the Khazar towns and adopting their ethical codes, their laws and their knowledge, that they acquired their first political structures, and first moved toward becoming a civilized society. At first Artamanov's study was ignored, then three years before Stalin died, he was condemned to death as a subversive anti-communist. *Pravda* declared his work 'a story of Jewish parasites.' Stalin and his cohorts did nothing more than continue a tradition initiated by the czars and carried on through the centuries."

Sofer wanted to smile. Her green eyes were full of anger as she voiced the fervent idealism of one who challenges the duplicity of the powerful. She glowed with a sort of admirable purity; a purity of cause that will always ultimately bring about a hero's downfall, for man or woman, they are always betrayed in the end by human unfaithfulness. Sofer wondered whether it was his age that made him think these thoughts.

"Is that how the group calling itself the New Khazars was started, the ones who blew up the oil installations at Baku?"

She looked at him slightly surprised, her anger dissipating. "No ... not at all," she replied coolly.

Sofer was immediately sorry. To cover his confusion, aghast at the implication of his question, he reached out to fill his glass. The bottle was empty.

"Would you like some more wine?" she asked.

"No, I've really had enough."

"Coffee?" She was already on her feet, walking to the stove. "You are the prisoner of a dangerous terrorist group," she said, with a touch of irony in her voice, "yet you can only think of wine, tea, coffee ... things you like...."

Hurt, Sofer replied, "Too right! I'm your prisoner! I realized that a while back. I'm shut up here just as if I were in Alcatraz, and, to tell the truth, I don't even know why!"

She turned around and looked directly into his face, an old aluminum coffee pot in her hand. Standing there, a laugh rising again in her throat, color in her cheeks, she was more desirable than ever. Although silent, it seemed to him she was saying with all her body, 'Oh yes you do!' Picking up two cups from a wall niche, she came back to sit down and declared in a calm voice, "You are completely free. You can leave here and go back to Baku whenever you want. I give you my word; now, at dawn, whenever! The passage out is not locked except to safeguard us. I'd only need to wake Lazir. The four by four awaits you in the forest, not far from the face of the cliff."

"*Us?*" queried Sofer. The word jarred him. "Who is *us*? Lazir and you?"

She shook her head, amused, filling her cup with delicious smelling coffee. "A dozen of us live here. We are dispersed throughout the hundreds of grottoes here; each of us has chosen one that suits us. We have been here several months and could be here longer, if we could make it a bit more comfortable."

"I see," murmured Sofer, smiling widely. "I must admit it's a great hiding place. Not very practical for launching attacks, however; the journey to Baku and back is hardly a snap!"

She hesitated, lips tight together, expression hard. "None of us has been to Baku. There is nobody here who is not a historian!"

"Wait a minute! What are you trying to tell me? You aren't the New Khazars?"

"Our organization is split in two. Here there are only historians and scientists. We are studying the contents of the library, making an exact copy of each document. The task is enormous and you have no idea how urgent it is!"

"Oh, yes I do!" Sofer continued to use irony in his tone. "And on whose account are you doing all this work?"

"For us all! For you! For humankind, Jews throughout the world, those here in Georgia and Azerbaijan!"

"What a list of patrons! Except that, as I seem to be included, I don't remember entering into any contract with a terrorist group!"

"We are not terrorists!" she protested vehemently, cheeks flaming.

"Ah! Then if it wasn't you who blew up the installations in Baku?"

"You'd need to talk to Lazir on that subject. If he's willing ... he's the one with connections to them."

"Them?" Sofer's query was so cynically charged that she looked away. "Those people?" he insisted, "you're part of them, aren't you? You are part of the same organization, the New Khazars! Whether you are a historian or a bomber, you are part of—"

"We only want justice!" she retorted, cutting him short.

"In my experience, terrorists always claim that justice justifies their violence!"

For some seconds they looked at each other in silence. Sofer was impressed by her calm. And also by the distance that was growing between them. Contrary to what he would like to think, it was not—at least not yet—the morals of the thing or the violence that had angered him. Quite simply, this discussion had broken the strange magic that had enveloped them in the synagogue and the library. They were becoming strangers again. She had ceased to be Attex! He was angry that the magic was dissipating.

Punctuating the folly of his thoughts, a sharp evening breeze blew in from outside. The young woman crossed her arms over her bosom to restrain a shiver. The gesture emphasized the contours of her breasts under her sweater. Sofer lowered his eyes, desire rising once more. Furious at himself and the young woman, he was on the point of standing up and leaving the room, but he discovered that she was smiling as she watched him closely, frankly amused at the bad temper showing on his face. She stretched her arm across the table and held his hand in hers.

"I wondered when you were going to lecture me! Remember, I have read your books. I know your opinions on violence." She laughed out loud, in the way that entranced Sofer. "Allow me the rest of the night before condemning me forever! I still have a lot to explain to you. I did promise you that if I can't convince you by dawn, then you can leave for Baku. Then you can denounce us to the Azerbaijan authorities, or forget us. You see, I am also taking a great risk, just talking to you."

Sofer forced himself not to look at the hand that held his. As if he were forcing himself not to be completely entranced by the sensation of this touch, not to dissolve in the movement of her lips formulating words he could only half hear over his own thoughts. She withdrew her hand, trailing the tips of her fingers as if in regret. She became serious and her face, for just an instant, was that of a dreamy child: astonishing, marvelous.

"A while back, when I joined you at the open cliff, you called me Attex. I wondered if you weren't a bit crazy. But in fact I couldn't stop thinking about it while we were talking and I realized that it pleased me. It pleased me greatly! Attex wasn't only the Khagan's sister, her life had purpose. She knew the complete power of love with Isaac, and that was almost like a present given to her by the Almighty. She knew it and yet had the great courage to offer her life for what she considered just: the survival of her people!" She laughed mischievously. "Like a terrorist!"

Without leaving Sofer time to reply, she stood up and crossed the room to search for something in one of the alcoves.

"Where are you going?" Sofer inquired, standing up, too.

She passed him a powerful flashlight. "Come with me. I am going to show you the last of tonight's surprises. Perhaps that will finally convince you that the New Khazars are fighting for a good cause!"

❧

This cave was lower, the roof so close that Sofer could touch it by raising his arm. Fine pale gray sand covered a floor that sloped downward gently. Sofer ducked his head instinctively. The beams from their torches finding only darkness in front of them, they continued on for another twenty feet or so. Just at that instant, a sort of low white wall appeared on the right. Sofer moved closer to it, and he saw that his torch beam was reflected in a strange way.

"What is it…?" he asked.

A metallic click made him jump. Soft light tinted the low roof of the cave yellow.

They were in an oblong pocket dug into the heart of the mountain, so vast that light from the spotlight could not reach the far end. Water, no doubt collected there via a formidable network of cracks and fissures, formed a large turquoise blue pool.

The water, perfectly still, fixed in its limpid transparency, could just as well have been a sheet of glass. One edge of the mirror-like surface licked a sandy slope, while to the right it was contained and framed by an amazing structure. What Sofer had taken for a wall was in reality the topmost curve of a large semi-circle whose steps, like those in a Roman or Greek amphitheater, led down underneath the crystal-clear water. The highest of these steps supported half a dozen columns reaching up to the ceiling at regular intervals. The tops of these retained traces of purple and blue paint, while on the pillars themselves could be distinguished, almost intact, subtly interlacing frescos of opulent foliage, roses, hummingbirds, golden butterflies and fruit.

"Eden! The Garden of Eden before the temptation of the serpent!" Sofer whispered, as if he feared that words spoken aloud might destroy this extraordinary vision.

"If you look at these pillars as you emerge from the water you can see Adam and Eve on two of them!" The young woman came up close to him. "It is a *mikvah*, a ritual bath for wives to purify themselves."

Once again, even more so than in the synagogue and the great grotto, Sofer felt he could literally sense the breath of the ages settle on him and restrict his heartbeat. There was no more need to imagine, to have recourse to study or play fictional games to feel in his being the presence of men who, long ago, had believed in the promise of the Biblical covenant. From the still water and this simple yet sublime edifice erected in the bowels of the mountain, the spiritual fervor of the Khazars still vibrated, so intensely that their belief in the Almighty was reflected even here in the depths of the earth.

He jumped when she touched him. They smiled together at

their difficulty in breaking the silence. She pointed out the opposite side from the steps in the bath. Wooden boxes had been piled up to allow someone to climb up to a large crack in the wall, at about eye level.

"We'll come back here after ..." she said, leading him toward the boxes.

Approaching the opening, Sofer reminded himself that the walls had been made with rock hewn from the mountain with ancient picks. They squeezed through the narrow hole. In the light of their torches, he could see a very different passage from those he had seen up till now. Very high, sometimes so narrow that they had to progress sideways, irregular walls, alternately smooth and rough, owed nothing to human endeavor. There was one moment when he felt as if he were penetrating the very flesh of the mountain, as if he were slipping between its chalk and sandstone, lubricated by the mucus of its dampness. But it was the smell, at first just heavy, then more and more of an irritant, that monopolized his attention.

After some fifty or so cautious steps, the young woman stretched out an arm behind her. "Give me your hand. From here on, be very careful where you put your feet."

Sofer hesitated for a second before accepting the proffered hand. He felt both ridiculous at being led like a child and yet unable to remain unmoved by the fingers softly entwined in his. The odor became almost intolerable, both oily and acrid, as heavy as evaporating gasoline, making his eyes water. A few steps more and it became so intense that he began to breath in small gulps. Suddenly, the luminous beams of their flashlights met nothing but a non-reflective opacity. The woman stopped short. "We're here," she whispered, glued to his side.

Letting go of Sofer's hand, she covered her mouth and directed the torch beam at the emptiness at their feet.

At first Sofer could distinguish nothing more than a rocky hollow, all black and cracked looking. But above the rocks, small bubbles, like hordes of minute insects, danced in the beams of the flashlights. Fifteen or twenty feet further down, the light ricocheted off a smooth, still, surface. Then Sofer identified the odor.

"Naphtha magma," she said, as if she had read his thoughts. "A real oil well!"

With the toe of his shoe, Sofer pushed a stone the size of a fist, making it roll over. It hit the oily surface with a dull plop, creating a lazy wave before sinking and disappearing. The young woman gripped his arm again, pulling him back into the passage behind them. "It's not good to stay here too long, unless you want to be asphyxiated."

❧

After having splashed her face with cold water, she took off her shoes and rolled her pants up to the knee. Without any further hesitation she entered the water up to mid-calf, grimacing at first at the cold then smiling at Sofer and confiding in him, "of all these caves, this is my favorite. I installed the floodlights so that I could come here to think quietly...."

When she broke the perfect immobility of the pool, it appeared to him that she had broken the unique sensation of melding with ancient times that he had been feeling, but then he consoled himself with the thought that thanks to this act, she brought life back into a place filled only with memories, and that she was right to do so. She joined herself to the limpid water of the *mikvah* as did thousands of women millennia ago, easing the tumult of their emotions and questions. She stopped walking around and leaned over to dip her hands in the water. For a moment, the small waves surrounded her with a set of sparkling reflections like silver dust on the water. Every one of her movements expressed itself with a grace that only left Sofer feeling sad.

In reflective silence, he realized he was staring at Adam, next to him, whose unhappy expression had been set in stone over a thousand years ago. Adam, father and son of the same torment, hoping that an embrace of flesh would achieve not only the knowledge promised by the serpent, but also, above all, that magnificent experience of life that a woman would bring and that, up till this moment, had escaped him.

Sofer heard her get out of the water and come and sit close to him. Despite the odor of naphtha hanging in the cave, he noticed her perfume. It felt almost as though she were touching him.

"There are millions of barrels of oil under this mountain," she announced suddenly. "What you have just seen is not just a simple naphtha well but the natural conduit to a huge reservoir. A veritable sea of black gold, so easy to extract that it would make any oil company green with envy...."

The words sobered Sofer. For the first time since he had entered the caves he thought of Thomson. "How do you know?"

"Last summer, an oil company carried out some exploratory tests in the Telavi valley, only a few miles from here. They included the cliff and spotted the caves from a helicopter while making maps of the topography. But it didn't interest them much until someone went to them and said, 'I know where there's oil! No need to drill, you'll only need a pan to scoop it out!'"

"Yakubov," muttered Sofer.

"Exactly! Yakubov! I don't know what he told you when you met in Paris, but he knows these caves like the back of his hand. Over the years he has walked every inch of every corridor, every little niche. Here, he scented the naphtha and found that fault…"

She pointed to the hole above the heap of boxes on the other side of the *mikvah*, the narrow passage they had just negotiated back from the well.

"He told me his father came here in secret from time to time to pray," explained Sofer, "and that one day he had followed him."

"That's possible," she agreed. "It's quite probable that for generations, Jews in the region knew of the existence of the synagogue and the library. But they would have guarded the precious secret well. Yakubov must have asked himself how he could profit from his knowledge. Happily for him and unfortunately for us, he was too greedy."

"What do you mean by that?"

"He wanted to cash in on both secrets: the oil and the Khazar treasure! To be more exact, at first he probably never even considered the oil, that would have made no sense to him. His idea was to sell, little by little, the objects from the guard-house, the manuscripts, and perhaps even the ark. But to whom? And how? Today's Georgia is not a country for trading in antiques. The markets here are full of much more mundane items. People are emptying their houses, selling their furniture, their carts, even the Soviet-era taps from their bathrooms. Nothing, however, of any value. Poverty is so bad in the towns that they have to swap everything for food. Vegetables for old eyeglasses, meat for rococo plates from Stalin's time. Yakubov quickly understood that he was sitting on a fortune, but that if he tried to sell the smallest piece in Georgia, some Mafia gang would soon hear about it. He could then say goodbye to the rest, and maybe even his life! Consequently he was going to have to be patient."

"He would have been able to sell them abroad," objected Sofer.

"Far too complicated for a Jewish peasant from the Caucasus! He would have had to get the stuff out of the country, go to Europe, convince some buyer. And then what? He was cornered. He could only take small pieces abroad, not the most valuable: the large weapons, the manuscripts, the ark. Even if he managed to convince a dealer in Berlin, Paris or London, who would take the risk of coming here to the Caucasus? Here to the Mafia's kingdom, next door to Chechnya and war? Nobody!"

"So…?"

"So, he walled up the corridors leading to the great grotto so that nobody else could discover its existence. It took patience, several years of patience. When the oil exploration began, he remembered the naphtha well. He must have thought to himself that he could at the very least earn some dollars for leading the oil technicians here. And that's precisely what happened, before things quickly became much more complicated. He never imagined that from the first tests, the analyses would reveal that the black pool we just saw is the top of a sort of natural pipe that has opened through faults in the rock. A geological accident. But down below, well below the bottom of the cliff, there is a field holding several million metric tons of oil! I don't have exact figures, but…."

"Wait a minute …" Sofer said. Without thinking he had placed his hand on her wrist and gripped it tightly. With a shiver of horror, he realized where this explanation was leading.

"Jesus! You're telling me that the oil companies have located an oil reserve under this mountain! Under the synagogue and the library. Then … then they will want to blow sky high to exploit that infernal oil!"

He didn't notice the victorious look in her eye. He hardly felt the hand placed over his own.

"Yes," she confirmed very quietly. "That's why we are here. That's why we formed the New Khazars! That is the reason, moreover, that we became terrorists, as you called us. We are under no illusions as to what we are doing. If we don't stop them, the oil companies will ravage this mountain and destroy everything in it to enable them to exploit the black gold!"

Transfixed, a moist anguish gnawing at his throat, Sofer looked at the beautiful water in the pool. She was utterly right! His eyes came back up to the Adam and Eve painted on the columns. He imagined them destroyed, reduced to powder by the transformation of the grotto into an immense pumping station. After so many centuries, one final, terrible act was going to claim victory and efface once and for all the last traces of the Khazars….

He stood up, stammering, "Take me back outside. To the cliff edge. I need some fresh air."

❧

Sofer was seated on a step of the staircase beside the cliff, in the light coming from the kitchen-cave, where she was once again preparing coffee. He looked at his watch. It was already four o'clock in the morning. In the east, barely visible, a little brightness appeared in the splendid obscurity of the starry sky. A cold, steady breeze was moving along the face of the cliff, refreshing him after the mild suffocation that had seized him in the *mikvah*. Yes, a real suffocation, that had frightened him. As if the labyrinth dug into the mountain was closing in around him. As if, in a sort of intuition of the flesh, the growing menace of the grotto and the treasures it contained were becoming a direct threat to him. Another relic of the Jewish world about to be effaced! Another destruction of memory! Another step toward the birth of a present completely cut off from its origins! His body and his heart had understood all of that before his mind, and was suffering for it. Doubtless it was excessive. He liked to think he was in control of his emotions. But everything, since he had arrived here, appeared excessive—at the same time threatening and extraordinary. Starting with his attraction to the woman whom he continued to call Attex.

He wondered whether he was truly in love with her. It had been so long since he had really loved in that way, a way that makes one feel good, open, welcoming of the other and accepting of their enigmas. Long ago he had barricaded himself behind the conviction that love was as impossible to share as a dream. Should he, could he, share a bit of this emotion with her? Was she just playing with him so that he would help her? He began to review the nature of the assistance he could give her. Better not to ask that question. Better to content himself with the fact that she had chosen him above all others. Was that not a sign?

She appeared on the rock balcony carrying an old Turkish style tray with a coffeepot and cups. She smiled, gracious and relaxed. From now on they were accomplices. Confidantes. She sat on the staircase, a step below him, pouring the steaming coffee into the cups and passing him his. He took it in cupped hands, warming his palms on the porcelain. With a slow movement she released her hair from its band. It was so light that the breeze expanded it around her shoulders. With a natural ease that made Sofer's heart beat even faster, she leaned back, her shoulder brushing against his bent knees. Through the cloth, he felt her warmth, the firmness of one breast pressed up against his thigh. He had only to move his hand a few inches to plunge it into her hair of fire, or stroke her neck or cheek. He held back, preferring not to break the strange covenant by which they seemed to be linked. They sipped their coffee as she continued the story of how she had met Yakubov the preceding winter.

After short negotiations and plenty of wine, a group of oil men had managed to obtain, unopposed, quasi-rights over one hundred square miles of mountain, forests and mineral rights, encompassing the cliff, the caves and the immensity of the reserves below, which extended under the adjoining plains.

"That means," she emphasized, "that we are in their territory at this moment. Completely illegally! They could throw us out whenever they want.

"Yakubov himself realized quickly that, in these circumstances, the time he had left to make money from the Khazar treasures was extremely limited.

"To sell them quickly, he would have to have some sort of network, but who could he use here without the risk of it getting to the ears of the Mafia? Yakubov is as sly as a fox, but his general ignorance and naïveté in certain matters trip him up. His first thought was that a history teacher would be certain to be interested in antiques." She stopped to refill their cups, moistened her throat with the fresh coffee and continued. "He came to my parents' house when I was home celebrating my return to Georgia as a teacher. He brought a spear, two or three daggers, some arrows and some coins in a sports bag. He said to me, 'It appears you know about old things. What is this lot worth, do you think?'"

Sofer could not prevent himself from smiling, remembering Yakubov's garrulous manner. He could easily picture him selling his wares!

"As soon as I saw the coins I knew that I was looking at Khazar artifacts." She shivered and snuggled closer to Sofer. "I was covered with goose bumps! To have suddenly right before your eyes, objects and coins that you had thought lost forever! You can't imagine the feeling!"

Yes, he could, thought Sofer. That feeling he knew perfectly well. At that very moment he could feel it pulsing all over his being.

Yakubov had, of course, refused to disclose where he had obtained the ancient objects. She had tried everything to convince him, from pleas to threats. She ended up insulting him, pointing out that his thirst for dollars was leading him—the son of a man totally committed to the Torah!—to sell the story and the memory of the Jewish people, not just some old bits of metal!

With the intention of forcing Yakubov to reveal his sources, she contacted—with the assistance of some of her Jewish friends from university—the community of Quba in Azerbaijan, the most important in the whole region. The rabbis there still had some power. In fact, she had hoped that they would be in touch with the Israeli authorities. They were not, but Yakubov was picked up one morning and questioned with a certain ... vigor.

"Well, it wasn't very legal, that's sure. But frankly, what else could we do? It was too important...."

"If I understand you correctly," said Sofer, "the inhabitants of Quba know this story. They know that you are here, why, and who is behind the New Khazars!"

"No, not everyone. Far from it! Only the mayor and some of his confidantes. They have helped us greatly...."

"Zovolun Buruth Danilev? The mayor?" murmured Sofer. "The one I asked to tell me where my coin came from and who tried to absolutely dissuade me. 'The mountains are full of rumors, Mr. Sofer. To believe them is to lose oneself....'"

"They are fantastic! It's they who take all the risks. They understood the situation in the blink of an eye. They had great pleasure in calling themselves the New Khazars! Under the communists, the mayor had organized a network to allow Jews to flee to the West."

"I see. Your 'action' arm. Father figures like me, or guys like Lazir who can use a bomb or two!"

"Don't make fun of me, it's not fair! We never thought of bombs when we started, I assure you! If the oil bosses were less stupid and obtuse, that wouldn't have been necessary. When Yakubov ended up leading us here, we were so enamored that we wanted nothing more than that the whole world share our good fortune. In front of the synagogue, before we even opened the door, we were all in tears. We were overcome with emotion. And when we were able to open the great doors of the library ... there are no words to describe it!"

No, there were no words. An image perhaps, as if the Adam and Eve painted on the columns in the *mikvah* had come to life, detaching themselves from the plaster of the fresco. As if they had become a man and woman of flesh and at last you could embrace them. But beyond this feeling, the questions raised in these last few weeks were at last finding their answers, like pieces of a puzzle coming together.

"We were naïve and full of hope. I was sure we would be able to make an arrangement with the bosses of the oil company responsible for prospecting. Once they learned about the extraordinary content of the caves, they couldn't but share our opinion. We tried to meet them in every way possible. They only have a local office in Tbilissi. We contacted their head office in Baku. They refused to talk to us. Finally a lawyer wrote to us advising us that everything that was in the caves belonged, from that moment on, to the ocoo."

"Offshore Caspian Oil Operations," groaned Sofer, thinking of Thomson.

"Yes, that's them. The lawyer's letter was a deliberate provocation. It stated that we had no legal right to come here without their specific authorization. You can imagine how we felt. Our first reaction, with the intention of giving ourselves a bit more credibility, was to create a society for the protection of ruins—the New Khazars. That's how the group started. I can assure you that we tried to move heaven and earth, as much in Azerbaijan as in Georgia. But the ocoo had imposed some sort of 'omerta' on everybody; in a matter of weeks, no one would talk to us. They didn't take our calls anymore, our letters disappeared into their garbage bins. We were treated as if we did not exist! The only thing we did learn, was that somewhere between now and the end of the year at the latest, a team will be sent in to evaluate the deposits. From then on the whole area will be forbidden territory. That means they will take away all the library contents and then destroy the rest, including the *mikvah*! That's why we decided to attack the ocoo installations. Unfortunately, they are so powerful that even our letter of demand was suppressed! No reaction! Silence!"

Sofer's mind was on fire. "Wait! Wait! The bosses of the ocoo know exactly who you are, don't they? And what you want from them?"

"By this time, I suppose they must have our photographs on their desks along with files containing the smallest details of our lives."

"The bastard!" Suddenly, Sofer understood what Thomson had been getting at. His intuition had not been mistaken; their meeting in the airplane owed nothing to chance. Thomson knew who he was and why he was going to Baku. Thomson and those who employ him knew everything: the location of the caves, the reason for the attacks and the identity of the people who perpetrated them. They knew about Quba, Yakubov and the rest. But why were they interested in him, Marc Sofer? Could they want him to become the messenger between the OCOO and the New Khazars?

For a moment Sofer closed his eyes and remembered the outline of Thomson's proposal the other evening, in the hotel, the one that had sounded like a threat: 'Give a message to your friends...tell them to let it drop. Not to attack a second time. That would be a sign to us, and we would remember ... and, if an explanation was given, perfectly anonymously of course, that would be even better ... with details implicating the Americans....'"

That didn't gel. What did the Americans have to do with this story, when Thomson and the OCOO already knew who had carried out the attacks and why? In addition, a second attack had taken place, but on an American installation, according to Lazir anyway. There must be a piece of the puzzle missing. Unless Thomson wasn't the only one taking him for a ride.

"What's happened? What's the matter?" She had placed one hand on his thigh and was looking directly at him, leaning toward him, a frown of disquietude on her brow. "Marc, do you feel ill?"

There it was! Using his first name with a voice of honey! And such a beautiful face. Why couldn't she just be happy being Attex, a fictional woman of his dreams?

A violent desire to embrace her ran through him, making him tremble. He contented himself with placing a hand over hers and squeezing it. One last reservation prevented him from telling her of his meeting with Thomson. Stiffening, he asked, "Why did you blow up the American installations this time, and not those of the OCOO?"

"Oh ... that was an idea Lazir and the mayor of Quba had. Since the OCOO wanted to ignore us, we would have to create a problem that would affect as many companies as possible, and the regional government in Azerbaijan as well. If the American interests were affected, perhaps they would publish our demands. Without understanding the background, but…."

"Unless the ocoo convinces them to do nothing! In which case you are only playing with fire and multiplying your enemies! There is something that I still don't understand; why don't the ocoo bosses just report you to the police? They could arrest you here, Zovolun and the villagers at Quba, and I don't know who else … since they appear to know everything and are well within their rights, it would be simple!"

"But that would create at least a few problems for them. At least a little. Some foreign journalists might hear the news. In Europe, England, France, all the member countries of ocoo would get to hear about it. Destroy all vestiges of the past? What civilized society would not respond in alarm? No, they have chosen the best weapon to beat us with … silence! Silence means we are in checkmate. They know we are weak. What's the strength of the New Khazars? Fifteen, twenty people. Who knows what we are and what we are fighting for? Nobody! What can we do when their silence kills us, wrecks us and destroys us more surely than a real war. I say this to you; they are strong enough to silence the loudest of our protests."

She shifted away from him slightly so as to be able to look directly into his eyes. Her mouth was suddenly twisted with anger. "We took photos and a film that we sent to them. I myself wrote a twenty-page report to explain in detail the historic importance of the library, the synagogue and the *mikvah*. Not only for Jews; it is quite simply the history of the Caucasus that is engraved here. You can be sure we also sent copies of the film and the report to Georgian and Azerbaijan newspapers, to professors at the University of Tbilissi, and some in Azerbaijan also. Do you know what happened? Nothing! As if we did not exist! And that's exactly what they want, for us not to exist! And for the caves to be empty except for barrels and barrels of oil!"

She was nearly shouting. Her voice ricocheted off the wall inside the cliff and echoed in the night. "We are not in Europe, Marc. Not even in Azerbaijan! There is no longer a State of Georgia, no law, no rules and regulations. When you have enough dollars to corrupt a minister, a person who possesses the power to sign a piece of paper, you can do what you like. If we lose this battle, what you have seen tonight will not exist within six months...."

She was right. He had only to let his eyes wander over the shadows that had begun to dissolve with the dawn to be convinced. This place was lost. Nobody cared what would become of it. If by 'chance' something unfortunate happened, it would be extraordinarily easy to attribute any kind of destruction to the war in Chechnya. And who would care about some old relics of the Khazars? The history books in the European academic world don't even mention them!

Yes, she was definitely right. And at last, without needing her to explain any further, he understood what he was doing there. The half-drunk cup of coffee had gone cold in his hands. He put it down on the tray and, that done, looked into her eyes. This time, the urge was stronger than he was. He turned toward her and placed his lips on hers.

He was surprised to find them burning. He was even more surprised to feel her embrace him as violently as if she had just been rescued, a low moan escaping from deep within her throat. The firm, supple body enveloped his. Their tongues met. The erotic tension restrained for so many hours expanded like drunkenness in their bloodstreams.

Chapter twenty-seven

Sadoue, Georgia
May 2000

She disengaged herself from his embrace as gently as a bee leaving a flower. She stretched out on the bed naked, heels under her buttocks, offering herself to his attentive gaze. Sofer felt as if he were seeing her for the very first time. Something had changed in her features while they made love, and it remained now. A trace of abandon, unrestrained pleasure, but something else too. Less assured, perhaps. Unless she was just simply disoriented by the difference in their ages now that they were both nude, and the violence of their passion was subsiding.

Surely she too must have felt, from their very first exchange of glances, that desire would prevail sooner or later. There had been too much pent up emotion that night for them not to give in to it.

She raised her arms to arrange her flamboyant hair in a loose chignon, and the points of her breasts hardened again. Her areolas were circles of fire, contrasting with the milky whiteness of her skin. Desire revived instantly in Sofer, surprising him. He held back and looked away from her green eyes so as not to embarrass her. Eyes closed, he rolled on his side to kiss her. "I haven't stopped thinking of you for weeks, even when I convinced myself I wasn't! To the point that it became worrying. You are so beautiful!"

She laughed her particular deep laugh, but he detected a slight distance, as if he had said something stupid. She pushed her head back, interrupting his kisses by stroking his cheeks. "Your beard grows quickly," she remarked.

He rubbed his chin. It was very rough. He grimaced.

"Don't do anything about it," she added immediately. "It suits you! Don't move, I've got a present for you…."

"For me?"

With cat-like agility she left the bed and went over to a metal trunk lying at the base of a wall. They were in 'her' grotto, just like the one Sofer had woken in, centuries ago it seemed. That was where they had gone, as quickly as they could, spurred on by the urgency of their kisses and caresses, undressing at each step, driven by desire. The only difference was that this room possessed a relatively comfortable camp bed and a battery connected to two small lights. Sofer was still admiring her as she opened the trunk and drew out a roll of paper. He hoped he had not upset her when he told her how beautiful she was. She was beauty itself, such that could make one believe in life as an achievement.

She came back to the bed, hips swaying, and handed him the scroll.

"What is it?"

"Look and see…"

He unrolled the scroll. Despite its appearance, it was not parchment, but paper, lumpy and of uneven thickness. Darkened by moisture stains, writing covered most of it, in an ink that had turned black. It resembled none of the careful calligraphy Sofer had seen in the library. When he had unrolled the whole of the manuscript, typed leaves of paper fell out onto the bed.

"You do read Russian, don't you?"

Sofer nodded. "What is it?"

"A letter. And its translation into Russian." She smiled broadly, picking up her sweater and pulling it over her bare skin. "I'll let you read it in peace. I'll be back in a moment. I'm hungry. Aren't you?"

Sofer did not reply, his eyes riveted to the first line of the translation, stomach knotted by something far removed from food.

My well beloved brother, Joseph, Khagan of the Khazars, Son of Aaron, May the Lord bless you.

May the Lord also will that this letter be delivered to you.

Joseph, I have two important pieces of news for you. One bad and another that I find good. I thought hard before writing this letter because it will tell you where I am, but that I must accept. The bad news is so important that you must hear it.

After having fled your protection in Sarkel, I went to our uncle Hanuko in his caves, you know the ones I am referring to. It is a miracle that Attania and I arrived here alive.

Alas, every day, the cave, the synagogue, the fabulous mikvah constructed by our uncle, all that and even our lives, all are in the gravest danger. Do you remember the vast valley that extends to the foot of the cliff? The troops of the Byzantine Emperor and of the Emir of Aleppo, Seif ad Daouleh, are camped there, day after day, fighting in a battle as ferocious as its outcome is uncertain. Uncle Hanuko says that the Greeks have engaged two Imperial divisions, more than ten thousand soldiers, with two battalions from Varegues. The Emir's forces are just as powerful.

That makes fifteen or twenty thousand men fighting each other three or four leagues from here, perhaps closer. The forest that hides the access route to the cliff was completely burnt down five days ago. We are nearly asphyxiated by the smoke. Incapable of washing, we are still black with soot. We will have to go and soak in the great bath of Adam and Eve, but none of us wants to be the first to desecrate it.

To tell the truth, Joseph, it was because of seeing us like this, dirty and stinking like animals, trapped in our caves, that I resolved to write this desperate message to you.

Since the firing of the forest, which as you must understand, revealed our presence to the Emir's soldiers, never a day passes without soldiers shouting to each other, searching for an entrance to the caves. *Their leader must be thinking he can use it as a fortress. Uncle Hanuko has always lived here in peace, protecting himself from evil by reading the Torah. We can only count on twenty men to defend us. And even then it has been so long since they bore arms that I doubt their efficacy.*

For the moment, the natural defenses of the place afford us the best protection, but for how much longer? Uncle Hanuko thinks that sooner or later the Muslims will make ladders that will allow them to climb over the postern gate, or they will wind ropes long enough to enable them to reach the highest caves from the top of the cliff. They are capable of anything.

There is another reason that I am taking the terrible responsibility of sending Attania to you with this letter. If we are not here tomorrow to tell you, you should know that this war between the Emir and Constantine is the reason the Greeks were forced to offer you an alliance. Apart from their vicious pleasure in leading you to a worse denial of yourself through marriage.

Joseph, my brother, open your eyes! How could you dream of a peace founded on the rape of the sister whom you love?

The bowing and scraping of Ambassador Blymmedes had no other meaning than to weaken you while the Byzantine forces confront the Emir. Constantine is weak today. He wanted to make sure that you did not make peace with the Emir against him. The peace he offered is nothing but a lure, my beloved Khagan. Think about this; if I had obeyed you, I would have reneged on the Law of Moses and submitted to the desires of a Christian without any benefit accruing to the Kingdom of the Khazars. Rather the contrary!

Joseph, listen to this truth: Byzantium hates the Jews and fears the Khazar warriors. There will never be peace between them and us. I am writing to you now because tomorrow I will probably be with the Lord, blessed be His name; you can only help the Jews in the rest of the world.

They think of you as a light in a dark night. You are a new star in their heaven. I beg you, receive Isaac, envoy of the Rabbi of Cordoba. Read the letter that he brings you and reply with compassion. Do not let yourself be blinded by jealousy. I know that bitter pain fouls your judgment, that that is a great part of your refusal to see Isaac. Don't fight against my love who took me in his arms; you cannot do anything against him.

Even if we only had one night to enchant each other, that night is eternal as the Almighty Himself is eternal. Yes, I say it to you, our love is the will of the Almighty!

I bear Isaac's breath in my bosom. His presence and the perfume of his passion will never leave me. He has purified me for always. I only have to close my eyes to know that it is the same for him. Nothing, oh Joseph, you who saved my life as a child, nothing can break this faith in my faith. If a Muslim soldier should rape me tomorrow, he cannot soil me more than the smoke from his fires.

Do you remember, Joseph, the teachings of Rabbi Hanania? One day he told us that we must consider the Torah as a young woman of great beauty and of high birth. He looked at me as he said those words. He told us of a young woman with a lover. Only she knows of his existence. Out of love for her, and even though he does not yet know her, this boy comes to her palace, passing again and again before her windows. He hopes to see this beauty of which his heart has already spoken but his eyes have never seen. And the young woman, she knows that he is there, that he will never go away. She opens her window for a second and for a brief instant shows herself to her lover. He alone, and no other, has seen her face. To him alone is she revealed, for only he possesses the heart and soul to be able to see into her window. And he knows from then on how great the love is that she has for him. And she knows from then on that the link between them is indestructible.

Isaac ben Eliezer and the Kathum Attex are thus, Khagan Joseph. They will remain so even through suffering. Even if the window can never again open. Even though there will never be an instant when he does not miss me.

Allow him an audience, Joseph. Save the Khazar Kingdom

and let my love come and save me. Then the Almighty can make of you what the forsaken and banished Jews already carry in their hearts.

❧

Sofer rubbed his eyes. They were moist. He would have liked to reread the letter immediately, to assure himself that he was not delirious. But the confusion in his mind was too great. Had what he imagined really taken place? There was a slight noise behind him. A whisper, a rustle of silk. Raising his eyes, he saw her, standing beside the door. She no longer wore her sweater, but a long green dress. A second skin, of green, reflecting like mother-of-pearl, stretched across her thighs, creasing slightly over the curve of her stomach, revealing the weight of her breasts and the sweetness of her shoulders. She spoke as she moved toward him. "It's a Khazar tunic. My mother made it for me from a description she found in a book."

Sofer thought it was exactly the tunic that Attex would have worn for her night of love with Isaac. He wanted to say so, but the words wouldn't pass his lips. It was all too much, too insane, as if two worlds had suddenly fused together.

She knelt down in front of him, her red hair swinging against her cheeks. She pointed to the letter. "It is a beautiful letter, isn't it? Beautiful and terrifying. From the moment I deciphered it, I thought it would interest you."

"Where did it come from?"

"From the library. It stood out from the other manuscripts because of the writing. It's almost certainly a copy. The original would have disappeared with Attania...."

She paused to look at him and whispered, smiling gently. "What's wrong?"

He looked at her as if he were lost.

"Why are you looking at me like that?" She looked completely thrown, almost fearful.

"Because you are so beautiful!"

"Bah!" she replied shaking her head in a pout. "What's that got

274

to do with anything? I don't like people saying that! Isn't it written in Ecclesiastes that one should never hire a man for his beauty, and never fire him because he's ugly? It is just the same for a woman!"

Sofer bit his lip. For the first time he felt embarrassed at still being naked. Annoyed at not being as beautiful as Isaac with Attex. However, he shook his head and used the very same words that the envoy from Cordoba had murmured on the barge, a thousand years earlier, during his sole night of passion, to reply to the same reproach from Attex. "No. You are not beautiful in that way. When I look at you, it seems to me that God, if He exists, offers me honey from the Garden of Eden. You are like His hand and His gaze. You are His voice and His sweetness. There is the light of the stars and the rivers in you. With you, I know what it is to be a happy man...."

She laughed. A happy laugh that rebounded from the vault roof. In her emerald eyes there was obvious pleasure. She pulled the tight-fitting tunic up to her waist, exposing her thighs and mons, hair the color of saffron. She seized Sofer's hands, kissing his fingers. "It's already daylight. But I'm sure the almighty oil lords can wait a little while longer before we need to bother ourselves with them."

She was asleep. Sofer was disconcerted. After they had made love, this time with less voracity and more tenderness, she had fallen asleep next to him, quite suddenly. In the middle of a muttered something or other, she rolled over onto her front, her cheek in the crook of one arm, the other across Sofer's chest, a hand resting on his shoulder. She slept with a stubborn yet peaceful look on her face. A smiling pout on her lips. Head raised on a pillow, Sofer could see the soft curve of her body, the two dimples in the small of her back, half hidden by the poor light of the room, while her buttocks appeared almost child-like. He smiled, moved. Moved, and happy to have told her how beautiful she was. She would probably never realize that from now on this beauty would be engraved in him, somehow imprinted in his body and his emotions like sustenance for the journey to come. He only had to lick his lips to savor the taste of her skin, remember the feel of her buttocks, the smell of her sex. That also troubled him. As if, at the height of their desire, she had offered so much of herself to him so that he would remember her perfume forever.

He would like to have been capable of feeling perfectly innocent. Capable of living this moment in sheer wonder, free from the encumbrance of experience and reason. To have been capable of accepting the magic and the mystery of this meeting that had all the appearance of waking into a dream. Even time itself had no landmarks. A strange sort of night seemed to perpetually pervade this grotto of love, while outside it was broad daylight. He no longer knew exactly how long it had been since he had left his hotel in Baku. Two days or three? Perhaps four? Perhaps even enough to ask himself what was happening to him. Thomson and his employers must by now have an idea. The second attack must have roused them to retaliate. How would they react?

Lying close, she sighed softly in her sleep and Sofer watched her skin gently perspiring. Immediately, his mind thought of oil, of Thomson, of everything that was waiting for him outside these caves that the Khazars, long ago, had believed impregnable. Out of pride, and to rebut his perpetual sarcasm, Sofer would have loved Thomson to have discovered him here, sleeping beside this new Attex. That would have been a sufficient reply to their last meeting and to all the Englishman's skullduggery. Perhaps she, this modern-day Attex, was also playing with him. It was unimportant. With the heat of her flesh next to his, her arm resting on him and the peaceful breathing from her lips, she was surely telling him the opposite. She had even managed to sow doubt in his mind as to what he had thought he imagined and that which appeared, in the end, to be nothing less than an intuitive reality.

Taking care not to disturb her, he lifted the letter Attex had written to Joseph to scrutinize once more the broad and ever-changing writing. Perhaps Attex had lived in this very room. Perhaps she had written the letter in darkness scarcely penetrated by torchlight, ears alert, waiting for an attack that might come at any moment from the Seljuks or the Byzantines.

Yes, it could be that the rock in the grotto retained the traces of those last moments. Doubtless there had been other letters, other scrolls in the library that bore witness to that time.

He knew so little about her. What were her likes and dislikes? Where did she go to dream of Isaac? Did she stay in the darkness of the caves or did she prefer the shock of daylight outside, worrying whether her beloved was on his way back to her, risking dangerous encounters with the soldiers of the Emir from Aleppo or those of the Byzantine tyrant? Did she go to the postern gate several times a day, throwing worried glances at the top of the cliff, fearing to see the assault ropes of the Islamic warriors?

How could she endure Isaac's long absence, endure the loss of his kisses and caresses? Did she never doubt their love, of which she assured Joseph so proudly in her letter, or did she pray each day that the Lord might preserve their young passion despite the distance and incertitude?

"Are you dreaming of her?" She hadn't moved, only opened her eyes. "You are dreaming of the Kathum Attex," she continued. "It's her you love, isn't it?"

Surprised at her intuitive grasp of the situation, he laughed, but less freely than he would have liked. He leaned over to kiss her breasts and then her lips. She moaned with pleasure and turned on her back. A coolness spread where their bodies had, up till an instant before, been locked together.

Sofer let the manuscript fall to the sheet. "What is it that you want from me?"

She threw him an amused look, slightly provocative, but with less surprise than he would have wished.

"I want you to speak for us. I want you to defend the continuing existence of these caves and all that they contain."

"For that you have more need of a good lawyer than a writer!"

"No." She shook her head and sat up. Everything about her was now awake. With the tips of her fingers she caught the bottom of the long green tunic, drew it over her head, and shook her hair back into place. In one movement, as maternal as it was sensual, she held Sofer's face in her hands and then to her smooth belly. Pushing him away just as suddenly, she went to the corner of the room that served as a bathroom.

Sofer heard her pouring water. She came back into the light, a sponge in her hand.

"No, it's you we need." She continued where she had left off. "Your words, with you speaking them. Not to go and speak with the oil barons. That's useless, we know. But to tell the rest of the world what is happening here...."

"The whole world!" Sofer teased. "How are we to do that?"

She sat down on the bed, kissed him gently, caressing his chest. Sweet but already distant. Almost a caress of goodbye, he thought as she took hold of the sheets and pulled them up over him, then lifted her serious eyes to his. "This is how I see things. Your friend Agarounov will already be worried by your disappearance, and will be stirring things up in Baku. I would think he will have already telephoned your ambassador. Lazir is going to phone him. He will ask him to alert your publisher. Agarounov will announce that you have been kidnapped by the New Khazars."

As she spoke her eyes were sparkling, although her tone and demeanor were serious. Sofer watched her with fascination. He had before him a true heroine, dedicated to reestablishing justice and truth with all the energy and intelligence at her disposal. At the same time, he could see a child announcing the rules of a new game.

"Listen to me!" she said impatiently, apparently aware of his straying thoughts. "For a few days we can keep the pressure on by maintaining a complete silence. Nobody will know where you are, Agarounov can tell those who want to listen that maybe you are even dead. The newspapers will make the connection with the Chechyns.... Perfect! You will have plenty of time to inspect the library. And there could be some time for us to..."

She paused with a sly smile, ambiguous, slightly questioning. Sofer caught her hand and kissed her fingertips. "We could have the time to...." He smiled and replied in the same tone. "Yes. And you imagine that during this time the newspapers—"

"Certainly the European newspapers!"

"… the European press, such as it is, will be interested in me, and therefore will be led to you!"

"I can imagine the headlines: Famous Writer Marc Sofer Disappears in Baku. Responsibility for kidnapping claimed by mysterious group, the New Khazars…."

"I fear you would only find such an article using a high-resolution magnifying glass!" sighed Sofer.

"No. Don't be so modest! You have articles published in all the important papers in Germany, Italy, France and Britain. Your books are published everywhere."

"Therefore, when I reappear again, you hope that a forest of microphones will be pushed at me so that I can tell the story of these caves, the synagogue and the oil!"

"The story of the Khazars! Now and then. Yes, certainly! Why are you so dubious? That's exactly what will happen. And then you can bring the journalists here and everything will be saved. The oil consortia will no longer be able to act as if we don't exist. Everyone will know that they want to destroy a sacred place, one of the treasures of human history. In spite of its money and power, the OCOO will have to take note. Israel will not allow them to destroy one of the sanctuaries of the Jewish people. No European government will allow it! Of course that's how it will happen. I tell you, their weapon is silence. If you want to, you, Marc Sofer, can break it. Then we will have saved the memory of the Khazars!"

Carried away by her own excitement, the pitch of her voice had climbed an octave. Sofer smiled again, but had to admit that this plan had more common sense about it than first appeared. Except that upon the official announcement of his kidnapping, the bosses of the OCOO would be certain to try to get there first. Perhaps they would come here. But in that case, he, Sofer, would be in a position of strength to negotiate the safeguarding of the synagogue and the library. She was right; it all depended on him.

He hesitated, thinking about telling her about the Englishman, but she was squeezing his hands, pressing for a decision. "You must not refuse. In Brussels you commented on having led too many unsuccessful campaigns. I am offering you the opportunity to save a fabulous part of our Jewish heritage. You cannot refuse!"

Sofer scrutinized her earnest face. He could see traces of far-off Khazar ancestry in her beautiful visage: the high cheekbones, the slightly slanted eyes with their smooth lids, the upper lip curved and full. He could not ignore the logical points in her argument.

He asked, "When you were at my conference in Brussels, you had already thought this all out, hadn't you? You wove your web around me like a spider around its prey. You didn't doubt for an instant that I would succumb to your trap."

"No!" she protested, shaking her head. "No! It was while listening to you that I realized and thought up how you could help us."

She leaned against him, touching his lips with a light kiss. "Later I began to think of you in other terms ... to tell myself that you might think of me simply as a woman."

Sofer leaned back gently with an amused smile. "I can never tell when you are telling the truth!"

She laughed capriciously, stood up and held out her hand to him. "Oh yes you can! Stay here three more days with me and you will never doubt again... Meanwhile come, I want to see daylight—it's nearly midday. You can make up your mind after we have eaten."

❧

The sun struck the cliff and lit up the forest with a light as bright as that of liquid steel. The air, full of small clouds of insects, smelled of dust and dry herbs. Accustomed to the cool air of the caves, Sofer felt suffocated by the heat when they had to climb the exterior stairway to reach the kitchen. Once there, a relative freshness pervaded, retained by the half-open wooden shutters covering the opening in the rock. Sofer expected to see someone, man or woman, but once again they were alone. He wondered if she was avoiding meeting other members of the New Khazars, or if her companions simply avoided meeting him for security reasons. Then, as he was sitting down at the table, she noticed the scroll of Attex's letter that he was still holding in his hand.

"You might just discover other letters from her in the library," she said. "But there are so many scrolls there that you would have to be very lucky to stumble on one without the whole collection being indexed first."

She passed him a bottle of white wine covered in mud and an old corkscrew. When he had poured their wine, he explained what it was in the letter from the Kathum that troubled him so.

"I didn't know whether she really came here to seek refuge and hide from the Greek ambassador. It just seemed logical to me. She would have had to find a secure hiding place. The thing that bothers me most, though, is whether she really loved Isaac ben Eliezer! For me, it was just a good idea for a story. Once again, life is stranger than fiction."

She cut into an enormous watermelon and placed the slices on a large blue and yellow ceramic plate before raising her eyes to look at him. "It wasn't such a safe hiding place as all that," she said sadly. She put the platter on the table and sat opposite him, pointing to the scroll. "That is a copy, but the Khagan never received the original. Attania never left with it. What Attex feared, happened. The Emir's soldiers invaded the grotto. It was a massacre. Attex died here with all the others."

Sofer put down his glass just as he had been about to sip. "How do you know that?" he asked, appalled.

"We found a document that recounts the event. It is in the library, you can read it for yourself."

"It's not possible! If the Muslims had come here they would certainly have destroyed the synagogue and the *mikvah*. They would have taken what they wanted from the library and burned the rest!"

She shook her head. "No! Attex and her uncle Hanuko had taken precautions against that. The document we found places the event in the year 4660 of the Jewish calendar, the same year Joseph finally decided to reply to the Rabbi of Cordoba. It is therefore the same year Isaac met Attex. There is no mention of the letter from the Kathum. The document only describes the drama in hindsight, some months later, in winter. The armies of the Emir and Byzantium had by then withdrawn from the plains. During the battle that was literally unfolding below their eyes, as we can read in Attex's letter, the inhabitants of the troglodyte village took pains to protect the things they considered most precious: all the corridors and stairways leading to the great grotto and the *mikvah* were stopped up with rock-falls that looked natural. That transformed the rest of the interior of the cliff into a labyrinth where it was easy to lose oneself."

"She died here," murmured Sofer. "Right here. I can hardly believe it!"

She placed her hand on his and squeezed gently. He felt himself ridiculously moved to tears. It was difficult to contain it. He shook his head, and smiled woodenly. "You can think me a fool, but I can still only imagine Attex waiting here for Isaac, completely safe. When Joseph finally decided to write that reply to Rabbi Hazdai, Isaac hastened to rejoin her and they ... they would have had time for some love, before he left for Cordoba."

He fell silent for an instant, on the point of adding, like us, in some ways. Struck by the similarity of their situation, he contented himself with suggesting, as if what had happened could still be changed by his statement, that possibly Attex could have accompanied him on his journey home.

She avoided his gaze, shaking her head, and biting into a slice of melon, she said, "No. When the Emir's soldiers invaded the caves peopled with the Jews, no allowances were made, no one survived. Especially not the women, who pass on the religion. Attex and her faithful Attania died that day. We can only hope that they died swiftly."

Sofer unrolled the manuscript and passed his fingertips over the rough paper. The premonitory sentence written by Attex in the dark ink hammered through his mind: *If a Muslim soldier should rape me tomorrow, he cannot soil me more than the smoke from his fires.* Then it must have come true! May God have granted her a death without humiliation, bathed in the love of Isaac, with her eternally! For a moment they ate and drank in silence. Outside, in the stifling air, the noise of crickets filled the void. Swallows glided the length of the cliff chirping, then swinging farther off above the forest, flying higher and higher.

While she poured them some more wine, some small stones fell, bouncing off the walls and the stairways. She frowned, listening carefully, then shrugged. "Pebbles ... they fall sometimes when it's very hot. The top of the cliff splits. It only takes an animal to...."

Sofer, who hardly heard her because he was so engrossed in his own thoughts, interrupted her. "But, then, Isaac knew nothing about it! While he was cooling his heels in Itil, waiting to obtain an audience with Joseph, he did not know that Attex was no longer alive!"

She nodded her head. "Yes, and the poor lad must have been on tenterhooks. Impatient to leave Itil to rejoin her, but obliged to await the goodwill of the Khagan, in spite of the help given by Hezekiah ... and all that for such terrible disenchantment!"

"Disenchantment? Why? At last he would have obtained the letter for which he had waited so long!"

"Yes. But what did it say? Joseph described his kingdom without any great enthusiasm. The only thing that seemed to stir him was telling the legend of the visit of the angel to convert King Bulan. As to knowing whether the messiah was going to appear in the Khazar Kingdom, he responded in very few lines ... he was very far removed from the passionate hope of Isaac and the Sephardi Jews for a New Kingdom of Israel!"

Sofer emptied his glass, incapable of ridding himself of the feeling of sadness and defeat that had invaded him on learning of Attex's death. Suddenly he found the room too small and the air stifling in spite of the cave's coolness. He noticed a slight groaning outside. Perhaps the sound of an engine, very far away. He stood up to go over to the opening and pushed open the wooden shutter.

Light flooded the room. The heat struck his face and body like a blow, but it calmed him. The shadows in the forest were lengthening. The plain was fixed in the immobility of death. Even the swallows had deserted the sky. He realized that she had got up and was standing behind him. She slid her arms around his chest and pressed her breasts against his back. When she planted a kiss on his neck, her breath was scented with wine and her lips still retained the sweet coolness of the melon.

"It's you who is the novelist," she murmured into his ear, "but if you want, I can tell you how it all happened."

Sofer, holding her hands in his, held her close to his back. "Go ahead...."

"As Hezekiah had said, now that Isaac had saved his life, his father the Khagan would have to receive him, to listen to him and, above all, read the letter from Rabbi Hazdai Ibn Shaprut. But that would take time. First they had to go to Itil. There, Isaac found Joseph's real palace. It stood on an island in the middle of the river and could only be reached by boat. Once there, under the surveillance of guards, visitors passed under a golden triumphal arch. The palace itself was of modest enough appearance, constructed in the Greek style as at Sarkel, adjacent to a synagogue and surrounded by brick walls. The interior was a curious mixture; over the centuries the Khazars had amassed a collection of some of the richest artifacts from the Asian, Persian and Byzantine peoples.

"With Rabbi Hanania's assistance, Isaac found lodgings on a neighboring island, closer to the mouth of the river and the Sea of the Khazars. He discovered that Itil was a town spread over a number of islets. Some were completely Jewish. Others were occupied entirely by rich Muslim merchants. The minarets there seemed impaled on the red sky that reflected off the sea. Another was uniquely inhabited by Christians who, very quietly, were building churches. When Isaac came out of the synagogue after evening prayers, it was to hear the muezzin's calls mixed with the chanting of monks. At last, one day, Hezekiah came to find him.

"'My father will grant you an audience,' he announced proudly. 'Come right now, a boat is waiting for us.'

"A little later, Isaac was bowing to the Khagan, heart beating fast. Rabbi Hanania and Borouh were there. Borouh looked solemn. The rabbi had reminded Isaac of the rules when attending an audience: prostrate yourself without lifting your eyes or uttering even a single word until the Khagan desires that you do so. Isaac lay there in fear and trembling.

"Joseph seemed to have aged several years in a few weeks. In spite of his thirty years, gray hairs showed everywhere in his beard and long hair. He did not keep Isaac in his position of submission for long.

"'Stand up, Isaac from the country of the Sephardim. Even though you have been living among us for some months now, I bid you welcome in my Kingdom. I must also thank you for the help you gave my son Hezekiah during our battle. Hezekiah assures me that you saved his life and I believe him. But I did bring to his attention the fact that his life would not have been in danger if he had not left our camp to join you. Am I right, Isaac ben Eliezer?'

"'Yes, Khagan,' whispered Isaac.

"'I thank you, then, but I am not going to offer you what a father must offer to one who has saved a son's life, showering him with gold and presents and granting all his wishes.'

"Joseph then used the silence to look at Borouh and the rabbi. Perhaps just to calm the remainder of his anger. Isaac could not be sure because he did not dare meet the Khagan's eyes with his own. 'There is another matter pending between us, Isaac: you helped my sister, the Kathum Attex, to avoid my orders. Beck Borouh himself assures me that she spent a whole night with you alone as only a wife should spend with her husband. I should cut you in two for that insult. Consequently, I thank you for saving my son Hezekiah's life and will allow you to live, thereby forgetting the way you soiled my sister's honor on that day. Am I fair, Isaac ben Eliezer?'

"'Yes, Khagan of the Khazars, you are fair. Save on one point. Attex bears no loss of honor because, although we were not united as a married couple, we were as lovers. Rabbi Hanania himself could tell you that there exists a teaching that compares the Torah to a young woman.'

"Joseph interrupted him. 'I know that lesson.'

"All fear dissipated, Isaac continued. 'Then you know that, Oh Khagan of the Khazars, only the Almighty can put such love in our hearts. It is His way of existing in us. Thus this love cannot dishonor us. On the contrary, it leads us down the right road, like a star on the horizon. As immense as is your power, Khagan Joseph, you cannot do anything against Him, nor against me, nor against her. That is the way it is.'

"Joseph, stunned by this answer, sat with his mouth open. Borouh's brow was more creased than an old tunic. Hanania's pupils sparkled like two jewels. He swayed to and fro very quickly to hide his chuckles.

"The silence in the audience hall was denser than a tomb. It lasted so long that Isaac thought his time had come to rejoin the Lord, blessed be His name, to whom he had, no doubt, attributed too much goodwill. Suddenly, Joseph's laughter boomed through the palace. A laugh such as the Khazars had never before heard from their Khagan.

"When Joseph, wiping his eyes with his silk sleeve, finally recovered his breath, he exclaimed, 'Well! I now know why Rabbi Hazdai chose you to be his messenger, Isaac ben Eliezer!'

"The rest of the audience was very different. Joseph left his throne and invited Isaac to share breakfast with him, Borouh and Hanania. There, the Khagan explained to Isaac what the real situation in the kingdom was. It was bad; the alliance with Byzantium was impossible, for even without the lies and tricks of the Greeks, it would mean a denial of the Law of Moses. The Russians from Kiev had only one idea in their heads; invade the Kingdom of the Khazars.

"'... and to beat the Khagan, who was their master and whose ancestors had taken their capital,' continued Joseph, sighing. 'It is as if they are obsessed with making us disappear and leaving them as the first men born on earth.'

"Borouh added, 'Their Queen, Olga, only became Christian with one end in mind: to bring the forces of Byzantium to her side. As for our southern borders, beyond the Great Mountains, they tell me that the Emir of Aleppo is leading a campaign against Rome. Let's hope the war goes on for a long time and exhausts them both!'

"'That is why,' continued Rabbi Hanania in a slow voice, resting his hand on Isaac's, 'the Khagan feels he cannot answer the letter from your rabbi with as much enthusiasm as we would all prefer.'

"'How could I make my kingdom the sanctuary for all the House of Israel? How could I assure all Jews, living far from Zion, welcome and peace, when I can hardly defend my own towns and villages?' asked Joseph. 'If the Lord wants to fulfill His word in our steppe, if He would wish David's prophesy realized here, then He should not give such strength to Kiev and Byzantium!'

"There was so much bitterness in this plea that Hanania twisted his beard and turned his face away. In any case, Isaac understood; he would have a letter to carry back to Cordoba and disappointment to transmit by word of mouth to—"

"Wait!" Sofer interrupted brusquely, detaching himself from her.

"What is it...?"

"Listen!"

From outside the cave came whistles, scuffling noises and shouts. Then, suddenly, before either of them could utter a word, a blue nylon rope dropped down over the mouth of the cave. A man, all in black, dangled on the end of it, pointing a gun at them.

"In God's name!" exclaimed Sofer. What the hell is going on?"

Chapter twenty-eight

Borjomi, Georgia
May 2000

He was several feet above the window, suspended from the cliff, hanging in the void like a huge spider. His black suit covered him from head to toe, down to gloves and a hood. Sofer had just enough time to think that in this heat the costume was ridiculous. Weird, imposing sunglasses that reflected silver took up half his face. He was pointing a semi-automatic at Sofer. The red dot of the laser range-finder was illuminating a point on Sofer's chest. The man waved his hand, and the red eye of the laser zigzagged from left to right. Sofer realized that he was being ordered to stand aside, the man fearing perhaps that he would try to close the shutter. He turned around, thinking that she was right behind him. He wanted to touch her, to hold her to him at that very instant, as if a unit made of the two of them could form a more solid defense. In fact he discovered she was on the other side of the room, standing behind the chimney that served as an oven, pressed against the rock as if she wanted to melt into it. She expressed neither panic nor unease and was looking at him with extraordinary intensity. Sofer thought he remembered an expression like that on her face an hour or so ago, at the instant of orgasm. He said, "Stay with me! Don't be afraid, they wouldn't dare kill us...."

She smiled. Not an ironic smile, but a tender smile, as if she were thanking him for having had the thought. Sofer's attention was distracted. He heard more noises and shouts from outside and turned around.

The man in black was endeavoring to swing himself on his nylon rope. He pushed away from the cliff face, swung in folding his legs and then straightened out, coming in through the window like a snake. He had scarcely regained his balance when the gun was again aimed at Sofer. The man hesitated, as if something puzzled him. The red dot left Sofer's chest, slithered over the table with the two wine glasses and the remains of the watermelon. Sofer risked taking a look over his shoulder. With one glance, he discovered what was wrong; she had disappeared.

Vanished.

She, Sonja Tchobanzade, his lover, his Attex.

Where and how, he had no idea. Neither had the man in black. In fact, in spite of all his sophisticated equipment, he looked totally dumbfounded. Sofer wanted to laugh, this was so like a game of hide and seek. Then he thought that perhaps he didn't really have much to laugh about. He hoped that she was not going to commit the folly of trying to fight against this commando.

A muffled sound issued from under the black suit of his assailant, and the muzzle of the gun waved toward the kitchen door that led to the stairway up the face of the cliff. Sofer went toward it shrugging his shoulders. "I'm going, I'm going!"

❦

The strange whistling noises that Sofer had heard were coming from thirty men descending in parallel along the cliff. Professionals, each one keenly aware of what he had to do. All were equipped with black outfits, infrared goggles and a semi-automatic. There were also three or four carrying rifles with telescopic sights. When they launched out from the cliff side from the top, they looked like a swarm of flies.

Some of them were standing on the highest steps of the stairway, others halfway down the cliff. Still others effected a controlled drop of several hundred feet to arrive down at the temple postern gate. As soon as the soles of their Reeboks took hold on a stairway or the flat shelves into the cliff, they released their ropes with a flick of their wrists. They entered the caves in groups of two or three, searching the darkness with the red beams of their weapons while changing their glasses from day to night vision.

They let off a few rounds to intimidate the enemy, not intending to penetrate deep into the caves. Most of the members of the New Khazars had the same reflex: when they heard the ominous sound of an attack, they ran toward the stairways and the openings in the cliff. Most of them were unarmed and had no way of fighting.

Only Lazir the boxing champion, woken from his deep siesta in one of the high caves, made it a point of honor not to be captured so easily. He faced one of his assailants in a hand to hand struggle on the edge of the cliff. Two men in black tried to immobilize him. In spite of that he managed to throw one of his adversaries over the edge into the void. At the instant the man broke his back on a platform lower down, Lazir turned around to face his other attackers, arms in the air like the champion he was. A bullet hit his left shoulder, breaking his shoulder blade and forcing him down on the ground. The marksman, equipped with a telescopic sight, was fifty feet away.

Sofer, who had just come out into the hot pulsating air, saw the fight from afar. He had just enough time to recognize Lazir by his black and white shirt, which was now rapidly turning scarlet. Calmly, but with urgency, the men in black herded the ten 'terrorists' to the front of the main cave. At last Sofer saw the faces of the members of the New Khazars. All men, all younger than thirty. Everything pointed to them being students, most of them frightened and apparently as dangerous as a cloud of dragonflies. Some showed anger and were gesturing angrily to save face. The commando attack possessed something so mechanical, so unstoppable, so perfectly dehumanized that not a word had been spoken and Sofer noted, nobody, not even himself, had thought to protest.

As soon as they were gathered outside one of the entrances leading to the main grotto, two helicopters surged out from above the cliff. One of them, apparently a military vehicle painted in khaki, had a pointed muzzle and was armed with what looked like guided missiles. Under its belly hung a metal container large enough to contain a motor vehicle. In a deafening roar and with the precision of a butterfly, the pilot deposited his charge on the platform in front of the postern gate. The second helicopter, in the red and white colors of a civilian machine, hovered some distance off. Sofer was able to distinguish a man in the cabin looking out at them through binoculars. The helicopter was far away from the cliff, but Sofer could have sworn that the man was Thomson.

⁂

Within a few minutes the men in black had gathered them together in the central courtyard of the great grotto, between the library, the weapons store and the synagogue.

Sofer realized that the commandos knew the complex network of caves and galleries well. Each time they had to choose between two directions, they showed no hesitation. Their infrared glasses permitted them to move without lights while he and the New Khazars, their way lit by one sole flashlight, progressed like blind men, stumbling and bumping into one another. A shrewd and humiliating way to dissuade them from any attempt at escape, thought Sofer. To run away was to lose oneself in the dark.

When they arrived under the immense vault where his lover had taken him earlier, Sofer hoped that she would be there, hidden in the library or the weapons hall. Some torches were burning there, hardly breaching the darkness. There were a thousand and one possible hiding places. Wherever she was at that moment, Sofer hoped that at least she had found a shelter in which she could escape from the commandos without getting herself lost. And, above all, that she would have the sense to do so without forgetting how quickly they might be evacuated. Because it was obvious that this was what awaited them.

They were grouped unceremoniously, gun barrels pointing at them unwaveringly. The commandos, difficult to distinguish now that

292

the black of their uniforms melted into the darkness of the caves, were doing something they couldn't see. Sofer heard metallic noises. He thought he saw a sort of wheelbarrow that someone pushed in, but just at that instant a battery of strong spotlights blinded them. The pale yellow light immobilized them as effectively as if they had been trapped in a block of ice. Protecting his eyes from the glare, Sofer discovered the boxing champion rejoining them, his face contorted with pain. Someone had quickly bandaged up his shoulder.

"Lazir!" exclaimed Sofer sympathetically. "Damnit man! Couldn't you forget to play the hero for once in your life?"

Lazir's twisted smile was belied by the look in his eyes. Sofer had no time to say anything more; a gloved hand grasped his shoulder. He turned around to disengage it, but a neutral voice ordered in English, "Follow us, Mr. Sofer. He is waiting for you outside."

Sofer tried to penetrate the gaze of the man behind the dark glasses. "In that case, why did you bring me here, into the grotto?"

The only response was the pressure of a hand on his back. "Please, sir."

Sofer glanced around at the erstwhile companions of his vanished Attex. The raw light of the spotlights transformed their faces into masks on which their fear and incredulity could be read. None of them were paying any attention to him, except for Lazir, who was staring at him; as if to encourage Sofer to follow the commandos, the boxing champ nodded his head discreetly in their direction.

The great explanation from the brave oil men was about to come. Sofer even had a good idea who this *he* was who awaited him outside.

He sighed and, in his most belligerent voice, said, "Give me a flashlight. I am not going to smash my face into a rock just because you can see in the dark with your Martian glasses!"

❧

He had not been wrong. Thomson was standing at the foot of the cliff, in a freshly opened clearing in the forest, near the red and white helicopter whose blades were still turning slowly. The Englishman was dressed in an impeccable gray linen and silk suit, slightly shiny, as extravagant in its way as the costumes of the men in black. All smiles, Thomson held out his right hand, as if he had never been so pleased to meet someone in his entire life.

"Delighted to see you, Mr. Sofer! So sorry for the upset; the men hadn't realized they were to bring you here right away. In this type of operation, you believe you have thought of everything but there is always something that goes slightly wrong!"

Sofer stared at him coldly, refusing the proffered hand. Over the throbbing of the engine that the pilot was already revving, he shouted, "Stop taking me for an idiot, Thomson! I would prefer it!"

Without waiting to be invited, he climbed up into the rear seat of the helicopter. Thomson sat beside him, retaining the gentlemanly smile on his lips. The pilot passed them earphones which included microphones, which reduced the infernal noise of the cabin to acceptable levels.

The machine rose gently and pivoted slowly in order to clear the unstable currents flowing over the face of the cliff. Sofer profited from this by absorbing as much as he could, searching for the silhouette of the woman who had told him to call her Sonja. All he could see were more men in black. Scattered in the openings to the troglodyte village, they were working on the rocks with some sort of tools Sofer could not identify. On the terrace near the postern gate and temple where the commandos had deposited the metallic container that now stood open, Sofer was surprised to notice that two men were installing a camera.

The cliff fell away rapidly, the dark mouths of the caves and the constructions that masked the entrances appearing to become as small as children's toys. Almost involuntarily, Sofer murmured her name. Sonja! He realized he had not called her that once, even when they were making love. Worse still, he had listened so inattentively to her family name that now he couldn't remember it!

Rendered sharper by the headset, Thomson's voice resonated in his ears, jolting him out of his reverie. "We will be in the helicopter for about an hour. If you are thirsty, you have only to say…." The Englishman brandished a thermos flask and filled a glass with fizzy water.

Sofer contented himself with a shake of the head. "Where are we going?" he asked.

Thomson pointed over the co-pilot's shoulder, directly ahead, in a southwest direction. They could just make out beyond the immense plain, yellow with drought, a range of bluish mountains shimmering in a heat haze.

"There. A charming holiday resort in the mountains. You will like it … we will give you the tourist's guided tour; we're going to cross the whole of the plains of central Georgia."

"And what are we to do there, in this charming holiday resort? Why aren't we going back to Baku?"

The Englishman's smile widened. "We will be perfectly at ease to chat there," which meant he would be able to avoid questions about what happened here, and give Sofer time to consider his own position!

Sofer loosened his seatbelt to look behind him once more. The cliff with the caves was already no more than a white strip above the forest.

⪼

Flying at low altitude, the helicopter wove between the valleys full of ancient trees. It was a magnificent region, where one could sense the vigor of the wilderness. The folds of the mountains, moving between sun and shadow, looked like drapes of ancient velvet. The highest peaks, delineating the border with Turkey, soared into the sky in the extreme south. Suddenly, they were flying over a river of dark water. The pilot followed the meandering river. In the headset Thomson explained. "We are nearly there. Below us is the Miqvari River. This valley was very well known about ten to fifteen years ago. Previously, in the time of the czars, Borjomi produced natural carbonated water for the Russian aristocrats. The Soviets took it over…."

"I know about Borjormi," Sofer interrupted dryly. He had been served the bubbly water several times in Moscow.

"Good! Because that is where we are going. I knew it would please you."

In all honesty, it was very difficult to believe that the little town they were to fly over a moment later had been one of the most famous spa towns in the Caucasus. The road that led there had more potholes than tar. Two of the three bridges that allowed one to cross the Miqvari were unusable; the factory where the water was bottled appeared to be abandoned. The ruined buildings allowed a view of the burst tanks, but there was no sign of any workmen. An old network of rusty pipes ended in a crossroads of railway lines that must have formed a station not so long ago. The rails had been lifted and wild grasses replaced them.

The pilot climbed a little. They found themselves fifty feet above several strange structures planted in the forest like debris from another planet.

"Great Soviet architecture," the Englishman said sarcastically.

It was difficult to describe them as apartment blocks. They were nothing but simple slabs of raw concrete with exposed iron reinforcements supported by crumbling pillars. Some of these gray buildings must have risen fifteen stories, dominating the old oaks and hundred-year-old beeches. Most were empty, without even a partition between the slabs. In others, plastic tarpaulins or panels of plywood defined the boundaries of the poor lodgings. Sofer could see inside to women's faces and children's eyes raised to watch the passing helicopter.

Leaving the village behind them, the helicopter plunged down toward a large bend in the river. Unexpectedly, a castle appeared in the middle of a vast parkland protected by a wrought iron fence. Once again, it was a strange building, but this time very tidy, with bright red balustrades, balconies, shutters and outbuildings contrasting with immaculate white walls. The whole structure was fussy in the extreme, as if the architect had no other desire than to place one roof on top of another. A small observatory tower crowned the edifice.

"Constructed by the Romanovs at the end of the nineteenth century," Thomson announced, as the pilot executed a sharp turn. "The family passed several summers here. You will see, the interior is even more interesting and surprising than the exterior!"

The helicopter settled above a sort of esplanade in front of the castle. The pilot, with a dexterity that spoke of long practice, grounded the aircraft gradually in a huge empty pool covered in blue tesserae. A dozen men in garb similar to the commandos at the grotto ran to them even before the blades had ceased to rotate. As soon as Thomson and Sofer left their seats, they formed a protective circle around them as if some hostile crowd was about to surge forth from the surrounding forest. The absurdity of the scene caused Sofer to smile wryly.

"What on earth are you afraid of?" he asked Thomson. "The ghosts of the Romanovs?"

The Englishman laughed. "No, of bears! There are at least a dozen bears in the grounds. At this time of year the females have their young with them and the noise of the helicopters makes them aggressive. But you are right, we have nothing to fear. Truly, nothing at all! You will be able to judge for yourself."

In the hall of the castle, standing beside immense snow-white marble fountains, Sofer suddenly saw a reflection of himself in a tall mirror. He had the strange feeling that he didn't look like himself; from his creased clothes rose a face made harsh by a thick gray beard. The contrast with Thomson, whose every step made his superbly cut suit glint, was gripping. Without a word, the Englishman climbed a grand staircase leading to the second floor. There, without waiting for Sofer to join him, he knocked respectfully on a door covered in leather.

"Eddy! Is that you at last?" exclaimed a fluid voice from the interior of the room.

"Mr. Sofer is here," announced 'Eddy' Thomson. "Arrived without mishap...."

Reaching the threshold of the room, Sofer saw a small, chubby man. About sixty, with curly white hair, he wore striped pants and a canary yellow Lacoste shirt with a pair of suspenders. He held out a hand to Sofer, who ignored it.

"Jeffrey Bellow," said the small man without lowering his hand. "I am the deputy administrator of the ocoo. In our jargon, that means I am the one who has to make the disagreeable decisions."

"In that case Mr. Bellow, why do you want to shake hands with me?"

Bellow looked taken aback. He had a rather feminine mouth, almost delicate. The lips trembled, then opened in a brief laugh. His arm dropped.

"Ah," he said, looking at Thomson, "you were right, Eddy."

"Mr. Sofer," explained Thomson, "I told Mr. Bellow that you could be depended upon to say the unexpected."

Sofer did not pay any attention to Thomson's remark, being too enthralled with the surroundings. He was in a very large room with a ceiling heavily worked in the Turkish style, covered in recesses and mirrors, with walls tiled with oriental ceramics. Bellow was leaning back against a small mahogany and elm desk. The marquetry on its surface formed the Hammer and Sickle. A pedestal at its side supported a bronze. Sofer moved nearer to ensure he was not mistaken. No, it definitely was Stalin, but in the classical pose normally adopted by Napoleon, a cape blown by the wind, his right hand inserted into a jacket buttoned up to the neck.

"Curious, isn't it?" Bellow remarked. "We are in Stalin's office, reverently preserved after his death. It appears he came here more often than the Romanovs ever did. The call of his native country, I suppose. Rumor has it that it was between these walls that he decided on and ordered some of the 'reforms' of his comrades, as the Little Father of the People was wont to call them...."

"Mr. Bellow, Thomson has already discharged his duty as tourist guide during the journey," cut in Sofer. "I would prefer you to tell me why I am here!"

Bellow's thin mouth firmed. "You are right. Even though we have plenty of time."

He walked around the desk, opened a drawer and drew out a shirt box, opening it and emptying its contents onto the desk surface. They were photographs, nothing but photographs, but Sofer froze as soon as he had them in his hand. Photos of him with Yakubov in his garden in Montmartre, photos of him at Cambridge, Oxford and Baku, with Agarounov and Lazir, and even in the mayor's company in the cemetery!

And photos with her. There, on the cliff-side stairway, in front of the kitchen cave. Kissing for the first time, spotlighted in the dawn light. In one of the pictures, Sofer's hand had pushed back Sonja's sweater and the curve of her bare shoulder was visible. Sofer's fingers began to tremble and a wave of nausea overcame him.

"You really are filth," he muttered.

He raised his eyes. Thomson was standing beside Bellow. He was holding a tiny digital recorder in his hand. He pushed a button and Sofer heard his own voice. "Wait! Wait! The bosses of the ocoo know exactly who you are!"

And she replied, "By now, I suppose they will have our photos on their desks and files containing our every detail!"

A silent laugh shook Bellow's cheeks. "Yes, Mr. Sofer. She was correct. We have it all. In sound and pictures."

"So what? What use are they to you?"

"The better to know you with, my dear sir!"

"We wanted to know who you were and what you were going to do in this affair, Sofer," Thomson intervened, placing the recorder on top of the photos. "We had to know who you were working for, and why."

"This is ridiculous! I am a writer. You didn't need to invade my private life to discover that."

"I must admit that there is truth in what you say," Bellow said sleazily. "That's what is so diverting about you. And nice!"

Rage flared in Sofer. To purge his anger he tore the photographs that he was still holding into shreds and flung the pieces on the desk.

"I repeat my question. What am I doing here?"

The small man's mouth continued to show its strange, tender look. His voice flowed like metal slicing through flesh. "You were on private property, Mr. Sofer. Your girlfriend Sonja Tchobanzade and her ridiculous companions the New Khazars have been breaking the most elementary of laws for weeks now. I had thought that you might be of use before they inveigled you into committing irredeemable errors."

"Yes...?"

Thomson leaned over the desk to pick up a bit of photo that showed part of Sonja's features. He shook it in Sofer's face. "She's just thirty," he said, gently scolding. "You must be nearly fifty and, excuse me for saying so, you are no Robert Redford. When a girl of thirty stages a whole screenplay to get you into her bed, do you never ask any questions? Do you never think that she is simply manipulating you like a puppet?"

Sofer clenched his fists but stopped before hitting him. His anger subsiding to a cold hardness, he began to smile. "My poor friend! I fear that your psychology is a little provincial. It is when a man like you offers me a box of caviar that I believe I am being manipulated. Not when a woman kisses me! As for you, Bellow, don't imagine for one moment that the cliffs and the caves could be your property or that of your fucking company. They never will be. They belong to a whole people—mine! The Jewish people. What they contain is sacred, Bellow! Their contents are a thousand years old! I know that doesn't mean much to you. But your problem is that you cannot act as if they don't exist!"

"But, Mr. Sofer ... that is precisely my intention."

Sofer's laugh was more of a groan. "Then you must be acting under some great delusions. I certainly will not stand in your way; I have no such pretensions... "

"Oh!" Thomson mocked. "I suppose you are dreaming about Miss Sonja Tchobanzade's strategy for using the media, then? Your kidnapping makes one of the European newspapers, you reappear, and then expose the noble cause of the New Khazars to the rest of the world... "

Bellow smiled and tapped the recorder. "Don't forget, my friend, that we have sound and pictures, as she told you."

Once more Sofer felt nausea mixing with his anger. Sonja had explained that strategy when they were in her bedroom. And therefore everything else had been recorded too! For the first time in his life he could have killed. Bellow must have sensed it, for he raised his hand in a protective gesture as much as to beg for calm.

"This is what I propose, Mr. Sofer. It is very simple: nothing ever happened."

Sofer frowned, silent for an instant. "I don't understand."

"Nothing happened," repeated Bellow smiling in the friendly

manner one assumes when explaining a difficult concept to a child. "You never heard of the New Khazars, you never met any of its members, you don't know Mr. Thomson or myself."

"And … the caves?"

"They don't exist."

"You're completely out of your mind!"

"Not at all. The caves don't exist. What you saw was nothing but the imaginings of your mind. That kind of thing is familiar to you, isn't it? After all, you are a novelist."

Sofer shook himself, petrified with fright. He thought about what she had said: the strategy of silence! The worst weapon, she had said, was silence.

"But why are you so keen on silence?"

Bellow smiled as if he were teaching an infant the elementary rules of survival. "I believe that Eddy has already taken time to explain the role of oil in this region. Here, Mr. Sofer, the whole world is at war. As usual, the Americans want all the oil for themselves. And, obviously, the Russians don't want to lose it all. The reserves discovered under the Sadoue plains, where your lousy caves are to be found, are immense. Unfortunately, they are badly located, as much for us as for you. Twelve miles as the crow flies from the border between Georgia, Chechnya and Daghestan … do I need to spell it out for you? If we reveal the existence of these reserves, war will break out tomorrow morning between the Americans and the Russians, just like the bad old days. But, you see, I represent European interests. And they don't want that, Mr. Sofer. They don't want to send missiles and young men to kill each other for oil. That's not our culture, as you may say, unless the Americans decide we must play it that way to give their GIs something to do! Consequently, it is in our interest at present, Mr. Sofer, for this miraculous pocket not to exist…. For the moment, at any rate, until the region settles down. In five years, maybe ten, who knows, our great politicos will integrate Georgia into Europe and then the game can begin! Only then will we be able to announce that we have just found a well of eighty million metric ton capacity that will assure energy autonomy for our beautiful countries in Europe for the following thirty years!"

Thomson and Bellow laughed like children. "And that, Mr. Sofer, is why we need silence! As you see, I too am defending a cause!"

"Wait a minute! ... Since you are not going to extract this oil, how would it harm you to preserve and publish the finding of the Khazar artifacts?"

"Don't be naïve! You saw the naphtha wells! It wouldn't take six months before some idiot, exploring the depths, would find them."

Sofer felt a shiver invade his being. Fatigue, but more than that, fear and heartache. "You can't do it," he murmured. "You can't! These are the only, and unique, material traces of the existence of the Khazars. You can't just destroy them with a wave of your hand! The whole world will punish you...."

"The whole world can fuck off, Sofer," growled Thomson. "The whole world wants cheap oil for their tanks. That's what counts!"

"The library? You could at least dismantle it, and the synagogue and the weapons room, for reconstruction elsewhere! It can't be necessary to destroy them...."

"And how would you propose explaining the provenance of these relics?" Bellow asked coldly. "And anyway, what's the difference between transporting them for miles and miles and leaving them where they are? A useless waste of our time, Mr. Sofer. There is only one solution and I have given it to you; none of it exists."

"It exists! I have seen it with my own eyes. I have held in my hands a letter of love and fear that a woman wrote more than a thousand years ago! You can't make it cease to exist...."

"Oh yes I can. You can go quietly back home and write some more stories. I never read novels, but my wife has read some of yours. She likes them a lot. Graceful love stories, she tells me. So, go and write one and forget all this. Not a whisper to the press, not a word to any of your girlfriends! Then everything will be okay."

"Mr. Bellow has let you into his confidence, Sofer," Thomson insisted. "And I can tell you this; it is a great favor."

Sofer's laugh hardly escaped his lips. "And what happens if I refuse this great favor? Are your men in black going to beat me up and feed me to the bears in the park?"

Bellow chuckled and walked up close to Sofer. "No, that won't be necessary. Come with me. Like your girlfriend in the grotto, I too have something to show you!"

⁂

"For the Romanovs, this was just a dining room. For Stalin, it became his Politburo. We have modernized it a little…."

It was a ground floor room, huge, a thirty-place polished rosewood table occupying the center between two marble fireplaces where one could roast whole beef carcasses. But, the rest, as Thomson said, had been 'modernized.' One whole wall was covered in large flat television screens. Three young men were seated behind a control console. Sofer paid them no attention, instead he followed the blossoming smile on Bellow's face. Thumbs in his suspenders, he was admiring the screens.

After his first look, Sofer knew that he had lost. Now he understood the reason for the camera installed in the temple-gate and the fierce lights in the great grotto. On the screens he had a half-dozen views of the cliff, inside and out. Held in a group between the library and the synagogue, the members of the New Khazars were still there, guarded by automatic weapons. Lazir, seated on the ground, supported by one of his comrades, seemed about to faint. Sofer could see the gold in his teeth as he moaned in pain.

Other screens showed men in black drilling holes with pneumatic drills. He could imagine the din, but not to be able to hear it gave much more power to the image. At the entrance to the great grotto one camera remained pointing at a red metal box bearing an aerial. On another screen, Sofer recognized the *mikvah* and the passage leading to the naphtha well. There too, men were working, some of them paddling in the water of the bath, shamelessly dirtying it. The largest screen was maintaining an overall view of the cliff. Mobile, unlike the others, it swept the troglodyte openings. Sofer realized that it was mounted in a helicopter.

Thomson leaned over one of the microphones on the console. "Tony, can you hear me?"

A voice came back from a loudspeaker. "Yes, sir."

303

"We are ready here. How much longer do you need?"

"It's practically done, sir. Four minutes at most."

"That'll take you ten with the evacuation."

Sofer searched for Sonja on every screen. He tried to see the kitchen-cave, but all the openings and stairways looked alike. He wanted to see her, and at the same time he didn't. She remained invisible. Was it possible that she had escaped? But how could she have reached the forest without passing the temple gate, which was totally under surveillance?

He felt someone take his arm. "Here's the deal, Mr. Sofer," murmured Bellow. "You go back home quietly. Nothing happened. You saw nothing. These New Khazar people are liberated after you have sworn them to secrecy. In a few years, someone may be able to find a solution to the problem of your relics, who knows? I have your word, and you mine. The first one to renege…."

With his fat little hand Bellow indicated the men drilling into the cliff, then the metal box. "In five minutes, the cliff will be completely mined. I will give the order from here. The little box you see there will receive it and … BOOM! As simple as that. Nothing will be left but the dust and a few articles in the newspapers accusing a local Mafia gang. Criminals of all kind are not lacking here!"

"You can't do that," said Sofer, devastated.

"I will do it if it's necessary, and without hesitation. Don't imagine you can do anything in return against us; you have no proof. And once the cliff is destroyed, everything will only be in there!" Bellow said, tapping Sofer's forehead.

"On the other hand," he added, "I have photos of you with dangerous terrorists—the New Khazars."

Sofer wiped his forehead with one hand. Although he was shivering with cold as if he were on a glacier, the sweat was pouring down through his new beard.

"Never! Never!" he murmured.

Bellow's fist hardened on Sofer's elbow. "Still four minutes for you to decide! I repeat, you stay quiet and everything will be okay."

"You will destroy the grotto in a year anyway! Quietly! I know you will!"

"Tomorrow is tomorrow!"

On the screens, Sofer saw the men in black leave the great grotto. Suddenly the lights went out. The screen went black.

"But they are inside!" he cried out.

"If the grotto blows up, sure, the New Khazars go too!"

The men in black were pouring out all along the face of the cliff. They were running toward the postern gate. The first of them were already running along the path to the forest. The camera on the helicopter zoomed in on the entrance to the great grotto.

"Three minutes," announced Thomson.

"You are absolutely vile!" choked Sofer.

"It's your choice," replied Bellow calmly, "not mine. You say yes, the lights will go on in the grotto, they will come out, and that's the end of it."

Sofer looked at the screens without understanding what he was looking at. The face of the cliff was now empty, strangely still. The blue ropes still hung there. The *mikvah* was also empty, the surface an immobile mirror. The metal box at the entrance to the great grotto, surreal.

"Sir!"

One of the young men on the console was the first to see her. She appeared to the left on one screen, well above the great grotto.

"Mother of God! What the...?"

It was Sonja. Sofer recognized both her hair and her silhouette.

"Thomson, what the fuck is she doing there?" growled Bellow.

Thomson shouted into the microphone. "Helicopter! Do not press the detonator!"

A brief and strange ballet ensued. The scene jiggled as the helicopter began to dance. Simultaneously, Sonja gripped one of the ropes and slid down the length of one of the outside stairways. The helicopter pointed its nose at her and a burst of fire rang out at the very moment Sofer shouted, "Look out! Look out!"

The bullets hit the rocks several feet above her, just as she grabbed another rope and slid down further. A second blast missed her; carried by her own impetus, she had moved sideways, then back to the left.

In the loudspeaker, an anonymous voice said, "Look out everybody, the vhs detonator is not stable, it's armed!"

"What does that mean?" Bellow demanded, without receiving a reply.

"Good God! Oh shit!" Thomson shouted. "What the hell have you done?"

Sofer watched as Sonja caught another rope to take her down to the entrance of the great grotto while the bullets continued to chip the walls of the cliff above her. One minute it looked like she was going to put her feet on a stairway, the next he thought he saw her fly down toward the forest, as if down a very long rope. Suddenly, the helicopter, too close to the wall, changed course, and the image showed only the top of the cliff. The first explosion had gone off. An opening, perhaps the one leading to the *mikvah*, filled up with dust and stones....

"The idiots!" whistled Thomson. "They tripped the detonator! It's all going to blow!"

For several moments they saw nothing other than the forest; the helicopter pilot was diving as fast as he could to get far enough away from the cliff. When he finally pivoted in a wide turn, they saw the apocalypse.

The long strip of the cliff was bouncing up and down. Explosion after explosion transformed it into a gray cloud, effacing everything, the cliff falling in on itself. Slowly, like a body falling, it fell to the peaceful forest below. Sofer closed his eyes. He prayed as if evil incarnate had just touched his heart and eyes.

"Well. That's that, Mr. Sofer!" Bellow said. "You need have nothing on your conscience!"

Chapter twenty-nine

I*t* was cold enough to split stones. A leaden sky weighed down

Sadoue, February 956

on the immense plains, presaging snow. It didn't worry him; Isaac's
heart was as warm as the campfire that was warming his hands. Beside
him, Hezekiah's mischievous laughter enveloped them in a cloud
of condensation. "This will be the last day of our journey. Tonight
you will sleep in Attex's arms. That is, if she wants you! After all, it's
been a long time since you have seen each other ... perhaps you will
discover that she has found some handsome young prince to replace
you...."

Isaac put his arm around the boy's shoulders and drew him
close. "Don't worry about that, she will be happy to see me, I can
promise you that!"

Hezekiah smacked his gloved hands on his thighs while watching the warriors of their escort saddling their mounts and piling the
tents onto carts. "Is everyone like that when they are in love?" he
asked. "Is everyone as happy?"

It was Isaac who laughed this time. "I don't know. It's the first
time I've been in love."

They both fell quiet for a few moments, each deep in his own thoughts. Then Isaac suggested, "Perhaps, today, we don't need to wait for the carts."

"Yes, you could almost gallop all the way to the caves from here!"

"Will you come with me, Prince? You know that this evening … you will do what you promised me, won't you?"

Hezekiah shook off Isaac's arm, brusquely. "Of course I will! I, Hezekiah, son of Khagan Joseph, will give you the authorization to be as man and wife, in the name of my father and Rabbi Hanania!"

"You could do it in the *mikvah*, where Adam and Eve are painted on the pillars, couldn't you? Like Rabbi Hanania said. And you can explain to the Kathum that she can decide whether or not to accompany me to Sepharad. If she did, she could deliver the Khagan's letter to Rabbi Hazdai herself."

"Isaac, we have rehearsed this scene almost every day since we left Itil…." Hezekiah hesitated, frowning. Over the frozen plains, three riders were approaching at full gallop. A cloud of vapor surrounded them as if the devil were on their tails. Isaac turned around. At the same time as Hezekiah, he recognized the men who had left as scouts the previous night to alert the secret city of their approach.

"Something's wrong," murmured Hezekiah.

Isaac felt a pain in his gut as if he had been stabbed. His joy, so obvious a moment ago, evaporated.

"Prince! My Lord Prince!" shouted the leading horseman, then only thirty feet away. With one bound, he leaped to the ground while his steaming horse continued on its course, leaping and bucking. In his hand he held a piece of a banner on which Hezekiah recognized the Cross of Byzantium.

"My Prince, a terrible tragedy!"

"What tragedy?" asked Isaac, already feeling anger rise in him, rather than fear.

"There has been a huge war in that part of the valley, Sire. Some months ago, and…." The man sucked in air, his gaze faltered. Isaac noted that his gloves and clothes were soaked in sweat.

"Speak!" ordered Hezekiah.

"It was terrible, Prince! The forest at the foot of the cliffs has been totally destroyed by fire. There are only cinders left. The cliff and the caves are black with soot...."

"And the people, are they alive? Did you see them?"

"No, Lord Isaac. We arrived in the dark. It would have been dangerous to wade through the cinders. And then ... we wanted to warn you as soon as possible...."

"But were there lights in the caves?"

"No, Sire, but...."

"To horse, Hezekiah! We are just wasting time!"

⁊⋲

They reached the foot of the cliff, which was as black as the world that surrounded it. Isaac shouted for Attex. Hezekiah shouted for his great-uncle Hanuko. There were only rooks and blackbirds to answer them. All along the path leading to the temple gateway Isaac continued calling for Attex. The name of the Kathum became an echo that rolled around the side of the cliff. The rooks started calling plaintively, ominously.

When they came to the gate, they discovered that the passage was still there but partially blocked with stones. There were only a few boards left capable of sustaining their weight. The silence that encompassed them from the open mouths of the caves was, to describe it properly, the silence of death. All the countryside and the light spoke of nothing but death. Tears began to run down Hezekiah's cheeks, thin skin-colored paths showed in the blackened sweat that covered his face.

Isaac crouched down onto all fours to cross the remaining boards of the passage over the void. At the temple-postern, he waited for neither Hezekiah nor the soldiers before mounting the steps leading to the first of the grottoes. Again he called for Attex. He ran into an alcove, still shouting. Then he ceased. He remained silent until the others joined him. In front of them was a pile of blanched skeletons, covered in remnants of clothing. It was impossible to know if they had been men or women, children or elders. Only the empty orbits of white skulls looked back at them. Delicate hand bones still retained a club, a rusty spear or a piece of cloth.

Hezekiah cried out and two warriors drew their swords. A scrap of tunic had moved as if stirred by a hand. A small crow emerged, observing them with his bright astonished eye. He flew off over their heads and even the tough Khazar soldiers fell to their knees to avoid being touched by the bird's wings.

Isaac fell to his knees, head in his hands. "Attex! Attex! Where are you?"

⋇

They searched the caves until dusk, but found nothing but bones. The birds now whirling about the cliff-face had not left even a trace of flesh on the bodies. All were now melded in the same death that forbade differentiation. Here and there, mixed with the bones, Hezekiah and the soldiers spotted several traces of Arab fighters. Here a helmet bearing the crescent on its point, there a broken shield bearing a picture of a falcon, emblem of the Emir of Aleppo. But after searching the corridors again and again, they could not find the great grotto containing the synagogue and the library, or the renowned *mikvah*.

"It's not possible!" Hezekiah maintained. They must be there. My father and Rabbi Hanania boasted of their splendor. They are there, we must find them!"

It was one of the escort officers who thought of it. "My Prince, your great uncle must have had them block up the passages. He must have feared the Muslims' attack and had the openings leading to the holy places blocked so well that now even we can't find them."

"That is why they have killed everyone," added another. "The Emir's soldiers must have been mad with rage at finding nothing of value. My Prince, men or women, these people who are now nothing but bones showed tremendous courage; none of them revealed the secret!"

Hezekiah wanted to share this news with Isaac to try and assuage his suffering, but the envoy from Cordoba didn't even hear him calling.

Haggard, his eyes swollen with tears and incomprehension, he was running from one grotto to the next, one stairway to another, returning dozens of times to lean over one skeleton, then another, searching in the color of a bone or the finesse of a skull for the face of his beloved. Any one of them could have been Attex, and none was. That such beauty could be effaced thus, without him even being able to see her disappear, without even being able to hug her dead body to him, rendered him almost insane. He started stammering that Attex was alive and could not be here in amongst these bones.

"No," cried Hezekiah, "she is dead like the others. I picked up Uncle Hanuko's tunic. She would have been with him. She died like a warrior."

"What do you know?" Isaac flashed, wanting to hit the boy to make him be quiet. "What do you know?"

Then he started calling for Attex again.

In the icy night that followed, like a madman, he screamed the name of his beloved to the cinder-covered plains.

"I will wait for you!" he howled. "You must purify yourself in the *mikvah*! Your brother wishes it, Rabbi Hanania wishes it! We can be a real married couple, just as I promised!"

Once again, only the birds replied.

Hezekiah, terrified, stayed silent in an alcove, closing his eyes tightly and covering his ears. The warriors too, in spite of the huge fire they had lit at the entrance to a cave, sat shivering at each howl. Then Isaac stopped. They could hear his sobs and his mutterings. "She is gone, she will never come back. She was beautiful, like honey. The Lord created her like that. No man could keep her. That is why she is gone…."

Hezekiah rejoined his friend. He was shivering, sitting on a stair, cold as a corpse. To warm him, Hezekiah put his arms around him, covering him with his own lambswool cape.

"I, too, want to be just bones," murmured Isaac with a weird smile. "The Almighty must also feed me to the birds. If not, I will never know whether she is alive or dead."

He began searching for the dagger in Hezekiah's belt. The boy unsheathed it and threw it into the void. "Isaac, you must live," he whispered. "You must. The Lord wants you to take my father's letter to your rabbi. Isaac, that's what the Almighty wants. You must go back to the Sephardim; they are waiting for you there, with hope. You must tell them that I, Hezekiah, son of Joseph, I may be this King of all the Jews that my father did not wish to be."

Epilogue

V

Montmartre, Paris
July 2000

iolent metallic noises broke into his sleep. It was still very
early. On the other side of the street, workmen were putting scaffolding up around a building. For three days now this had been
Sofer's wake-up call. Since his return from Baku, Sofer had not had
one calm night's sleep. His night hours had been filled with dreams
and nightmares. There seemed to be something missing all the time.
He had to keep waking up to grasp the absence, to find peace. Alas,
when he opened his eyes, there only remained dreams of a face. A
face and a body, a whisper and a laugh. *Her.* The same vision assailed
him; Sonja holding on to the end of a rope and then the cliffs and
the caves turning to dust.

Had she succeeded in escaping in time? Without being injured
or buried like her companions, under hundreds of tons of rock? He
had not been able to return to the cliff at Sadoue. Thomson and Bellow had the area sealed off by the Georgian army. Officially the affair
was over. Reuters had transmitted the news to all the editors in Europe
and America: the New Khazars were nothing more than a group of
Chechyn bandits, a gang more Mafia than political. Their attempt to
blackmail the OCOO had failed thanks to the official security services

313

of the consortium. Over a few weeks, they had identified the terrorists' hiding place, a troglodyte village near the frontier of Daghestan and Chechnya. When the Georgian Police had encircled their position, an explosion, doubtless caused by some clumsiness on the part of the terrorists, had literally blown the caves in Sadoue apart. The violence of the explosion gave some idea of the impressive arsenal that the terrorists of the New Khazars must have stored there.

Of course, there was not the slightest hint about oil and even less about the Khazar relics. Sofer could not help admiring the simplicity of the lie; an evil which took on such a benign appearance was capable of obviating the truth of history. But he, Marc Sofer, how could he forget? He looked at his empty hands as if he could find there some trace of the acacia wood from the ark with the Cherubim in the old Khazar synagogue.

He thought of the marvelous library that no longer existed. Of the letter from Attex to her brother that Sonja had given him.... Damn! Why hadn't he slipped it into his pocket at the moment of the attack? It was on the table, in the kitchen ... but he didn't have any pockets when the commando captured him. His jacket was back there too, in the kitchen, under the debris of what was left of the cliff. And in his jacket ... the coin Yakubov had given him. He had nothing left. Absolutely nothing. Not even one drop of water from the *mikvah*.

He closed his eyes in an attempt to see the frescoes of Adam and Eve again. They would still be there, but for how long? He could see Sonja walking in the purifying waters. The obsessive image of the woman he had called Attex, the woman who had disappeared from the end of a rope like a dryad, assailed him once more. How many times since his homecoming had he told himself that she was not dead? How many times had he called himself an old fool?

He shook himself and prepared his breakfast. As he installed himself on the small terrace, he noticed that in the soft morning light his roses did not have their normal fire. He walked over to look at them more closely and discovered they were covered in greenfly, the foliage attacked by a vicious mildew. He would have to treat them and care for them. In a flood of no doubt excessive emotion, the odor of some jasmine he had planted the previous year overwhelmed him. It seemed that this floral disaster was a living image of what he had just been through.

He thought of Cordoba and imagined that Isaac, on his return, had sensed the same sadness when he found himself back in the splendor of the Sephardi gardens. Both of them had known the beauty of love and the horror of its corruption. A corruption born out of the unnecessary and deceitful violence of men. Like him, Isaac had been frantic and had completed his return journey buoyed up with the mad hope that Attex was still alive. He had accomplished his duty as Hezekiah would have wished. It had taken him nearly two years to carry King Joseph's answer back to Rabbi Hazdai Ibn Shaprut. Yes, a Jewish empire really did exist at the other end of the world, it was no dream, and he, Isaac, was the bearer of this fabulous news. But this same Isaac ben Eliezer, as he delivered the king's letter into the hands of the rabbi, knew that the words made no sense; a rumor from Asia was already spreading through the markets of Sepharad like dirty smoke—Itil, the capital of the empire of the Jewish Khazars, had been occupied by the Russians. Hezekiah would never become the great king that he had dreamed of being.

Sofer was inclined to believe that some of the Khazars survived in the area between the Caspian Sea, the Black Sea and in the Caucasus Mountains. In 1245, the traveler Jean du Plan Carpin, a disciple of St. Francis of Assisi, tells in his *Historia Mongolorum* how he met, in the Caucasus to the north of the Alain country, some Circassians, and 'some Khazars observing the Jewish religion.' It could therefore be possible that Agarounov and his friends the Jews of the Mountains were direct descendants of the Khazars....

As for the others, the hundreds of thousands of 'Aryan' Jews threatened with death on the collapse of their empire, they had been exiled to the West, in that part of Central Europe composed of nascent kingdoms such as Poland, that had been ready to welcome them. They must have arrived there at the same time as other Jewish refugees, the Ashkenazim, expelled from France, Flanders and Germany by the first Crusades. What percentage of these two groups must have been in the six million Jews who, centuries later, the Nazis sent to their death?

Sofer himself could even have been a descendant of the same line as Attex. Was such a hypothesis so absurd? From now on, whenever he would look in a mirror, ignoring the beard that had grown to give him the appearance of the Patriarch that he was not, he would search for and see the slightly slanted eyes and the high cheekbones.

⁊

The Wind of the Khazars had blown through the steppe, chasing the Khazars themselves, pushing them toward Europe, through the Mountains of the Caucasus. The Wind of the Khazars had blown through the centuries, effacing all traces of the Jewish Kingdom, patiently and obstinately, until not even a spear or a love letter remained. The Wind of the Khazars had disseminated and carried off forever the vestiges of ancient times. It had blown for the very last time to bring down the dust of the cliffs at Sadoue.

Nothing more remained in Sofer's hand but the memory of Attex's skin and, at the tips of his fingers, the shadows of the words that perhaps, one day, might build a memory of the Khazars.

THE END.

Acknowledgements

I t only remains for me to thank all those who helped in the research of the Khazar documentation: Jean-Pierre Allali, Maria Iakoubovitch, Clara Halter, Vladimir Petrukhin, Oksana Podetti; for her editorial work in *Editions Laffont*, Nathalie Thery; for having guided me and accompanied me to the Jews of the Mountains in the Caucasus, Mikhail Agarounov.

About the Author

Marek Halter

Marek Halter was born in Warsaw in 1936. When he was five, he and his family escaped from the Nazis by crawling through the sewers under the Warsaw ghetto. He has lived in France since 1950. In addition to being a writer, Marek Halter is also an artist and a human rights activist, and has served as President of the European Foundation for Science, Art and Culture. His book *Le Fou et Les Rois*, which recounts his experiences working for Middle East peace, won the *Prix Aujourd'hui*.

The fonts used in this book are from the Garamond family

Other works by Marek Halter published by *The* Toby Press

The Book of Abraham